THE ALBINO STAG WITNESS

D1711925

THE ALBINO STAG WITNESS

Robert W. Feragen

Writers Club Press
San Jose New York Lincoln Shanghai

The Albino Stag Witness

Writers Club Press
an imprint of iUniverse, Inc.

For information address:
iUniverse, Inc.
5220 S. 16th St., Suite 200
Lincoln, NE 68512
www.iuniverse.com

ISBN: 0-595-22255-2

Printed in the United States of America

For Madlin Ann Melrose Feragen
***Who made the challenge and gave the
encouragement***

Acknowledgements

The author is deeply appreciative of the assistance of friends and family during the writing of this story. I was given information about South Dakota law by my attorney nephew Thomas J. Farrell and his colleague Sidney B. Strange, Sioux Falls, S.D. Additional information about South Dakota legal procedures was provided by my friend, attorney David Blair. Any errors made herein regarding these laws arise from my ignorance and are not the product of my advisors. I also thank Diane Krueger for permission to refashion an episode in her life, fictionalized here to advance the plot. Finally, my sincere thanks to my Texas neighbor Jane Tompkins and my wife Madlin for giving this story its first critical readings.

CHAPTER 1

Cottonwood Acres was the newest addition to Hamilton, South Dakota, its winding streets and cul-de-sacs suggesting an opulence missing from the rigid gridwork of the town's north-south, east-west streets laid out a century ago. The only movements evident in the neighborhood were from buried sprinkler systems raised and active this hot, dry August afternoon, spraying jets of water back and forth over new lawns. In the humid afternoon only the muted hum of air conditioners could be heard emanating from beside the most expensive homes in town. There was no human movement up and down the street when a lone, blue Ford 150 pick-up drove slowly to the end of the cul-de-sac, turned and came back down the broad curved street.

The noise of the rifle shot and the shattering of the picture window of States Attorney James Henslow's home went unheard in the closed-up, air conditioned homes, nor did anyone hear the roar of the truck's engine as it sped out of the development and toward the center of town.

Inside the wounded house, Sheri Henslow got up on her knees on the tiled kitchen floor where she had thrown herself at the crash of shattering glass in the living room. She was at first aware of an acid taste in her mouth, then the pain in her left arm which had hit a kitchen cabinet as she had dropped to the floor.

"Oh my god, my god," she gasped.

She did not move at first, waiting for another assault. She noted that the clock on the kitchen wall said four thirty. The silence in the house was deep. There was only the whisper of cooled air passing through vents along the perimeter of the room.

Sheri crawled to the doorway between the dining room and kitchen, peered into the living room beyond and saw where the window had exploded into shards across the carpet, some fragments onto the seven foot sofa. She stood up then, anger overcoming the fear she'd first felt. She ran to the dining room window and looked out upon the empty street. Lawn sprinklers rotated lazily in the yards across the street.

When she telephone her husband at his office in the courthouse, she began to shake, anger and fear urging adrenaline into her bloodstream.

"Jim, someone shot out our window," she nearly shouted into the telephone.

"What are you talking about?" Henslow replied, confused by the urgency in his wife's voice.

"The goddam living room window. It just got shot out. Glass all over the place. Call the police. Come on home and see for yourself what happened."

"Dammit," was all he said and hung up.

By six that evening Jim Henslow had the lumber company come to the house and nail a four by eight foot piece of plywood over the outside of the window. He and Sheri spent more than an hour picking up large pieces of glass and then vacuuming the carpet and furniture.

"Rogers, that s.o.b." Jim said the name like a curse. "That goddam Art Rogers threatened me, you know. When I got his brother Clarence sent up, he said something to me right at the end of the trial. Said I wasn't so smart to have gotten his brother sent to the pen."

"Who is he, anyway?" Sheri asked.

"Lives in Chesterton. Both he and Clarence have been arrested for fights in the bar out there. Couple of rough characters. I'll get that bastard for this."

"If you don't, I sure as hell will. I swear to god I will. He scared the wits out of me. What if I had been in that room? He could have killed me."

Events at Pioneer Village east of town that same afternoon were to divert their attention and concentrate it upon Jim Henslow's stepfather Horst Henslow. Jim Henslow was soon to focus all his attention on his skills as States Attorney of Chautauqua Country, for in the next year, he was certain, he would have kicked off the biggest real estate development in the state and become South Dakota's newest state senator.

❦   ❦   ❦

With his one good eye Rasputin watched every move Assistant Professor Jack Oliver Traid made while eating an early dinner. Sitting in a baby's high chair without a tray, the brindled colored tom cat commanded the table. Where the right eye had been was a pucker of skin sprouting tufts of fur. Rasputin had known treachery at the hands of trusted ones. Jack talked to him about it from time to time, commiserating, silently comparing. But it was dinner time now.

"You want a bite, Rasp?" Jack asked, cutting pieces of baked chicken breast on his plate. He placed a morsel before Rasputin on the brown plastic placemat reserved for just these ceremonies.

The cat sniffed the meat, thought about it, then nipped up a piece from the mat.

"Gourmet cooking, wouldn't you say?"

The cat's good eye blinked.

"You're getting too fat, you know," Jack said, an unheeded complaint which got response from neither the cat nor resolve from the man. If any of Creation's creatures deserved spoiling, Jack reasoned, Rapsputin was one of them.

"Found him in my garage," Jack would explain to friends once Rasputin made himself visible to them, an act of bravery that often took weeks, and with some people, particularly men, months. The cat had little reason to trust of homo sapiens.

Declawed and neutered he clearly had once been someone's pet; domesticated, not yet feral, he had found refuge on a cold October night in an empty cardboard box in Traid's garage. A tight knot of skin and bones, of dried blood and pain, he had hardly looked like a cat when Jack found him.

"My guess is that he had been abandoned on some country road," Jack would explain to friends. "Whether the owner had also attempted to shoot him after letting him out of a car, or a hunter walking a pheasant-less corn field felt he needed target practice, is a crime never to be solved."

Jack Traid spoke with a bitter edge in his voice. He spoke from experience. After nineteen months in Vietnam followed by twenty years on the Dallas police force, the last ten as detective lieutenant, he was no longer shocked at the varieties of human violence against its own and other species. He believed he had witnessed in his lifetime most varieties of treachery. When he dared think of it, he admitted to himself that he had been a participant—victim as well as perpetrator—in a few treacheries.

In telling Rasputin's story to new friends, Jack would explain that the veterinarian had removed six shotgun pellets from the cat's hind quarters and head. It was not the vet's bill of one hundred sixty dollars that bothered him so much, he would explain, but the sight of the pitiful condition of an animal once taught to trust humans. Forever scarred and wary, Rasputin now had a secure place, provisional as he might regard it. In the house he had a hundred hiding places, emerging only for Jack or Jack's friends of proven reliability. Rasputin never ventured outside this refuge.

"In someone's eyes" Jack would conclude his tale of Rasputin "a cute little kitty had become an expendable cat, a disdained animal, just part of a throw-away society."

Rasputin would seldom meow, but now, watching Jack continuing to eat, he emitted a deep purring rumble which signaled he wanted another piece of chicken.

Except for sharing bits of chicken from his plate, Jack concentrated on a sheaf of papers to the right of his plate. These were the last of the final examinations he had to grade before finishing the summer session. As the red pencil scanned the answers, Jack let out a cry of despair. Startled, Rasputin prepared to jump from the high chair.

"Don't worry Rasp, it's okay. It's nothing to do with you," Jack said, reaching over to scratch behind the cat's ear.

"It's my failure to teach these prairie chickens the basics of binomial theorems," he muttered, more to himself than to the cat.

For five years he had been teaching mathematics and general science at Hamilton State College, a liberal arts school with fifteen hundred students, more or less, and little in the way of a reputation. Hired as a provisional instructor because he lacked a Ph.D., he was then at age forty-eight, a widower and starting what he did not regard as a new career so much as securing a refuge from urban streets and persistent memories of Vietnam. What he could not express to others was his search for escape from his past self and the violence that had been at the core of most of his life.

It was Elliot Morris, publisher of the Hamilton *Times* that he had to thank for the job. Elliot, an old friend from graduate school days at the University of Iowa, was a member of the State Board of Higher Education and champion of struggling Hamilton State College. Their meeting again in 1989 on the Iowa campus was pure coincidence, Jack thought, or perhaps, he conceded to close friends, Fate taking over his life of aimless wandering after Alice's death. When she had been killed in the automobile accident in May, 1988, he resigned from the police force, taking early retirement and setting out to wander on back roads through the geography of his past.

He'd been on the University of Iowa campus most of the day of his visit that June, feeling out of place among the ebb and flow of young people who crossed the Quad where he sat on the steps of Old Capitol. He had spent the morning wandering the campus and had just climbed the hill from the newly expanded Union Building to the Quad. He had needed to catch his breath. Elliot caught sight of him first and left the three men he had been with, each with a name tag signifying a conference of Mid-west Publishers and Editors. He stood before Jack, silent a moment, then said, "Skipping class again?"

They had spent the rest of the day together reciting autobiographies. Minerva Morris, Elliot's wife, joined them for spaghetti dinner at the Airliner, patiently listening to their reminiscences. It was she who made the suggestion that he come to Hamilton, sensing immediately, Jack later concluded, his need for a place to come to rest.

"Elliot will talk to President Adams," Minnie had said. "I am sure Franklin be pleased to have you teach at Hamilton State. That will give you a chance to settle into our little community."

For the second time in his life he left the Iowa campus—in '63 as a second lieutenant headed for Vietnam but this time in search of peace.

The house Jack and Rasputin shared was a two-bedroom bungalow on the north side of Twelfth Street which defined the north city limits of Hamilton. His garden and back yard looked north over corn fields and distant rows of trees of shelter belts. The prairie of low, rolling hills rose gently to the horizon. In the winter Jack would watch from his house the approach of blizzards across open fields, his view unobstructed. The previous owners had insulated the house against northwest winds which had few barriers to impede their force as they swooped down from the Arctic Circle. Jack Traid felt little threat from weather. There were demons more destructive than weather with which he had to deal in the quiet of Hamilton, South Dakota.

In five years he'd proven himself a popular teacher. When promoted to assistant professor his second year, President Franklin Adams had made it clear that there would be no further promotions because Traid had only a Master's Degree in mathematics. And then, Adams explained obliquely, there was his age. His were considered second-class credentials in academia. The second-class status pleased Jack. He felt an even greater security in not having ambitions for advancement. Hired at forty-eight years of age he had been on a self-described plateau of resigned contemplation. The institution could not induce in him envy for academic achievement at this late date, for his pride had no need of another career, or institutional recognition. The president and dean looked to others to chair committees, pressed the younger instructors and assistant professors with fresh doctorate degrees to bring fame to the college with their publications. Traid was exempt, left to teach his freshmen and sophomores, valued for his stoic acceptance of remedial sections without complaint. He fit the niche perfectly.

Hamilton College was wholly rural in character. It was located just three blocks from Traid's house and occupied a campus three city blocks on a side. The college complex was a park-like retreat for students and teachers alike. The campus of broad lawns, shaded in summer by century old oak and elm trees, was remote from urban clamor. A safe haven. It was nearly possible, he thought, to purge memories of twenty years picking through blood-splattered crime scenes and spending endless nights searching for the enraged and crazed. This campus was nearly quiet enough and safe enough in being surrounded by fertile Dakota farm land to allow him to suppress further the submerged anger for the treachery that had resulted in his nearly losing his left arm.

❧   ❧   ❧

Second Lieutenant Jack Traid gunned the Jeep up the street of
Hué, June, 1963, swerving to miss robed figures lurching out from
side streets and temples. A swelling crowd of Buddhist monks was
rushing toward the center of town. Ahead of them South Vietnamese
ARVN troops in weapons carriers were pushing into the center of the
street to block the way of the crowd. Lieutenant Colonel Vance Bonnier stood next to Traid, a forty-five in his right hand, his left clinging to the windshield of the Jeep. Bonnier was yelling in Vietnamese.
He urged Traid to go faster.

"The sons of bitches. They promised," Bonnier cursed.

He didn't have to explain to Lt. Traid. They had both been part of
the negotiations with General Nhu's officers. U.S. demands for an
end to persecution of Buddhists would be met. President Ngo Dihn
Diem himself had promised. Buddhists would get a share of power,
and would be able to fly their flags as had the Catholics during their
holy days. Here in Hué, where eighty percent of the population was
Buddhist, a new round up of monks had begun as the demonstrations increased in size. It had been only weeks since the agreement
with Diem's brother, General Nhu. But it was Madam Ngo Dinh
Nhu who had effectively vetoed the agreement and urged the sup-
pression. Madam Nhu's strident accusations enflamed the situation.

"Buddhist bonze are murderers," she broadcast in every Diem
media. "Communists," she screamed on state radio. "The monks are
all communists."

Bonnier was trying to reach Nhu headquarters in the center of
town, but the streets were becoming impassable. After edging the
Jeep by the first rank of uniformed ARVN soldiers, Traid and Bonnier found themselves in a sea of Vietnamese, many of them saffron-
robed monks. The Jeep crept ahead slowly, its horn honking, Bonnier yelling in Vietnamese. Into the midst of the mob came another

squad of ARVN troops, their rifles held at high port. They began to jab with the butts of rifles at any demonstrator within reach. Officers would grab a monk and pull him up against a building. Both monks and civilians tried to stop the arrests. A full riot was imminent.

"Keep moving," Bonnier yelled at Traid.

But their Jeep was mired in a sea of humanity. Jack could only edge their vehicle deeper into the congealed crowd of shouting, angry demonstrators. It was then that a monk, a mere boy, pulling free from an officer trying to jerk him from the crowd, was felled when another soldier brought the butt of his rifle down on the boy's head. The crowd opened momentarily where the boy lay. A cry went up from the mob. Blood oozed from the boy's shaven head.

"Bloody bastard," Bonnier shouted.

Jumping to the ground he lifted the limp body into his arms as if it were weightless and placed it curled up in the back seat of the Jeep.

"Get us out of here," he commanded Jack. "That side street, there," he said, pointing.

The soldier who had brought the boy down stepped in front of the Jeep, his rifle pointed just above Bonnier's head.

Bonnier yelled at him, but the helmeted ARVN did not move. Jumping from the Jeep again, Bonnier walked up to the soldier, pushed the barrel of the ARVN's U.S. M-16 aside and put his face inches away from the frozen soldier. He muttered something in Vietnamese and turned and walked back to the Jeep.

In the Jeep once again Bonnier swore, "Some goddam allies they are."

The way cleared for them gradually as Jack shifted into second to accelerate. It was then the rifle fire exploded about them, shattering the windshield, popping into the metal body of the Jeep. Bonnier turned to the rear, taking aim with his .45, but the crowd was too dense to risk shooting. He was crouched over the boy's body in back. The ARVN soldier who had shot at them was struggling with the riotous crowd that was beating on him.

It was then that Jack felt the pain in his left arm, the hot flow of blood down his side under his shirt. He could not move the arm, which hung at his side. He sped down the side street, steering with his right hand.

"You hit?" Bonnier yelled.

"Yeah. Left arm."

"Stop the Jeep. Get over here. I'll drive."

They raced to the U.S. compound and the military hospital at the outskirts of Hué. Traid fought off faintness by reaching back with his good arm to hold the boy monk as the Jeep careened through narrow streets. The child moaned as they bumped over pot holes, giving Traid hope that the boy would survive.

Medics took the monk from the Jeep as Bonnier helped Jack into the hospital. In the next month Vance Bonnier resigned his commission in protest of Diem's regime and the faint-hearted efforts of United States officials to stop the persecution of the Buddhists. His actions made headlines for a brief time in the *New York Times* and other major dailies.

By the time Traid had been rotated back to the States for rehabilitation, Bonnier was all but forgotten by newspapers. From his hospital bed Traid followed the news in August of Diem's declaring marshal law; television pictured more monks setting themselves on fire in protest. On November 23, 1963, just before he was given a disability discharge, he watched on the television set in the hospital lounge the assassination of President Kennedy.

Traid returned to graduate school at Iowa and continued physical therapy. It was a year after that he became a member of the detective division of the Dallas Police force, accepted with a veteran's preference and a waiver in the physical examination for the left arm that had regained most of its former strength. The grip of his left hand had actually become stronger than his right. A compensation, he thought to himself.

He was once again working in downtown Dallas where the building in which his parents' Traid Print Shop used to be located. It was now part of a delivery service garage. The familiar territory provided him a new base in the beginning. He found police training and the early years of service challenging. But he had to learn to hold his tongue when fellow officers railed against the rising tide of opposition to the Vietnam war and the student demonstrations on college campuses which had become more frequent and strident.

The assassination of President Kennedy seemed to him the heavy hand of fate dealing a terrible retribution soon after Diem had been murdered with U.S. complicity. He did not know how to tell fellow officers his feeling that their own country was becoming like South Vietnam, painfully divided and with a leadership blindly convinced of its invincibility, submerged in the profound error of believing in its own metaphors. In those last years of the war, Jack Traid maintained an uneasy resignation to duty as a crime investigator.

During the first years of his career as a police officer Jack Traid believed he had found escape from the lawless chaos of war. He learned to accept the commonplace of violence to which his job took him each day, believing he might make a difference as part of the rule of law. His first wife Mary Geats, a brilliant fellow graduate student at Iowa who at first shared his idealism about law enforcement, could not bear the reality of living with the demands made by his service on the Dallas force. They divorced after three years. It was not until six years later that his second bachelor life was ended by Alice, the desirable Arlington debutante. She had encouraged his interest in her, and had urged from him the offer of marriage. Their marriage too was another dream cut short before fulfillment.

❧   ❧   ❧

Under Jack Traid's red pencil the last math paper was marked A+, one of two nearly perfect exams. His spirits rose. Getting up, he cleared the dishes from the table. The freshman class had not been a complete disaster after all.

Rasputin slipped from his high chair, thumping to the floor and, despite a limp in his right rear leg, hurried into the living room to curl up in the over-stuffed chair they both understood was his alone.

In the kitchen Jack glanced at the clock. Five-thirty. Ellie Easton would be home by now, he thought, and pressed the seven numbers on the wall telephone to reach the Easton farm.

The casual voice of a young man answered, "Yeah, Eastons."

"Hi Gordy. Is your mother home?"

"Hi Jack. Mom's just coming in the back door," the sixteen year old replied, his voice familiar in a way that made Traid pleased with the friendship that had developed over the past year with son and mother.

Jack had read the story in the Hamilton Times when Ellie's husband Ralph had been killed. A year and a half after the accident he had been allowed to enter into Ellie and Gordy's lives. He and Ellie had met at Roger and Ann Faregold's Thanksgiving dinner. During the year that followed he and Ellie had attended college and community concerts and plays together. Friends began to treat them as a pair. It was a convenience for both in the intimacy of the small town, but required fending off suggestions that the path would inevitably lead to marriage and a common household. In defense Ellie would refer to Jack as "my good buddy" in front of friends, signaling to them the character of their relationship.

There was an understood bond of mutual support between them which neither tried to define but wondered about to themselves. That they had not bedded together was regarded as unlikely, even suspicious, in the minds of some people in town. Gossips preferred that middle-aged men and women who dated get in bed together without delay. But Ellie and Jack had in their minds a logically undefined arrangement. There had been too many accidents in both their lives to commit easily to any permanent arrangement or premature commitments. Both were wary of presumptions about the feelings of the other, as well as of their own. A reserved friendship had served them well these first few months. For Jack, Ellie's commitments to son, the farm and memories of a dead husband, represented a clear contrast to Jack's ever-present memory of Mildred Singer, art professor at Hamilton State and lover until she left to teach in Minneapolis. Mildred's passion, her restlessness and dissatisfactions were a stark contrast to Ellie Easton's quiet acceptance of what life dealt.

"What's up?" Ellie's voice was brisk, echoing the tone she used with patients at the Hamilton Community Hospital.

"Dan Morris is coming over to my place for a short rehearsal in a few minutes. He's promised to play trombone with the sextet. Okay if I come out later this evening after we're done?"

"You can come out if you remember that I'm a working girl. You've got to get out of here by eleven." She has the voice of a young girl, Jack thought, belying her 45 years.

"Wouldn't think of staying a moment longer. By the way, do you have to work tomorrow? Saturday duty?"

"Nope. But Gordy and I've got to get caught up with chores out here, then I have to do some shopping in town. Why?"

"I thought you might like to go out to Pioneer Village with me in the afternoon while I work on the flat-bed press. Won't take too long. Then we can go out to dinner tomorrow night."

"I remember. You and Mike Wilkins promised to do the special edition of the Pioneer Voice for Pioneer Days. What time are you going out?"

"About two o'clock. That okay?"

"Sure. Are you driving that beat up Toyota?" Her tone was knowingly skeptical.

"That's the problem. I have to drop off the heap at the garage early tomorrow morning. I thought you might like to drive?" He had

decided to gamble on a valve job with the hope of another fifty thousand miles from the tired Corrola.

"You sly dog. It's the transportation, is it?"

"You found me out. But dinner's on me."

"Okay. See you later tonight."

"Great. You're a nice person." His tone of voice said more about
his feelings than the cautious words.

CHAPTER 2

$\mathcal{J}$ack finished putting dishes in the dishwasher after his call to Ellie. He went out the back door into the eight by ten foot breezeway leading to the print shop. With an exterior door and window on the east wall, the room had been made into a small gallery. The framed paintings, printed ephemera, and memorabilia on shelves spoke of his many interests. An autographed photo of Duke Ellington hung above a picture of the original Dakota Dixieland Ramblers, only two of its original members still meeting in Jack's living room twice a month to rehearse. The session tonight with Dan was to familiarize him with the group's charts. The sextet would rehearse in three weeks to prepare for the College's Halloween benefit dance.

An abstract oil painting in bright reds and blues by Mildred Singer, painted while she was still at Hamilton College as art professor, hung next to the door to his studio. Mildred had left it for him as a gift the day she left Hamilton two years ago, placing it inside the front door of his house. She'd left town two days after the semester ended, having told no one the day and hour she expected to leave. The note inside the envelope attached to the painting read: "The title is 'Love's Splendor,' my dear. I would stay here with you and wait for your healing, but I am not a martyr, for love or teaching. I hate good-byes, too."

The bold reds and yellows of the painting were cheerful and defiant at the same time. For Jack it was the portrait of the one woman in his life he had come to love since Alice had been killed. A wild swath of deep blue cut through the field of reds and yellows, like the doubt, he thought, that held him back from where passion should have lead with Mildred.

Mildred had great talent as an artist, and he thought, as a caring person. She had made him feel whole. He was excited by her creativity that glowed in each new work. This painting was no different. It swelled with memories. It declared, too, her impatience with small town life. And, he thought, in a contrary way it clearly defined his satisfaction with living in Hamilton, for the painting was grounded nowhere—there was nothing to circumscribe its internal vigor. Where Mildred had felt trapped, he had found a comfortable freedom. We have different furies, he thought.

They had become coffee-break friends at first by virtue of having adjoining offices. Mid-mornings at the Student Center cafeteria, they would report to each other on their reading, sort out campus gossip, and later when they had begun to date, talk about the symphony concerts they had shared in Sioux Falls. Their one heated and persistent argument was over the benefits vs. the short-comings of a small town. His portrayal of Hamilton as a sanctuary had not impressed her.

"More like Siberia," she had said, "especially in January. And art? There are a few valiant souls like Sarah Riemer and the Arts Association who struggle here on the prairie, but their battle is too sad to bear."

Mildred had a passionate love of the book arts, of fine bindings and hand-crafted books which she collected. The subject had provided them with hours of talking about this shared interest. She had helped him design a monograph which he had printed and bound for one of the faculty members. And then she was gone.

It was late in April, 1993, when she told him she was leaving Hamilton at the end of the school year for a college near Minneapolis. His anger could find no expression. He could not speak to her for a week, feeling betrayed and left to figure out the reason on his own. Their conversations until the day she left were as between strangers.

The hollow in his life diminished slowly over the past two years. Nothing had replaced their making love, at times in his house, most often in her apartment, which was a magical place to him. He missed her reading poetry to him after they had made love on a winter's evening. The sense of betrayal had not left him.

It was only Ellie Easton who six months after Mildred left had been able to distract him from the sense of loss, and from the older, persistent guilt for Alice's death.

Centered on the solid white door to the print shop was a brass plate, a birthday gift from the Faregolds last September which announced "Atelier de Jack O. Traid." It had been good for a laugh among friends. Under it he had mounted another and smaller brass plate he had had made by the local jeweler announcing "And Master of None."

The door opened into one corner of the studio which formed an "L" with the entryway. The north wall opposite had but one high window over a row of type cases. To the right two platen printing presses stood in the middle of the room. Both were old, but the smaller was a certified antique of more than 100 years age.

The south wall of the shop had three large windows which looked out across his garden to the street beyond. Beneath the windows was a workbench where mock-ups of work in progress lay. In the center of the shop near the presses was a table carrying a large imposing stone with a type form at its center. The first edition of Roger Faregold's poems, *The Tenured Heart*, was nearly ready for printing. He had yet to set in type the colophon and a title page that satisfied him.

Jack picked up a steel composing stick and began to pick lead type letter by letter from the compartmented case which was set at a slant on top of a type stand. His fingers moved quickly, each piece of type dropping into the composing stick with certainty. His eyes darted from manuscript to the letters set up-side down in the stick. Time stretched out. An enveloping quiet came over him. Memory of smells of childhood in his parents' shop filled his mind—the hot metal of a linotype, the dry, grainy smell of the paper storage room, the lingering pungency of ink and solvent. The smells helped him recall a serenity of family life that he had not achieved again in his life, and he now clung to its remembrance with these out-dated, now antique molded letters in lead. The lingering memories of Mildred, and deeper, of his being Alice's trophy husband–"Alice's very own cop," her Vogue-inspired friends liked to comment–dissolved into the quiet of the shop.

The extension to the front door bell buzzed in the studio. Jack hurried from the shop and back through the house. Dan stood at the front door as Jack came into the entry just off the living room. Rasputin had disappeared.

"This a raid?" Jack asked referring to Dan's uniform and the .38 caliber service revolver in its holster. His trombone case seemed incongruous baggage.

"I'm on call again. Hopson's choice—Friday night duty or Saturday night duty. And I'm sorry I'm a little late. Had a call from Police Chief Ford at five-thirty. Damndest thing. Someone shot out the living room window at States Attorney Jim Henslow's house. Luckily, his wife was in the kitchen."

Dan stepped into the living room. Rasputin scurried up the stairway and out of sight.

"Drive-by shooting in Hamilton?" Traid asked.

"Sure was. Luckily no one was hurt, but they'll need a new window and repair to the living room ceiling. Looks like it was a thirty caliber rifle."

"Who'd do that to the States Attorney?" Jack asked.

"According to Ford, Henslow says he thinks he knows who did it. A guy named Art Rogers. Henslow sent his brother Clarence to the pen last month."

"I read about that. Cattle rustling, modern style."

"Right. But Henslow's got no proof that Rogers shot out his window. Anyway Chief Ford wants the Sheriff's Department to poke around a bit in Chesterton where Rogers lives."

"I've got the trombone parts all together in a couple of folders for you," Jack said, taking the folders from a tea table. "We better work on folder A first. We play those most often."

Dan began to look through the book. He had an athletic build and at six feet two inches, one hundred ninety pounds he had the appearance of a college fullback, despite a slightly stooped, relaxed posture. Jack guessed him to be twenty-five years old.

His first year out of law school, Dan was at loose ends about his future. He had been made a deputy sheriff of Hamilton county two months earlier. As the son of Elliot and Minerva Morris, owners and publishers of the *Times*, the daily and only newspaper in Hamilton, the job had been a cinch to get. Even that sometimes critic of the *Times* coverage of crime, Jim Henslow, Chautauqua County States Attorney, said publicly that Dan was a good choice for the Deputy Sheriff's job. Dan explained to friends that he was "waiting for something worthwhile to put a law degree into."

"I'm surprised you never took an interest in newspapering, like your father?" Jack said as he watched Dan study the music. "You have probably heard that my parents were in the printing trade—got ink my blood early."

"Nope, not me. Never did particularly care for it. I did fool around the back shop when I was a kid, but mostly I was in the way. Being a reporter or publisher just isn't for me."

"Law is?"

"By a slow process of elimination it has turned out to be a trade I seem to qualify for—love of language and history, love of research. The other option was to play trombone full time."

Dan continued to leaf through sheet music in the folder, commenting, "Lots of old favorites here: 'Tiger Rag,' 'Maple Leaf.'"

He chuckled.

"Some real old timers too," he continued. "I'm not so familiar with 'Livery Stable Blues.'"

"That was also known as the 'Barnyard Blues.' One of the early Dixieland numbers."

Jack went to the hi-fi console and put a record on the turntable.

"What say we blow along on 'Jazz Me Blues'? This is the Dukes of Dixieland. Same arrangement as ours."

They both got their instruments ready. Jack sucked on the saxophone reed. Dan worked the slide. Jack lowered the needle and after the first chorus they joined in, softly, tentatively.

The Dukes whetted the enthusiasm of the two men. Standing in the center of the living room, neither looking at the other, concentrating. Jack reset the phonograph arm to repeat 'Jazz Me Blues.' Dan was better than he had any reason to hope. This was no audition, he thought. This was the beginning of a new sextet.

When they finished, Jack said, "Didn't you say you played with the University's stage band?"

"Yeah, most of the five years I was there. Good experience and an occasional buck."

At Dan's belt a pager peeped.

Dan pulled the instrument off his belt and looked at the display.

"The dispatcher. Can I use your phone?"

"In the kitchen on the wall."

Dan hurried into the kitchen and punched the numbers.

"Dan here. Where? Pioneer Village."

He waited, listening and then said a clipped "Right away."

As he put the phone in its cradle he hurried toward the front door.

"There's been an explosion at Pioneer Village. Someone's hurt. Want to go?"

"Sure," Jack said without thinking, caught up in Dan's excitement. He put his saxophone down on the sofa and hurried after Dan to the patrol car parked at the curb.

Dan spun the unit across the middle of the street and turned east on Twelfth Street. The patrol car's flashing lights reflected off windows of neighboring houses.

Jack noted his watch. Six fifteen. The sun was approaching the western horizon of the late August sky behind them. Long shadows of trees and houses reached across the north-south streets. The air was still and dry. The siren echoed through the quiet streets.

The quickest way to the Village was to skirt the town by taking 12th Street east, past the college campus to the last through avenue, Badger, then south seven blocks to State Highway 43. From that intersection at the city limits it was five miles east to the county road that ran south, parallel to Chautauqua Reservoir for less than a mile into Pioneer Village grounds.

"Dispatcher said the explosion was near one of the tractor sheds," Dan explained, concentrating on the street ahead.

"Who go hurt?"

"Didn't say. Just a 911 asking for help."

The tires squealed as he took the corner at Badger, then accelerated to fifty miles an hour for the seven blocks to the highway, siren echoing off houses. Turning left onto the four lane concrete road, Dan accelerated to seventy-five miles an hour. The patrol car's siren wailed across the countryside. Its flashing lights cast jumping patterns onto the hood of the patrol car.

"I can see the ambulance coming onto the highway," Dan said, glancing up into the rearview mirror.

As they sped east cars ahead pulled off the highway to make room. Jack began to feel his chest tighten. It was a dreaded sensation, unexpected. It had been a mistake to come. He realized then that he had not traveled at high speed in an automobile since leaving Texas. In the tension of the speed, he imagined he could smell gasoline.

Jack felt his breathing beginning to be short. He turned away from Dan, and gazed out at the blur of the fence posts, a car parked on the shoulder of the road. "Dammit, dammit" he thought to himself. A blurred memory of Alice returned. She was sitting next to him in the front seat of their Chrysler as they sped down a Texas farm-to-market road outside Denton. They had been at one of her friend's dinner parties. She was trying to explain her cute remark at the table about her abortion. Her abortion! And he had not suspected. He, the hard-nosed detective hadn't had a clue. Was the authentic version of the memory, he wondered. But every memory of the moment was authentic and vivid as reality. He could hear her sobbing through the words. He saw his arms flailing, pounding on the steering wheel. She had tried to explain why she didn't want a family. Not then, anyway. Blinded in anger he hadn't seen the movement on the right. Memory played the blurred image of the farm truck without headlights skidding onto the highway into the glare of his lights. It was all he could remember. Yet, overlaying the memory was the pungent smell of gasoline that engulfed his mind. He smelled it when he awoke in the hospital. It was only then he had learned the truth about the truck bursting into flames. They told him about his having been thrown out the driver-side door thirty feet into a ditch. In his anger departing from the party he had failed to fasten his seat belt. He had been unconscious two days. It had been someone from the sheriff's department of Denton County who explained that the driver of the truck had been drunk, and had been killed. Alice had been killed instantaneously by the impact.

He had taken responsibility. It had been his carelessness in anger that caused the accident. If he had been alert he might have seen the truck failing to slow down. He had judged himself unfit any longer to deal with the scenes of stabbings, beatings, violence arising out of animal rage. He never returned to duty. Alice's parents buried her before he was released from the hospital. He visited the grave the day he left Dallas. After that he wandered the roads they had taken together until he had returned to Iowa City, Iowa, searching his memories of a time past that had been filled with vigor and meaning. It was then that he and Elliot Morris ran into each other on the university campus.

As Dan turned onto the county road leading to Pioneer Village, Jack knew that the smell of gasoline and the sight of blood right then would make him sick. "Please don't let it be a gasoline fire," he thought. As the car slowed he began to feel calm. Dan had not noticed his tension.

The patrol car rumbled over the cattle guard at the Village entrance. Jake Bickerson, head of the Village Board, was standing at the souvenir shop door, pointing down the street toward the south end of the block-long tractor shed. The directions were unnecessary, for there was a thin, wavering jet of steam still rising from near the lean-to shed. A diminishing whistle of released pressure was the focus of attention. Half a dozen men stood across the street and watched the old Avery steam tractor weakly jetting steam from one of the pipes into the cab. The tractor sat half-way into the Village street.

Ten feet from the crowd of men, Dan pulled up and was out of the car before Jack had the door open on his side.

"Who's hurt?" Dan yelled at the nearest man.

"Henslow. Horst Henslow. Looks like it got him in the arm."

Standing away from the group on the other side of the steam-breathing tractor was a barrel-chested man in bib overalls. He was about five feet six inches tall, a muscular man in his sixties. Hatless, his hair disheveled, he held his right arm with his left hand. The right sleeve of his shirt had been torn open and was wet. As they got closer they could see the skin on part of the lower arm blistered and red.

"Come over here to the patrol car until the ambulance gets here," Dan yelled at Henslow over the hiss of the steam leak.

Jack admired the young man's authority. A cool one.

"It vas no accident, dat tractor!" Horst shouted, ignoring Dan. "Der vas nottin' wrong yesterday. Somebody try to ruin dis machine."

"Okay, Mr. Henslow, We'll figure that out later. But you have to get that arm attended to."

Their voices were no longer raised over the sound of steam, now whistling softly from the breeched pipe inside the cab.

The ambulance was coming down the Village street, its red blinking lights and siren announcing its arrival. The driver pulled past the patrol car and stopped near Dan, Jack and Henslow.

"Can he walk over here?" the medic yelled at Dan.

"What about it, Mr. Henslow? You want some help to the ambulance?"

They could see that Horst Henslow was shaking, his hands trembling.

"I don't need no help. You yust find what crook did this to my machine."

"You better get into the ambulance before shock sets in," Dan said as he and the medic led Horst to the back of the ambulance, helping him up onto the stretcher. The medic applied a cold pack to his arm and then fasten straps across Horst's broad chest, and then his legs.

Horst raised his head and shouted to Dan, "Dat safety valve vas good yesterday. Someone jammed it, I bet."

"We'll check it out Mr. Henslow. You better take it easy now. It could have been a lot worse for you."

The back doors of the ambulance slammed shut and with the siren going again the square white and red vehicle crunched over the gravel street toward the Village entrance, moving slowly, the emergency lights still flashing.

Back at his patrol car Dan was on the radio reporting where he was. He gave the dispatcher Horst Henslow's name.

"The ambulance will notify the hospital. It doesn't look life threatening, but he's got a steam burn on his lower right arm. Lucky it didn't get him in the face. I'll take a look at the tractor when its cooled down. When Sheriff Taylor gets back from Sioux Falls tell him I'll have a report for him, but I think he better get out here to take a look for himself."

As pressure dropped, a weak jet of steam wavered in a whiff of breeze off the reservoir. The early evening air coming over water cooled anxious faces. The hot August afternoon had turned cooler, and there was calm once again in the make-believe village.

"It's nearly done," someone said.

"Better let it cool a bit before you mess with it," another offered.

Dan opened the trunk of the patrol car and took out a roll of yellow plastic ribbon marked "Police Line—Do Not Cross."

"Can you guys find me four stakes of some kind. I'm going to put this tractor off-limits until the sheriff can take a look at it."

One of the men went into a metal storage building opposite the tractor shed and brought out four steel fence posts and a sledge hammer. Another helped him place the posts as Dan directed.

The sun was settling onto the horizon, the glow of sunset on a direct line with the Village street they had come down earlier. Jack looked at his watch. Seven ten. The emergency had been over quickly. He began to relax. It was a strange accident, he thought. But he knew he was going to like getting to know Dan Morris. Here was an accomplished jazz musician who could also take command of situations like this. That was cool in every way.

For his part, Dan talked to the group of men who had gathered near the yellow ribbon. Bickerson had come down from the entrance and was taking the lead in the explanations. Jack walked half way around the tractor. Steam no longer leaked from pipe on the left side of the fire box. Instinctively, his mind began to picture the tractor and Henslow just before the pipe ruptured. The tractor had been turning up the street, according to the tracks in the gravel. The Avery had had enough of a head of steam to move out of the shed and into the street. There was one conclusion he was certain of: if it were not an accident but sabotage, it was a strange and complicated way to hurt a man.

Bickerson and Dan approached the tractor and looked up into the cab at the controls.

"The valve looks okay to me from here," Bickerson said. "No visible damage, at least. Could be stuck. But that steam line is too hot to handle now."

"Well, let's just leave it as it is," Dan replied. "Sheriff Taylor can decide what to do."

As Dan returned to the patrol car with Jack, he commented, "The rest of those guys don't know much about what happened. Most of them were inside the barn there, and two were working on their own tractors. But they're a close-lipped bunch."

Dan frowned and added, "You know that Horst was picked to be Parade Marshall for Pioneer Days. You don't suppose someone is that jealous?"

"Well, Horst sure sounded as if he thinks someone sabotaged the tractor," Jack said. "Who'd try to get Henslow that seriously?"

"Good question. From what I've heard from my Dad, old Henslow can get pretty touchy, especially if he thinks the *Times* stories about Pioneer Village aren't fair. Dad said that when they ran the story last week about his being elected parade Grand Marshal, he came into the office furious about the story also including a paragraph about his being in the German army during World War II. It appears that his son Jim had let the new writer Carla Garza know that Horst had been taken prisoner at the end of the war when he was a guard at one of the concentration camps. She included the fact in a positive way. You know, enemy prisoner-of-war becoming a successful South Dakota farmer. But he complained bitterly to my Dad.

Said that had nothing to do with Pioneer Village. It was private information. Poor Carla. She'd just got on the job a couple of months ago. Jim Henslow blind-sided her by offering that information about his old man and the Nazi concentration camp. Bickerson says that Horst Henslow is one of the most active participants in the Village, although not the most popular in its affairs. He is on the board of directors that runs the place. Bickerson gives me the impression that old Henslow doesn't much like the town of Hamilton, when you come right down to it, but treats the Village as his residence, in a way."

"You don't suppose we have a serious attempt on Henslow's life?" Jack asked.

"Well, what do you think?" Dan replied. "Ex-detective like you should have some ideas from the scene."

"It's a hellova an uncertain way to kill a man," Jack replied, "Hurt him, sure. Or just scare him. It has the appearance of a prank gone awry. The picture will get a lot clearer when you have a closer look at that pipe and boiler. If the valve is actually okay, maybe it was just an old steam line letting go. On the other hand, if it were sabotage, there were plenty of opportunities to get to the tractor. These old things sit out here most of the year before being fired up for Pioneer Days."

Dan expanded the idea. "And it took some doing, if it was a prank. But it is interesting to note that Bickerson thinks Horst Henslow is one of the most particular tractor collectors around. He keeps his two steamers in tip-top shape. Bickerson said he was surprised that Henslow wouldn't have noticed if something was wrong when he was getting the steam up."

"That certainly suggests that it might have been deliberate sabotage," Jack replied. "When you and Taylor look it over together, you might want to see if there are any tool marks near where the boiler piping breached."

Dan and Jack got into the patrol car. They moved up the Village street slowly. Dusk was thickening. It would soon be dark. Several security lights on power poles had come on throughout the Village. As the patrol car reached the entrance, they saw that Bickerson was back at the office, standing near his car. Dan pulled over and rolled down his window.

"Try to keep that tractor off-limits, will you Jake? You going to be out here for awhile?"

"Well, Rachel's saving dinner for me at home. I'll get Elmer to watch it, if you want. We close the gates at ten."

"I think that's a good idea. Sheriff Taylor will be back sometime tonight. I'd like him to look it over before anyone moves it."

"I understand. If you need me I'll be at the farm."

"Strange coincidence," Dan said as he rolled up the window and pulled through the gate and out of the Village, "Jim Henslow's window was shot out this afternoon about four thirty, and now his step-father's tractor blows a steam line."

"Step-father?"

"Yeah," Dan continued, "Jim Henslow was adopted, I've been told. Makes one wonder what connection there might be, of course."

"Off hand," Jack offered, "I'd say the style of the two incidents are a lot different. Pot shot a window from a car. Tamper with a steam boiler line. The latter takes some serious planning and execution."

"Yeah. That seems about right."

The ride back to town was at the speed limit.

"Guess we'll have to pick up on a rehearsal later," Dan said. "I better get back to the office now."

"Sure. You can pick up your horn whenever. The sextet will get together at my place week after next. I'll let you know the exact time, okay?"

"Great. Look forward to it," Dan replied.

"Would you mind dropping me off at the Easton place?" Jack continued. "My Toyota is being temperamental. It's in Bud's Garage and I promised Ellie I'd drop by tonight."

"No problem. That's Ralph Easton's farm just north of the highway, right?"

"That's the place."

Jack could not be sure if he heard an attitude or not in Dan's voice. The young man had been away at college at the time of Ralph's accident. He likely didn't know the family very well. But then in a town of six thousand, even the people on the surrounding farms were part of the community.

The patrol car rumbled over the washboard gravel driveway into the Easton farm, pebbles pinging the under carriage. Two security lights at opposite sides of the farmyard bathed the house, garage, and barn in light. The white house and red barn were protected on the north and west side by a shelter belt of trees and bushes. Tall pine trees lined the driveway on the left as they approached. A white picket fence, recently painted by Gordy and Jack, flanked the wide driveway on the left and enclosed a front yard to the three-story, square house. A carefully mowed lawn was divided by a concrete walk, on either side of which were flower beds.

CHAPTER 3

$\mathcal{T}$he muffled whine of the siren penetrated the assuring words of the medic.

"You'll be okay, Mr. Henslow. The cold pack should ease the pain for now."

"Ya. I'm not hurt much. Somebody make mischief mit my tractor."

As Horst spoke he felt exhausted. Under the blanket, held by the straps of the gurney, he'd became drowsy, did not want to say more.

He'd been hurt worse in his life. To suppress pain by sheer will was the mark of a manhood he'd achieved at age thirteen in the Hitler Youth. This was nothing, his wavering consciousness assured him.

Gravel rattled against the underside of the wheel well of the ambulance as it accelerated toward the Pioneer Village gate.

"It's okay," the medic was saying. "Go ahead and rest. Just relax. We'll have you to the hospital in a few minutes."

Horst let his eyes close, gave in to the warmth of the blanket and the calming inside him, but the ringing in his ears echoed the screaming steam jet of the tractor. Then he forced himself to open his eyes again. The medic was sitting upright at his head. A green tank was strapped to the wall behind the attendant. Horst's eyes closed again and the sound of the tires under him changed as the ambulance rode up onto the macadam highway. The interior became quieter. The sound of the siren seemed distant.

Dream or memory returning? It melded into the calm that enveloped him. It was nineteen forty-five. He was thirteen. He and his friends Hans Steiner and Ludwig Krainer were called out of the school room and told to go to the front entrance. A light drizzle misted the roadway and had turned the stone houses opposite a dark gray. Everything was wet. The March air was cold, dank under a lowered sky. There in the street was their former teacher, Herr Martin Mathison, who had retired from teaching a year ago. Now in his sixties and wearing a loose-fitting uniform of the Volksturm, Mathison looked like a comic soldier, a character in a festival play. The uniform hung from his shoulders and the trousers were too big, baggy. Beside him stood an SS officer whose long leather overcoat glistened from the rain, as if it had been varnished. On the high collar of the officer's jacket was the insignia of the rank of Obersturmfuehrer. Hitler Youth had to know the military ranks, memorize them. It was not a high rank but the officer's manner was commanding. His deep set eyes looked at them without blinking.

"Heil Hitler," the officer snapped.

The boys returned his salute.

"You are late. Were you not told the order?"

"What order, Sir?"

Other boys were coming out of the school building and began to assemble before the officer, who now raised his voice and addressed them all.

"All Hitler Youth are to report in uniform. Today. Teachers were to tell you. You are now to serve your country. You now have the honor to fight for our Fuehrer."

"Where are we going?" one of the boys asked.

"Herr Major Mathison is your officer. He is in charge of this village's Hitler Youth contingent. You are to be in the service of the Fatherland tonight, to serve the Fuehrer."

The order came at Horst like a punch of a rifle butt in the chest. The war had closed in on him. He would disappear into it just like his father had.

"But my mother. She is alone," he blurted aloud. "I take care of her. My father is on the Eastern Front and she has no one."

The SS officer fixed him with a stare and in a commanding voice lashed out at him with an answer.

"Then you will be a hero like your father, not a stay-at-home shirker."

The SS officer turned to Mathison.

"The trucks will be here at 1800 hours. Get all the other boys from the school. Have your troop ready to go when the trucks arrive."

They saluted each other with raised arms, Mathison listlessly.

When the officer had departed in his staff car, Mathison turned to the boys.

"It will be alright," he said, "it is only guard duty. We can be glad we are not being sent to Berlin with the other boys to face the Russians."

"What about my mother?" Horst pleaded.

"She will be all right, like all the others. They will have to help each other. Maybe the bombing will be over soon. Maybe everything will."

It was March,1945, and food was scarcer than ever. Some markets would no longer accept official ration cards. Most food had to be bought on the black market. How would his mother get food if he were not there?

"Come on Horst. Quit being a cry-baby," Hans said. "This is what we trained for." Hans ran off to his home to get into uniform.

"Hurry, young Horst," Herr Mathison said, "the SS is shooting those who do not obey. And be sure to tell your mother not to put a white sheet out her windows while you are gone. The orders are for the SS to shoot whoever gives signs of surrender. And if you run away now, they will shoot your mother. So go, quickly, if you love your mother."

At home Horst got into his Hitler Youth uniform while lying to his mother. It was to be a training camp exercise like all the others, he told her. Only a few days.

"Mama, you must ask Herr Schmidt next door for help getting food. Stay in the house, in the basement, when the fighting comes to the village."

He told her about the order not to show white flags.

She was not yet fifty years old, Marta Henslow, but looked older than sixty. Her frail figure stood before him, a short, trembling woman who had comforted him when he'd been hurt as a child. When his time came to join the Hitler Youth she would tell him quietly at night when he returned from drill that God was more important than what the politicians and soldiers were telling him.

"Trust God, not these pagans," she'd say. "I pray for you every night, Horst. Trust God and he will save you."

He was fearful someone would hear her call the authorities names and would turn her in. He was confused by her talk of God, a vague, undefined god that had shown him none of the glory of his nation's rule over Europe. His mother was not like so many of his friends' parents. They praised the Party, the destined leaders of all Europe. The Fuehrer said that Communists, Jews and all the unfit people would be eliminated so that a greater nation would rise from the striving required today. For a thousand years Germany would show the world the glory of its superior way. The massive meetings in Hamburg where his Hitler Youth troop had been taken were thrilling. One time the Fuehrer himself appeared, rising up from behind the podium between towering torches, spot lights illuminating a halo around him. He looked like an ancient warrior; his voice pierced the night like a high trumpet call of victory.

Horst's spine had tingled with excitement and he had shouted with the others. Over and over they shouted "Heil Hitler." And then at the top of their voices they sang songs as they marched before the Fuehrer who had made them into one indestructible body. They would create the greatest nation ever known. He loved his troop, his friends, the Fuehrer. What need had he for his mother's little god that could not be seen or heard? He feared that his mother and her hatred for the Party would be found out. He felt ashamed and a little sorry for her. In those days she did not understand the great changes taking place, the meaning of Germany's victories over inferior nations and races. Now, as he stood before her in his uniform, he wondered if she had been right. The world was crashing down upon them. They had heard nothing from his father. The enemy leaflets said Germany was already defeated.

She kissed him on both cheeks, holding his face close to hers. Tears were streaming down her cheeks and wet his face.

"No, no mother. It will be all right. A short training exercise."

"I know better, Horst. I can hear defeat in the voices of those trying to tell us on the radio of our valiant fight. They say victory will be ours. But the battles are closer and closer. The enemy leaflets say their troops are over the Rhine and the war will soon be over. Now, the SS are forcing you children to fight where they have not been able to hold back the enemy."

He could not argue with her. The same empty feeling that swept over him when the SS officer ordered them into uniform now made him feel weak in the knees. But he could not let the feeling take hold him. He had a duty. He knew he had a duty, for it was the one lesson learned above all—his duty to the Fuehrer, to the Fatherland.

"The radio also says we have great reserves yet to put into battle."

"Ach, children!" his mother cried out. "Yes, children they will use now."

"Don't mother. Don't say those things. They will take you away."

"I don't care. They took my husband, now my baby."

"I am no baby. I have a duty."

He left then, turning from her. When he looked back from the middle of the road he saw his mother standing in the doorway, holding both sides of the frame, as if to keep herself and her home from collapsing.

"I will pray for you my dear Horst," she shouted after him.

It was the last thing he heard his mother say. It was the last time he was to see his home, the only house he had ever lived in. The image was indelible in his mind.

The sound of the back door of the ambulance being opened awakened Horst. The medic seated next to his head scurried to the rear. He and the driver were pulling out the gurney. Two others assisted them to lower it and the two-hundred pound Horst to the pavement. They were under the emergency entrance canopy. Horst could see three or four people and two children standing to one side watching. They had heard the ambulance coming to the hospital and were to be the first to know who in town was in trouble.

In the emergency room two nurses and the medic helped Horst onto an examination table. He felt dizzy, unable to steady himself. His chest hurt from the strain. Lying down was better. His age was telling on him, he thought. He felt older than ever before in his life. Sixty-three, he thought. Never did he think he would live so long, or go so far from his home.

"We'll take care of that burn, Mr. Henslow," one of the nurses was saying, as she examined his right arm.

"We'll have to take your shirt off so we can see all of it."

Part of the right sleeve of the flannel shirt was already torn where he'd pulled it clear of the burn. The nurse helped him take his left arm out of its sleeve first, then eased the fabric over the blistered lower arm of the right.

"Could have been worse," she said. "What if that steam had hit you in the face?"

"Ya. Dat vould hurt. Somebody tried to hurt me bad."

"Don't worry about that now. We are going to treat the burn and then you must rest here until the doctor comes."

It was done smoothly, the treatment. The nurse took his temperature and then his blood pressure.

"Just routine," she assured him.

Doctor Wilson arrived a few minutes later. His examination was done quickly.

"Not as bad as it looks, Mr. Henslow," Dr. Wilson said. "You'll be okay in a day or two. But your heart is racing from the shock. I want you to stay here tonight and get a good rest. Just a precaution. We'll see how things look in the morning."

Dr. Wilson listened to Henslow's chest with a stethoscope again. Taking the instrument from his ears and letting it hang about his neck, he frowned as he looked at Henslow.

"Your blood pressure is elevated too. Probably not surprising, considering the excitement. But I'd like you to come in for a thorough exam sometime late next week, after your arm has healed some."

Horst listened and rejected the invitation in his mind. It was too much concern about a little thing.

A nurse's aide took him to a private room in a wheel chair. They would not let him walk.

"I can valk, you know. I'm not so hurt," he said again, not wanting to give into the warm feeling of helplessness which all the care had created.

But such care, he thought. Here in this little town, good care of the sick and hurt ones. He had never before been in the Hamilton Community Hospital as a patient. But he was comforted by the security.

The hospital room where the attendant took him smelled of freshly laundered sheets and pillow cases. A tall window looked out on houses across the street, their windows lighted from within. Peaceful little town, he thought, remembering the recent image in his mind of his own torn village in Germany, and the rubble pile that had been his home.

As he began to feel himself sinking into sleep again, he was fully awakened once again by his son's voice.

"What happened, Papa?"

Jim Henslow, stood at the bedside. Just under six feet tall, he stood squarely upon his two feet, looking down at the injured man. His curly, dark hair, inherited from his father, was carefully combed. To Horst he looked the successful professional man he had become, dressed as he was in his suit and vest, a deep red tie set off by a blue shirt. His dark eyes were deep set. They reflected impatience. A frown crossed Jim Henslow's brow. He made a tentative gesture to touch the old man's shoulder, self conscious of the move.

Jimmy was not Horst's natural son, but had been adopted when he was two years old. Horst looked up at the frowning face of the man who was now his only family. The "Papa" greeting surprised him. Jimmy had not used the term since he was a child.

"Someone made the boiler pipes of the Avery blow up," Horst said. Why, he wondered, was Jimmy concerned about him. He never came to the farm any more, this important lawyer. Now this boy of his was a big shot in town and the States Attorney.

"Don't you vorry none," Horst added quickly. "You go about your business. No use vasting time on me."

He was surprised by his own tone. He tried to hold back, not wanting to sound peevish like a father talking to a child again. An old habit. He had tried to train the boy to be correct and a good worker. That was all he wanted. But it didn't matter any more. He's not really my son, he admitted. Not any more because he doesn't want to be.

"They called me from the emergency room. Said it wasn't serious. What did Doc Wilson say?"

"I'll be vell soon. A week, maybe two, and its all healed. I can be in dat Pioneer Village parade next month."

"So what happened?"

"A steam pipe blew open. Steam came out of the return flow pipe near the fire box."

"Doctor says you have to stay here at least overnight. That okay with you?"

"Ya, sure, yust like the doctor says. But it vas no accident."

"I don't think it was either. Something is going on about us Henslows. Someone shot out the picture window in our house at supper time. Now this."

"Ach. So," Horst replied, "Den it vas no accident. Someone monkeyed wit that machine to hurt us."

"Maybe, Papa. But why would anyone do that?"

"Smart alecs out to the Pioneer Village, maybe. Try a trick on old Horst. Some of them guys are jealous I got picked to be parade marshal for Pioneer Days last week at the board meeting. Maybe they tink I haven't lived in this country long enough to be a pioneer."

"Well, it's not a very funny joke, if you ask me. I'll talk to the sheriff. If we find out who did it, we'll press charges of assault."

"You don't bother. Don't make a big ruckus."

"You can't ignore it Papa."

"Vell, dat new deputy vas dere, so you don't have to trouble yourself."

It didn't sound the way Horst wanted it to sound. Still grudging. He didn't want to sound as if Jimmy didn't matter to him, but there was not much more to say. Since Marie Henslow had died two years ago, her body reduced to a skeleton by cancer, the son had ceased coming out to the farm. Horst missed having a son, a family, but Marie could not have other children after Jimmy was born. Baby Jimmy had been like his own. The formal adoption made Marie very happy. They were family. Today he would admit to no one that Jim Henslow's coldness toward him was painful, that this son's treatment of his stepfather had been like taking away his only family. It was almost like denying him the citizenship he had worked so hard to prove.

The strife began when the boy was in junior high school. He resisted every direction Horst gave, worked at chores with a sullen reluctance. Marie tried to negotiate, quick to intervene when Jimmy resisted his stepfather. But the antagonism grew on itself, the boy and man barely speaking to one another for weeks.

"He doesn't treat me like a father any more." Horst would complain to Marie. "I've been a good father since he vas a baby. Vhat did I do to him?"

"You are too hard, sometimes. And don't ever whip him again. He's afraid of you. Maybe you could be more friendly, not command him so much when he's doing chores."

But there was a right way to do things and a wrong way, Horst thought. The boy could learn from him if he only tried. Jimmy was twelve years old when he had talked back. Horst had used a rein of an old harness to discipline him. Not hard. Just across his back. In his anger he had shouted in German and the boy began to cry and then ran into the house. After that Jimmy resisted every direction. Horst's memory of the feeling was vivid. He didn't want that boy growing up soft. He loved him like he was his own. But the words never seemed to come out right, as if the English language he'd learned so quickly didn't have the feelings in the words that he wanted to say to make up to the boy.

The depth of Jimmy's anger showed itself later in one outburst, which surprised them both. He was a sophomore in high school, already on the first team of the football squad and a popular student. Alert of mind and a fast, agile runner, Jimmy Henslow attracted attention of the varsity coaches when he was still a freshman. The Hamilton *Times* printed his picture. His quarterbacking was by the book, plays carried out to their full purpose. But the coaches liked his initiative, which transformed even the most mundane of plays into opportunities for another yard, another foot. By mid season his freshman year they had him dress with the varsity team. The next year he played in every game, earning a letter earlier than any in the classmates his age.

It was on a cool autumn Saturday, a good day to work. There was no game that day so Jimmy was home. They were cleaning the milk parlor. Jimmy was too slow, upset because he had to stay on the farm to work.

"You aren't too proud to vork in the barn because you're a big shot on the football team, are you now?"

Horst knew as soon as he said it that it would hurt the boy's feelings. It wasn't what he meant to say. He had really wanted to say, 'It's all right not to like work in the barn when you're a young man. I'd like to tell you to go to town, and be with you friends. But everyone has to work. It is good to do your work before play. That will make you a strong man.' But it didn't come out like that. It had sounded all wrong.

Even then he was surprised at the ferocity of Jimmy's reaction.

His face red, his fists clenched, Jimmy Henslow shouted at Horst, breaking a silence of weeks.

"What do you know about being a big shot. You're just a damned farmer. Damned Kraut farmer. You don't even come to the games because you don't understand them. You don't give a shit about me. You just married Mama for her farm."

Horst had raised his fist and stepped toward him.

"I'll kill you if you ever touch me again," Jimmy shouted.

He had turned and run from the barn and was gone. A half hour later Marie came to the barn to tell Horst Jimmy had left. Her eyes were red, glistening with tears.

"He took some of his things. Said he wasn't ever coming back."

It was as if Horst had broken her most precious possession. He didn't know how to undo the damage. His anger was more at himself. He could not talk to her all that day. He stayed in the barn, doing work that could have waited weeks.

Three days later Marie had negotiated Jimmy's return from his friend's house in town. Later she told Horst that when he wasn't with them she had scolded Jimmy for the outburst. She explained to her son how she grew to love her husband and how Horst Henslow had struggled to fit into the American way of life after his uncle in Pennsylvania had brought him over from Germany in 1952. He had been in the war and a prisoner of war. All his family there had been killed. His mother had been killed when their village was bombed in the last days of the war. It had not been easy for him, she explained. Jimmy should understand how hard it had been for Horst.

"When your father died you were only two. Horst worked on the farm for us. Good, hard working young man. He is a good man, Jimmy."

She told Jimmy the whole story about how polite Horst was.

"A year after your father died, I asked Horst to go to church with me. He was too shy to ask me. I liked him very much, Jimmy, before we were married. People in the community got the idea that we were lovers even before that was true."

"Don't tell me that stuff."

"No. You have to hear it because your step father saved my life and made it worth living after your father died. Horst was a very proper young man. Never presumed. He tried very hard to be a good American. After we were married we were able to pay off the mortgage on the Pennsylvania farm. Then we came to South Dakota because your Uncle Randolph Meyer knew about this farm which was far better than the little acreage we had out there."

Marie explained that Horst had done everything he could for the two of them.

"Affection is hard for him, Jimmy. He wasn't brought up in Germany to show his feelings. But he cares. He really cares a lot for you. Loves you like his own, even when he feels like he is a foreigner and not really your father. Can you understand?"

The truce was made, but its terms did not include healing. Jimmy could not accept what his mother said and kept to himself the image of what his step-father meant to him—the usurper, the opportunist who moved into a good deal, the tyrant. He remained silent for his mother's sake. But there was no peace where there were no words. For his part, Horst had no longer tried to put into words what he felt, the loss. It was as if one edge of the security he had long ago achieved in America was now eroding, slipping into an unknown, dark abyss. The solid ground which Marie had made for his life had become less sure. And he blamed himself.

At night in the dark of their bedroom he would whisper to her. "I don't understand that boy. I do everything wrong for him."

"Give him a little room. He's proud and lets his temper go too easy. You do too."

Marie made excuses to get Jimmy alone to tell him again and again her feelings. She would talk to him about Horst's hard work to make the little Pennsylvania farm profitable, assuring Jimmy that his stepfather was a real success as a farmer. When they sold the Pennsylvania acreage and came to South Dakota, it took a mortgage again to get on and keep the 320 acre place east of Hamilton. That was in 1959 and through the good years and bad, Horst made the farm pay. He was proud of making the payments to the bank on time and buying more acres.

"And I made him promise that someday you would have the farm, to keep it in the family. He has worked for both of us, Jimmy. You should let your father be proud of that, of something. Every man needs to be proud of his work."

"He's not my father," was all Jimmy had said. He clamed up and said only what was required of him. Three years the truce ran on until he went away to the University and got his law degree. When he returned to join the Pettigrew Pettigrew Johnson firm in town, Marie was the proud parent. By then Horst had given Jimmy to the others, to the town. Horst came to town less frequently. It was then that Pioneer Village became Horst's passion. Marie thought that the pretend village, by its looking back at the history of prairie farming and settlement in the Dakotas with its old restored buildings, a sod hut, all the antique tractors and cars had become Horst's way of being more American than the others. Horst Henslow had given today's Hamilton to his stepson the lawyer. The make-believe Pioneer Village was his community.

"I'm sorry you got hurt, Horst," Jim Henslow was saying as he stood in the hospital room doorway, ready to leave. "Maybe someone is trying to seriously hurt you because of your past." And with that he left.

"With my past?" Horst shouted after him. But the door was closed. Why had Jimmy said that? Just like the newspaper article. Making his life seem bad. There was no past that he hadn't told Marie and the boy about long ago. Was he talking about the Pennsylvania farm, and his courting Marie after Harold died? Or was it about the war and his being in the Hitler Jungen? He had told Jimmy about those last days of the war. Jimmy was in eighth grade and read about the war and Germany and had asked him.

"You were on the other side, weren't you," Jimmy said one night, looking up from the book he was reading at the dinner table.

Horst explained about growing up and being in the youth program, the Hitler Yungen. "Like your boy scouts. That vas the way it seemed to us." He had shown Jimmy the two arm patches he'd saved from his uniform, souvenirs of a brighter time.

He then told Jimmy about being drafted into service by the SS. Twenty-four of them were in the truck that went to Bergen-Belson. They were given guns and ammunition. Guard duty, the SS said. They were ordered to patrol the fences of the camp and stand at the gates. The dead were everywhere. They weren't told what to do with the starving ones or the dead ones.

"I can't tell you how terrible the place was," Horst said. "It vas like a nightmare. But ve had to walk guard. Sometimes a boy vould be found crying in his bunk. Ve vere yust kids. I vas only thirteen. Most of us vere afraid. Our guard duty vent on for a week, maybe only five days."

Horst then explained that the SS left the camp in civilian clothes after the Hitler Youth had been there only a day or two. They and their old teacher Mathison were left to guard the dead and dying. Then the British soldiers came. It was April by then. Nineteen forty-five.

"I remember the date," Horst told him. "The 15th of April. Ve had been told that vhen the enemy came we vere to become Werewolves and fight underground. That's what they called them. Werewolves. Every German vas to kill allied soldiers, and be an underground fighter. Before the British took over the camp Herr Mathison had read us the order from the high official Martin Borman. I remember some of the words: 'Only scoundrels will leave their post. Stamp out your weakness.' But our old teacher told us not to take such an order seriously. He told us to surrender quietly vhen the enemy troops came. Not to shoot at them. One or two of the boys ran away then so they wouldn't be captured. My friend Hans did. But most of us vere taken by the British to the POW camp. It is hard to explain to you vhat a boy of thirteen felt by the defeat. All my life I had thought our leader knew the answers for our nation. We had glorious achievements. But my mother had been right and I vanted to tell her so after they let us go home. I got back to my little village after walking most of the way. Dere vas no home, no house left and my mother dead and buried after an air raid, one of the last. All dat happened to me in less than two months. From glorious days, Jimmy, like your football games, ve in the youth group felt like victors every day. Den after defeat ve had nothing. We became nothing. My parents vere dead. Germany defeated. My school destroyed."

After Jimmy's outburst Horst forced himself to tell his story again to Jimmy and Marie. He tried to explain how everything in his life had been wrecked, about trying to get work in his village and going back to school when teachers were found to conduct the upper grades, the gymnasium. The Schmidt family let him live with them six months but he knew they could not bear the burden of him in their family. Then for two years he worked part time on farms in the area, being paid with meals.

"The authorities in our sector put up tar paper covered buildings for those of us who had no houses. I lived in one of those on and off while working on farms for a year. Vhen I finished gymnasium in 1947 I moved to a farm near Hanover and vorked until my Uncle Randolph sent me money to come to America."

During the bitter winter of '49-'50 food was scarce, and farm work uncertain. Among the letters the Schmidts had salvaged from the bombed out house were those his mother had kept from the Meyer family in Pennsylvania, her mother's brother Randolph Meyer. All the letters were dated from before the war. Horst had written the Meyers and asked for help. Could they send a little money until he could find better work. The reply was beyond his dream or expectation. They would try to get him a visa to come and work on their and neighboring farms in Pennsylvania. In German Uncle Randolph wrote that he would send the money for the trip by boat when the permit was obtained. Six months later the money came and he went to America.

"Maybe you can understand that coming to America then vas like I got born all over again. I had a new life vhere there was plenty of food, plenty of vork, and relatives dat helped me get jobs on farms all over dere. I soon vanted to be as good an American as I could."

After that night when he had told Jimmy his story, there were no more outbursts, no more arguments. Jimmy did his work without complaining, but shared little of what he was doing in school. He seldom brought friends to the farm except in the fall when three or four would come out to hunt pheasants, walking corn fields in a rank to flush out the birds. Jimmy never invited him to hunt with his friends. Horst came to accept being outside Jimmy's world. He would be cheerful about it, he decided, and encouraged Jimmy to bring friends to the house. At least, he thought, he had made Marie happier.

❧   ❧   ❧

Jack Traid thanked Dan Morris for the ride and got out of the patrol car.

"I'll give you a call to confirm the rehearsal time," he said as he began to shut the door. Dan gave him a quick salute.

A single large oak tree sheltered the house in the front yard on the south. A soft golden glow of light filled the Easton house. Jack relished the feeling of sanctuary he got from this place, the groomed lawn and garden, the protection of the row of evergreens on the north. There was an atmosphere of timelessness seclusion about the place. He could see Ellie through the kitchen window as he went around to the side door. It was a peaceful domestic scene, her moving from stove to sink. The side door entry reinforced his feeling of the familiar, for it was used only by family and friends. Front doors are seldom used on farms, he mused. What would an architect decide about how one should design a farmstead strictly for function rather than the borrowed Victorian ideas of these four-square houses built on the prairies? Yet, the antique feel of the Easton place pleased him tonight and he was grateful for the friendship that had developed over the year between him and Ellie. And Gordy, he added thoughtfully.

Traid did not easily tell others what Hamilton had come to mean to him. Uncomfortable about sharing personal history casually, he'd lightly brush off the obvious questions about his left arm and Vietnam and about his retiring early from the Dallas police force to teach elementary mathematics in rural South Dakota. He would offer the flip observation: "Not that much different, you know. Track down a murderer, search out a kid doing violence to Pythagorus. Just a day's work."

But it was more than that, living in Hamilton. He had shared his true feelings with only a few. Elliot and Minerva Morris knew why he was in Hamilton and why he had fled Dallas. Mildred Singer probably understood his retreat better than anyone, for she too had been recovering from the loss of her only child, and a divorce from an abusive husband. After a year of Jack's holding on to the promise of their love, she had quit her job at Hamilton State and left town. She had explained little. His sense of having been deserted had been diverted by Ellie Eaton, who had skills at prying some of his history from him piece by piece over the past year. But in the beginning there was a polite sparring between them in a neutral zone.

Her first comment to him was, "A gentleman, no less," as he held a chair for her at the Roger and Ann Faregold's Thanksgiving dinner the past November.

Quick to respond he said, "Mere reflex. Mother's training."

Ellie had smiled. His tone had been just right.

Since Ellie's husband Ralph's death in a tractor accident three years earlier, her attitude toward men about her own age was mildly sardonic, signaling a suppressed bitterness about her loss and a preference for distance. She would explain, if urged to talk about her marriage, that she and Ralph had met at State College—she in nursing, he an ag major. Love at first sight, she'd say. She talked of their marriage matter of factly. It was, she'd explain coolly, a partnership, a "sound marriage because we both had the drive to make a success of farming and rural family life." As she spoke she would manage a whimsical tone that excused the edge of bitterness, as if to say life goes on, pushing a person every which way into the future, making the past more difficult to hold in memory. Her perspective of what was valuable seemed to Jack to be so certain, sustained by clinging to the security of the farm even though she had lost her husband. The attitude made her attractive in a wholesome way he had trouble parsing into analysis. At one point he had the strange notion that Ellie was the kind of mother Alice had needed but never had. Ellie maintained a stubborn resolve in life's arena as she wished it to be defined.

"My son Gordy and I are on our own now. We intend to make our lives and Ralph's farm work."

Traid caught her mood that first night. Here was a safe female companion who presented no threatening entanglement. It would be no repeat of his passionate attachment to Mildred. Here the landscape of relationship was well marked, an expanse of no serious commitments as far as the eye could see. That suited him fine since he had not settled his feelings about Mildred leaving Hamilton, the college and him.

"You and your son run the farm still?" Jack had asked at the Faregold dinner.

"With hired help. Gordy is sixteen now, and does a man's job when he's not in school."

"And you work at the hospital too, I hear."

"Five days a week. Makes me a part-time farmer"

"Worth it?"

"I want to keep that farm. It cost too much to get as far as we did, Ralph and me. I'm not going to sell it, not yet anyway. My job at the hospital makes it possible to hang in there."

It was clear to Ellie that Jack Traid was more comfortable asking questions than answering them.

A muscular, six footer with dark hair just receding at the temples, Jack Traid stood squarely on two, slightly parted feet. He had the appearance of an ex-athlete not quite in shape any longer. She noticed too the awkwardness with which he moved his left arm. He noticed and commented only, "Vietnam." With his rough cut and weathered face he did not fit her idea of a college math teacher, but she found him pleasantly masculine in an unthreatening way.

"Traid," she said, "certainly not Scandinavian like half of the folks around here."

Jack chuckled. "Not so far as I know. Would you believe it is an Anglicizing of Traidovsky, the name my grandfather brought from Russia. The Ukraine."

"Like so many others."

"What?"

"Changed their names to fit the North American tongue."

The Thanksgiving dinner which Ann and Roger Faregold offered each year to friends was a town-and-gown mix that was not unusual in a community where the college was a major employer and central to its cultural life. Roger, now Finance Officer of Prairie Rural Electric Cooperative, had once taught college English. According to his wife Ann, Roger's heart had not quite left academia. Among the twelve seated about the expanded dinner table that night were John and Sarah Riemer. A decorated veteran of World War II, John was a professor of history and close to retirement. Sarah was chairperson of the Hamilton Arts Association and an amateur painter. Carl and Margaret Engstrom, both full professors, he of English and she of chemistry, were the only couple that were both teaching at the college. Randy Spies from the art department and recognized in the region as an accomplished sculptor, was in his late thirties and unmarried. Elliot and Minerva Morris, relaxed and urbane in their late fifties, were regulars at these affairs, bringing with them the full weight of the town side of the party as well as news from the inner workings of the state legislature, such as the annual threat to cut the funding for the college.

"And where did your Russian ancestors settle?" Ellie had asked, pressing on with their introduction to each other.

Talking about himself inevitably led to having to tell about his marriage and the accident, memories of which he tried to keep hidden, even from himself, awake and asleep. If he could keep the subject on ancestors, he was safe.

"My grandfather came to Texas from New Jersey where he and his brother had landed, refugees from Czarist pogroms against the Jews in the Ukraine."

To those he felt might be sincere in their sharing of families, he would add, "It was a great deal easier for my Grandfather to live in Texas, not as Vladamir Traidovsky but as Vernon Traid—an ironic but iron-bound fact about attitudes in our great melting pot.

"Grandpa Vernon became isolated from his brother in New Jersey, from his American roots, as it were, as he moved from town to town as a tramp printer. He was probably nineteen or twenty years old when he traveled around Texas. Then at twenty-two he married my Grandmother Esther Mueller in Fredricksburg. That, apparently, was a romance and marriage celebrated only by the lovers. They quickly got themselves to Dallas and settled down to work in and later buy a small job-printing shop located in the backwaters of downtown. That's where I came from—from a Russian Jew and first generation German-American girl trying to make a life together in the printing trade."

Ellie noticed that Jack was watching her expression carefully as he talked, as if he needed reassurance. Here was a man with a tough exterior but trying to cover up the conflicts that ran deep within. Here, she thought, was a safe companion, an interesting man. This fiftyish man offered protection, she realized, which she still needed from the expectations of Hamilton match-makers, and from her own sense of incompleteness.

"With my Grandfather Thorson," she offered in exchange for his story, "it was the Lutheran Church that drove him from Norway to America. Couldn't wait to escape official religion. And he never went to church after he got here, except for weddings and funerals. This is probably the reason his wife and kids became Presbyterians."

But Ellie had soon returned to his history.

"Printers," Ellie said. "That explains the print shop I hear about."

Jack's private printing shop was equipped with antique machines. It was regarded as a curiosity among his academic friends. To those who took an interest in why an ex-cop was also a printer, he would describe his experiences in the little job shop in Dallas where his parents and grandparents worked at their trade. It was there he got printer's ink in his blood stream. Today it was to his own hobby shop that he went to renew what he regarded as an essential part of his life.

"My grandmother taught me to set type. She could set type by hand faster than anyone in the shop, including the two or three journeyman printers who worked for my father from time to time. She'd come into the shop long after Grandpa Vernon died and sit at a California job case part of a morning. I think she did it as a kind of ceremony of remembrance—and to show off how fast she was even in her mid seventies."

He might then add to the story about the little Dallas shop and how it was then the family's bread and butter through good times and bad, while explaining what he liked to call his "studio" shop. It had nearly as much equipment as his parents' little business, but was merely a hobby—a private place of remembered skills, a place for his own ceremonies of remembrance.

As Jack approached the back door to Ellie's house, he felt the familiar surroundings take hold of him once again. The place was a kind of security blanket, he thought, an island sheltered by the trees surrounding the property. His knock was greeted with a call from inside, a ritual welcome by now, he thought. It was as if Ellie knew only the sound of a warm homecoming.

"What's with the sheriff's car?" she asked when they had briefly hugged, the lightly touching embrace of cousins. "And the sirens we heard out on the highway?"

"There was a steam tractor accident at the Village. I went out there with Dan Morris. Horst Henslow got burned."

"Seriously?"

"Well, it didn't look that bad. But I guess I couldn't be sure."

The heavy, rapid descent on the steps on the stairway from upstairs announced Gordy Easton, nearly six feet tall, skinny but broad shouldered. He wore a plaid shirt and jeans. He was in stocking feet.

"Hi, Jack."

Gordy's friendship was remarkable, Jack thought. A teenager who paid more than a moment's notice to a fifty year old was to be cherished.

"What say, Tiger?"

"Not much, but I bet you can't guess what I saw in the shelter belt tonight."

"Wolves?"

"Nope. The albino deer."

"Really. It really exists?"

Ellie joined in. "He came running in to tell me. But it had gone by the time I got out past the barn to look."

"Yeah, they've been talking in town about people seeing this white buck north of town," Gordy explained. "Not too big a rack, but then I couldn't see that well. But it was there, just bright white among the pines."

"That's wonderful!" Jack offered, "Did you know that in some cultures an albino animal, or human for that matter, was thought to possess magical powers. They were treated as having sacred spirits. They had to be preserved as a way to protect the tribe from evil spirits."

"Well, Charlie's Bar is offering a hundred bucks prize for whoever bags the albino deer in season," Gordy said.

"Not much magic or sacred coming out of that place," Ellie offered.

"Yeah. Wish I could keep it hidden here on the farm," Gordy said.

"Maybe you could encourage it to stay close by. Put out a salt block and some corn," Jack suggested.

"If you want to," Ellie said to Gordy. "We can get a salt block at the Farmers Co-op tomorrow. If you can get Jack to help you shell the corn from the crib right now while I fix some dinner, we'll let him stay to eat."

"Great," Gordy said.

Jack smiled. It was what he had expected, part of the ritual of the past year as the three of them fashioned a friendship that posed no burdens, not for any one of them. He wondered if the gossips in town would understand that. Ellie and he were not piling into bed, the only goal worthy of their gossip. The comfort of their relationship was undefined, undemanding. It was just there. They liked each other. That was good enough for now.

As Jack and Gordy were leaving, Ellie announced, "Left-overs again, since I had to work late today. The working girl's answer to Martha Stewart."

Outside the air was becoming cooler after sunset. The late August afternoon sun had scorched the open fields and heat seeped into the recesses of the barnyard. The security lights flooded the area with light.

"Was your dad much of a hunter, Gordy?"

"Nah. Guys thought it kinda funny that he never hunted, not even pheasants. You know, everyone has a gun out here on the farm, but not my dad."

"How come?"

"He told me. It was a special thing to him that he didn't want to kill animals. He used to say, 'We live on other living things, like beef cattle. But I don't do individual killing if I don't have to.'"

"How did he come to think that way?"

Gordy explained as he pulled ears of corn from the open hopper of the corn crib and filled the bushel basket he'd taken from the barn.

"Dad said that when he got home from Vietnam he went hunting with a friend. He said he loved to hike across the fields. Didn't care if he saw pheasants or not. Then, he said, one time a rabbit broke out of the grass suddenly and ran down the edge of the corn field. He said he up and shot it with his twelve gauge. An automatic reaction, he said. He hadn't wanted to kill the rabbit, but there it was. He said it made him ashamed. That's all he'd say, but I figure it was connected to what he saw in Vietnam, what he had to do there."

"It probably was, Gordy. I was over there early in the war."

"Yeah," Gordy replied. "Mom said."

"Your dad had every reason to feel that way, about killing, I mean."

Jack listened to this child now becoming a man, maturing fast because of the loss of his father. It was as if the genes of maturity, responsibility, seriousness had kicked in as protective devices. Gordy Easton had grown up fast, understanding what his father's death had meant to his family, to his mother and his life on the farm.

For fifteen minutes they twisted corn kernels from the cobs, half filling a pail before quitting.

"Where do you want to put out the corn?" Jack asked.

"I think we better put it away from the buildings. Maybe out near the east end of the shelter belt, about where I saw him. I can just leave the pail out there where we can see if he comes back."

"Good thinking."

They walked out along the pine trees, the yard lights casting enough light to show the way down the lane. The penetrating odor of pine reminded Jack of the mountain vacations he and Alice had taken in Colorado to escape the July heat in Dallas. Vivid though the memory was of Estes Park resorts in Rocky Mountain National Park, the time seemed remote. Another life, he thought, not fully lived, taken away senselessly. In the twilight of this late August evening, the smell of sun-warmed blue spruce and Norwegian pines eased the memory further to the back of his mind.

"Right here," Gordy said. "I saw the white buck when he was standing right here. Look, there's some scat."

Gordy looked for a level place to place the bucket, twisting it into the dirt for support.

"That ought to do it. I'll watch early in the morning and in the evening to see if the albino comes back."

"Well, it might very well. Probably has a territory it wanders in," Jack said.

"Race you to the house," Gordy challenged.

"No you won't, not in my lousy condition. But we can jog it."

Together they trotted back along the shelter belt, angled off across the packed earth between the corn cribs and barn, past the separate garage and workshop, and in through the side gate of the yard.

"You want to work out with me on the track sometime?" Gordy asked.

"Yeah, maybe. What are you thinking?"

"I'm going out for track this year and I figure I could get some extra workouts over the weekend. Like tomorrow morning."

"What time you planning?"

"Early. Right after I get some chores done here. How about meeting at the college track at seven? The college track's not far from your place."

"Seven? That's about when I get up. But sure. I'll make it. Ellie and I are going to the Village tomorrow afternoon so I'll have plenty of time. I'll be at the track at seven. It'll do me good. That your idea or your mom's?"

"Not telling." Gordy grinned broadly, party to a private talk he and his mother must have had. It seemed strange, Jack thought, to be feeling this happy in the midst of such a conditional relationship. Take the full measure of this moment, he told himself. Cherish the unfolding. Don't rush your feelings. Don't push on those of others. How long it had taken him to understand that simple way.

They went inside to a table already set. The smells of squash and hash hung invitingly in the air. Three places were set at one end of the kitchen table. It was as it must have been when Ralph, Ellie and little Gordy sat as a family those years when their lives were held in a seemingly secure, sound vision of life on their own place. The tranquility of tonight seemed to highlight Jack's imagining their lives before the accident which took the father.

Feeling that he was becoming Ralph's substitute, that it was not just on his own merits that he was welcomed at this table, Jack seated himself opposite Gordy. Ellie sat at the end of the table, now, although unspoken, head of the family. He had become a provisional part of this family, as a borrowing, he thought, that worked for each of them. An honor was being accorded to him. His care for these two he knew to be in each of his gestures, but was not yet ready for words of commitment. He knew that Ellie also was comfortable with this non-committal relationship, just at the edge of intimacy, their friendship enveloping and securing them to these moments that were at a casual level.

As they ate and talked of Gordy's sighting of the albino deer, Jack reminded himself to absorb the moment, to quit analyzing every relationship. Accept the gift for what it is now. It was a lesson that had escaped him for most of his half-century of life.

Jim Henslow left Hamilton Community Hospital feeling irritable, irresolute, and angry with himself. He had meant to give some comfort to the old man, extend a hand. Instead the old hurt had returned as he looked down at Horst and heard him dismiss even this tentative offering of care.

Sheri Henslow was waiting for him in the driver's seat of the Lincoln Continental parked near the front entrance. It was her car. It was birthday present they really couldn't afford. But, oh how proud she was of that new car, Jim thought. Maybe it had not been a good idea to get it for her. To go further into debt. But she liked appearing to be in the same class as the wealthier members of the Minnehaha Country Club in Sioux Falls. She certainly felt as important as the Pettigrews, or the Johnsons or Morrises, those three families in Hamilton acknowledged by most to be 'leading citizens' by virtue of what had to be described as 'old wealth' in the terms used by this prairie town.

But he worried that the big car might not be good for his political future. Being states attorney was only a stepping stone, and one he wasn't going to pause on for much longer. Its low profile in the welter of state politics made it an unsteady blip on the radar of promising political futures. And the public perception of one's wife, he knew, could make or break any political future. Sheri's reputation as a photo journalist was already considered to be a bit off-beat. No charity work for her. But he'd bought the Continental on impulse, to assuage her discontent that had been growing during the past year. He had asked her to quit taking new photo assignments from the Sioux Falls *Argus Leader* and other publications because it gave the wrong impression in town. The car was to show her that they would soon enjoy real money. He had even encouraged her to drive in style to Sioux Falls to shop at Silverton's, the upscale women's clothing store. That image was saleable to Sheri at least. The Lincoln had brought weeks of peace between them during which she had not complained of having to live in Hamilton.

"Well?" Sheri's voice was pitched to a mild irritation.

"He'll be all right. The steam burned his right arm."

"Did you tell him about our window? About Art Rogers?"

"About the window. Not about Rogers."

"Why not? Maybe that bastard is going after all of us."

"Maybe, maybe not. I don't think he's that clever to work over the old man as a threat to me."

"Get the son-of-a-bitch arrested."

"We don't have proof yet that he's involved in any of this. Dan Morris is going to go out to Chesterton to talk to him and see what kind of alibi he has."

"Well, did you talk to the old man about the development deal?"

"Of course not. Do you think he's in any shape to talk business? I just wanted to make up with him, make him think I cared about his getting hurt."

"And?"

"And maybe I didn't make it sound quite right. So cool it. The deal will keep, at least if the Carpenter Group doesn't change its mind and go for the North Sioux City development."

Sheri emitted a sigh of disgust.

The Chautauqua housing development project was his promise to her that they would soon have money that counted for something, and enough to assure his election next year to the state senate, meaning they wouldn't be living in Hamilton the whole year through.

It was the new real estate deal that dominated Jim Henslow's mind these days. Plans were being made for a gated village on the east side of Chautauqua Reservoir, across from Pioneer Village. The Henslow farm was situated in the center of land on which the Carpenter Group already had options. Chautauqua Manor would be a convenient commuting distance to Sioux Falls. The low, rolling hills and waterfront of the Henslow farm offered an ideal rural setting. The plans were hardly known in Hamilton. Jim had talked to potential local investors, including his law partners, but few others in town knew that a major housing project was possible in the county. There had been no news stories yet.

"Mark Peterson gave me the impression that I have a couple months to get Horst to agree to the arrangement. If I didn't succeed today, I will before long, after we are talking to each other again."

"What do you mean? Did you blow up?"

"For Christ's sake, lay off. I didn't blow up. I just didn't make my concern sound right. He as much as told me to shove off, that he didn't give a damn whether I cared or not."

"And you said something. Right? The last-word lawyer."

Sheri backed the car into the street. The new smell inside the quiet interior of the Continental took the edge off her irritation. The power of its engine pleased her as she accelerated down the street.

Jim couldn't relax; she knew that. He couldn't deal with the old man the way they agreed it had to be. It was time that Horst was convinced that it was time for him to retire. He needed to give up the farm. The eight hundred acres were rightfully Jimmy's. His mother made Horst promise it would become Jimmy's. But there had been too great a chasm between Horst and his stepson in the past ten years for the subject to come up between them. She fought off the frustration of Jim's failure to get close to the old man, no matter what, and to change Horst's mind about living on the homestead to the end—that is, Horst's end, which couldn't come any too soon.

"Well?" she accused.

"I didn't blow up, but when he brushed me off I said something like there were people who didn't like his past, what he was back in World War II. It just came out."

"And he said it didn't matter, I suppose. Like that little addition you got put in the *Times* story about this ex-Nazi being chosen parade marshal last week. I bet he was thrilled to have the world learn he was a guard at a concentration camp."

"I told you why I did that. It's the one thing he fears. His past and what happened at the camp. Maybe its his fear of the Nazi hunters or someone he was with in the camp. I have never been certain, but it's a past he wants to forget but can't. I figured if he gets nervous enough about it, if it was all out in town, maybe he'd decide that Arizona is a good place to retire to."

"That's one helluva long shot. So what did he say to you?"

"I don't know what he said. I just walked out then. Left him to wonder about what it might mean. Who knows. Maybe he'll get so uncomfortable about everyone in town knowing about his past he'll want to get away from here, even away from his beloved Pioneer Village."

"And maybe he won't. And maybe now he'll be even more pissed at you. And you won't have a chance in hell of getting the farm. You make me sick sometimes with all this fumbling. You're getting it all fucked up."

"Can you use some other word, Sheri. You sound no better than a slovenly bar maid when you use that kind of language. You'll sound just great among the other legislator's wives."

"Well, fuck you very much for the compliment. You thought I was a pretty sexy waitress when you met me at the country club. And don't you forget my folks were just as damned good as that screwed up family of yours. And what's wrong with working in a bar, anyway, you stuck-up prick."

"Oh for god's sake don't let's start on that. It's just won't help when I announce for state senate next spring and have you cursing like a foul-mouthed bitch of a journalist."

It was Jim's rap on her when she insisted she ought to get busy and keep up her reputation as a news photographer. A journalism major in college, she had some success before their marriage in getting special assignments from several dailies in the region. They liked her aggressive pursuit of news photos. It was during the first year of their marriage that she first made her reputation as a gutsy photographer. She had gotten dramatic photos and the inside story of the riot at the state penitentiary in Sioux Falls. She had made stunning photos of the fires, prisoners stripped to the waist brandishing clubs. When she got news of the rioting and the fires inside the compound, she had driven alone to Sioux Falls and with a press pass and charm turned on high she persuaded guards to let her into a secure section that overlooked the yard where the fires were burning. Then she got the inspiration to talk to the rioters herself. She found her way to the first floor level where there was a barred door to the open yard, a door that prison guards had secured, and stood at with guns at the ready.

"Let me talk to them," she'd ordered. "I'll start a negotiation. You guys get back down the hall a ways."

And she had succeeded. She had talked to a six foot six, bare-chested Sioux Indian who was one of the leaders. The exclusive story and dramatic photos she'd made were a sensation among media people.

Sheri knew Jim resented her daring, her drive to get into a story. He wanted a wife that would make him look good. For weeks she would not go on assignment just to please him. But when she felt she was about to suffocate in Hamilton, she would go to the Country Club and drink with Derrick Holmes, assistant editor of the *Argus* and talk first about assignments she could have, and then about themselves.

As the Lincoln moved slowly through residential areas, they fell silent. It was her old tactic, Jim thought, to bring up her working in a bar when he first met her. She liked to goad him with the fact that her father was a junk dealer in Sioux Falls. There were six kids in the family and a domineering mother who made the whole bunch of them stick together long after they needed to leave the family for saner territory. It was Sheri's badge of honor that she had survived her dysfunctional family and had finished college and had married well. Her marriage was more of a personal victory than achievement of some ideal. But she made believe that it was a leap into success when she talked to her sisters and brother. But she resented having had to live in Hamilton instead of Sioux Falls, or Minneapolis. Jim insisted that his political base was in Hamilton and that Chautauqua County was politically safe for him.

Sheri muttered as she had to wait at a stop sign at an intersection for three cars to cross.

"Traffic jam, Hamilton style!"

"Calm down. And I'm sorry for what I said. We just have to get it right if we're ever going to get Horst to agree to a deal about the farm and to make good on his promise to my mom. It's the only acreage on the other side of Chautauqua Reservoir and right across from Pioneer Village. It's right in the middle of the land the Carlson bunch has already got options on. It's perfect for a housing development. And the Carlson Group knows it. But they're also interested in one near North Sioux City, too. Convincing Horst to get off the farm will be tough. But if I can get this done we'll have the money we'll need for the campaign and then some."

"And I suppose that means we'll have to stay in this rinky-dink town forever."

"It means that if we get in the state senate now that Pettigrew has decided not to run again, then with a little luck I'll get to Congress. Then you can kiss this place goodbye."

"Oh yeah, when I'm fifty years old. Wouldn't it be a lot more money to move to Sioux Falls and you get in that law firm that offered you a partnership?"

"And do divorces and real estate closings? We've gone through that before. No way. Not after all the years I've invested in Chautauqua County. We've got to be just be a little more patient. I'll go see Horst in the morning. I'll help him get home when he's discharged. He'll need a ride."

Sheri pulled into the driveway of their three-bedroom ranch in Cottonwood Acres, the newest addition to Hamilton. Sapling trees recently planted dotted the sodded front laws. Curbs and sidewalks that were not to be found in all neighborhoods of town announced that this was the development of choice, advertised as "homes of distinction." Today their house stood in the midst of the manicured neighborhood as a wounded structure, the shattered picture window covered with a sheet of unpainted plywood.

The garage door opened at her pressing the button of the opener clipped to the visor above the steering wheel. The car eased into its stall next to Jim's Ford Explorer.

Inside the house, which still smelled of new carpet after only eight months of occupancy, Jim and Sheri went their separate ways. They had agreed that she would have a bedroom and dressing room suite to herself and he the other bedroom with a bath.

"When you have to have it," she assured him with a smile, "we can do it any place you want. But I want some privacy, ya know."

Sheri enjoyed talking about their love-making as if it were a contracted commitment to be dispensed per agreement. To goad him further she would sometimes suggest they might set a schedule for having sex. Mark the calendar.

"Okay by me," he'd said. He supposed that it was the newest thing, separate bedrooms, separate living, routine sex. Sheri was tempting any time of day, none the less. Besides, having separate bedrooms was a lot more convenient than bumping into each other to get socks out of the dresser. The arrangement suited him fine.

"Stuffed peppers okay for dinner?" she shouted down the hallway from the kitchen. "I'll zap them after I've changed."

"Sure. Whatever."

Jim went to the dining room located in the corner of the house, between the kitchen and living room. The window in the dining room looked out onto the street. He pulled the drapes closed over the window before going to his room.

"What are you doing?" Sheri called from her bedroom door.

"Closing drapes. Just in case."

Neither Jim or Sheri Henslow felt at ease in their new home that night in August.

CHAPTER 4

*T*he Hamilton Country courthouse stood at the center of the city block dedicated to it, its Works Project Administration architecture of polished gray granite relieved only by an intended elegance offered by a two foot wide green marble trim around the double-door entrance. From the wide, raised concrete entrance porch designed for ceremonial events, one looked out across Main Street at the Carnegie Public Library standing guard over its square city block of Library Park. The latter periodically excited local real estate promoters into proposing a high rise office complex on its sacred grounds to accommodate the commercial needs of the growing town. The citizens were not willing to give up listening to the Hamilton Municipal Band concerts on summer evenings in Library Park as they had for the past fifty years. It was also a place of revered memories of once young lovers. It was here where engagements had been made or broken, where families had been started or just avoided. Those who would subdivide the park soon learned they were no match for the awakened defensive action by an otherwise contented populace.

Hamiltonians were proud of the foresight of their founding fathers who had provided a park at the center of the town and who had also envisioned the main thoroughfare which flanked it as a grand concourse. The park and Main Street were made fit for parades, public celebrations of every kind. Main Street was a wide backbone of the village, extending from its northern most limit to the Chicago and Milwaukee Railroad tracks to the south, both ends since extended as the town grew. In the 1880s it was a dirt street, packed and dusty in dry seasons, a quagmire in wet. During the good years at the beginning of the century, Hamilton's town council, with the urging of the boostering Merchant's Association, predecessor to today's Chamber of Commerce, had the then full length paved with red granite cobble stones. Inaugurated on the Fourth of July, 1902, this public concourse of a town of 3500 patriotic citizens became the talk of the eastern Dakotas. In the more urgent war-time of 1917 the maintenance-hungry street was covered over with macadam, a concession to the municipal budget makers and mayoral promises of frugality. Yet, the broad reach of the street, some one hundred twenty feet curb to curb, remained a matter of town pride, once designated by a poetically inspired editor of the Hamilton *Times* as the "Champs Elysee of the Dakotas." The older buildings at the center of the business district retained their turn of the century appearance, showing off fine tin work of entablatures bordered with acanthus leaves in relief and dates of their completion: "Johnson Block, 1909." "Pettigrew and Sons, 1896."

The uncluttered stretch of Main Street was a convenience on most days of the year for those who sought its arterial way north or south through town. In the nineteen thirties there were parking places provided in the middle of the street, but after World War II the town fathers judged that convenience too messy for an otherwise unique public way. In recent years from seven to eight on Saturday mornings the southern end of the street was closed to traffic to give the Hamilton High School marching band its wide expanse for rigorous training sessions that might one day take it to Macy's Thanksgiving Day parade in New York City.

Jim Henslow, forsaking on this Saturday morning a suit and tie in favor of Levis and a plaid short sleeved shirt, stood on the entrance platform of the courthouse and watched the ragged rank and file of high school youth in bright shirts and blouses, skirts and jeans. The band's instruments flashed brightly in the late August sun. The drummers were keeping time with the metallic beat on the rims of their snare drums. Pete Jorgenson, band director, was shouting the cadence and urging "eyes left" and "keep the line straight." Fall was already in the air, if not in temperature certainly in the anticipation of the football season and the first game scheduled for the following Friday night at Severson Field.

Jim Henslow felt the pull of nostalgia, the attraction of vaguely remembered problems, which in those days had simple outlines and easy solutions. For him high school had been a time of escape from home into the acceptance of his peers, who presented no threats or barriers to the future. If one could go back to…But he interrupted his own thought and turned and went into the courthouse, taking with him the challenge of today's problem. He carried with him the new .32 caliber pistol he'd just purchased at Mork's Hardware.

"Expecting more shooting out in your neighborhood?" Gustav Mork queried.

The news of the window to his house being shot out was already circulated throughout town. The assault had not required a *Times* story, which did not publish Saturday or Sunday editions. By Monday the threat against him would be old news, as would the boiler incident that had injured his step-father.

"Never know, Gus," Jim explained to Mork, "I'd better be prepared just in case whoever shot out that window decides to get a little more serious."

He had done the paper work for registering the pistol, bought a box of shells and was prepared to leave when Gus asked if he knew how to fire a pistol.

"No problem. We got training in ROTC at the U."

As Jim entered the courthouse his mind was on his step-father and not on his new purchase. How could he make Horst believe it was time to give up farming, move into town and make good on his promise made long ago to deed the eight hundred acres to him, the step-son who had warred against him?

The States Attorney's office was a simple arrangement of two rooms in the southeast corner of the building. Behind the frosted glass door bearing in block letters his name and title was the reception room, the domain of Mary Pettigrew, a distant cousin of the Andrew Pettigrew family of Hamilton's ruling class, and a legacy that the Republican Party honored with the sinecure certain until her retirement. At fifty-six Mary Pettigrew, trim in her dark blue jacket and skirt, a white blouse with its neat black ribbon tie, presented to the world just the image Jim Henslow liked his office to project. Sitting upright at her yellowing oak desk, a smile on her face through tempest or calm, Mary Pettigrew suggested stability, an unchanging bureau of government that no freedom-loving citizen need fear, nor look to for excessive progress or expansion. It was the latter image Jim Henslow offered in his campaign pronouncements. Here in his office it was Mary who represented the ideal, an intended check upon ambitious lawyers who might temporarily hold this office.

"Good morning, Mary. Any calls yet?"

"Good morning, Mr. Henslow. Nothing. Quiet as can be, like most Saturdays." The tone was Mary's usual oblique complaint about having to work until noon Saturday.

"I'm expecting a call from Mark Peterson, Minneapolis," he explained.

"Oh, yes. He was the man you talked to when Sally in the Registrar of Deeds office told us he was looking at the plat where your dad's farm is. Is that the man?"

"That's the man. Interested in Chautauqua County. Might be the answer to the Chamber of Commerce's dreams. Interrupt whatever I'm doing if he calls. By the way, I've got to be gone for awhile this morning. Just lock up when you leave at noon. My step-father was hurt out at Pioneer Village last night…"

"Oh, I know." Mary exclaimed. "Is he all right?"

"Nothing very serious, but he got burned from a steam leak in one of his old tractors. I'll have to take him home this morning. The hospital said he will be released at ten."

The States Attorney's own office was located at the corner of the building, two tall double sash windows in each wall let in the bright August morning. Closing the door after him, Jim went to his desk and seated himself in the new, high back leather chair he'd dared to purchase after two months on the job. That was more than six years ago. Elected in 1988 without serious opposition from a Democrat who presented a threat to him only in rural areas but thought too radical by town voters, James Henslow had launched a political career that pleasantly alerted party leaders, at least those living east of the Missouri River. Here was a comer. His campaign was mentioned in the Sioux Falls *Argus Leader*, usually mute about states attorney races outside of Minnehaha Country. But fifty-eight percent of the vote had meaning, the paper opined, beyond that election season. At the state Republican convention the next year those who mattered suggested to him the way he should head. The obvious route was that he could be next in line for the state senate when Andrew Pettigrew II, his law partner and mentor, retired. That time had come. Pettigrew was making it clear that the way was open. A politically safe seat in the senate was his for the asking and Jim Henslow was about to ask.

The ease of his election in '88 and the now-familiar office enveloped him with its aura of security and importance. It was a feeling to be feared, he thought, that sense of ease of office during the six years he had become a fixture on the political landscape of the county by winning each election by a larger margin. But he had rejected the feeling, the certainty that the office could be his indefinitely if he continued to receive the favorable notice for his handling of cases, including the success this summer when he prosecuted the eldest of the Rogers brothers for stealing cattle. Both Art and Clarence Rogers were involved in the theft, Henslow was certain, but it was Clarence who was caught transporting stolen cattle. On that occasion the *Argus Leader* printed Henslow's picture under the caption, "Prosecutor's Roundup." The compliments on Main Street had been even greater rewards, ample return for challenging Clarence Rogers and his brother Art. Praises from voters were chips for later use, and not, he intended to make sure, only an investment in a Chautauqua County office.

The bachelor Rogers brothers farmed a rocky, shrub-covered hundred and sixty acres at the northwest corner of the county. A few acres of corn were in evidence, and a feed lot for cattle. The farm was mostly the domain of Clarence since Art operated a welding shop in Chesterton, a village of two hundred souls northwest of Hamilton. His skills as a welder were well known in the area, skills acquired during twenty years in the Army. Local farmers valued Art's careful work if not the life style of the brothers.

The Rogers brothers were best known for their wild sprees at the Roundup Bar in Chesterton, an occasional activity which was troublesome to the community. Sheriff Tom Taylor had been called out to the Roundup on half a dozen occasions to break up fights instigated by the Rogers. Nearly as infamous as their carousing, in the minds of the tidy Scandinavians and Swiss farmers in the county, was the junkyard appearance of the Rogers' farmstead where rusted auto bodies blossomed among ancient hay rakes and manure spreaders long past usefulness.

After the judge announced the five-year sentence in July and Clarence was being led out of the court room, it was Art Rogers who muttered to Jim Henslow from behind, "Now that wasn't too smart, was it." The whispered threat did not register at first. Clarence had not been too smart? Then it occurred to Jim Henslow that it was he who had made the mistake, not the cattle thieves. The veiled threat had faded in Jim's memory over the past month as the solution to three years of missing cattle brought accolades from every quarter.

The rural voters would now have more reason to support him for higher office, Jim thought. That vote was a key part of the equation that would open the way to state political office. Praise for bringing in the conviction of Clarence was worth whatever Art might have in mind. As he sat at his desk and opened the box to look again at the pistol, he wondered how rough Art Rogers was intended to play.

The muffled sound of the high school band playing a march pulled into his office the quiet assurance of a peaceful town, a feeling he could enjoy in the few quiet moments of his life. It had been an orderly world being States Attorney of Chautauqua County, and for many would be satisfying enough for a lifetime. He knew that. He had been told as much by his law partners. But it wasn't enough, not for Jim Henslow and not, he was certain, for Sheri Henslow. He knew that his own ambition was rooted in Sheri's ambition and he had promised her when he asked her to marry him sixteen years ago that living in Hamilton was not going to be permanent. He had not yet made good on the promise. But in those days he had not been able to resist the sumptuous attraction of Sheri Morton. It had been a risky union in the minds of his staid partners, but since their marriage he and Sheri had avoided serious censure from the Pettigrews or Johnson.

Sheri Morton was all energy and revolt against convention. To be with her was like accepting a dare, uncertain where she might lead him. In the early years of their union she offered a sexual adventure he had only imagined. She was ruled by impulse. They were in bed together within in a week of meeting, Sheri's supple body surprising him with its wild reciprocity. The week before they were married it was she who took them to a hidden place on the shores of the Chautauqua Reservoir at two in the morning to undress and make love in high grass at the water's edge, massaging him with mud packs, then locking her legs about his back as they plunged as one into the cold water. He never discovered how she knew of the place. In those days

Sheri's not fitting into the prescribed Hamilton mold bothered him not a bit.

It also pleased Jim Henslow during the first years of their marriage that Sheri was winning recognition as a daring photo journalist, independent of Hamilton mores, winning by-lines repeatedly. But he felt uncomfortable about how his law partners felt about her. He knew they had expected him to marry Martha Mork, the librarian and daughter of the respected downtown merchants Gustav and Tina Mork. Martha was admired as an intelligent and steadying influence on the young people of Hamilton. The children's library she had built up over the years was an achievement touted in regular articles in the *Times*. But it was Sheri whom he could not resist. She had been working part-time between news assignments as a bar waitress at the Minnehaha Country Club. After their first date his limpid interest in Martha eroded in hours. Sheri had just received her degree in journalism and political science at the University. With their marriage vows was an agreement to do without having children. They were both going to get on with real careers

The phone rang. Mary announced "Mr. Peterson on line one."

Jim snatched up his phone.

"Hi, Mark. Glad you phoned."

"Jim, happy to find you in. How's the weather treating you this morning."

Trivia about weather provided each the assurance of a handshake before settling into business.

"Still pretty warm. Like summer," Jim replied.

"Did you get those preliminary drawings I sent you last week of the layout we're considering for your site?"

"Yes. Very nice. Impressive."

"You'll be glad to know that the board of Carpenter Properties is leaning pretty strongly toward the Chautauqua County location over the North Sioux City plan. They went over the plat of the farm property this past month. They like the location between the reservoir and the interstate. Now, if they can get something solid to work on from your end. How's the situation developing with your father?"

"It's going to be all right, Mark. Dad wants to quit farming and move to town. And soon. I just have to work out the arrangement between us."

It was a risky lie. Jim knew the assertion was more of a promise to himself than a fact, a condition that just had to be a reality and soon. The farm had been promised to him, after all. By rights it was practically his. Mark didn't need to sweat the details.

"Well, we'd be ready to make a commitment in two weeks if you can be a bit more definite."

"Jeez, two weeks. That may be rushing it from my side of it."

"Those who wait too long, Jim, get left in the dust. The deal to develop Chautauqua Acres has to be put together soon. The target is preliminary site prep before freeze-up this year, with layout of the golf coarse and construction started on the first units early next spring. Our investors are in place, for the eighty-five percent of the first phase. But you need to get commitments locally for the other fifteen percent of the required initial money. The board thinks the location is right for commuters to Sioux Falls and for retirees wanting to live on water. Don't forget, the North Sioux City location is a hot competitor, but I think we can swing it for your property if you can sign a contract no later than October fifteenth."

"That's a definite date then, October fifteen?"

"'Fraid so. But, I tell you what. If you can get into the Twin Cities Thursday, the Carpenter executive committee is meeting and maybe we can work out an interim deal, give you a little more leeway to work out the arrangement with your dad and get local investors on board. And the other detail is for you to get the tax deal sewed up, too, don't forget. The Committee members would like to meet you, anyway."

"Thursday? Kinda quick notice. But sure. I can make it."

"The meeting is set for ten o'clock in the morning, Radisson South."

"I can catch the early morning flight from Sioux Falls. That will get me to the Radisson by about eight."

"Fine. Let's have breakfast before the meeting. I'll meet you in the lobby at eight-thirty. We can have breakfast there at the hotel and I'll bring you up to date."

When he hung up the phone Jim knew the deal was moving in his direction. The excitement in Mark Peterson's voice, of the certainty of rapid development of the Chautauqua Acres project caught him in its rhythm. This was big time, real money. He rehearsed in his mind the unfolding of events. Horst would come to see that it was only right to put the farm in his control now, especially when reminded of the promise made to Jim's mother. Horst might also have to be reminded that this estate started in Pennsylvania with Jim's real father's farm. He might have to remind Horst of all the years his mother had contributed to the present farm's success. Horst might even remember the work he, Jim, had done over the years on the place. It was clear enough that he had rights to the eight hundred acres, to what was now known throughout the county as the Henslow place.

He had already worked out an idea for the arrangement that would provide Horst with security and give him, Jim, control of the farm and freedom to bargain with its true worth as a development site. Under a trust agreement Horst would get an annuity like those written by insurance companies, its value based on the market price for farm land in the county. It would provide a steady monthly income, a fair income for the rest of Horst's life. Nothing would be taken from him. The development deal was something he, Jim, had parlayed, the benefits of which were rightfully his. Horst didn't need to know too many of the details.

Jim Henslow swiveled his chair away from the desk, his head back on the headrest. He knew without putting into words in his mind

that the trust arrangement was an idea that Horst would have difficulty visualizing, to hand over his land for a piece of paper. "Lawyer
paper" Jim had heard him describe all contracts. But now was the
time to overcome the years he had shunned Horst as not fit for his
family.

Just bringing the past into memory brought the whipping incident into sharp focus, and the anger smoldered once again in Jim's
memory. The sound of Horst's swearing in German echoed in his
mind. At ten years of age he had been powerless against this foreigner, this intruder and former enemy of America. Horst Henslow
had succeeded in ruling him and his mother. He remembered thinking, even in junior high school, that America had been too good to
this former Nazi. It had given too generously of its wealth to a person
who had carried a gun at the Bergen-Belsen concentration camp a
fact he had learned when the old man tried to make up after their
argument. It had taken more than his step-father's version of history
to piece together those last days of the war. Jim Henslow had read the
books and clipped news stories about the search for former Nazis
hidden away in both North and South America. The role of the
Volkssturm battalions and the Hitler Youth were of special interest.
He could imagine clearly what this stocky, well-built man who had
married his widowed mother must have looked like in his youth. In
Jim's memory Horst's commanding voice was dressed in the uniform
of a Nazi, the broken cross on the armband blazing its message. Still
in his ears was Horst's taunting tone, his criticism of every chore Jim
performed on the farm. It was a vicious authority Jim knew he neither deserved nor had earned. It was those thoughts which had built
up over the years, compressed into an impossible silence that finally
exploded in the clash with Horst when he was in high school.

Since returning to Hamilton with his law degree and quick success
at passing the state bar exam, he refused to have his step-father to his
house. When he was elected and then sworn in as States Attorney
someone asked if his father had been invited, to which he replied

that Horst had no interest in Hamilton or its affairs. Now he confronted the high barriers he, Jim Henslow, had built to exclude that rude, awkward old man with a hateful past from his life. And now he wanted everything from him.

The clock showed ten after nine. He got up from his desk, and went to the south window to watch the band retreating toward the high school two blocks away, the cadence quickened by the beating drums. He would have to try, he thought. Convince Horst it was time to make good on his promise and give up all the responsibility of caring for the farm. It was time to convince him that now was the time he should honor the promise he had made to his dead wife. In the past five years Horst had already made it clear that he didn't care to actively farm the entire acreage. He'd been renting out most of the fields, keeping only the homestead and acreage bounded by Highway 43 and Interstate 29 as his own operation.

Jim returned to his desk, put the revolver back in its box and the box in the paper bag with the box of shells. He put the package in his brief case and went into the reception office.

"I'll probably not be back by noon. So just lock up, if you will Mary, when you leave."

"Tell your dad I hope he heals up real quick."

"Thank you, Mary. I'll tell him. Your thoughts will please him a great deal."

The muscles in Jack Traid's legs reminded him of his fifty-two years, of his sedentary ways since becoming a math instructor. Three miles of jogging around the Hamilton State track had been at least a mile too much, he thought, but Gordy's steady progress about the oval, his passing him with words of encouragement only to catch up to him again before he had completed a circuit had pushed him on.

Ah, the vanity of old men, he thought, when confronted with reflections of their own lost vigor. At the police academy as an instructor fifteen years before he would have run stride for stride with a young man Gordy's age, his then thirty-seven year old body had been trained into hard muscles toned for instant exertion and for endurance. Well, he thought wistfully, I have traded that muscle development for studied inaction, for developing a different strength. Then he revised the thought with a "maybe." He supposed that Socrates was flabby, short of breath when exerting himself, having succumbed to the peace provided by sitting with his students in the deep shade of an olive tree. It was necessary, he thought, that now before entering old age he would have the peace to understand what Vietnam had taught him, what the sum was of his career as a detective, and the meaning of a troubled marriage to Alice. He felt he had failed to put any of those parts of his life into a meaningful context. And for Alice he bore the greatest guilt, the deepest question of his inadequacy.

He and Alice had had a brief courtship, a small wedding with only a few friends attending. It had been a seven year marriage that seem to him to have hardly started when it ended in tragedy on a back road of Texas. What had all that meant? As a police detective he had earned two or three awards from the City of Dallas and there had been recognition by the FBI. Colleagues at the Christmas party playing a joke on him with the "Accounting Award," after he'd been temporarily assigned from homicide to lead the investigation of a corrupt city auditor who was convicted and sent to prison. In those years he had been in the midst of the gears of society, he thought, in which he had been a small cog. But Alice's death had stripped away that central structure of his life about which he had sought meaning.

With help from Elliot Morris, his roommate at the University of Iowa in 1962 while both were in graduate school, he had come to Hamilton after Alice's death and had found a classroom and the acceptance of the administration and faculty at Hamilton State.

Surely, he thought, Ellie and now Gordy might become the centering point about which he might get a hold on his life deep in middle age. Mildred Singer had seemed to promise that prospect two years ago, before she fled from Hamilton. It had nearly been spoken, but not quite made, a lasting commitment to each other. Then she had left without much explanation. He did not understand why.

A measure of trust, of an emerging sense of security, had returned to his life since he had begun dating Ellie. She and Gordy were reliable, and being with them had come to seem necessary to him. He had accepted that feeling in the beginning with wariness. What, he thought, was beneath this feeling he had for Ellie? Was it her strength and competence? She was totally unlike Alice, who had played at life and seemed only to merely tolerate his long hours on a case, and was embarrassed by the modest life style they could afford and which did not measure up to the affluence of her parents. Alice's bridge group made up of friends from that other life had been the focus of her married life. Their seven years together had been like a pause in time, as if both were waiting for something to happen. After a time it was no longer a novelty for Alice to show off her "private cop" at fund raisers sponsored by the Young Matrons Club. He had accepted beautiful Alice, her easy life, her early having fun at being married to a detective, but he did not know what it was supposed to become. The anger he felt in his working life, that he felt at the city, and at those he pursued and whose lives were spent preying upon others, had become like a veneer to his entire life. He would explode at Alice for some imagined stupidity, some inconvenience or slight. It flashed between them that night on their return from a dinner party and she had confessed to aborting their child, blinding him fatally to the pickup that had come from the side road. It was the anger that he had yet to understand. Mildred's love had nearly healed that raw anger inside him, but some fear she had not confessed to him took her to Minneapolis, a new teaching job, and success with placing her art work in galleries.

The session at the track lasted a little more than an hour.

"I've got to get back to the farm, Jack," Gordy said, running in place. "Mom said she wanted to start for town before nine to do some shopping. How about coming out about sundown to see if the albino shows up? I'm going to put out a salt block this afternoon."

"Well, your Mom and I are going out to dinner, but maybe that will work out just right. You and I can watch awhile before we go."

So they agreed and Gordy took off down the street on the return mile and half run to his home. The sight of Gordy free in the morning sunlight, his blond shock of hair bobbing as he moved with ease down Twelfth Street, struck Jack with the simple reality of their entwined lives. There was simplicity and wholeness to their friendship. That was because Ellie had provided a new stability in his life. He was, he realized, becoming dependent upon this young man's friendship. Was there, he wondered, such a thing as a fatherly instinct that had to work itself into one's life, regardless?

The directness and the wordless drive of the mutual passion which had enfolded him and Mildred Singer for the eight months of their relationship was like another language entirely from Ellie Easton's reserve. The afternoons in Mildred's apartment-studio, where they make love without questioning the present or future, were still felt as much as remembered. The smell of her oil paints had become for him a signature of their desire. He could not yet imagine he and Ellie approaching bed with as little negotiation or with as much freedom as Mildred had given him. As attractive as Ellie was, desirable by any measure he could conjure, he knew that they both needed assurances from the other. They would need some kind of final assurance from the ghosts of their pasts to verify their fitness for each other. Mildred had not dwelt in the past, seldom speaking of her divorce, the death of her daughter. It had seemed to him that Mildred required no assurances about the future, but he may have been mistaken.

❧   ❧   ❧

When Jim Henslow reached the hospital room, Horst was dressed and sitting on the edge of the bed. There was a pathetic aura about the old man. Jim could almost feel sympathy for him. Horst's large head with its uncombed wisps of white hair was bent forward, which made him seem defenseless, vulnerable. It was an aspect Jim had never seen in this man before. Horst had become an old man. And now, sitting slumped on the hospital bed, his vulnerability was heightened by the ragged right sleeve of the plaid shirt which had been torn open over the bandaged wound. He was buckling the straps of his bib overalls when Jim entered.

"You're dressed, I see," Jim said. "I figured you would need a ride out to the farm."

"Nurse said you called and vere coming. You don't have to bother, you know. There are cabs."

"No, I'll take you home. I'm worried about you, just in case you wonder. That steam leak could have been really serious."

When Sheriff Taylor and Dan Morris came into the room and made their report, a new meaning of the tractor incident emerged.

"Tampered with for sure," Taylor said. He was using his official voice. "The safety valve was forced onto its expanded seat. We couldn't get it off at first. Then we saw where someone had drilled a hole half way down one of the return steam lines."

Taylor paused as if to remember the facts. He looked at Dan for the detail, since it was the latter who had made the close inspection and had written the report while Taylor talked with Jake Bickerson about the horse show during Pioneer Village Days.

"The hole had been filled with lead or solder," Dan explained, "so it would hold until the heat and pressure built up. Whoever did it knew what he was doing."

"Ya, I knew something was fishy," Horst replied. "Dat vas a good machine."

"When did you last get steam up on the tractor?" Dan asked.

"A veek ago, about. Ya, it was on Friday before."

"It was all right then?"

"Ya."

"Someone tried to hurt you Mr. Henslow," Taylor said, interrupting Dan's query. "We'll do our best to find the perpetrator. Your son here can bring serious charges against anyone we find responsible for this attempt on your life."

"No. No, don't you bother yourself. Maybe I made a mistake myself. No big stink about this. OK?"

"You didn't make any mistakes, Mr. Henslow," Taylor said in disbelief. "I think you and Jim should be serious about this. It was a deliberate act to hurt you. Maybe kill you."

"Maybe I did. Maybe I didn't. But you yust forget it. I'll fix that boiler pipe myself."

"Well, whatever you say, for now anyway. But when we find out who's behind this we'll have to act. This is a case of assault to do bodily harm. Your son can tell you that's a serious crime. The intent was clearly to hurt you, maybe worse."

Taylor then addressed Jim Henslow, States Attorney,

"The Sheriff's Department doesn't overlook this kind of thing, Jim. And we haven't forgotten that the window to your house was shot out the same day."

Horst Henslow was frowing. "Maybe these are just jokes," he said.

Taylor ignored the comment and went on. "We'll let you know if we turn up anything. I'm sending Dan out to question Art Rogers, to follow up your suspicions, Jim. Even if we haven't any proof, we'll just keep him on edge a bit if he's our man."

"Sure, Sheriff," Jim Henslow replied. "I'm really concerned that this is more serious than Dad is admitting. For all we know it may be a threat against Dad's life just to get at me, as I told you yesterday. Or maybe something else, from the past, is going on here."

In Jim Henslow's mind the potential for convincing his step father he should leave the farm changed from his having to offer convincing arguments to doing what he might to enhance the fear Horst had of the past. His appeal to Horst would be shifted into a new argument based on Horst's need for protection. That tactic offered greater potential than urging Horst to understand his, Jim's needs for the future.

It was a seed to be planted in the Sheriff's half-alert mind, Jim thought. Horst's past was a clouded and forbidden territory the old man did not want explored in public media.

Turning to the elder Henslow, Taylor turned down his voice, as if to speak to a child or the very old.

"Now you just be on guard, Mr. Henslow. We'll do our part to catch whoever is after you."

With that the Sheriff and deputy left the room.

"Why did you tell them to forget it, Papa?"

"They'll make a big story about it and it will get in the papers some more. I don't want a big fuss."

"Well, it's going to be in the papers regardless of what you or I say because the *Times* reporter will pick up the Sheriff's report. They'll probably even suggest a connection between our window being shot out and the boiler blowing."

"That's not good. Maybe you could get the paper to not print anything? You said last night that someone didn't like me because of vhat I vas. That's just vhat you said, 'Because of vhat you vere.' Vhat was I, Jimmy? A German? Yes. A little boy in a uniform in the vor? Yes. But I didn't kill those people in the camp. I didn't do any of dos horrible tings. I vas thirteen years old. Now that is going to be in the paper again and sound terrible."

"Look, I'm sorry all that got in the Pioneer Village story. I wasn't thinking. But that new writer made it seem you have really accomplished a lot. She wrote that you had become a success. It didn't come out bad."

What I should have been imagining, Jim thought to himself, is that someone out there is trying to tell Horst Henslow something about his past, about the concentration camps. Maybe Bickerson. He goes to Sioux Falls to temple Beth El. His and the Marritz family are the only two Jewish families in town. Good families, to be sure, but maybe they have some deep resentments. The Bickersons had farmed south of town for two generations. And the Marritz family had had the Hamilton Shoe Store for as long as he could remember. It was hard to imagine that either family would be turning on Horst Henslow with memories of the holocaust.

As he watched his step-father sitting listlessly on the edge of his hospital bed, Jim began to realize that regardless of who was trying to scare the old man, the incident opened many possibilities for a new and convincing argument to be made to Horst. He, Jim, would have to become Horst's protector against the threats, this one and the ones that he, the stepson would make sure were made in the next few weeks. As he turned the thought over in his mind, he realized that the little mystery of who fixed the boiler pipe had opened a new way for him to hasten Horst's decision to leave the farm.

"What you have to face, Papa," he went on, "is that the steam leak was not an accident. It wasn't something you forgot to do. You are too careful with your tractors. Everyone knows that. I know that. That's right, isn't it?"

"I keep doz tractors like new. There vas nothing vrong with the Avery last veek vhen I got steam up. I vas making sure it vas ready for the Labor Day parade a veek from Monday. I'm supposed to drive it in the parade to advertise Pioneer days. Then yesterday, I just got the tractor into the street vhen the steam came out at me. It got me on the arm vhen I vas checking the fire box. Then I jump."

"Yes, and maybe the whole boiler was supposed to blow up."

They had said more to each other in this half hour in the hospital room than had been said in the last ten years, Jim realized. He could see in the old man's eyes a shadow of fear.

It was that look which convinced Jim Henslow that fear was going to be far better than reason and logic to convince Horst it was time to acknowledge and act upon his, Jim's, right to the farm.

"There are people, you know, who don't care how old you were when you were at that camp. Details get blurred. I've read about groups hunting down ex-Nazis in America."

"But I vas a little boy. Ve even tried to give some of the prisoners bread. But there vasn't enough."

"You know that. You know what was in you mind—yes, even in your heart—in those days. But people in organizations that still hunt for Nazi's may not care about that. It's revenge time."

"Now? So late. So long ago those things happen."

"Maybe now that the big fish have been caught, or are dead, the Nazi hunters are going after the small fry. Maybe they just now learned about your past."

"Past? That sounds terrible! I came to my uncle in Pennsylvania. I vas legal. Not a new name or trying to hide like I read about the SS officers who vent to South America. I read about them in the papers and I know I vas just a boy and did not make that kind of terrible thing."

"Yes. I know. But we have to be prepared to keep you safe from those who don't care how old you were. Maybe all they know is that you were a German soldier, and you were a guard at Bergen-Belsen concentration camp."

The name of the camp struck a dark note. Jim paused to let it sink in. The potentialities were opening up. The arguments for Horst to give up farming were becoming even more persuasive.

Horst hung his head, shaking it slowly. When he spoke his voice was nearly a whisper.

"Forty years I am a good American. I take citizenship. I take no handouts and vork hard. I vork to make the Pioneer Village, too. Now this? Now they will try to kill me because I was a little boy that didn't know anything? What kind of country is this now, anyway?"

"Maybe you should come stay with Sheri and me. For a little while, anyway. Until this blows over."

"No." The old emphatic command returned to his voice. "I'll go to the farm. I got my guns, you know, if they try to monkey around out there."

"Well, whatever you want. But you better be on your guard"

As Horst rose from the bed, Jim reached for his arm to steady him.

"Can you walk okay? Should I get the nurse to wheel you out?"

"I walk. I'm okay."

Horst stepped away from the bed and started toward the door. He stopped and held the door for support.

"Just a bit dizzy, you know."

Perspiration was on his forehead.

Jim took the old man's left arm. It was a surprising move for him, a reflex that broke through the years of disdain. The tyrant was an old man, he thought. He's becoming more feeble and vulnerable and he knows it.

"Take it easy. There's no hurry. You're all checked out. I got your prescription filled at the pharmacy. It's an antibiotic so you won't get an infection. So we can go out the front way where my car is parked. Can you make it okay?"

"You don't like doing this, do you Jimmy? All the years you hate your step father?"

"Let's forget that. I mean, if you can forget it, put it aside for now, I'll just try to help you."

Jim could feel Horst's weight on his supporting arm. He was accepting help, this man who once needed no one, who could do everything on his own and was the authority. Now he leaned on the son who had denied him. It was ironic, Jim thought, how fragile he seemed. He could remember no time he had ever touched his step father, not since he was in grade school. Now he was helping him into the Explorer, supporting him as Horst hiked himself up onto the seat.

They rode in silence through the town, past Hamilton State, down Main Street to its intersection with State Highway 43. They turned east into the morning sun. Once beyond the city limits with five miles to get to the Henslow farm, Jim prepared his argument.

"You know, Papa, it's time for you to think about getting off the farm. It's not good to be all alone out there where someone might try to get at you."

Horst did not reply. He was shaking his head slowly, perhaps not hearing, or perhaps not totally refusing the idea of leaving the farm but trying to resist the force of its logic.

"Like Ole Halverson. He and his wife sold out, went to Arizona. People say they got a nice, new place in Sun City. Most of the successful farmers your age are getting off the farm. Like Peter Mitchell after his wife died a year ago. He now has an apartment in town."

"Pete is an unhappy man, I tell you," Host replied emphatically. "He comes to the Village and hangs around vith nothing to do. Says, 'Can't play vhist all day.' That's vhat it comes to."

"But you don't farm much any more. You're renting most of the place on shares."

"Ya. It's home too, you know."

"We could find you a comfortable place. You could pick it out and fix it the way you wanted."

"Jimmy. You have thought about this, I can tell. Don't you vorry about the farm. Vhen I die you vill get your share."

It was in the open, the fate of the inheritance, of the farm.

"But the farm, the eight hundred acres. What will happen to that?"

"I have an idea, maybe. I tell no one yet. Just an idea. But don't you worry Jimmy. Even if you didn't ever talk to your step-father, he won't forget his duty to you. Your mama was good to Horst. For her I won't forget my promise."

It was now that the argument had to be made to this jury of one, jury and judge. It was time to pry Horst's intent into the open, and change it on the basis of the new evidence that someone was out to harm him.

"What I have been thinking," Jim began, "is that the farm can be preserved without your staying out there alone. We can keep it in the family without big estate taxes. You know that the tax is big after $600,000. Wasted. Goes to the federal government and doesn't do anyone any good."

"I know about the taxes."

"It doesn't surprise me that you do. But we can avoid all that. I can set up a trust, a legal arrangement, that will provide you with a steady income, a very good income, the rest of your life, and the farm will be protected and we will find you a safe place."

Horst looked up at the lawyer speaking to him and tried to see the little baby he'd adopted forty-one years ago. He wanted this baby to be a son. Now he was talking to the lawyer.

"Protected?"

"The trust. And you too. Somewhere safe. I will administer the trust until you pass on, then the assets will naturally go to your heir."

In the cool interior of the air-conditioned car the hum of the tires on the road was as a monotone of suspension, a background of sound effects that enveloped a proposition too new, too complex for Horst to grasp. Maybe, Jim thought, it sounded too much like a scam. Maybe he was selling it too hard.

"I have to tink about that Jimmy. I had some ideas. This is another one."

"You will think of it, then?"

Jim was turning into the macadam driveway of the Henslow farm, a broad swath of newly mowed grass lay on either side. The house was set back thirty yards, nestled among blue spruce, a tall cottonwood towering over it from the rear. The clapboard siding was newly painted and brightly white, the window frames dark green. Despite the freshness of the buildings shining in the diffused morning light coming through the trees, in his mind Jim saw it as a dark place, a foreboding place. This was the house where he had been like a prisoner all through high school, just to please his mother. But now, what was rightfully his was being kept from him. The property that could launch him into the world of finance and political position was also the place where this hard man had laid the lash to him. It was both a place that could open a new beginning for him. It was the place he had tried for years to purge from his memory.

The driveway lead directly to a double garage, the doors of which were closed. Sixty feet to the left of the driveway, across the packed gravel farmyard, was the mansard roofed barn painted a traditional bright red, the window frames painted white. Behind the barn, between it and the grove of trees, was a feed lot enclosed by a white fence. Horst kept no cattle now, but the fences remained in good repair and were freshly painted. A machine shed to the right of the barn was also freshly painted white. Horst's pride in the farmstead spoke loudly and showed itself to the world passing by on State Highway 43. The farmstead offered itself as a model operation.

"Can I help you in the house?" Jim asked.

"I'm okay, now."

From the car seat Horst picked up the white paper bag with the bottle of pills. He opened the door and eased himself out. When he had both feet on the ground he paused, held onto the open door and turned to Jim.

"You are an important man now, Jimmy. I'm sorry ve didn't get on all those years. Just because I vas a dumb ox, I guess. I'm sorry I vas hard on you those times."

"And I was stupid too, Papa. Maybe we can forget about it," Jim replied. It had to be said. Try to start a new relationship, he thought. Become the protector, while more threats are made. There was not much time. He'd already led the Carlson Group to think the farm was as good as being his.

"Maybe," Horst said. "Maybe that happen."

"And you will think about the trust idea? Everything arranged for you? You safe somewhere?"

"Ya, Jimmy. I'll think about vhat's best."

"And you better lock up at night. Just to be safe."

Horst Henslow stood blinking in the sunlight as Jim backed the Explorer around and prepared to leave. He watched as Jimmy drove out onto the highway. Leaving him was the hope he once had for his own family.

❧   ❧   ❧

When Jack Traid returned home from the college track he showered and spent the rest of the morning in the print shop. The first two pages of Roger Faregold's book of poetry were ready for printing, locked in a chase and mounted in the Chandler and Price press. On the press's tympan sheet he'd adjusted the pins to which the paper would be fed during the printing. Without turning on the motor, he rolled the fly wheel of the press to print one sheet. He then folded the sheet to check the precision of the margins. He started the motor powering the press to begin printing the fifty sheets of this run. In the repetitive feeding of sheets to the press, he felt as if time became suspended. There was at least order in the universe of his shop.

The slow, jazzy rhythm of the press evoked old memories of Traid's Print Shop in Dallas where job work arranged the day, the craft of each step organizing one's mind about the duties, as if that carefully proscribed commitment to life was wholly contained in these simple skills. The repetitive, steady feeding of sheets to the press was, he thought, like a religious ceremony in which forgiveness could be found. If, the persistent "if" of his life since Alice's death focused on him. If he had only noticed, had had only a fraction of a second more; if he had cherished more when there was a chance to reach out with care. But his anger had betrayed him. And when disaster struck and Alice was killed, he was powerless. It was then he left Dallas to wander through the geography of his past.

The press continued its clatter and stamping at the slow speed he needed to interleaf a sheet of newsprint between each printed page to prevent the fresh ink from off-setting against the next. It was the end of August, 1995, and the morning sunlight made the day radiant. Be at peace in this moment, he told himself. The past cannot be undone. Accept forgiveness, just as Mildred had urged. The angry spirits of those other times can be calmed, she insisted. Here, in his print shop, he could begin to understand what Mildred tried to tell him. Here he had begun to make another realm in which to breathe. The rich texture of each sheet of handmade paper received the deep imprint of lead type, the printed page a beautiful object made in propitiation of wrathful gods.

It was his hunger that could not be denied at twelve noon. Since he had skipped breakfast except for a cup of coffee and a piece of wheat toast, a western omelett seemed justified, he told himself. It could be justified, too, he mused, in view of his valiant effort to recapture muscle tone by the early morning jog with Gordy and by spending three hours devoted to his craft.

❦   ❦   ❦

When Jim Henslow returned home for Saturday lunch, Sheri prodded him with her questions.

"Well, I suppose he said, 'Okay. You treated me like a shit all these years but I want to give you the farm.' Right?"

"Don't be stupid. Your irony stinks."

"Well, just what did he say?"

"He was nice to me, surprising as that may seem. He said he wasn't going to forget me. And said he would think about the trust agreement I explained to him. That would put me in control of the farm and how it is used. I think he understands."

"Oh I bet that old codger understands. He knows about deeds and property."

"Well he does, and the fact that he didn't boot me off the place is promising. And there is a new element in the deal. He's afraid. The accident wasn't an accident and it's scared him."

"What do you mean?"

"I mean that Sheriff Taylor and Dan Morris came to the hospital and told us that they had clear evidence the tractor had been tampered with. Someone deliberately tried to hurt Horst."

"How clever of you!"

"For Christ's sake, don't ever say that, not even as a joke."

"Just kidding, dear one. It would have done you credit though."

"If anyone began to think that I was responsible, we'd have about two cents worth of a chance to get the farm, not to mention being elected to the state legislature. Whoever sabotaged the tractor hates Horst, either because of his past or maybe because he is being honored by Pioneer Village. What I have to do is convince the old man that he needs to retire and forget about being a big shot at the Village."

"Well, I was just thinking about how capable you used to be at such things."

"Yes, and what might that be?"

"What it ought to be now," Sheri said in level seriousness, "just as damned rough as it needs to be. That I know for sure. Like at the U and your dirty tricks operation you told me about. How was it you fixed old what's-his-name's ambition to become chairman of the Young Republicans? What was it, stolen property found in his locker? You got what you wanted, right?"

"You can forget I ever told you about that."

"But, my dear," Sheri's voice mocked him, "think how clever it would have been if you shot out your own window to make people believe both you and your old man were both targets of a guy like Art Rogers. That would be like a man who had imagination and wasn't going to let anything stand in his way."

"Well, keep tuned, smart ass," Jim snapped. "The Horst Henslow saga isn't over yet. But I didn't shoot our window out and you better face it, it's a bit scary. If Art Rogers is getting even, what's next? I got us a little protection just in case," He added, opening his briefcase and showing Sheri the revolver.

"Well if he comes around here again and I see him, I'll shoot the bastard. I by god promise you that. Put it where I can find it."

"It'll be in my dresser drawer. But if I were you, I wouldn't be too frisky with a gun. But in the middle of the night I'll feel safer knowing we've got one in the house."

Jim softened his tone to change the subject and added, "And just to remind you, I've arranged dinner with Tommy Johnson, the Pettigrews and Morris's at Andy's tonight. I think Tommy and Pettigrew may be about ready to put some money in the project. I don't know about Morris, but I've got to get them off the dime."

"Do we really have to go? That place bores me. Stuffed birds, guns and traps hanging from the walls. The place smells of dead animals."

"And serves the best steaks in the state. Yes, to answer your question. We have to go. Now that Andy Pettigrew has announced he won't be running for re-election, I need his endorsement. And I need Tommy to engineer the nomination at the convention. And it doesn't hurt for us to be seen with my law partners in public, either."

"It would be more fun to go to the Sioux Falls Country Club."

"We will, but not tonight. And I've already told Tommy we'd be at Andy's at seven. When I show them the drawings of the project Mark Peterson sent me last week, then maybe they will get a little more serious about investing in Chautauqua Acres."

❧   ❧   ❧

Ellie's honking in front of the house hurried Jack Traid from the kitchen where he had finished feeding Rasputin and putting his own lunch dishes into the sink.

On the way to Pioneer Village they talked about Gordy, about the workout at the college track that morning, about his putting out salt blocks in hopes of seeing the albino buck again. For Jack the domestic chit-chat was strangely comforting, without the stress of undercurrents in Mildred's life. The subject of Gordy Eaton was a safe one for them, the love of the mother, and his, Jack's own admiration for a serious teenager coping with the loss of a father.

He and Ellie had been able to talk of personal feelings since their first date alone. He had taken her for a Friday night dinner at the Quarry Resturant in Dell Rapids months earlier. They had confided in each other, sharing biographies in detail for the first time, including his being shot in Hué, Vietnam. He knew that his was an inadequate description of the suppressed anger he came to live with because of the futility he felt after the war. His inner sense of anger was exacerbated following the war by the seemingly endless legions of criminal humanity he pursued as a police officer in the back streets of Dallas. He told Ellie of the drinking problems of fellow officers, of the stress they endured, and the infectious cynicism among members of the force. He tried to describe his own wavering idealism about the need for civic responsibility. When Ellie asked about his marriages, he was able to force himself to make a brief recitation of how his first wife Mary had left him after only three years. He'd just gotten on the Dallas force in '72 and decided they could afford to get married. She'd then decided she couldn't take being married to a police officer. Then there were bachelor days again before Alice found him. Telling Ellie about the crash in which Alice had been killed was painful. He told her about the dark aftermath of the accident when he quit the Dallas force and had wandered alone through Oklahoma, Kansas, and west into the Rocky Mountains—revisiting the roadways on which he and Alice had vacationed together. He retold the story of how he had sought out remembrances of his past on the University of Iowa campus where he and Mary had met, and how that search had led to his accidentally meeting Elliot Morris on the Quad. It was, he explained to her, the reunion with Morris which resulted in his coming to Hamilton to teach. He didn't describe the town as a refuge, but Ellie had been a sympathetic listener and seemed to understand.

Ellie had opened up during that first dinner and told about her first dates with Ralph at State College when they had been too poor for restaurants and had shared peanut butter sandwiches for impromptu picnics on campus between classes. She told about their marriage in a Brookings church, family and college friends surrounding them. It was a time, she had said, when both of them believed they would live and love into great old age. She described the difficulty they faced in arranging financing to purchase the Chautauqua county farm and how she became pregnant with Gordy at a time when they needed her salary from the hospital. Ralph's accident and death she lingered on, saying she could talk to few people about those weeks and months of the aftermath, but that because of Jack's willingness to talk about Alice and the accident it was easier for her. There had been a bond made that night, Jack felt, one that had suggested to him over the following months that they could trust each other. Being with Ellie made Mildred's desertion of Hamilton, and of him, haunt fewer of his hours.

When they got to Pioneer Village and the Pioneer Print Shop, Ellie perched on a stool and watched as Jack began to adjust the huge ink rollers of the flatbed press. An antique but in good working order, the press had been donated to the village print shop by the Dell Rapids *Tribune*, which like hundreds of country newspapers had abandoned letterpress equipment for computers and remote offset printing plants operated by others. The old press was a great prize for the Pioneer Print Shop, which was equipped and laid out to represent a turn of the century country newspaper office. To the right of the front door as one came into the narrow, frame building was a roll top desk with a hand-lettered sign on top: "Editor and Publisher." Cabinets of type cases lined the wall on the right, and two antique job presses sat against the opposite wall. The flat bed press filled the back end of the shop.

"So what will the first issue of the Pioneer Voice have to tell the world?" Ellie asked, looking over his shoulder as he reached back under the feed board to adjust the height at which the rollers would sweep across the two newspaper pages of lead type..

"Now that is interesting subject, and a big secret out here in the Village world. Jake Bickerson told me just yesterday that he might have a very important announcement and that we are to save the headline for it. And I figured we better reserve at least eight column inches for the story. Jake said we would get the announcement at least two days before opening day—just enough time for Mike or me to set the type. But Jake says if we print before the first day of Pioneer Days, we have to keep all copies locked up until after the noontime announcement which will come right after the tractor parade."

"Don't you ever get a kind of spooky feeling out here on the make-believe main street of old buildings? They are empty most of the time with only their ghosts to occupy them."

"Naw, we don't allow ghosts out here, except next door at the Davidson Funeral Home and Mortuary. There the antique caskets on display are reserved for the few ghosts we do have out here."

As they were talking they saw through the bay window which looked out onto the Village street Dan Morris pulling up in front of the print shop in a Sheriff's Department patrol car. He soon filled the frame of the open front door.

"Oh, hi Ellie. What're you two up to on a nice Saturday afternoon?"

"Jack's trying to convince me that the only ghosts that live in Pioneer Village stay at the mortuary."

"Well, he may not be right about that," Dan offered. "There may be at least one or two prowling about down at the tractor sheds. Capable of a little mischief, maybe a little steam engineering poltergeist."

"Oh?" Jack questioned, coming from behind the press. "What did you find out?"

"Sheriff Taylor and I got a good look at Horst's Avery this morning. Looks as though the safety valve had been jammed and a boiler steam line weakened with some kind of insert put in a drilled hole. I've been taking pictures of it just now."

"Someone deliberately tried to hurt Horst, then."

"Sure looks that way. It's pretty clear that someone rigged a plug in the quarter inch hole. Bits of solder-like material were found along the edges of the hole. When Sheriff Taylor and I told Horst and Jim Henslow about it at the hospital this morning, old Horst said for us to forget it. Said it was maybe his own mistake. But it certainly wasn't."

"And what will the Sheriff do about it, then?" Ellie asked.

"The question is what is the connection between the shot through Jim Henslow's picture window and the boiler explosion? Jim suspects Art Rogers but when I went out to Chesterton and Rogers's shop this morning, he seemed to have an airtight alibi, at least for the shooting. He named two men who live in Chesterton he said he was drinking with them that day from four to midnight in the Roundup Bar. When I questioned them, they backed his story. I called Jim Henslow about the alibi, but he still thinks Rogers is involved.

"And the boiler?" Jack asked.

"Art is smart enough and has the skills to tamper with the boiler. He's worked metal most of his life, including his twenty years in the Army."

"Possible he did both," Jack said, "But the style sure seems different,"

"Style?" Ellie asked.

"Yes. Every crime scene has a personality, a style," Jack replied. "It's as if every criminal act has a signature. These two are about as different as they get."

"Yeah," Dan said.

"Do you suppose," Jack went on, "that competition among these collectors of old steam tractors can get serious enough to lead to a prank like that? Do you think a couple of them are jealous because Horst was voted Grand Marshal for Pioneer Days? "

Ellie answered. "After your Dallas experiences you know the answer to that!"

"I guess. But that kind of violence out here in rural South Dakota? Pretty vicious reaction."

"Oh sure! These nice, placid rural folk," Ellie snorted. Her cynical tone surprised Jack.

"Not so peaceful as you might image," Dan reminded them. "Don't forget the little incident that happened south of Sioux Falls a couple months ago. Guy shot his neighbor dead for messing with a ditch and sending water into his field. There's plenty of envy and anger to go around out here. Maybe a touch of greed mixed in. And don't forget, it was a couple of country boys who blew up the federal building in Oklahoma City last April."

"Yeah," Jack conceded weakly. "People with their arrogance and non-solutions."

It was nearly five o'clock when Dan left.

"We better get back to town," Jack said, "if we're going to change before going out to dinner. Did Gordy invite you to watch for the deer with us tonight? I kinda promised him we'd spend some time with him staking out the salt lick."

"Well, he got the salt block and set it out near where you put the bucket of corn. He told me he'd asked you to watch with him. Maybe I'll just let the men do that while I gussie up for Andy's Steak House. Saturday night, you know. Everyone in town will be wanting to get served out there. The great community ritual."

"Should I call the Faregolds? They might like to go out with us."

"Sure. With that Saturday crowd at Andy's, our dinner isn't likely to be much of an intimate affair."

"Speaking of which…" he left it hang in the air a moment. "You are an inspiration today, Ellie. Spending a couple of hours watching me wallow in ink and grease."

"A girl's gotta do what a girl's gotta do."

"What does that mean?"

"It means I think you are a nice guy!"

He leaned forward, kissed her lightly on her lips, holding his grime-covered hands up in a gesture of surrender.

They embraced and kissed, lingering at the taste of each other. The silence and warmth of the old print shop excited them and drew them closer. For the first time their bodies pressed tightly together.

Ellie eased away, both hands on his chest.

"Hmm," she whispered, "we appear to be getting a little too serious."

"A wonderful bit of seriousness, Ellie."

"And maybe…" Ellie started, then paused to seek the words. "…more wonderful when we have both made peace with our losses. When we are more sure of one another. You know that don't you?"

"Yes, I know. It's hard to explain how much I appreciate being with you. I like the time we share. It makes some memories disappear for awhile. I know that sometimes I can't see the world for what it can promise."

"If it's meant to be, we'll get there," she said, taking his hand in hers, then removing it. "And now we'd both better wash our hands of the print shop for the time being."

Using waterless soap, they removed ink and grease from their hands, sharing one of the industrial cleaning rags Jack had brought to the shop.

The ride back to town was in silence, a warm comforting silence, Jack thought. They were a step closer. He felt he was, at least. But it was frightening. There was a commitment being suggested that both had skirted these few months. There had been a salving lilt to the tone in Ellie's voice all afternoon, he thought. It was as if a new mood was developing between them. He stopped himself. Don't analyze, he said to himself, slowly repeating each word. Don't...an-al-yze. But with Ellie he was left with the feeling he didn't quite understand what he really felt.

Ellie pulled up in front of Bud's garage west of town where the ten-year old, blue Toyota sedan waited for him in front of the shop.

"I'll phone the Faregolds," Jack said as he got out of her car. "I'll tell them to meet us at Andy's about eight. I'll be out to get you at seven, okay?"

"No later. And we'll take my car to Andy's, not that heap." She smiled to accentuate her comment upon his chosen vehicle. "And remember, you're going to watch for Gordy's magical deer. "

"I won't forget. And I won't forget a wonderful afternoon, Ellie. Thanks."

"And I won't forget a wonderful afternoon, Jack. Thanks."

She smiled again and drove off.

❦   ❦   ❦

Horst Henslow stood in the living room looking out the front window at the reddening sky in the northwest. The sun had moved back from its northernmost post at the summer equinox, its setting now nearly out of view of this north-facing window. The old house was empty behind him. Marie was gone, now these five years, and that child who should have been his son but was not because they both had failed. Now Jimmy was being pleasant, acting as if he cared what happened to his old step-father. He was being nice because he wanted the farm. There was no hiding it. Jimmy wanted the farm. Then, what about Horst? Go to Arizona? What had Arizona for him? Another empty house? No friends or a Pioneer Village where he was needed?

He turned from the window feeling his knees weak, trembling. He never before felt so exhausted. Settling into the recliner before the television, he did not turn on the light or press the remote button to watch the evening news. He stared toward the front window and the gathering darkness and felt again the empty fear that had gripped him in the middle of the night at the hospital. What was it? Ludwig Krainer in his dream?

There had just been Ludwig's face, coming closer and closer. He was shouting but Horst could not hear, as if the dream were a silent movie and the looming figure was all shadow and eyes that pierced into his soul. Ludwig, who wanted to surrender to the advancing Allied troops, saying it was all over and there was nothing left for them to save by fighting. Horst's dream shifted into a memory scene from that time. Ludwig was standing next to his Uncle Martin Mathison at the prison camp. He was afraid to escape the on-coming troops and Herr Mathison was telling him it was all right to surrender. They were both traitors. Hans Steiner was shouting at them, waving the pistol. Hans had become a werewolf, following orders. Horst was watching. Just watching. Helpless. He then awoke with a start. The old dream again.

It was dark by the time Horst got up from his chair and went into the kitchen and pushed up the light switch. The bright overhead light revealed Marie's kitchen. He had not changed a thing. The hot pad holders she had made hanging next to the electric range. The framed devotion, a poem about holding on to each day, was hung on the wall next to the kitchen table. Horst felt the emptiness seep inside him and he was fearful. Who was trying to wreck his tractor? Trying to hurt him with the steam leak? If Marie were here she would be able to tell him how to be calm, how the old phantoms were long dead, not to be feared.

❧   ❧   ❧

The diffused, pink light of sunset filtered through the branches of the ranks of trees in the shelter belt which reached a protective arm around the Easton farmstead on the west and north. A whiff of ripening corn seeped into the protected compound on a northeast breeze. Jack Traid noted the wind direction to Gordy.

"If the wind were blowing the other direction, out from here, we'd probably have little chance of seeing any deer."

Man and boy sat on their haunches, backs against the east end of the barn. The shadow of the building provided their cover, and stretched down the dirt drive paralleling the shelter belt. The salt lick was a hundred yards away.

A benign stake-out, Jack thought. During all the times he'd had to watch from an unmarked car, or from a rented room overlooking a dismal Dallas slum, smelling the poverty of those who struggled under the weight of neglect, never could he have imagined this sweet watch on a Dakota prairie. The excitement and intensity of Gordy's desire to see again the albino buck deer, charged the air about them.

"You gotta see it, Jack. You just gotta, before someone scares if off, or it gets killed."

"Sure hope I do."

"You said albino's were magic. Like how?"

"Well for one, the Sioux Indians have the white buffalo story. When a white bull calf was born they regarded it as a sign of their coming success against the flood of settlers. They would be able to overcome all opposition because the albino calf was a sign."

"Yeah, I can see that. Like it's really special."

"You can read it that way. People do. Actually its a genetic flaw that causes a creature or plant to develop without color pigmentation. A freak of nature. Often such abnormalities result in poor health and short lives."

"Maybe that's why people think they are so special."

"What do you mean, Gordy?"

"Oh, just that when people or animals live a short time there is something special about them, like they have something in them that made them different. Maybe they have to have more life faster."

"You mean like your dad?"

"I guess. I feel him around the place all the time. Sometimes I think I can almost see him, or hear him. It's like he is helping me finish restoring his tractor when I work on it."

"I know the feeling. Someone so special to your life doesn't just disappear forever. They do live in you—hold on to you."

Gordy nodded. The shadows were deepening in the approaching night. The striation of high clouds above the fence line at the end of the shelter belt had turned from pink to deep gray and purple.

"Do you think human spirits ever get into animals?" Gordy asked.

"I don't know, Gordy. Some people would scoff at the idea. It's our human arrogance. We're superior. 'Have dominion over all creatures of the earth,' the Old Testament says. So the idea most people like to believe in is that humans are special, above nature. But I like to think we are deep within nature and that we can thrive on understanding how miraculous that is, for us and the animals."

"I kinda think like that. You know, like my dad could be showing himself in the white buck, like he was around here, protecting us."

"That's a fine way to think of it Gordy. Your believing your dad is still with you keeps his spirit alive."

As they talked Jack felt the warmth of this open, generous acceptance of him as a confidant. Here on this quiet farmstead he was not a cop or a teacher but a friend of Gordy. The unspoken trust was a gift unexpected. But then too, he thought, it may be erecting a barrier around mother and son. Friendship can penetrate such a screen but the way is more treacherous for sexual love of the boy's mother, for the passion of a total commitment beyond their past. Now he was challenged to navigate the shoals of trust, friendship, and love where another man's huge spirit moved in the shadows of trees, through the outbuildings, the house, on the freshening breeze from the now dark prairie.

"Looks like we're out of luck, Gordy. Maybe your deer hasn't discovered the salt block yet."

"Yeah, maybe. You and mom going out to Andy's for dinner again?"

"Yup," Jack said casually. Then directly to Gordy, saying what needed an answer, "You don't mind do you Gordy? I mean about your mom and I dating, going out with each other?"

There was silence as they walked toward the warm yellow lights of the house. Gordy was translating a complicated thought into the words he had available.

"I don't think so. It's nice that you come out here to the farm and are our friend."

"But your mom and me. We're becoming pretty good friends. Is that okay?"

"Mom says so. She says she will always love my dad. But she says she likes you a lot. So it's okay."

A simple answer, Jack thought. Nothing more needed to be said. Much more needed to be lived.

Gordy's dinner was on the kitchen table. Ellie was dressed in a dark pleated skirt, a blouse in fall colors under a light tan damask vest. As they stood in the doorway to go Jack remarked to himself at the womanly transformation from the afternoon's casual jeans and loafers. Her perfume tonight was understated, a spicy aura that presented itself then faded to emerge again. Hints of Oriental nights, he thought, then chuckled at this romantic reflex.

"And what are you chuckling about?" Ellie asked as they went toward her car parked at the fence outside the yard.

"At how lucky I am tonight."

He put his arm around her waist and pulled their hips together as they walked.

"You are a beautiful woman, Ellie."

"And you are a generous man, Jack Traid, even if you are an ex-cop."

"There is always hope, even for the most lost of souls, like old cops gone out to pasture."

On the way to Andy's Country Restaurant west of town on highway forty-three, Jack described his and Gordy's vigil for the white stag.

"That boy of yours has some pretty deep thoughts about people, and about his dad."

Ellie turned and looked at him, saying nothing. In the dim light of the dash he could see her eyes misting.

"He misses his dad, of course." Jack said. "But he also has him close to him. It's interesting that he associates the white deer with the spirit world. He even said that maybe it was his dad telling him that he was around still."

"He told you that?"

"Yes. It was a great compliment, Ellie, to have Gordy trust me with those thoughts. He trusted me not to laugh, and I didn't, of course."

"He is a very deep kid. Sometimes I think too serious."

"But it's his strength. He'll survive with that kind of strength. We could all use some of it."

"Yes, couldn't we."

"But he said it was okay that I liked you, and take you to dinner."

Ellie reached over and squeezed his hand on the steering wheel.

"That's two of us."

The entrance to Andy's Restaurant was a small vestibule turned into an exhibit of hunting photos and a featured painting of the Rough Rider. The oil painting of Teddy Roosevelt in his Badlands cowboy incarnation had been done by a local artist. Primitive in its execution, the full-length portrait at times required identification for those who did not quickly recognize the subject.

"That's the old Rough Rider himself," Andy would explain, "when he was up to North Dakota on his ranch. Helen Pillsbury did that for me. Almost was going to call this place the Rough Rider, but decided that seemed too much like North Dakota where he went in summers. But he was some guy, that Roosevelt."

Among the framed pictures of men posing with strings of pheasants, and one of a hunter holding up the head of a buck deer with a wide rack of horns, was a hand-lettered notice: "Andy's Restaurant offers $500 to the person who bags the white buck seen in these parts. Andy will have it stuffed and put on display."

Jack gestured at the notice.

"See that reward offer? The ante has been raised for whoever brings in the albino buck. Andy is outbidding Charlie's Bar. Gordy isn't going to like that."

"That's terrible. I ought to tell Andy I think its disgusting."

"Cultural hangover." Jack opined. "Years and years away from hunting as a necessity, the habit goes on. Frontiersmen for an afternoon, I guess. But I really don't find anything wrong with true sportsmen. They have their skills, their rules."

The interior of Andy's was also frontier rustic befitting its log cabin structure. On the knotty pine walls over booths hung photographs of hunters standing next to their deer kills hoisted by hind legs to tree limbs. Here and there on the walls hung three antique muzzle loading rifles and traps with rusted chains.

Faregolds were waiting for them in a corner booth. Roger untangled his six foot four frame from under the table and stood to greet them.

"Hi Ellie. See that you got that printer's devil cleaned up pretty good."

Roger and Ellie embraced lightly, then she slid into the booth as Roger and Jack seated themselves. Ann reached across the table and touched Jack's hand.

"Maybe I get my hug later? On the dance floor."

"It's a sure bet," Jack replied.

Their conversation ranged through their day, the mundane becoming necessary to report. Roger and Ann had spent the day in Sioux Falls shopping for drapery material and a kitchen fixture for their house. Into the fourth year of restoring a stately Queen Ann house on Main Street, which was located halfway between downtown and the college, the Faregold's weekends were spent together rescuing the old place from its abuse as an apartment house and turning it into a spacious home ready to celebrate its one hundredth birthday. With their three children grown and living in distant metropolitan centers, the Faregold's had opened their home to Hamilton friends for the casual get-togethers as well as traditional holiday feasts.

"I just couldn't do a typical Victorian thing with the drapes," Ann explained. "Too dark. The house has such beautifully arranged windows, oriels, that the drapes had to emphasize the light those old builders wanted to get into the house."

She described the vine and delicate flower design of the parchment colored drapery, and explained that she'd have to get help from Audrey Simpson to sew the heavy material, mentioning Hamilton's most reliable seamstress.

Roger offered his story about the plumbing. When it was her turn, Ellie explained how she'd overseen the restoration of the printing press at Pioneer Village. Jack shared the story about a surprise announcement that would be in the inaugural edition of the *Pioneer Voice* on opening day of this year's Pioneer Days.

Patrons continued to arrive. State senator Andrew Pettigrew III and his wife Patricia waved to Roger and Ann as they moved toward the back room to the "Duck Blind" alcove, which they and Tommy Johnson often reserved for their Saturday night dinner parties. As a state senator, Andrew was Hamilton's voice in legislative wrangles about little Hamilton State. Jack and Ellie turned and waved.

Elliot and Minerva Morris came into the main dining room minutes after the Pettigrews. Sighting the Faregolds, they came to the table on their way to the back of the restaurant.

"This is a likely looking crew," Elliot offered. "Rural electric plots or college plots tonight?"

"Pioneer Village plots," Roger replied. "Jack has been telling us how he's going to put you out of business with the Pioneer Voice."

"Maybe he's got a job for a skilled writer," Minerva offered, reminding those at the table who knew her talent as author of three books. "Elliot won't print a word I write."

Elliot smiled wanly, shrugging helplessness.

"Can't have Hamilton's leading daily turn into a family album, can we. Besides, young journalists need the work."

"You can work for the Pioneer Voice any time you're of a mind to, Minnie," Jack offered. "How about doing a story about how Chautauqua got started and later got incorporated into Pioneer Village."

"Serious?" she replied.

"Sure. It would be a great piece for the souvenir edition. Lot's of people don't know how Pioneer Village grew out of the old Chautauqua grounds."

They agreed on the project, which Minerva Morris promised she would produce by the end of the following week. Since she was the unofficial historian of the town, no one doubted she would have it done well before any deadline Jack might have.

After the Morris's, coming in the main dining room from the front entry, were Sheri and Jim Henslow. They quickly greeted people at nearby tables and hurried on to the back and the Duck Blind party.

"We better scoot," Elliot said, waving to the Henslows, "Looks like the Pettigrew, Johnson, Henslow offering for this Saturday is about to begin. You must have heard about the Henslow's front window being shot out and old man Henslow's steam tractor blowing up. Both on the same afternoon."

"Sure did," Jack replied. "I rode out to the Village with your son when he got the call. Strange coincidence."

"Yes," Elliot replied. "And good copy for Monday's paper. Maybe you can use your Dallas experience to give Danny a hand."

"I don't think he'll need much of my help," Jack said, but recognized a friend's request none the less.

The Morris's left and filed past booths and tables, now with diners deep into Saturday's gossip. His old friend Elliot's request was more than a casual remark, Jack knew, and in his mind he accepted the assignment as it might develop. He owed Elliot and Minnerva more than that.

As much a community center as a public restaurant, Andy's on Saturday night offered Hamilton's citizens a time for a civic roll call, each group noting the presence of this and that person, what common intelligence was for this week about them and theirs. Arriving patrons often went from table to table to greet friends, and as Roger noted, to check the reaction of rivals or old enemies. Henry Raymond, local area manager of Dakota Gas and Electric Company, the commercial competitor in some rural areas to the rural electric cooperative, was working his public relations way among the tables. Trailed by his smiling but silent wife Shirley, Raymond approached their booth.

"How are these fine folks, tonight?" he said, directing the comment to no one in particular.

Roger was quick to reply, his tone sincere, "Just great, Henry. Hello, Shirley. Good to see you both."

"Looks like summer is going to drag on into October," Henry observed.

"Don't complain," Ellie said. "The first freeze will come soon enough."

"Well, you folks enjoy your dinner," with which Henry and Shirley moved on to the next booth.

When the couple had moved out of earshot, Ellie commented on Roger's cordiality.

"You sounded like Henry Raymond was a long lost buddy of yours."

"Yep. Annoys hell out of Henry when I'm friendly like that. His company tells them the cooperatives are part of a communist conspiracy and Henry is not quite sure how to deal with us lefties face to face."

"Is there real competition between your companies?" Jack asked.

"Not any more, or at least not between legislative sessions. The state law today pretty well spells out the service areas, so raiding of customers stopped long ago. But the campaign to discredit consumer-owned systems, like the cooperatives and municipally-owned systems, surfaces every now and then. Mostly they try to drive up our costs with special taxes, or other restrictions, like saying we can't serve loads over a certain size regardless of whether or not they are in our service territory. But old Henry is a decent enough guy. Not a part of company lobbying. Actually he hates it when his company runs a series of advertisements about how they but not us fit the mold of good old free enterprise. During those times I like to be especially friendly with Henry."

Their drink orders given, menus discussed, and the warmth of friendship encircling them, the four friends turned to Jack's report on the progress of the "Tenured Heart," collection of verse.

"How many copies are you printing?" Ellie asked.

"Fifty," Jack replied.

"Turns out that the handmade paper from Twin Rocker in Indiana," Roger added, "is not only some of the most beautiful to be found, it also vies as the most expensive. Fifty copies of the fifteen poems was the limit of the budget Ann allowed me."

"And how does one get a copy of this special work?" Ellie asked.

"You're on the list, Ellie." Roger promised, "And Jack of course will squirrel away the printer's copies."

They had not noticed Dan Morris's approach until he stood over them at the end of the booth. Out of uniform and wearing a rugby shirt, chinos and loafers, he radiated his youth which the Sheriff's department uniform hid.

"Hi Roger, Ann. Ellie, how is everyone doing tonight?"

Greetings accomplished all around, Dan turned to Jack.

"I was wondering if you could do me a favor tomorrow sometime?"

"What would that be?" Jack asked.

"I'd like you to go over Horst Henslow's tractor with me one more time. Taylor said for me to finish the report. But before I do I'd like to take one more look with your help."

"I've been out of the detective business a long time, Dan. But, sure, if I can be of help."

It was clear, Jack thought, that Elliot Morris had suggested to Dan that he should involve him in the case.

"What time tomorrow?"

"How about two in the afternoon. A lot of the tractor guys will be out there getting ready for Pioneer Days. We can do a little talk-talk with them about who would be interested in seeing that steam pipe sabotaged. Maybe we'll even get a hint if there are some strong feelings brewing out there."

"Village politics?" Roger asked.

"Well, it wasn't an accident, but we don't have a clue why it happened. Old Henslow is no big help," Dan explained. "But my bet is that there's more to our little excitement than meets the eye. Time to call in a big-city investigator."

"I help on one condition," Jack interjected. "No publicity. I'm serious. I'll be glad to help you any way I can, Dan, but you've got to remember that I'm a math teacher now, which fits me just about right."

"No problem. I'll take all the credit."

As they laughed at Dan's remark, he turned and started toward the "Duck Blind" to join his parents and the lawyers.

"He's a bright one," Roger offered.

"And a handsome one, too," Ann added. "Do you suppose he'll stick with the deputy's job?"

"My bet is, not for long," Roger said. "Looks like daddy used his influence to get Dan a job in town until he makes up his mind where he's going. Law or newspapering."

"Well, it's not the newspaper, from what he told me," Jack noted. "But if he wants to become a professional musician he's got what it takes. Great addition to the sextet."

"About which. When are we going to hear you guys again?" Ann asked.

"Appropriately enough, Halloween. It's the college scholarship benefit. A dinner dance. We're the talent."

"We'll be there," Ann voted, "Won't we Roger?"

"Of course. Where else could one hear jazz saxophone played by an ex-Dallas detective who knows all about Euclid?"

At that moment there was a commotion at the entry. Jim Henslow who had returned to his car for papers stormed into the restaurant, swearing aloud.

"Some bastard punctured my tires. Where's Dan Morris?"

He pushed past a waiter and rushed to the back of the restaurant. Soon he and Dan hurried through the room and out the front door. Two men diners followed the excitement and went out the front door. The flurry of agitation subsided into a murmur throughout the restaurant.

"What was all that about?" Roger asked.

"Sounds like Jim Henslow took another hit," Jack replied.

᠅   ᠅   ᠅

Arriving late at Andy's Restaurant, Jim Henslow had had to park Sheri's Lincoln Continental at the end of a long row of cars facing the ditch along the country road that defined the property corner with State Highway 43 where Andy's Restaurant sat. The security light high on the power pole near the side entrance to the restaurant illuminated this far end of the black-top parking lot, but the shadows of cars obscured the condition of the Lincoln until one came next to it.

"I came out here to get some papers and found this." Jim Henslow was nearly shouting at Dan Morris, pointing at the flattened tires in front. "And the back ones too. Dammit all, Dan. Some son of a bitch is going to pay for this."

Dan circled the car, looking at the ground. Two men came out of the restaurant and watched the scene.

"Anything missing from the car?" Dan asked.

"Nothing. Had it locked."

That was a curiosity, Dan thought, locking car doors in Hamilton. He guessed that of the fifty cars in the lot, not more than one or two had locked doors.

"Well, I don't see anything that would tell us who did it. I suppose whomever it was parked along the county road, ran over here and did the job and sped away. Wouldn't take thirty seconds."

"Son of a bitch," Jim said. "Be damned sure you make a report on this. I'll need it for insurance, at least."

What Jim Henslow did not tell Dan Morris as they walked back to the restaurant was the name of the person he saw getting into a pickup and speeding away to the north on the county road. What he didn't tell the Pettigrews, Johnsons and Morrises when he returned to the Duck Blind was that he had seen Art Rogers at the rear of the Lincoln, crouched over. Nor was he going to tell them he yelled at Art who bolted from the car and jumped into his pickup. Rogers had looked back a brief second and then high tailed it down the country road. They had seen each other eye to eye. As Jim had stood there all four tires were going flat. In the left rear tire was a switch blade knife stuck deep into the side where Rogers had abandoned it. Jim had pulled it out and folded it before putting it in his pants pocket. It was at that moment that he knew he had Art Rogers by the short hairs. With a little thought he would know the best way to make use of Mr. Art Rogers' talents. But it required a night of rest, a day of rumination, a delight in directed purpose. That night in his room as he looked at the switch blade with a bone handle, the initials AR neatly carved mid-way, Jim Henslow knew he was up to the opportunity offered by this new if involuntary ally in the scheme to remove Horst Henslow from his farm.

CHAPTER 5

A warm drizzle persisted during Sunday morning. Church-goers scurried from their cars, some of the women with plastic head covers to protect new permanents, others with brightly colored umbrellas to shield Sunday finery from the rain. Whether by some long-forgotten design of the town founders, the four principal churches were sentinel to North Main Street where no commercial enterprise dare invade. State Highway 43 was the Rubicon between the secular world of the village and the spiritual. These days the Catholic and the Lutheran churches glowered benignly at one another across North Main Street on opposite corners at its intersection with Highway 43. The spire of the Catholic church reached higher, pointed more decisively heavenward than the squat Gothic bell tower of the Lutheran church. More than one pundit had remarked about the Lutheran's "spire envy." But each maintained a silent resolve by remaining unchanged.

In the 1920s a stern commitment to the congregants respective faiths permeated town politics and business. Buy from the merchant who attends your church, a priest or minister would suggest. Contribute to projects of your own church but shun the fund-raising turkey dinners in the other church's parish hall. But on this rain-freshened morning in late August, 1995, members of each saluted members of the other as they left their parked cars. It was as if these citizens, most of them thoroughly committed to this place, to their work and to the routine of their lives, were as much a part of this prairie earth, of life and death, as was the passage of the seasons. Two world wars, Korea and Vietnam had each visited upon this prairie town the sorrow of loss, and unspoken, half-realized shame of the failure of their species. Articulated or not, merely sensed or brought into meditation, it was as if on this humid August Sunday each of them was pleased to be a loyal parishioner of their chosen religion, each wrapped for the moment in his or her understanding of their faith, but grateful for the friends, rivals, fellow citizens who made their village thrive. It was a time of peace. It was a time for gratitude. Hour-long services silenced the streets of Hamilton. Then the rain stopped.

Two blocks down the street, at their appointed posts were the Methodist and Presbyterian churches, the modest facades of their structures facing each other with a quieter resolve than the older faiths down the street. Their members emerged into the bright sunlight from the staid rituals of the hour. Members of both churches mingled on the street corners near their parked cars. The rain-washed town had become steamy by mid-day as the sun emerged from misty clouds into full prairie blaze. Men departing from church shed their suit jackets as they prepared to get into their automobiles. Umbrellas remained furled.

Jack Traid and Ellie and Gordy lingered on the porch just outside the double doors of the Presbyterian church to talk with Pastor Clyde Masters. Ellie offered the minister today's dinner at the Easton farmstead because his wife Charlene was in Rochester where he had been with her yesterday and would return tonight. Masters declined, explaining that the Clintons, Maureen and Joe, had put in an earlier bid for dinner before he left for Rochester. A rain check was agreed to.

Following Masters' report on Charlene's grave condition, talk shifted to the subject of the Easton farm, its progress without its man. Ralph's name was not mentioned by Masters, the understanding being that the inquiry was not too probing. Masters' concern was considered a courtesy by both the interrogator and widow. Here on the church steps the minister did not seek to know too much of the troubles of each parishioner today, preoccupied as he was with his own concerns. At other times Pastor Masters's natural optimism sought to hear more about the successes of parishioner's lives. Ellie assured him that Gordy was helping her with the farmstead, that the rest of the acreage was in the good hands of George Carter who had been renting the cropland on shares since the year following Ralph's death.

As Ellie, Gordy and Jack moved down the steps, Jack suggested he take them to Sunday dinner at the Dakota Diner, which was situated in the middle of the business district and the oldest eatery in town. Site of both Kiwanis and Rotary meetings each week on different days, the Dakota had its reputation for plain but reliable food. It would be crowded Sunday noon, as it was on every Sunday, assigned the ritual of respite for housewives.

"That's a nice offer, Jack," Ellie said, "but I have dinner in the oven, waiting for us. I thought maybe Reverend Masters would be able to come, and you, too, of course. Now there will be more for Gordy and you. Ham and sweet potatoes sound okay?"

He had wanted to be with Ellie and Gordy this day, to be inside the safe routine of Sunday in small town America. The ordinariness of expected events enveloped him. Although he counted on being included in their Sunday dinner, Ellie's invitation was necessary. This was still the slender wedge of formality that remained between them. Would he be able to dissolve it into lasting intimacy? Was it his barrier or hers? Or both?

"Wonderful, Ellie," he replied, "but next Sunday you and Gordy have to come to my place. I'll do the cooking."

"What a nice idea. Next Sunday, then. But today, we eat at the farm."

"I'll have to drive out in my car," Jack said. "Remember that I promised Dan that I'd meet him at the Village at two."

They departed in their cars, into the brief but busy traffic up and down Main Street as the faithful dispersed into their own routines, their own sanctuaries. At the Easton farm the meal was like that in a hundred households, the talk not much different from that of little families throughout the town. The choir was sounding better. Reverend Masters had been a bit harsh about some parishioners not pitching in during church cleanup day. His text on false pride had been familiar and reassuring to the committed.

He and Ellie spoke of church on her terms, her unquestioning faith. During the sermon Jack Traid's mind had shifted into its translation mode, changing what Clyde Masters said into terms that accommodated his own uncertainty about a personal deity of which this earnest pastor spoke with great assurance, as if speaking of a personal acquaintance. The translation hardened when Masters expanded his text into the political realm half way through the sermon, expressing his wish that Christ had been made emblematic of the nation, wishing aloud for a different history for the nation, opining that the Deist authors of the Constitution should have been more solidly among the Christian faithful.

"What glory it would have been if the founding fathers had declared us to be a Christian nation."

For Jack Traid, it was a piercing and discordant note on this quiet Sunday. The implications of what Clyde Masters was yearning for, Jack thought, escaped the pastor totally. The image that came to Traid's mind was the throng of Vietnamese Buddist monks on the streets of Hué being beaten by agents of a Catholic regime. Had Masters missed that sad chapter in world history, the duplicity of official religious policy? Had he forgot the rule of New England's Puritans? Did Masters not understand the magnificence of that fragile constitutional freedom which sheltered this country from just that scourge which in earlier centuries had sanctified rulers' every brutality? It had been politicized faith that filled dungeons with cries of martyrs whose beliefs differed from those officially sanctioned. Minority faith had burned brightly at the stake. Beneath the innocence of Clyde Masters' desire, its heartfelt sincerity, was a dangerous wish that had been voiced that morning.

During the sermon Jack thought contrary thoughts, countering Masters' polemic by thinking how much this minister to a small flock was diminishing the glory of creation. It seemed to him that Masters was pulling the drawstrings of imagination tightly around a proscribed brief which came out of a misty past and held it up as the one by which all must live. Jack rejected the narrowness of this vision. How could this good man fail to understand that the geocentric world had been destroyed centuries ago and that mankind had to face not being at the center of creation's interest. Man was something other than a mere pawn in a late Roman deity's tight little game. Jack silently countered Masters' words with his own idea that man was a peculiar and favored witness who was gifted with the intelligence to contemplate the vast galactic array of time and space. Homo sapiens had been invited, Jack thought, to send the mind and soul into a vaster miracle. It was a far more profound existence which the Creator had offered the human spirit to contemplate on its way to understanding the mysterious gift of human life.

Jack did not speak of his wariness of religion with Ellie and Gordy. He feared the implication for their relationship of Ellie's brief comment at dinner praising Masters argument that the country should have been designated a Christian one. He quickly suppressed the anger that rose in him. Ten years earlier he would have exploded into an account of his Vietnam experience, and what he had seen of the grinding injustice of a sect dominating a government and its policies. Now he remained silent. His heated reaction to Masters' bland assurances he knew he could not explain to Ellie. Not yet, anyway. She went on to commend the day's sermon with casual praise.

"Reverend Masters has such good ideas. He's such a sincere, good man. It is so sad that he has to go though the pain of Charlene's illness."

Jack knew that his revulsion at Masters voicing the simplistic idea of a Christian nation was remote from the immediacy of the sermon's message offered this Sunday morning: false pride exacts its own terrible punishment. Why, Jack thought, should he, struggling with memories of Dallas, of Alice, attempt to refute a teaching he knew for certain was true, and of which he was guilty that very moment. It had not taken supernatural guidance to teach him that lesson; it was a failing, he admitted to himself, of his own spirit which was yet to be resolved, yet to be taken down into the arena of personal struggle. But he did not have the words to link that acceptance to the larger agenda that Masters proposed. He feared the stain might begin to seep into his attraction for Ellie.

Jack resolved he would remain silent, holding back from Ellie another part of himself which was not yet ready to live within this creed of exclusive certainty. It took the homeyness of Sunday dinner to calm his irritation and his feeling that on Sunday mornings he was as a stranger in this town. Ellie did not question Masters' political agenda. The breach, Jack knew, which separated him from Ellie, however hairline it might be, threatened to jeopardize their mutual desire for a safe, comfortable relationship. Yet it troubled him that these thoughts silently intruded upon his affection, just as the voice and image, the sharp presence of Alice persisted in being seen and heard at these times when he began to feel domesticated and free from the past.

❧   ❧   ❧

At Pioneer Village the committed collectors of antique machines were busy in the sheds that lined the far end of the east-west thoroughfare which ran from the entrance gate to intersect with Chautauqua Avenue. Its street signs had been painted freehand: "State Street." The Village was laid out in a grid of town blocks, except along the waterfront where Chautauqua Avenue followed the natural curvature of the lake shore. Along the western side of Chautauqua Avenue and facing the sand beach of the reservoir were the Good Spirit Restaurant, a Victorian bandstand, the Town Hall, White's Mortuary and at the far southern end, the tractor sheds.

The old buildings had been moved from towns throughout the area, each of them repaired and painted. Today the bright aggregation of restored buildings appeared as an 1890's village, alive once again. A flawed memory of the past energized the vision of the organizers, idealizing into tidy charm that which had been a world of commercial uncertainty. The weathered buildings spoke of the vulnerability to harsh Dakota weather which battered the little settlements that had briefly flourished along the railroad rights of way.

Each activity at Pioneer Village had its committee, its hobbyists. The weavers reigned in the school house, organized by Ann Faregold. Sheriff Tom Taylor lead the effort of the horse lovers who had their stable and corral at the far south end of the village, in the area that had been in the teens and twenties the region-famous Chautauqua Park. Local history recorded that William Jennings Bryan had once given his "cross of gold" speech at Chautauqua Park. It was a time of high ideals about public education that had driven the Chautauqua movement. The name of this very county, which had been named Hamilton at its founding, was changed in 1922 by an act of the state legislature to Chautauqua County. Capturing that name for the county had been a triumph for city fathers of the day, eliciting editorial comment and historical stories in the two local papers competing at the time.

Still necessary in 1890 was the blacksmith. Pioneer Village's blacksmith forge sat close by the stables. Here Art Rogers, when sober and with the intent of advertising his own welding shop in Chesterton, demonstrated horse shoeing and metalwork during Pioneer Days.

A more somber attraction was to be found where Chautauqua Avenue and State Street intersected. Here Donald White, owner of the White Funeral Home in Hamilton, and Chautauqua County Coronor, had moved to the Village and furnished a two story build-ing as an antique mortuary, complete with old instruments of its trade, and caskets typical of gone-by days. White had only his wife Sarah as the other member of his committee, mortuary science not yet a popular attraction for hobbyists. Next to the mortuary on State Street, the Pioneer Print Shop was the domaine of Jack Traid and Mike Wilkins, amateur and journeyman respectively.

Jack parked his battered Toyota at the Print Shop where he would return to work after meeting with Dan Morris. Feeling the mood of the place, the optimism of history seen as well painted and orderly, he strolled down State Street toward the lake front and then turned left onto Chautauqua Avenue. He saw the Sheriff's car pulled up next to the Town Hall in the center of the block past White's. On the main thoroughfare were a few Sunday tourists peering into buildings or sitting on rude benches on the front porch of the Electric Museum maintained by the Prairie Rural Electric Cooperative.

Admission to the Village was five dollars for adults and one dollar for children, an entrance fee which gave the curious tourist free run of the village. In six weeks Pioneer Days would be in full swing. The streets would be jammed with thousands of people from all over the region. For an afternoon they would believe they were witness to a simpler time, a kinder era. It took commitment and hard work of Village volunteers to create this illusion of a pleasant world that never existed.

A central hallway divided the Town Hall in half, two offices to the right, two to the left. The door to the first on the right bore the sign "Mayor" and was opened. Dan and Jake Bickerson sat at the end of an eight foot long oak conference table. Curved backed, oak chairs were arrayed around the table and along one wall of the room.

Jack greeted both and sat next to Dan, waiting for him to continue what he had been saying when interrupted.

"But you can't think of some incident out here that would give us some clue as to why someone would tamper with Henslow's tractor?"

"I can't make myself believe there was vicious intent. Sure, there is a gentle rivalry that goes on. These guys joke with each other. All except Horst, who does not kid other guys. But most of them have fun with each other. Like one of them will say to another 'Do you call that pile of junk a tractor?' or something like, 'When you breakdown I'll tow you back.' Most of these men have no serious conflicts with each other that I know of."

"It may not be involved, but have any of the regulars out here said anything to Horst about being German?" Dan asked. "You know, about his once having been a guard at a concentration camp?"

"Oh they know about it, and they knew about it before the *Times* article last week. Those who know him pretty well will kid him about being in the German army. Like, Hank Severson is Commander of the VFW and I've heard him ask Horst if he'd like to join. You know, a veteran of a foreign war. But it's all a joke."

"No bitterness? No one who wants to embarrass Henslow?"

"Well, that's possible. Horst isn't the easiest guy to get along with. His way is always the right way, and he likes to make that known. On the board of directors there are arguments from time to time and Horst is usually in the midst of it. But the regulars out here know how much Horst has done for the Village. My gosh, he donated lots of money for the tractor sheds. He gave up land for the reservoir when the Department of Interior wanted to construct the flood control dam. The Village is as much Horst's project as it is mine, or anyone else's in the Village."

"What about any connection between Horst and his son Jim?" Dan asked. "Has Jim Henslow influenced the board's decision, you know, to get Horst elected Grand Marshal?"

"We never see Jim Henslow out here, except maybe on Pioneer Days, along with the rest of the politicians."

"So you don't see any connection that might explain why Jim's window was shot out on the same day as Horst's tractor blows a pipe?"

"I guess not. None I can think of. Pioneer Village is Horst Henslow's love, not his son's." Bickerson was emphatic.

"No jealousy because of Horst's very commitment to the Village?" Dan asked.

"Well, some, I suppose. Horst isn't very modest about what he contributes. He loves the idea of being Grand Marshal this year and did all he could to get the board to choose him. It wasn't a popular choice. But it was a necessary."

"Necessary?" Jack asked.

"Well, it was Horst's bargaining in the board meeting that finally persuaded them to select him. He's done an awful lot. Probably will do more."

"But maybe others are envious of his getting the honor," Jack said.

"Well, it is true," Bickerson replied, "that some of the fellows think that he doesn't have any real connection to American pioneer days. Volunteers like to be recognized and being elected Grand Marshal is the big prize out here. Kinda patriotic like. I don't mean there aren't other rivalries, like who's going to take my place when I retire from being Mayor and chairman of the Village board. There are a couple of guys who think they can do a better job. Horst is number one in that category. He's made it clear that he is interested even though he knows his taking over the board would be pretty controversial."

"What you're saying," Jack offered, "is that there is actually something more than a mere undercurrent of hard feelings about Horst Henslow, despite all his contributions."

"Sure. But I can't believe anyone of the regulars would actually sabotage his tractor on that account."

"Still," Dan said, "it is clear that something went wrong with the Avery steam pipe and that it was deliberately tampered with by someone. Who is more likely to know how to do it but one of the regulars, as you call them?"

"What about Jim Henslow's window being shot out? The tire slashing? Maybe someone was trying to get at Jim through Horst." Jack suggested.

"Jim thinks Art Rogers might have done that. He says Rogers threatened him when he sent his brother to the pen," Dan said.

"Art comes out here during Pioneer Days," Bickerson replied, "does demonstrations at the blacksmith shop. He'd certainly know how to jigger a steam line. But we don't see him very often."

With Jake's remark Dan was ready to drop the questioning and began to rise.

"Why don't we go down to the tractor sheds," he said. "I want Jack to have a look at what Sheriff Taylor and I found."

"Before we go there," Jack interjected, "I'd like to go back to what Mr. Bickerson said about some of the men kidding Horst about the war. I'm getting a hint that there may be some serious resentments out here on that score. For example, can you remember any definite reference to his being in the German army? Has anyone said anything about his duty at a concentration camp which has now come out in the *Time's* story about his being Grand Marshal?"

"Well, we all know that he was in the Hitler Youth, not the regular army. He told us that himself. Said he was just a kid of twelve or thirteen. He said the SS made kids do guard duty at one of the camps. I can't recall which one he said."

"And what was the reaction to that out here?"

"I do remember Hank Severson telling a story about the Hitler Youth and how some of them acted at the very end of the war in Germany. He told three of four of us after Horst had left that time. Said his tank unit was with the Seventh Army entering a small town in the south of Germany. They went in without opposition and then this kid threw a hand grenade at Hank's tank. It didn't go off. Severson said he jumped from the tank and knocked the kid down. Pinned him to the ground. The boy was maybe fourteen or so and crying, and saying something in German. Severson asked a buddy who knew German what the kid was saying. He wasn't asking for mercy. He was saying he failed the Fuehrer. He was saying he wanted to die. I guess some of them who never knew any other world but Hitler's teachings were like that. Their religion had failed them."

"Do you think Severson is bitter about Horst having been in the Hitler Youth?" Jack asked.

"If he is, he is pretty good at hiding it."

"Who are the other board members who had to vote for Horst?" Jack asked.

"There are six of us. Horst and myself. Hank, George Carter, Tom Killian, and Roland Smith."

"And they all get along with Horst okay?" Dan asked.

"Well, mostly. Tom Killian squares off against Horst sometimes, mostly taking Severson's side. But I'd say he and Horst seem to get along with each other most of the time. But he didn't like the idea of Horst getting Grand Marshall. He voted for Hank, his buddy. Tom Killian does a lot for the Village too. As you probably know, he's the accountant at the coop elevator so he is the natural one to keep all our Village accounts."

"Does Killian have a tractor?" Jack asked.

"He has a small Case gasoline model. I forget what year. Not much of an antique, I'd say, and he's pretty casual about it. He isn't the great collector like Hank and Horst are."

"So maybe he just hates Horst's guts," Dan offered.

"If so, it doesn't show," Jake replied. "You got to remember, I try to keep the peace out here, so any of this rivalry stuff I smooth over if I can. But yeah, if you want to put it into columns, Tom and Hank vote against Horst sometimes just out of plain cussedness. They certainly voted against his being marshal this year. The ballot vote was four to two. Horst voted for himself"

"And Hank Severson is also Commander of the VFW," Dan said. "I hear he got wounded in Europe. Purple Heart. Maybe he has stronger feelings than we know. The so-so successful farmer resentful of a really well-to-do farmer who was in the German army and is now getting all this recognition."

"You'll have to ask him, I guess. He's out here somewhere today. Even if Hank didn't get marshal this year, he'll make it next year and he knows it. So he shouldn't have any gripe. Hank has a fine Case but the Committee decided Horst's Avery was really in tip-top shape, and that it was time to recognize all his contributions. So Horst got the votes."

"So Hank could be harboring a few hard feelings," Dan said.

"Severson is a nice guy," Bickerson commented. "So it's hard for me to picture him sabotaging someone else's tractor, even if he is in a race with Horst for being chairman of the board. He sure wants it bad enough."

"Rivalry with Horst about that, too?" Jack asked.

"Like I said, Horst has made the village his life and he likes the idea of running things out here. Severson is sure that he can do it better. I guess you would call that rivalry."

"Well, let's go take another look at Horst's tractor," Dan said, getting up.

"And maybe we can find Hank," Jack added.

Bickerson lead the way out of the Town Hall. They walked down Chautauqua Avenue, three abreast in the broad, graveled street. Volunteers cleaning the Good Spirit Cafe, which was operated by the Hamilton United Church Charities, paused to watch the three men. The stories about the steam leak and Jim Henslow's window being shot out and the tires of his car slashed had been told throughout the county by Sunday afternoon. That an investigation had begun by these three men did not have to be explained to the onlookers.

"You guys may not know it, but this is one of the best collections of steam tractors in the region," Bickerson explained as they walked. "We've got one or two from the late 1880's, like that 1885 six horse-power Nichols and Shepard. And the Russells are well represented. We got a 1919, and a 1925."

Bickerson's enthusiasm was showing. He knew his village and the farm machinery museum it had become. They stood before the city-block long line of open sheds that were arrayed on the south side of Steam Street which ran west from Chautauqua. Over each stall was the name of the tractor and its owner. The ailing tractor which had become the center of talk that weekend had been pushed back into its stall in the middle of the tractor shed.

"This is Horst's 1920 Avery. It is one of three Averys we have in the Village. One older, one newer. Some of the names of the steamers you'll recognize, like the Case machines. There's also a 1908 model. And down at the end is Horst's other machine, a Case built in 1886, a real historic piece."

Dan and Jack stepped up on the tractor's operator platform. The levers and brightly polished brass gauges were reminders of the earlier industrial age when a machine's working parts were in full view, where streamlining was not an objective. There was an honest appearance to the machine, Jack thought. It seemed to hide nothing.

"See where we pried off the safety valve?" Dan pointed to the top of the boiler where the valve cap lay next to the open piping. "The valve seat had been forced open and the valve hammered down tight onto it. No way it would have released. So boiler pressure built up. Now, just about at knee height you will see the return steam line with the hole where the steam came from. Its pretty clear where it had been drilled into with what must have been a quarter inch bit."

Jack leaned over to get a closer look.

"Have you any idea how it was made to let go after the pressure was built up?"

"Well, Bickerson told me these models develop about one hundred twenty pounds of steam, or thereabouts, so someone figured out that a lead plug would let go at that pressure. Not really high pressure."

"Heat and pressure," Jack commented. "Something that would loosen up as the boiler got hot and the pressure went up."

Taking a small knife from his pocket, Dan probed the small round hole in the pipe.

"You can still see bits of metal here. Most likely solder, or just pure lead. See this flake."

"Yes." Jack said. "Makes it certain that Horst wasn't just careless about his machine."

"Yeah," Dan agreed. "There is no doubt that this was a booby trap. Hole deliberately drilled. Fixed with some sort of soft metal. Meant to hit the legs of whoever was at the driver's spot after the boiler was fired and steam had built up enough to run."

"One thing seems clear to me," Jack said. "This has all the marks of a prank. Give a man the hot foot. But this was not designed as a serious attempt on Henslow's life. And at the same time it serves to disable the tractor for a time."

"For certain."

"The hole is too small," Jack went on, "to give off a serious amount of steam all at once, even if it turned out to be enough to burn Henslow in the legs. But he was bending over, reaching for wood to feed the firebox when it hit him in the arm. Now, if someone wanted to kill Horst Henslow, they wouldn't have gone to this kind of trouble. At the worst, this was maybe a warning."

The two men jumped back to the ground.

"What about security out here, Jake?" Dan asked Bickerson. "Can you think of how someone might get in here at night?"

"It would be no problem to walk in." Jake replied. "There's no one here at night, except during Pioneer Days. The gates are locked. But lots of the regular folks have keys. Usually the place gets closed up about eight or nine in the evening, depending on how many tourist are out here. The Village doesn't have anything like guards. Each person takes care of his own area. For example, no one messes with the Print Shop. Jack and Mike Wilkins each have a key for the front gate and for the shop. The office has a key to open each exhibit area of the buildings but the volunteers pretty much leave the other things in the exhibits alone. Guess you'd say the place is wide open."

"When I've been out here to work in the print shop I haven't noticed the signs identifying the owners," Jack said. "They must be new. How long have they been up?"

"The signs were done this summer. We put them up a week ago to get ready for Pioneer Days. The guys like getting credit for restoring these old tractors."

"So, someone not familiar with the Village could still find Horst's tractor," Jack commented.

"Oh, sure," Bickerson replied. "Ownership is well advertised. Each man has a sign on his tractor during parades. Every one of these tractors works, you know, as you will see during the parade of tractors during Pioneer Days."

"Would anyone beside Horst drive his tractor?" Jack asked.

"I doubt it," Bickerson replied. "Some of these are jointly owned and one or the other of the owners will run them. But not Horst's machines. I've never see anyone but him run his tractors."

"Well, anyone who wanted to target Horst would have no trouble finding his tractor, that's for sure," Jack noted. "And what about last winter? What goes on with these tractors?"

"Not much, unless one of the owners comes out on a mild day. The steamers are drained of all their water to prevent freeze-up. The Village is closed December through February, as you know," Bickerson explained.

"So where does that leave us?" Dan asked.

"Knowing that there was a deliberate tampering with the tractor," Jack noted, "very likely with the intent to scare Horst but not seriously hurt him. And it was done by someone who knew only Horst would be driving this tractor and that person knew how to make a metal plug that would give way when the pressure was increased because of the jammed safety valve."

"Okay." Dan replied. "So we just file that away because there is no other evidence on the tractor that I can see."

"We should note," Jack said, "that the steam pipe did not blow while it was in the shed. Horst must have gotten steam up for awhile before he headed into the street. The tractor was at least fifteen yards away from the shed. The wheels were turned and the tracks showed that he had begun to head up the street. Whoever did this probably wanted to make sure that the tractor was moving and that Horst was operating it."

"Yeah. Sounds logical," Dan said.

"In my opinion," Jack added, "it was a fairly well thought out piece of business. Maybe this won't be the first attempt. There's a lot of intention behind this. Does Horst's son know what happened, the likely sabotage?"

"Sure does. Sheriff Tayor and I suggested as much to both Horst and Jim Henslow when we went to the hospital Saturday morning. I think Jim takes it seriously, but Horst shrugged it off."

"Time will tell, I guess. It usually does," Jack said.

"Jake," Dan addressed Bickerson, "Thanks for your help. I'll be getting back to you again later. Now we better talk to a few of the other men."

They left Bickerson and walked west up the long line of tractor sheds, away from the reservoir toward two men who were standing in front of a huge Hart Parr that just fit under the shelter of the shed.

"Hey, Danny, what's up?" the younger of the three, Tom Reed, said as they approached.

"Hi, Tom," Dan said in recognition, holding out his hand to the younger. Turning to the older man he said, "You're Mr. Carter, aren't you?"

"That's right," replied the wiry man whose weathered face marked him as a working farmer. "George Carter. Know your dad pretty well, Danny."

"Sure. I remember. I've just been gone from Hamilton too long. You men know Jack Traid, I suppose." Dan added.

The three men shook hands.

"Mr. Carter, you farm some of the Easton land, don't you," Jack said.

"That's right. Fine family the Easton's. Just too damned bad about Ralph."

Jack wondered if Carter's comment carried an implied opinion about his, Jack's interest in Ellie.

"Jack's giving me a hand looking over Horst's machine," Dan explained. "You fellas have any idea why someone would tamper with the tractor?"

Neither Reed or Carter spoke immediately, then the older man replied, "You probably know that I serve on the Village board with Horst. Much as he does for this place, he isn't in the friendship business. Put simply, he's an arrogant son of a bitch who always has to have it his way."

"Enough to make a few of the guys get together to teach him a lesson?" Jack asked.

"More than enough, I'd say, but I don't know who did it. Could have been any of a dozen people, especially the tractor owners. You'd think Henslow owned this whole tractor shed the way he orders people around."

"Yet, the board voted him Grand Marshall. Didn't you vote for him?" Jack asked.

"Seemed the thing to do, despite his attitude. He got us the lake, contributed heavily to the tractor sheds. Guess we think he's about to do even more for the Village."

"But you have no doubt about a motive behind this little prank, then?" Dan asked.

"Plenty of motive for a joke, at least," Carter replied.

"Kinda serious joke. Henslow could have been seriously burned by the steam," Jack commented.

"So, who should we talk to next, Mr. Carter?" Dan asked.

"Maybe Hank Severson could tell you something. He's out here as much as anyone. He's Henslow's big rival for board president next year. No love lost between those two."

"Has Hank been around today?"

"He was working on his machine half an hour ago." Tom said. "Maybe check the Good Spirit. He probably went over there for a cupa."

Dan and Jack turned and retraced their steps, turning left onto Chautauqua Avenue and walking back half a block to the Good Spirit Cafe. As they approached the front door Dan commented, "Bickerson says he doesn't really believe one of his regulars would do this. I don't believe him."

"But remember," Jack said, "he's the chairman, the peace keeper. He doesn't want to say anything negative about one of his fellow board members."

"Unless he's involved, of course."

"Sure," Jack continued, "but Carter leaves no doubt that plenty of people hated Henslow's guts and Hank Severson is first in line."

Inside the Good Spirit Cafe they found Severson sitting at a table alone at the front window. A solid built man in his early seventies, his tanned face spoke of hours spent in fields under the Dakota sun. Above a starkly white forehead, thin, whispy hair signified greater age than was suggested by the alertness of his eyes and the ready poise of body. Hank Severson sat upright at the table, his big right hand around a heavy porcelain cup in front of him.

"Mind if we talk a bit?" Dan asked.

"Not at all."

"You know Jack, of course," Dan said, turning to indicate Traid. "He's giving me the benefit of his experience in trying to figure what happened to Mr. Henslow's tractor."

"Oh I know Jack. He's our Pioneer Voice editor," Hank said, offering his hand. "Used to be a big-city cop, right?"

Jack smiled and the two shook hands. Hank indicated for them to sit down.

"You've had lots of experience with steam tractors, Hank. Do you have any idea why the steam line on Horst's tractor blew?"

"Can't say I do. Never have seen a thing like that."

"It was sabotaged," Dan said flatly.

"Oh yeah? Who'd do a thing like that?"

"We get the impression from some of the guys that you and Horst aren't exactly good friends. That right?" Dan asked.

"Well, we manage to work together out here. To be frank, he ain't the most lovable guy. Some times he goes around acting as if his contributions to the Village are the only ones ever made. Likes to think he gives more than anyone else."

"So, is it possible that some of the tractor buffs engineered a little prank to embarrass him?" Jack asked

"I guess you detective fellows will have to figure that out, won't you."

"That's what we're trying to do, Hank," Dan said, tension rising in his voice. "You know about Horst being in the German army, I take it."

"Hitler Youth," Hank replied. "Nasty little bastards. I ran into them over there. One of them threw a grenade at my tank. A dud. But it sure put us on guard about the little sons a'bitches."

"Do you hold that against Horst?" Dan asked.

"Not especially. No. Not now. He can go his way. I'll go mine. But ain't it just a little ironic that he's a big shot at Pioneer Village. Pioneer. Shit, there ain't no American pioneers in his kraut family!"

"So some of you real pioneer's fixed his tractor?" Dan said.

"If you ask me, he probably screwed up the safety valve on that Avery himself. Possible you know."

"But that's not the way it was, Hank," Dan said decisively.

It was clear to Jack and Dan that Hank Severson wasn't going to admit to what he may have thought was going to be a practical joke. Maybe he knew more, but his steady gaze at them said they were not clever enough to trap him into admitting anything.

"What escapes me," Jack said, "is why with all his unpopularity, the board elected him Grand Marshall for Pioneer Days."

"Maybe he's just pretty good at bribes, even if all of us ain't taken in."

"What do you mean by that?" Dan asked.

"Nothing much. Old Henslow will do anything to take over the board, even make lots of promises."

"Promises?"

"Yeah, about what he can do for the Village in the future. Don't impress me much, but then I got only one vote. Most of the rest of them want to believe him."

It was clear to Dan that Hank had told them all he was of a mind to tell. It was also clear that Bickerson and Severson and the other members of the board were holding back information.

"Well, thanks, anyway, Hank," Dan said. "I'll probably be getting back to you later."

"Okay by me. Maybe send Sheriff Taylor to do the job," Severson said, the implied insult hanging in the air.

"Maybe I'll just have to do that," Dan replied.

He and Jack got up and left the resturant.

"He either did it or got someone else to do it," Dan said.

"He had the motive, certainly the means and opportunity," Jack replied. "But evidence? That's a bit tougher to get at."

Dan's beeper went off and they parted quickly with the promise to get together later to discuss what they had found.

"Think about it," Dan said over he shoulder as he hurried toward his patrol car.

When Jack returned to the Village Print Shop, he felt the old sense of the hunt return. The hundreds of crime scenes he had investigated had all told a story, some obliquely, some as obvious as if the perpetrators had written a confession on a wall. Some revealed the rage of a violent act; others spoke to him in a quieter, a more sinister voice of jealous intent. Horst Henslow's tractor spoke to him in that manner. But Jim Henslow's shot-out window, tires slashed? Those acts were motivated by simple anger. No subtle motives behind that mind, he thought.

CHAPTER 6

*D*an Morris had lived for two months with his parents in their sprawling ranch house in Cottonwood Acres when he returned home after receiving his law degree from the University. He felt a tinge of guilt in having to return to his parents' home, a place where he was warmly welcomed but one he felt he had not earned. Elliot and Minerva Morris prided themselves on their contemporary taste, their knowledge of modern architecture, of the Prairie School of Frank Lloyd Wright and Walter Burley Griffin. Henry Potter in Sioux Falls was their choice of architect for designing their home to reflect their appreciation of the prairie style. Potter's reputation had reached as far as Sioux City and the Twin Cities with his revival of the style.

The muted modernity, slightly aged, with Prairie School elements Potter expressed in the house plans was pleasing to the Morrises. The low roof planes had generous overhangs and presented to the street a rich but modest welcome. A broad expanse of windows at the rear of the house was focussed inward onto the two acre lot, newly planted with trees. The Morris wealth was never to be flaunted, but always stated in terms that Hamilton would understand, perhaps appreciate. For Danny Morris the house was a statement that spoke too readily of an unchallenged claim on power and influence. This new house, built while he was at the U and not the one in which he had been reared, made him uncomfortable. It was a clear expression of his parent's success and was not about him. He was not yet willing to play the part of heir apparent waiting for him in Hamilton and at the *Times.*

It was Sheriff Tom Taylor who suggested it to him a week after he'd gotten home. Having a law degree certainly wouldn't hinder one from carrying out the duties of Deputy Sheriff, Taylor argued. It did not surprise Dan that his father urged him to take the assignment.

"Maybe a year or two in law enforcement will convince you that the newspaper is not all that bad a place to work," his father argued, reasoning privately, Dan knew, that the job, or any job in Hamilton, would keep his son close by and open to taking the role all expected him to play in the Hamilton scheme of things.

"In any event," Elliot Morris added, "the experience will likely teach you some things about the law that you can't get in school."

After successfully completing the ten weeks of police training at the Rol Kebach Academy in Pierre, Dan was sworn in and put on a deputy sheriff's badge. That same week he moved from his parents' home and took an apartment downtown over Mork's Hardware. Parental arguments fell apart at his insistence that he had better try living by his own lights in Hamilton now that he had a job, even if the family name would continue to enfold him in its history.

"I probably should have gone to Sioux Falls," he explained to his parents, "and taken the law firm offer, but I don't feel ready for practicing law. But don't worry. I'm not going to throw away all that college. I just need a little time to sort things out in my life."

Minerva Morris accepted Danny's indecision about the family business. She understood that his breakup with Cynthia Jeans during his last year at the University had had a greater affect than he was willing to share. He seemed to have withdrawn from young people his age, dazed by the first rejection by a lover.

"Thank god," she reminded her husband, "he hasn't taken to drinking or drugs like some of his age when the significant other wanders into someone else's arms." Danny's compromise was acceptable. He was here in town but on his own.

Sheriff Tom Taylor liked having a Morris on his staff. Dan's being a deputy served a number of good purposes. At least that was the Sheriff's fond hope. The *Times* would likely pay closer and more sympathetic attention to the good work of the sheriff's office. And more important, Dan's being full time permitted the sheriff to concentrate on quietly campaigning for next year's election. And yet more important than any reason, the sheriff concluded, was that Dan's competence and attention to duty permitted Taylor to spend more time out of his territory. Lilly Brown in Sioux Falls needed Tom Taylor's attention, which neither Mrs. Taylor nor the voters of Chautauqua County would understand, nor needed to know about. Besides, he rationalized to himself, as a wounded veteran of the Korean War he deserved a little extra freedom. He'd paid his dues for this community over there, having come back with one leg shorter than the other where a land mine had smashed his left femur. He would think to himself while entering the back door to Lilly's apartment that there were debts that never get paid. But he had the right to collect interest. Lilly Brown was interest. He felt all the more secure in his pleasure now that Danny Morris was on the force, Danny who did not question his explanations about the frequent Sioux Falls trips.

"Auto theft case. Minnehaha County has some records that will help us out. I need to dig around them a bit if we're going to find out who's been stealing automobiles in Chautauqua County with such regularity. Appears to be a syndicate operation. Sheriff Jeff Harlan in Minnehaha has been working on it too."

After two months on the job, Dan Morris found himself in charge of the Sheriff's Department a good number of days and nights. He soon learned the division of labor between the Hamilton police and the sheriff's office.

Albert Ford, Hamilton police chief was nearing retirement and after twenty years as a police officer, knew very well the boundaries of his duties. The Hamilton police force territory was described by the city limits, outside of which was, to Ford, a great *terra incongnita.* His officers were well instructed not to cross over into Sheriff Tom Taylor's territory, for the uproar from Taylor was not worth abiding.

Dan received a call at his apartment from the Hamilton police dispatcher at eleven Sunday night telling him that Sheriff Taylor could not be reached, and that an emergency call, "a life and death matter," had come from Mrs.Reinhart who lived just outside the city limits, and that Dan had better get out there quick.

"Seems that someone she's caring for has attempted suicide."

"Notify the EMS to get a medic and an ambulance out there. I'm on my way."

He descended the stairs to Main Street two at a time. Main Street was nearly deserted. The patrol car was park diagonally at the curb. With lights flashing he made a U-turn across the broad street and sped toward the north city limits.

Dan knew the Reinhart place. He'd gone to high school with Matt Reinhart, a businessman now living in California. Matt's mother Thelma was one of the staff at Comfort Retirement Home, and known in town for her devotion to the job of easing the elderly of their worries, making easier their halting steps toward the end. It was Thelma Reinhart who people cited as doing "her Christian duty."

The two story, clapboard house was set back in a grove of elm trees. The shabby lawn and unkempt driveway spoke of commitments made elsewhere. The ambulance was coming east on Twelfth Street at the city limits as Dan pulled into the drive and rushed up onto the porch. The flashing lights of the patrol car and soon those of the ambulance raced across the front of the house and through the trees. Mrs. Reinhart was standing in the doorway.

"She's upstairs. I think she took an overdose."

She was frightened. Her directions were confused. She didn't say who she was caring for this night.

As Dan rushed up the narrow stairway, Pete Gillay was coming into the front hallway with his emergency bag.

In the upstairs hallway Dan confronted two closed doors. Flinging open the closest one he found the crumpled form of a young woman, her face deep into a pillow, sound asleep. He began to shake her.

"Wake up. Wake up. You gotta stay awake."

Pete was beside him.

"Keep shaking her."

Patty Reinhart's eyes opened slowly, then wide, startled by the two men bent over her.

"Did you take pills," Pete demanded.

"Ya, my noth was all snuffed," Patty tried to explain. "Flu. I took aspirin."

"Not her. Not her," Mrs. Reinhart yelled from the stairwell. "In the other room. It's Gloria."

Pete led the way, flinging open the door to the other room where the three of them found Gloria Miller standing at the window, staring out at the flashing lights of the ambulance and patrol car.

"What the hell do you want?" she said over her shoulder.

"You okay?" Pete asked.

"What do you think?"

"Mrs. Reinhart thought you had taken a bunch of pills," Dan said.

"You all right now, honey?" Thelma Reinhart asked through tears. "I was so afraid for you when you said you were going to end it."

"I should've. He called me 'a useless broad.' That's what he said. Then he left for Texas. Said he would write when he had a mind to, but 'Don't you expect no love letters.' That's what he said. 'And don't expect no checks for your brat either.' It's his baby, ya know. It just has to be his baby."

She was crying by then. Mrs. Reinhart came into the room and went to Gloria, putting her arms around her. The two men backed out of the room.

A false alarm, Dan thought. A necessary false alarm. But a needed public service. A case of the abandoned needing attention. And sometimes they need more attention than the Mrs. Reinharts of the world can give.

Wrapped in a terry cloth robe, a smiling but sleepy, forty-year old Patty Reinhart stood in the doorway to her room. Dan and Pete nodded to her and smiled sheepishly to acknowledge their confusion.

"Mom's always doing that. Getting excited. Gloria depends on her so much now."

As Dan was leaving the house, Mrs. Reinhart came down the stairs and caught up to him.

"I'm so sorry to have bothered you, Danny," she said, remembering the teenager who used to come to her home with her son. "I've been so worried about Gloria. That man she was living with, just up and left. He had promised to marry her, but walked out after the baby was born. Poor thing. Gloria's mother is caring for it while Gloria is getting treatment at the hospital. Depression."

Dan nodded his understanding. The mess people make of their lives, he thought.

"She just needs a job of some kind. If she could get back on her feet, somehow. She was just too dependent on that good for nothing."

"Yes, I can see," Dan said feebly.

"If you hear of anything…" Mrs. Reinhart let the sentence hang in the air, her voice reaching out.

Feeling helpless, remote from the emotions of Gloria Miller and Mrs. Reinhart's concern, Dan returned to his apartment to seek refuge. He turned to his high fidelity CD player with its Bose speakers for calm and reason. A Mozart piano concerto described a larger, immutable order in the universe, holding within it the soaring beauty and complexity of creation. For Dan the music described a crystal brightness shimmering above the darkened flesh of man's folly, over the farce of the mistaken patient this night. What has Mozart to say to the Gloria Millers of the world? How much less complicated was Cynthia Jeans dropping him for Howard Edmons, son of the merchant king of Sioux City. Edmons Department Store. How much more logical and how much less painful. Yes, he thought. How much less painful it has been for my having myriad routes of escape and compensation. Gloria Miller? That young woman who had none of Cynthia's resources. Cynthia who could pick and choose. Who had chosen and told him why.

"You don't have a clue where you're going," she'd said. "Play a gig one night. Study all the next. Sometimes you hardly know I'm here, unless you need to go to bed with me."

And she was right. It was her stunning beauty that had attracted him just as it had left half the male population on campus lusting after her. Rush Week Queen, runner-up Homecoming Princess, she gave status to her escort. He had failed to learn that her kind of beauty demanded keen attention. Her farewell was abrupt, announced the morning after they had made love three times during the night. What he could not forget was Cynthia's flawless skin. It was naturally a light tan, without blemish, almost unnatural in its silky perfection. He could not get enough of touching it when they were together, kissing her back and buttocks. Aroused by the attention of his eager lips, she made love with intensity, laughing and describing with delight his maleness to him, urging him on. She gave herself without reservation. That morning she was smiling as she brought coffee from the kitchen.

"That was a very nice goodbye, Danny."

"Goodbye?"

"Yes. That has to be our last wonderful screw. I'm engaged to Howard Edmons. We told his parents last weekend. The wedding is set for June, after we graduate."

There was nothing for him to say or do. Cynthia expected no reply. It was typical, he thought. He should have known, and been more alert. She would make up her mind as if none other deserved explanations. Cynthia had done that before; she disappeared during spring break to go to Padre Island, Texas, with a sorority sister without telling him. And in the final analysis, the Hamilton *Times* registered her mind as a small-time enterprise compared to the Edmons Sioux City mercantile empire. Cynthia knew how to weigh the elements of security and importance. The equation just didn't come out with his name on the other side of the equals sign.

Rejection had been a new experience for Dan Morris who had been about to receive his law degree with honors. His family had provided for all his needs. His popularity and leadership in high school and at the U. had made life's path smooth, without obstructions. But Cynthia left with part of him, as if she had taken a piece of his self assurance with her, leaving him feeling incomplete and ignorant of the ways of the heart.

Dan knew how innocent he was of the life around him, even of this village on the prairie where he'd grown up unaware of the Gloria Miller's of the world who were destined to suffer deeper wounds. They were not part of the "in" crowd. Most had to work after school. Thinking of those with hidden wounds, Dan's thoughts turned to old Horst Henslow. Dan imagined him as caught in two half understood worlds, his past and his present. And Dan had lived all his life in a world absent of someone intent upon hurting an old man at play with his tractor. He felt the wound of Hank Severson's evasiveness and condescension toward him. It baffled him that George Carter and Jake Bickerson had voted for Horst despite their feelings about him. Dan knew he was challenged. The time had come to burrow into the real life of this place, he thought. The deputy's job was, after all, what he needed. "Smart pills," he thought, thinking of the old story about the kid who was fed rabbit droppings by his older brother, being told they were smart pills and would make him really smart. When the kid finally figured out what they were, he was told, "See, they worked!"

Mozart played into the early morning hours of Monday, arranging the universe to perfection. Thunder sounded over the town of Hamilton.

❧   ❧   ❧

A cold front had moved through the Dakotas on Sunday night setting off thunderstorms that boomed over the town of Hamilton into Monday morning. A cold rain had been falling steadily since a gray daybreak, bringing down the summer-like August temperatures with a reminder of colder days to come. It was not to Jacob Bickerson's liking, the rain that would turn his corn fields into deep mud and delay the soy bean harvest until the sun had dried crop and ground.

The Bickerson 640 acre farm was eight miles south of Hamilton on the main north-south county road 70. From the kitchen window of the ranch house, new five years ago, Rachel Bickerson watched the gravel road begin to show puddles. Would the school bus be safe? Who would be driving this route this year? Her family sat in the oak breakfast nook. Jonah had his nose in a school book, doing a lesson he should have done last night instead of watching television and talking on the phone to David Marritz for half an hour. A week into the school year and he was already complaining about assignments. "Dumb," was his summary. But he was well-liked at school and on the football team. She had to make sure he did well. She worried about Jonah but not yet so much about Sarah, now in eighth grade and beginning to merge into womanhood. They were the future of this little family, but did their future include the farm, their parents? Rachel worried about the future. Today's future. Tomorrow. Ten years from now. Her husband clung to the present. As she prepared scambled eggs, she half listened to Jacob telling the children about the accident at Pioneer Village.

"Accident? Maybe. Maybe not," he was saying. "Sheriff Taylor and that new deputy Dan Morris say it was deliberate. That Avery is a pretty old tractor. Horst might have jammed the safety valve somehow. Although that is hard to believe."

"What happened to him?" Sarah wanted to know.

"He got burned by the steam that came out of the leak. Not too serious but could have been much worse when you think of it. Scalded his arm a bit. But it could have hit him in the face. That's what's so strange. Why would anyone want to hurt a man who has worked so hard for the Village?"

"Maybe because he's an ex Nazi," Jonah said, looking up from his book, "like it said in the paper last week about his leading the parade at Pioneer Village this year."

"He's an American now," his father replied. "All that business about his being in the German army is dead history. I don't know why they printed that. He was just a boy, forced to carry a gun the very last month of the war. He told us."

"Sure. And he didn't know about what the Nazis were doing in the concentration camps," Jonah said with disgust.

"He was a child. Too young to make decisions."

"How old was he then?" Sarah asked.

"He said he was thirteen when he was made a prisoner of war by the British. That seems about right, considering his age now."

"Well," Jonah said, "you can have him for your friend, but once a Nazi always a Nazi."

"No, Jonah. You shouldn't be so hard. He has been a good man. His farm is one of the best. He has worked hard. Sometimes he isn't easy to get along with, but if it weren't for Horst Henslow Pioneer Village would be much less of a place."

"Maybe you should read what the Hitler Youth were like, Dad," Jonah argued. "There are books in the library about what they did. They weren't boy scouts, you know."

"Don't blame one man for the whole terrible chapter in German history."

"'Never Again!' that is what we better not forget."

Rachel disliked the verbal sparring between father and son. Jacob would accept, forgive. He had such a heart. But not Jonah. Since his bar mitzvah he had become more Jewish than his family. It was Jonah who urged the family to go to temple in Sioux Falls on Saturday. He reminded them that this year the New Year began September 25 and Yom Kippur was on October 4. He marked the calendar in the kitchen. They should not forget, he insisted.

The clock over the sink showed seven forty-five. The school bus would be at the drive in five minutes. Rachel made sure Jonah had his backpack for the overnight trip which the football team was making to Vermillion for a special football camp that afternoon and tomorrow morning which was offered by the University coaching staff.

"Wear your rain coats. The umbrellas are in the closet by the door."

She knew they would not take the umbrellas. Having wet hair was bearable compared to the ridicule of the others on the bus. Umbrellas were for the old and feeble.

"After you're done with the football camp are you and David still going to see about the University entrance?" Jacob asked.

"Sure. Like you agreed. David's applying for entrance at the U next year, too, so we've been working on our applications together. We'll be out until real late tomorrow because after football camp ending tomorrow noon, we have to go to the orientation which is tomorrow at two. David's driving his car. If we are real late getting back to town, I'll stay over at David's."

"Well, you two behave yourselves," the father said, almost as a chant, imagining the troubles young men found in girls or drink. But Jonah had never been in trouble through all of high school. He was a good boy.

Rachel watched from the windows as her two children ran toward the road as the yellow bus came into sight over the hill a quarter mile south. They were growing too fast, she thought, and the close family on this rich farm land was changing. She wondered if she and Jacob would be ready to live here alone after all these years as a family that worked together on their own farm? She wished time would pause, or turn more slowly upon the delicious security she held to her breast at this moment. A good husband. Smart and beautiful children. Accepted too, here in Chautauqua County. Jacob elected chairman of the Village. They could be Jews here in South Dakota and not fear the night riders, the Klan or the skin heads that raged with hate in other parts of the country. She worried about her family, about the future. But for the moment she relished the warmth of her kitchen, the arms of her strong husband around her from behind.

"That was a good breakfast, Rachel. You make a good home for us." And he kissed her neck.

❧   ❧   ❧

The Hamilton *Times* was at subscribers' doorsteps by six o'clock Monday evening, setting the agenda for many a dinner discussion. National news swirled about the Oklahoma City federal building bombing and the continuing investigation. Whitewater had become a national marker in conversation, conclusions of guilt suggested by columnists uncomfortable with the president of the Baby Boomer generation. But Hamilton's own news was more compelling on this night. In the minds of many there was no doubt about the connection between the triple events of Jim and Sheri Henslow's picture window being shot out and their Lincoln automobile tires slashed and the boiler pipes blowing on Jim's father's tractor. The favored story was that it was probably Nazi hunters who had at last found the concentration camp guard Horst Henslow and were exacting revenge. The simple facts reported about the incidents, inadequate as they seemed to most, were now part of local mythology. Too much had been left unreported. Readers checked the story against the rumors they had heard, then elaborated upon the details and passed the revised story on to others.

For some good citizens of Hamilton the newspaper account of the attacks upon the Henslow family was the whole of the story. The world was full of nuts. For Jack Traid it was a mere summary which was lacking the nuances of reality and without comment on what he was sure were two different elements of private intent. But the headline coupled the three events in a question: "Accident, Shooting, Slashed Tires Connected?"

The story was by-lined by the new reporter at the *Times*, Carla Garza. The Friday afternoon shooting incident and the Avery tractor boiler pipe leak at Pioneer Village at 6:05 p.m. that same evening involved father and son, the account reported, although no connection had yet been made by the Sheriff's Department. Sheriff Taylor was reported as saying that the coincidence of these attacks upon the Henslows suggested the family had become specific targets of someone's intent to harass them. No arrests had been made, although an unnamed suspect had been questioned about the vandalism to the Henslow residence.

The newspaper account went on to report that Horst Henslow, according to Taylor's report, sustained burns on his right arm and had spent Friday night in Community Hospital.

As Jack Traid read the account he found himself reviewing the supposition to which he and Dan had agreed. The drive-by shooting was a sudden lashing out, as was the incident with the tires. Juvenile acts. But the boiler pipe tampering was a well-engineered, thought-out piece of business.

Jake Bickerson was quoted by the *Times* as saying "Horst Henslow is a good friend of Pioneer Village and a valued director on its board. He has contributed a great deal to its success. This tampering with his tractor was a mean and senseless act."

The report concluded by noting that Henslow had farmed in Chautauqua County since 1954, coming to South Dakota from Pennsylvania with his wife, the late Marie Henslow and their son James, currently Chautauqua County's State's Attorney. The front page story continued on page three where it was reported that in 1963 Henslow had contributed more than two hundred acres of property to the Department of Interior flood control project which provided Pioneer Village with lake-front property.

Dan Morris, Jack Traid noted, had been left out of the report, the quotations coming mostly from Sheriff Taylor. The Hamilton official world was not that much different from that of the big cities, he concluded.

❀   ❀   ❀

As Jim Henslow read the Hamilton *Times* article Monday evening sitting in the violated living room of his home, the picture window now an expanse of unpainted plywood. An emerging sense of drama filled his mind. He had discovered in himself a new resolve. Elements of suspense and danger were as certainties in the plan that unfolded in his mind. He had no doubts that Art Rogers was responsible for shooting out the window. The act had been only a prelude to his slashing the tires on Sheri's Lincoln at Andy's. A crude revenge, Jim thought. But by these acts Art Rogers was to be made the agent for getting the decision needed from a frightened Horst Henslow. Whether or not Rogers had sabotaged the tractor was irrelevant for now. What Jim knew for certain was that it was Art he had seen on Saturday night, and Art knew he had been seen and he knew Jim had his knife as evidence. Rogers the intimidator was about to be transformed into his ally. Author of a simple-minded strategy of threats through vandalism, Rogers would learn how these petty acts with his, Jim Henslow's editing and advancement, would be put to use in a grander strategy.

The publicity about the accident and his step father's past suggested to Jim that the story of Horst Henslow needed development into a more harrowing tale arising out of the murky depths of that old war. Horst might fend off the implications of a failed boiler, but he would not treat lightly further peril, a spotlight out of the past revealing secrets, real or imagined, long forgotten and now about to be revived as a long-delayed repayment for concentration camp atrocities. Once he had become a pariah in Hamilton and Pioneer Village, Horst Henslow would seek Arizona as a quiet haven of retirement. And he intended to help his step-father get there. Art Rogers, Jim reasoned, would be the instrument by which that outcome would be assured. It would be but a modest payment for Rogers' acts of retaliation meant to even the score for his brother's incarceration.

Sheri had gone to her own bedroom by eleven Monday night. Jim sat at his desk in his bedroom sorting the legal size sheets of the trust agreement which he had prepared on his computer. This bit of security, this trust, would be offered in concrete form, he reasoned, but only after Horst believed he was adrift in a storm of his past life. He, Jim Henslow, would make that past come alive now that the prologue had been written by someone else.

These thoughts made it clear to him that he needed to leave his house Wednesday evening, telling Sheri he would be staying over in Sioux Falls in order to be fresh for the early morning flight Thursday at seven. That would give him the security of an alibi certified in the motel guest register forty miles away while the nighttime hours advanced a long-delayed retribution against Horst Henslow, ex-Nazi. His restlessness to get on with his plan carried over into a dream that night. In the dream a dark form crept across the Henslow farmyard, crouched, threatening the bright house where his step-father, and disturbingly, he waited in terror.

All day Tuesday he rehearsed in his mind the drama that he would author in which Art Rogers and Horst Henslow were to be the antagonists. Jim Henslow left the court house at four o'clock in the afternoon with the mission clearly in mind and drove in the lingering drizzle through a countryside of pastures and corn fields where the stalks hung heavy with ripening ears. The black earth glistened with puddles. Past Andy's Restaurant, Highway 43 took a sharp curve to the north and then turned west again, track of the surveyors' adjustment for the curvature of the earth as their chains had long ago laid out the civilizing gridwork of government applied to broad prairie. Two generations earlier there had been gravel and dirt roads, fewer fences, a horse-drawn culture. It was a young country. A rich country, boundless with opportunity. And he would have his share, he mused, and Art Rogers was going to help. The arrest warrant he had prepared that morning was the leverage that would make Art Rogers his ally of many skills.

The faded red garage building on Chesterton's side street had a simple sign over the service bay door which was opened to a workshop. "Rogers Machine Shop." Paint was peeling from the white background of the sign. The blue letters had been faded by the hot Dakota sun. There was no one in the shop when Jim pulled up in front of the doorway and got out of the car. He had decided not to carry the revolver he'd bought. The warrant was greater protection.

There was some traffic on the main street of Chesterton, but here on the side street there were no other cars, no people to be seen. At four-thirty in the afternoon the farmers who had taken a rainy day to come to town for supplies, or to have repairs made to machines, had headed home. School kids were home, out of the cold drizzle, watching television.

"Hello," Jim called.

There was no answer. He stood in the doorway of the shop, waiting.

"Art Rogers," he called out.

He waited a minute.

"Anyone here?"

The voice almost right next to him was startling. Art Rogers leaned against the corner of the shop. In his hand he carried a piece of angle iron, as if it were a club for defense.

"Whata you want, lawyer?" It was an epithet, made the more menacing by the disgust his tone conveyed.

"I brought a piece of paper to show you, Mr. Rogers. Thought you might be interested."

Art moved passed him and went into the shop. He began to lock the angle iron in a vice and was about to use a hack saw to cut a piece from it.

"I think we should talk in your office there," Jim said, indicating the jumble of file cases, a desk and chair which had once been an office for a service station.

"Say what you're going to say and get the hell out of here," Art snapped.

"Have it your way. I have here a copy, note I said copy, of a warrant for your arrest."

"Bullshit!"

"Not so. Very real. It says you are wanted for malicious mischief for shooting out a window in the James Henslow residence and for slashing four tires on the Henslow family car. It notes that there is evidence of a knife with your initials on it found in one of the tires. It goes on to cite you on suspicion of attempting to do grave bodily harm to, if not actually attempting to murder, one Horst Henslow by sabotaging his tractor."

"Who says?"

"I say, Mr. Rogers. You know I saw you Saturday night. You and that pickup as you left the parking lot at Andy's."

"Your word against mine."

"I have your knife with your initals on it. Panicked a bit, didn't you."

"Screw you. Could be anyone's initials."

"Maybe. But then I can also arrange to have a witness or two who will swear in court that they saw you leaving the parking lot."

"There wasn't anyone else there but you."

"Ah. You didn't see anyone but me, but it isn't difficult for me to get two sworn statements saying you were seen, clear as day. That and the knife will pretty much do the job."

"So I let a little air out of your tires, but you can't prove I shot up your house, and you sure as hell can't pin attempted murder on me. I didn't touch your old man's tractor."

"Well, that's to be seen. And for now it is neither here nor there."

"Whata ya mean?"

"I mean, my friend, I have a deal to make with you. I will clear you of charges without the inconvenience of having to serve the real warrant on you, of convening a jury and then putting on a trial which would mean you would have the expense of lawyers to defend you. All of which would certainly result in your serving some hard time with your brother."

"You trying to blackmail me? Money?"

"Oh jeez. You have little imagination, Mr. Rogers. It's not money that this is about. It has to do with your skills, your wonderful talents with the torch."

"Don't get smartass on me Henslow. I don't know what you're talking about."

"Then let me make it clear. A simple deal between you and me. Since it was probably you who fixed my old man's tractor, and you had guts enough to drive through my neighborhood with a rifle sticking out of your pickup window, I figure you can do some other creative acts to advance civilization. Case in point: I will drop all charges. No one will ever know that a warrant exists, unless of course, something happens to me and they look into my desk. I will drop these charges, tear up the warrant, even give you back your knife. And I will make it worthwhile for you do a couple of easy jobs, like burn down a shed."

"Fuck you, lawyer. You're setting me up."

"It may look that way to you, but the alternative is for you to answer to the charges in this warrant. Which way do you want it?"

"What the hell are you up to, Henslow? What shed you talking about?"

"Well, not the sheds and barns folks around here think you probably have already torched. You know, those little bits of revenge you had for fights you didn't win at the Round-up. No. I would like you to put the torch to the Henslow place. Not the big barn. Too nice a building. But the machine shed out there. You have to make it look deliberate. You know, a couple of gas cans, rags. It has to appear to be another threat against Horst Henslow."

"Your old man? You're going…"

"Don't try to figure it out, Rogers. It has to do with the kind of persuasion you ought to understand. Just do what I ask, tomorrow night, after midnight, and we'll have the beginnings of a nice deal all around."

"And if I tell you to go to hell?"

"Then Sheriff Taylor will be out here tomorrow morning and you will be in the Chautauqua County jail for a few days, rather than having the freedom to move around, undetected I might stress, in the dark of night."

"You want me to burn your old man's machine shed? Out at his farm?"

"You have it right. Just after midnight, Thursday morning. And, just to make the deal a little more interesting for you, I have two hundred bucks here to pay for any expenses you might incur."

"I don't like this one damned bit," Rogers said. He stared at the ground, considering.

"Okay," he said finally, "I'll do it, but only on one condition."

"What's that?"

"Find a way to spring my brother."

"Now, that isn't so easy to do. Since he went up just last month, he won't go before the Board of Pardons for another year."

"But there's a parole hearing coming up in a month. You could do something then. Get them to include my brother. That's my deal."

"Well, okay. But I can't promise he'll walk free, but I can give it a try."

The money passed. The contract had been made. An interesting partnership, Jim Henslow mused, was to give the Chautauqua County State's Attorney additional persuasive power in the interest of helping launch a more powerful political life, and he felt sure, acquire one of the best farms in the region which had long ago been promised to him.

❧   ❧   ❧

Horst Henslow had spent a restless Sunday night. His right arm throbbed in the quiet of the slowly turning hours. He felt nervous, his chest tightening with anxiety. His sleep disturbed, he wandered the first floor of his house, moving from the bedroom in back off the kitchen, through the kitchen, then the dining room and into the living room. The security light on the front of the barn illuminated the front yard and driveway. As he stared out the front window he saw a raccoon scurried across the driveway entrance. At two in the morning there was little traffic on Highay 43. A semi rumbled past, going in the direction of Hamilton.

Under doctors orders not to exert himself, Horst spent most of Monday in the house fixing meager meals, trying to read the *Dakota Farmer*. The empty house spoke to him with loneliness for Marie, and with the sad echo of his son's curses, the almost son he had wanted to have as his family. But the wish had failed, that hope evaporated. He knew it was his temper, his failure to be gentle when it was necessary. Now there were only memories and confused thoughts about the past. No longer were there thoughts of the future. The vigorous hours he had spent creating his model farm had become empty recollections for him. All was different now. There were no cattle to care for, no crops which were his to harvest since he had rented tillable acres on shares. But it was still a good place, he thought, a beautiful place that was his own.

Despite the drizzle that continued most of Monday afternoon, Horst went outside, crossed the farmyard and wandered through the barn. He then looked into the machine shed where a workbench and equipment were carefully organized. Every tool was hung in its place and the welding tanks were in their dolly. He knew his decision about the farm had needed to be made, and soon. Jimmy wanted it so badly, but not for farming. He'd heard from some of the men at the Village that Jim was planning some kind of development and wanted local people to invest in it. Surely that was why he wanted the farm. It was a sad end to his own hard work, he thought, that this man, his stepson, who had learned to hate him and now wanted everything.

The resentment did not go away when he argued with himself that Jimmy, who had been promised the farm, was owed at least some of its value. Maybe he should get some of the land and not just money. It was true that Marie had made it possible for him, Horst, to have a good life in America, to own property and make it into something. There was that legacy and somehow he would make good on it. But all the farm? He could not think of Jim Henslow taking over the farmstead where he never came, for any reason. Jimmy had hated it too deeply.

Monday night and Tuesday morning Horst felt a little better. Tuesday was spent restlessly, walking his acres until he was weak, his legs trembling. He'd gone down to the reservoir dam thinking he'd cross over to the Village, but changed his mind and turned back toward the house. The old strength would not come back, he thought. The farm was too much for him. He could admit that. Tuesday night Horst went to bed after the ten o'clock news and slept for a few hours, his arm bothering him less. But he awoke with a start early Wednesday morning. A noise at the front of the house brought him wide awake. His heart racing, he took a loaded twelve guage shotgun from the bedroom closet and moved slowly into the shadows of the kitchen. A pale yellow light came in from the security light out at the barn. The wall clock showed five past one. Slowly he moved into the dining room. The noise came from the living room wall. As he entered he could see shadows against the front windows back lighted by the security light. Two men moved back and forth beneath the windows. He raised the gun and almost pulled the trigger, imaging the blast of curtains and glass exploding into the faces of the intruders. But he paused. They were not trying to open the windows. Then the two shapes turned and ran.

Anger and fear electrified his spine. Still in his pajamas and bare footed, he flung open the front door, stepped onto the concrete stoop, the shot gun at the ready. The two figures were nearly to the barn when he fired, aiming high to be sure he missed hitting them. It was then he smelled the fresh paint. Turning he saw the black scrawl under the front windows. A two foot high swastika dripping with black, shiny paint. And next to it, crudely lettered, was a word he did not know—"Barzal."

From beyond the barn and the grove behind it came the sounds of a car speeding away toward Interstate 29. Horst stepped back into the house, closed and locked the front door. He was trembling and had to steady himself as he stood in the dark next to the overstuffed recliner chair where he had spent hundreds of evenings peacefully reading or watching television with Marie. Now the distant past was being hurled at him, distorted and made ugly with the swastika. Over and over during the years in America he had reasoned that he had not done wrong. In church with Marie he had prayed for forgiveness from his dead mother, knowing that he bore the guilt of knowledge, that he knew which of the Werewolves had killed Herr Mathison the night before British troops came to the camp. Hans accused them all of being traitors to the Fuehrer and that Mathison was responsible. Only Hans had been strong enough to confront their leader. Why shouldn't they fight? But Mathison said all was hopeless, that they should surrender peacefully. He told the youth that they shouldn't listen to the orders coming down to fight to the last man and boy. Hans yelled at Mathison, saying it was cowardly of him to quit. When Herr Mathison turned abruptly and left the barracks, Hans made himself leader of a small band, insisting the Horst come with them. Little Ludwig Krainer refused to go with Hans. He was crying, saying his uncle Mathison was right.

Five of them marched to Marthison's quarters, Hans in the lead. There was an argument among them. Who was on whose side? Some wanted to escape then. Forget Mathison. We better run before the enemy show up, Horst had argued. Hans was armed with a pistol and commanded them to wait. He would not listen to the rest. He went in. Then there was a single shot. In a moment Hans stood in the barracks doorway, Lugar pistol in hand, and announced that Herr Mathison had been judged a traitor and had been executed. Who was going to join him now as he made his way to Hamburg to fight underground against the enemy? He stood there and shouted at them. None of the others moved. Traitors, traitors, Hans shouted. Looking at Horst, his friend since childhood, he aimed at him with the pistol.

"I should kill you too," Hans had shouted. "I hope you rot in hell."

The details of those terrible minutes were confusing in Horst's memory. The way he remembered it was that Hans stuffed the pistol under his belt, buttoned his jacket over it, and left running with only one of the other boys going with him. Ludwig Kainer, Mathison's nephew, then showed up and went in to where his uncle lay dead. When Krainer came out of the barracks he looked Horst in the eye. It was he, Horst, who was responsible for killing poor old Herr Mathison, Krainer said. Hans was **his** friend. He could have stopped him. Someday Horst would pay for this crime, Krainer had said, sobbing. The memory in its confused details had haunted his dreams and memory for fifty years.

Mixed with the lingering guilt about Mathison's death was the feeling that Hans was right when he accused them of being traitors. The fleeing SS were traitors too. But up until that night before the British troops showed up, he had been faithful. He had believed that one true leader was their salvation, and it had been only in the last hours that he had turned from the bright light of that dream of glory into the demeaning surrender to British toops which happened the next day. The stark images of that night and the sound of Hans's accusing voice shouting at Herr Mathison had remained with him as the stain of treachery through all his years. But who was it who had now come to haunt him with those days. The ghost of Hans who was killed by American troops before he got to Hamburg? The ghost of Herr Mathison? Or maybe Ludwig Kainer wanting revenge before both of them grew old and died. Or perhaps the ghosts of all those dead and dying within the barbed wire. Maybe they had come at last.

Other fears filled his mind. Maybe the Nazi hunters had found him. They did not care that the thousands of Hilter Youth were mere children. No one would understand now that he had been a child and that none of that brief part of his life was anything but a bad memory for him. He had suffered for it again and again. Krainer's accusation and Hans's curse on him that last night in the camp were memories he could not erase.

Horst sat down in the chair, holding the shotgun across his knees. He was shaking, his heart beating heavily. His breath came in short bursts. He could not make himself calm. There were too many ghosts from the past to fear.

When he drove into the farmyard Wednesday morning, Jim Henslow found his step-father wiping paint from under the front windows of the house. Still apparent was the swastika form under the smeared paint. The word "barzal" had not been touched. Jim jumped from his car.

"What are you doing? What happened?"

"Two men did this last night. I should have shot them."

"Shot?"

"I had my gun. They ran but I could have hit them before they got round the barn."

"You said two men? Did you see who they were?"

"Na. They had masks. Ski masks. I saw them through the vindow vhen they vere painting. I came out vhen they run. Shot over their heads."

"Well, don't touch anything here. You should have left it the way it was. The sheriff has to see this."

"No, Jimmy. Then the paper vill print another story."

"It doesn't matter. Someone is trying to hurt you. Maybe after both of us. I'm calling the sheriff."

Jim hurried into the house followed slowly by Horst. The telephone was in the kitchen. As he dialed he noticed the clutter of unwashed dishes piled in the sink, open cereal boxes on the counter. Anger filled his mind. What was going wrong with his plan with

Rogers? The sheriff's dispatcher connected him with Dan Morris. He explained what had happened.

"Horst was trying to clean it up, but you can see what they painted."

"Well, leave it the way it is. I'll be right out. Sheriff Taylor is in Sioux Falls this morning."

While they waited, Horst went into the bathroom next to the back bedroom and washed his hands. Jim sat in the living room which was unchanged since his mother's funeral. While he wondered if Art Rogers had acted on his own to harass Horst, Jim surveyed the familiar room. On the west wall over the sofa was a print of Millet's "Gleaners," in a dime store gilted frame. The archway was defined by bookcases on each side. His mother's meager collection of books included one set of encyclopedias, a reader's reference book, "Bible Stories for the Young," and novels long since forgotten by the world's readers. On the left side of the arch was a recliner chair, thrown over the back of which was a many colored wool afghan she had knitted before he was born. The afghan had been in this house and in his memory from the beginning. It, the books, the sentimental print signified the pathetic scope, he thought, of his mother's life. How close the horizon of possibilities had been for her and for this man she had married. And now, with this new and unexpected gift of a painted swastika, that horizon had tightened about this farmstead for Horst. He must be made to believe that this house and farm offered him little security. It was time for Horst to leave.

When the sheriff's department patrol car arrived and Dan got out, Jim and Horst went out onto the front stoop. Dan began to take pictures of the smeared swastika and the word "barzal."

Dan turned to Horst and Jim, frowning.

"What the hell does that mean?"

There was no answer.

At Dan's urging Horst described what he had seen. There were two of them. They wore ski masks. That was clear in the bright light of the security light. They had hidden a car in the grove beind the barn. He heard it speed away toward the Interstate. No, he hadn't seen the car.

"It's probably not safe for you to be out here alone," Dan concluded as he finished taking notes. "Whoever is threatening you has too easy a target. These attacks are getting too serious to ignor."

"Maybe you'll come to town now," Jim added, turning to Horst. "Move in with Sheri and me until we can get you a proper place in town."

"No." Horst's shot back, his tone verging on anger. "I stay right here on my farm. Next time I shoot to hit them if they come on the place."

"Maybe if you had someone living here with you, like a housekeeper, you wouldn't appear to be so vulnerable," Dan suggested. "I think I know a young woman, Gloria Miller, who would be a big help to you. She needs a job. She can cook meals. Keep the house clean for you."

"That's not a good idea," Jim blurted out.

It was a terrible idea. It was totally outside his plans. A woman on the place would make Horst's staying on the farm all the more feasible, and would undercut the argument that it was time for the old man to retire in town.

"Well," Jim continued, "I don't think Dad wants someone living out here in his house."

"Just an idea," Dan replied.

"Maybe that would be okay," Horst said, his voice tentative as he tried to imagine how it would be.

"Doesn't need to be permanent, you know," Dan offered.

"Dad should really come in town. You'll be safe there," Jim repeated, touching Horst arm softly in appeal.

"No, Jimmy. I stay on my own place. You send that woman out, Deputy. I talk to her. But no newspaper stories about this." He gestured toward the front of the house.

"No control over that," Dan said. "Now, which way did they run?"

"Over to the barn. They ran around the side. Fast runners. Then I heard their car speed out of the grove. Vent out to the highway and vent east, toward twenty-nine."

"I want to walk along where they went. See what I can see."

"Papa, you better get some rest. You look exhausted. I'll send someone out here to get this cleaned off and repainted."

Horst agreed. He felt tired. The anger and fear had drained him of energy. Jimmy and young Morris being with him now was reassuring. Whatever was happening to him, others were concerned. Together Horst and Jim went back into the house to wait for Dan to return.

They sat in the living room. Jim Henslow knew he needed to call Art Rogers soon. What kind of trick was this painting? And who was with him? And the swastika and the word? Why would Art do that? He had the feeling that his own plan was slipping out of control just as it was supposed to get started. Maybe Rogers was too unreliable. He should have known that. And even now, with this new threat there was no resolve on Horst's part to leave the farm. He needed to press the issue, Jim thought, immediately, to show Horst the trust agreement now as he had intended when he came out to the farm. Get everything in the open.

"Papa, I came out this morning to talk about the future of this place," he said to Horst who sat in the recliner, head back, eyes half closed. "I know how much you love the place, but it's just too much for you. And now its dangerous."

"Not so much, Jimmy," he replied dreamily. Then more alert, he opened his eyes. "And that Dan has a good idea. I just need a woman out here to do the cooking and cleaning. Then I'll be okay."

"But Dad…" Jim started to say.

"No, Jimmy. I got everything here. And it's just a little vay across the dam over to the Village. I valk there on good days. If I lived in town I'd have to drive all the vay out. Now I get my valk vhen its nice."

Horst's view of the future meant years of his staying on the place. He was ignoring the threats. Jim could see how Horst relied on the familiar routine, a comfortable daily round of keeping the farmstead in shape, playing with his tractors across the lake at the Village, being a farmer by dealing with the rental of his land. It was clear that he had not been considering changing the status of the farm at all. The idea of an annuity, of living off the money the trust would provide had not penetrated into Horst's vision of the last years of his life.

"What about me, Papa? What about my part of the farm? My mother's promise about my getting the farm?"

"Oh don't you vorry, Jimmy. I already put you in my vill. You vill be fine."

The satisfied tone of Horst's voice was infuriating. It had been all settled in his mind. There was finality to it. There was no more to be discussed about Jim's getting the farm. Jim felt his face flush.

"Damit, Papa. This is more of a place than you really need. If you will just agree to the trust agreement, you will be set for life and…"

"Jimmy, boy. I am set for life, aren't I. Even if someone is planning to kill me. Vho is doing deese things against me? Dey find me any vhere. Ya?"

What could he say. The old man was immovable, even after this latest threat. Horst had only this world of the farm he'd build and the world of Pioneer Village. Maybe Art Rogers had more work to do than was in the first plan.

"You don't want to help me now?" Jim said, exasperated.

"How help you? I guess you have some plan for the farm. Folks talk about you trying to raise some money for some kind of houses development. Is that vhat you vant for this farm?"

There was no way to finesse the deal past Horst, Jim thought to himself. The old man already knew the outline of it. The town talk had made keeping the development details secret impossible and he should have known it. His own clumsiness made him angry. He needed to spell it out, now, cut the old man in on the deal.

"I've been working on a major deal, Papa. A Minneapolis group wants to build a model housing project right here in Chautauqua County, convenient to the highway and bordering the reservoir. They have options to buy land surrounding your place. This farm is the central part of the project and there is big money to be made if we do it right."

He talked on, describing the quarter million dollar homes that would be built, the architects' plans for landscaping the eight hundred acres, and making the lake front prime residential property, adding a golf coarse. He started to say that he would get a cut of the sales, but then revised it to say that they, Horst and he, would get a percentage of the sales. He spoke of the planned towns of Reston near Washington that Chautauqua Village would be modeled on, complete with stores and restaurants. The modern world was coming to Chautauqua and he would share with Horst all the plans and profits to be made.

"Dat is a nice plan, Jimmy. But I don't tink I want to lose my place. It is all I have now."

"You won't even consider it?" Jim tried to keep the anger out of his voice.

"Don't be angry, Jimmy. Just try to tink of how it is to be an old man, vith his wife dead and a son that doesn't love him." Horst paused, staring directly into Jim's eyes as if accusing him. "Just tink of that, Horst said, his voice breaking. "Den maybe you know vhy I can't let go of this place, not to some fancy houses. Then I be vorse than dead."

From Jim's childhood years the tone of the words was familiar. There was unmovable resolve. The decison was final. Jim hung his head in silence, his hands clasped before him. He could think of no other way to present his case. Horst would not buy into any plan for the farm. He could not be convinced by potentials for money he did not need. He had no concern for reputation or political power. He had no interest in being influential and recognized in the Hamilton community, nor did he even understand what that meant. His life was centered on the farm and Pioneer Village. Other means would need to be devised to convince this obdurate old landowner, for that is what he was, an old fashioned owner of land, land he valued beyond investments and position. Beyond progress.

When Dan Morris returned from his walk around the barn he carried a spray paint can in a plastic bag. Jim came out on the front stoop.

"What did you find?" he asked.

"Well, this is a piece of evidence that might tell us something," Dan said, holding up the plastic bag. "Found it along side of the barn. Akrin brand spray paint. Common enough."

Jim descended the steps from the porch stoop and inspected the can Dan held. Horst stood in the doorway.

"Maybe fingerprints?" Jim said.

"Yes, if they were really dumb and didn't wear gloves," Dan replied, then added, "Before I go, do either of you have a statement to make? Who do you think might be doing these things to harass Mr. Henslow?"

Both Jim and Horst shook their heads.

"It is strange. The tractor thing was meant to hurt Mr. Henslow. Without a doubt. Maybe not seriously, but hurt him. But this. This is some kind of threat with a message. What do you think Mr. Henslow?"

"I don't know who vould do this. I am not a Nazi. I am a farmer. I am an American citizen. I mind my own business."

"But you were once in the German army…"

"No. Not the army. I was a child in the youth group. Ve vere forced into the var. It was the last days."

"But there is some connection here. The swastika. Do you know what 'barzel' means? A German word?"

"No. Not German. I don't tink I know dat vord."

"Why would anyone paint a word on your house unless they thought you'd know what it meant?"

"I don't know dat. It is no word I know."

"Mr. Henslow," Dan said, addressing Jim, "My advice is that your father requires protection. But we don't have the resources to post any guards. We'll patrol out here, now and then, but that won't prevent someone from trying again."

"I understand. I wish my father did," Jim replied, looking up to Horst who still held the front screen door open where he stood.

Horst said nothing. Then he pointed toward the gate. A car and a van entered the farm yard. On the side of the white van in bold red and blue letters was painted KOLO TELEVISION.

"Get dem out of here," Horst said to Dan. "No newspapers or television." Saying that he went inside, slamming the door after him. Jim could see him look out from behind the blinds.

A young woman got out of the car and approached Dan.

"Hi Danny, what happened?"

It was Carla Garza, the Hamilton *Times* reporter.

"Heard on the scanner there was another incident out here."

"See for yourself," Dan said, gesturing toward the house. The KOLO cameraman was already taking pictures. Jerry Holt with microphone in hand stepped in front of Dan.

"We're here at the Henslow farm east of Hamilton." he said into the mike. As he extended the microphone to Dan he asked, "Sheriff, what happened here?"

Jim Henslow watched as Dan talked to the camera. He was about to intervene, assert his legal role as State's Attorney when Carla turned to him.

"Pretty serious crime, don't you think, Mr. Henslow?"

The KOLO cameraman and reporter turned to Jim. Carla let them know who they were talking to since the Sioux Falls crew had no idea about the local officials.

Holt held the microphone out in front of Jim. The red light of the video camera came on.

"State's Attorney Henslow, we understand that an attempt was made on your father's life last Friday and that windows were shot out of your house. Do you think the swastika and message is part of a campaign against your family?"

"We can't be sure, yet. Maybe the incidents are connected. Clearly this painting is an attempt to threaten my father. When we find the perpetrators they will be prosecuted to the full extent of the law."

"Can we have a statement from your father?" Holt asked.

"I'm sorry. He is too disturbed to talk to you. I have advised him to stay in the house."

The camera continued to roll. Jim Henslow realized that what he had first thought was a local plot against Horst was becoming a regional news story. The publicity would not hurt, not his political reputation nor his plan to move the old man off the farm.

"What's the motive for these threats?" Holt asked.

"My father has been a hard working farmer here in America since the 1950s. He's an American citizen. The few days he was forced to serve in the German army during World War Two as a teenager should be ancient history. If this is the basis of this harassment and threat of a decent man, it is not only unfair, it will lead to prison terms for the guilty."

"Deputy Morris says there was more than one person seen running away from the house after painting the swastika," Holt was saying as the cameraman panned away from Jim and focussed on the smeared black letters and symbol.

"Apparently so, according to my father. If there is a conspiracy to harm this poor man, we will find it out and put these people in prison."

Holt put the microphone down as the cameraman panned across the farmyard, taking pictures of the barn, machine shed and then

·back across the house. The Henslow place would be on the six o'clock news.

Carla Garza continued to take notes as she talked to Dan. The KOLO crew thanked her and got into the van and drove off.

Jim walked over to Carla and Dan.

"How did the KOLO people find out so quick?" he asked.

"They were out at Pioneer Village doing a story on Pioneer Days. I was out there too and told them what I heard on my scanner. Pretty neat. They really appreciated the tip. Great story for them."

"Mr. Henslow isn't going to like it much," Dan said.

"I don't suppose," Carla replied. "Must be scarry stuff for him, someone doing that in the middle of the night." She nodded toward the crude message.

Jim straightened up to his full State's-Attorney-in-court height. This young woman was just learning who was important in Hamilton, having been on the job only a few months. He had better make an impression to make sure she came to him for information about crime in the region.

"Felony offense," he said. "When we get those people before a jury, there is no doubt in my mind they'll end up doing hard time."

"Do you think local people are involved?" Carla asked.

"We don't know, yet. That's possible, I suppose. But then, it may be one of those Nazi-hunting outfits." It was, Jim knew, another opportunity to plant seeds in the press of intimidation coming out of Horst's past.

"Nazi hunters?"

"Well, sure. As I told you for the story about his being selected Grand Marshal for Pioneer Days, my father was in the Hitler Youth as a kid. He served for a short time as a guard at one of the concentration camps. Bergen-Belsen. Who knows, he may be on a list of some outfit looking to get revenge."

Carla scribbled fast as Jim told the story. It wouldn't hurt, he thought, to get the story in the papers again. Constant exposure of the implications of Horst's past life might shame him into reconsidering Arizona, if not scare him into it.

"I better get back to the paper," Carla said, looking at her watch. "Deadline for tonight's issue is two o'clock. Can I phone either of you if I think of anything more to ask," she said to both Jim and Dan. Her bright smile and dark eyes impressed both men.

"Sure. I'll even stop by this noon to see how it's going," Dan said.

"You can call my office too," Jim said.

When Carla had got into her red Camaro and wheeled around in front of the barn and sped out through the front gate, Jim turned to Dan.

"Looks like we have a big story on our hands."

"Yeah. And I'm worried about your dad out here alone."

Horst had come back out on the front steps of the house.

"Well," Dan said, "Mr. Henslow, if you are still interested in a housekeeper, I'll have Gloria Miller come out to talk to you."

"Ya, you do dat," the old man replied.

"Having another person here might discourage any further attacks," Dan added without conviction.

He got into the patrol car and hurried down the drive, turning left onto 43 and sped away toward Hamilton.

"I better get back to town, Papa. Sure you won't come with me?"

"I stay here. I'll be fine, Jimmy," Horst said, his voice softening. "Don't be disappointed. You have a big future mithout taking my farm."

Jim Henslow left the farm not knowing what he would tell Sheri, or more confusing, what he would tell Mark Peterson and the Carpenter Group tomorrow morning in Minneapolis. He had to keep the deal alive in their minds and that would require concrete evidence that the arrangements with Horst were as good as made. The trust agreement would be presented to Mark as signed and sealed, regardless of what Horst planned. A computer-scan of Horst's signature was easily put on the trust agreement. He would show the Carpenter group a document he would say was a copy of the original agreement. A forgery would have to serve for the time being.

To add to his frustration was young Morris's suggestion about a housekeeper. He had to check out this Gloria Miller. Just who was she? She was going to be just another uncontrolled element that intruded upon his plan. But first he had to confront Art Rogers. He knew it would not be wise to be seen in Chesterton again. People would make connections if the State's Attorney was seen meeting too often with Rogers.

At the Mobil station at the east edge of town was a public drive-up phone booth off Highway 43. A tattered directory had enough remains to reveal the number in the yellow pages of Rogers' Machine Shop in Chesterton.

"Yeah?"

"What in hell is this about painting the old man's house?"

"Who is this?"

"You know damn well who it is. I said the tool shed and tonight, not last night."

"Sure. So what?"

"So why were you out there last night at my old man's place and…"

"I wasn't out there. No way. We have a deal. Early Thursday. After midnight. That's it. Like you said."

"Are you kidding me?"

"That would be just a lot of fun, but off my back lawyer. I wasn't out to your old man's place last night. I'll do what I promised, and that's it. And just so's you remember why, it's because you're going to get my brother off early, like you promised. Understand."

"Okay. Okay. I'm working on his early release. Listen. Forget tonight. Something happened out there and we better put it off for awhile. I'll call you later. In a few days."

"Have it your way. Whenever you say go. Okay by me."

"All right, then. No fire tonight. Later, after I talk to you."

He hung up and started toward his office where he was preparing to prosecute a petty theft case. There would be time to get a signature on the trust agreement before he left for Minneapolis because he didn't need to go to a motel in Sioux Falls for an alibi after all.

❦   ❦   ❦

There was a feeling of luxury for Jack Traid in the three weeks of free time between the summer and fall semesters. An hour in his office at the college to pickup mail and look over the next semester's schedules of classes required little attention. Walking back to his house Wednesday morning, he contemplated a pleasurable day in the print shop, arranging the forms of type for *The Tenured Heart*. Among the letters in his box in the Mathematics Department was one from Mildred. She wrote that she had spent the summer in Canada hiking the Rockies. She ended with "wish you'd been there!" The scribbled pages paid little attention to punctuation or capitalization. It rambled on about Banff, Jasper, the backpacking trails. Bears sighted. Elk on main street. She did not say whether or not she had been alone.

Back in the print shop he pinned her three page note to the bulletin board over the desk near the door, a reminder that he needed to answer her letters, now two that he'd received during the summer. He had not replied to the first, uncertain about what he would say. Except for a Christmas card, it had been the first communication since she left Hamilton. She had written in that letter about her life-drawing classes. "Strange models. Some luscious. You should see them." She'd underlined "you." Oblique invitation? Humor? Probably the latter, he decided, remembering Mildred's acid wit when she was of a mind to use it. He missed her urbanity, her comfortable connection with art and literature. Their love making had been a counterpoint to their talk about books, about art. There were none of the unspoken barriers he and Ellie seemed to be trying to maneuver around, the distance from which it seemed Ellie, even in her most carefree mood, was assessing him. With Mildred there had been no tentativeness about sex. For the few months they shared she had made him feel vital, enfolded in the excitement of lovemaking, of ideas and creativity, all part of the same fabric of their relationship. In her apartment was an eclectic collection of prints, her own paintings and small sculptures both impressionistic and realistic in detail. Her letter reminded him how much he missed her, missed the tenderness of afternoons and evenings together in her magical, and in his mind, always exotic apartment. He imagined she had found an arty crowd in Minneapolis-St.Paul, and a lover.

The remembered aura of Mildred bothered him most of the morning while he tried to concentrate on Roger's poems about love. It could be, he thought, that the elegant paper, rich black ink with carmine colored florets here and there as accents, would be in the end superior to Roger's verse, written in a commonplace meter, with rhymes that seemed obvious. The emotions Roger evoked verged on sentimentality. Yet, the sincerity counted, of course, and the books were for his children, his wife, and for a few friends. The pretense was mostly in the fine printing he, Jack Traid, was capable of producing. Poets with reputations were being printed letterpress in limited editions by private presses which sold them for hundreds of dollars a copy. Not so Roger Faregold's work.

It was noon when the extension phone rang in the shop. Dan Morris was on the line about Horst Henslow. His son Jim had called him out to the Henslow place. According to Horst a couple of men had sprayed a swastika on the front of his house in the middle of the night.

"Black gloss, too. A mess where Horst tried to remove it. But the strange thing is, there was a word painted next to the swastika. 'Barzel.'" He spelled it for Jack.

"Does that ring any bells for you?" Dan asked.

"No. I can't say that it does. It suggests itself to me, as if I once knew it. But, no, I can't tell you what it means, not right off."

"We thought it might be a foreign word. Or maybe the name of some person or group. Could it have been a name Horst once used? He says he doesn't know what it means."

"Let me think about it, Dan. It seems to me I ran across something like that in Dallas, but it won't connect in my mind just now. I've been working on poetry, not threats."

"Give me a call if you think of something."

"Barzel," Jack said aloud to himself after hanging up.

He reached for the American College Dictionary on his desk. Nothing. He repeated the word to himself as he worked on the type forms on the imposing stone. Another two pages were ready to be locked into the chase for printing.

The word obviously had meaning in the context of the swastika. In Dallas there had been an incident of swastika painting on tombstones in the Jewish cemetery. It had been the work of a small group of skin heads who were caught with cans of paint matching that in the cemetery. The only word they slopped on headstones was "Jew" along with swastikas. The hateful vandalism had energized the community. More than fifty volunteers that included Protestants, Catholic Hispanics, Unitarians, as well as members of the temple showed up that very day to scrub and scrape the desecration from the monuments. For the first time in his life he realized that this graveyard and its people were a part of his own heritage, even if he had little part in their traditions and religious observances. His grandparents had not become part of the Jewish community, and had acknowledged only casually the traditional holidays. His parents attended a Unitarian church, and he for a while in his youth its Sunday school. Yet, there had been no doubt in his mind that he too had been under attack, as had the entire community. The realization had sparked an emotion he'd never felt before. Because of the accident of his birth, he could become, like the millions in Europe, a target of hate and death. It was the sickness of inhuman hate which had been splashed across tombstones. His part in the speedy arrest of the perpetrators had produced a quiet pride he seldom felt in his work.

It was strange, he thought, that Horst Henslow, once a child marching to the martial music of racial purity had become the victim of unknown assailants in the night. What had this farmer done to deserve these two attacks so late in his life? Why were they so dissimilar in nature—what appeared to be a meticulous sabotage of the steam boiler, and now the crude spraying of paint? How did the shot-out window at the Jim Henslow residence and the slashed tires fit into these threats?

The memory of the Dallas cemetery brought to his mind the group of demonstrators who had formed later that day in Dallas. Six young men from the Jewish Defense League carried hurriedly painted signs: "Never Again! Fight the Hate!" In two days the incident had been over. His own anger faded and the episode became lost in other daily crises. The word "barzal" seeped into memory in the voice of his grandfather. Steel. No. Not quite. It was Hebrew. He was certain. Then it came to him. It meant "iron." As he was about to call Dan back he received a second call which was from Gordy Easton.

"I saw him. Last night just before I went to bed. Right there at the salt block. I could just barely see him move. It was so dark because of the rain. But he was there."

Jack shared Gordy's excitement.

"It's working then, the salt and corn. Maybe he'll stick close by your place."

"Mom says I can put up "No Hunting" signs around our fences to keep out deer hunters this season. Think that will help?"

"Sure won't hurt. Want some help?"

"Maybe if you come out after school. I'm going to get some signs at the variety store during lunch break."

"Okay Gordy. It's a deal. About four o'clock?"

"Yeah. I'll be home then. There's no track practice today because all the coaches have some kind of meeting."

When Gordy hung up, Jack dialed the sheriff's office. Sally Edwards, the dispatcher, told him Dan had left.

"Tell him it means 'iron.'"

"What?"

"The word he wanted to know about. Tell him barzel is Hebrew for iron."

"That's weird. A Jew word."

"No, my dear, it is simply Hebrew. Another and ancient language."

Her provincial, biased tone irritated him. He calmed himself and continued, "Dan wanted to know what that word painted on Henslow's house meant. Tell him I am pretty sure it means "iron." It's used by a Jewish organization. The Jewish Defense League. But I haven't the faintest idea why it would be painted with the swastika on Henslow's house."

"Probably because he was a Nazi," Sally replied.

Her off hand remark surprised him. Was there a general perception in town that their village was shielding a Nazi war criminal? What rumor had been circulating since the newspaper article about Horst being selected Grand Marshal for Pioneer Days and now the tractor accident?

In ten minutes Dan phoned him back. Jack explained about the Dallas incident and the demonstrators from the Jewish Defense League.

"Maybe there is a connection with that group?" Jack suggested.

"Okay. Worth a try. Never heard of them here in town, or anywhere in South Dakota."

Perhaps, Jack thought, the world was getting smaller, much smaller, crowded, its hate and envy closing in on the rural quiet that had protected him these past few years.

❧   ❧   ❧

"More Threats Against Local Man." The inch-high banner head-line in the Tuesday evening *Times* stood over the sub-head, "Horst Henslow Again a Target." Carla Garza's by-lined story stuck to the information she'd gotten from Dan Morris and Jim Henslow. There were no leads on who the perpetrators were. According to the sher-iff's office it was not clear if the boiler pipe leak and painted swastika and word meaning "iron" were connected. That Horst Henslow had been a guard at Bergen-Belsen concentration camp might be behind the incident according to State's Attorny Jim Henslow, son of the vic-tim, but he said he could not be certain. He promised full prosecu-tion for these crimes.

A picture of Horst Henslow's house was at the center of the front page. The caption read: "Swastika and Hebrew word meaning 'iron' apparently meant as threat against Horst Henslow at his farm east of Hamilton."

For Carla Garza it was a thrilling day. Editor and publisher Elliot Morris stopped by her desk and congratulated her on the biggest story so far that year.

"Good reporting," Mr. Morris had said. "Keep it up. You're doing a great job here, Carla."

Carla felt she was going to like working in Hamilton. The first month she had had some doubts. Weddings and baby showers were not her idea of journalism's highest calling. The Henslow story was more like it would be when she got to a big city newspaper. And then there was the handsome deputy sheriff to think about, she mused to herself. She cautioned herself that she should think of him princi-pally as the best source of information in town.

Across town Jim Henslow watched KOLO TV's six o'clock news-cast. Horst Henslow was the subject of the lead story. The anchor-man introduced Jerry Holt's story with the assertion that the swastika painting suggested that Nazi hunters were operating underground in South Dakota. The idea had a satisfying ring to the ears of Chautauqua County State's Attorney Jim Henslow.

CHAPTER 7

*J*im Henslow's return flight from Minneapolis to Sioux Falls Thursday evening was nearly full. The boarding process had been slow and irritating to him as he shuffled forward to his seat. Ahead of him a large, middle aged woman struggled with two shopping bags in the narrow aisle. Jim was certain she would not be able to lift one of them into the storage bin over the seats. It annoyed him that the airlines permitted so much to be dragged onto flights. He was relieved when a young man ahead of the woman politely offered to help her, freeing him from what had appeared to be an unavoidable obligation. With relief he slipped into his seat next to a window, put his briefcase on the floor under the seat ahead of him, and turned to watch the ground crew below loading baggage into the cargo bays.

Mark Peterson and the Carpenter Group executive committee of three were pleased that Jim was able to deliver to them a copy of the trust document bearing Horst Henslow's signature. He explained that it was a photo copy of the original which was secure in his safe at home. It clearly gave him, James Harold Henslow, complete control of the 800 acres of farm property. The legal description of the land in the trust agreement reassured them, for Peterson had it marked on the maps laid before them on the conference table. Henslow had shown copies of these maps to his law partners at Andy's restaurant the night Sheri's car tires were slashed.

"It will take a month or so to make arrangements to get my Dad off the place and moved into town. But there's no problem," he had said with confidence.

He knew the lie was a high risk move, but he could think of no other way. He couldn't let the Carpenter Group get out of his grasp this late in the game.

"We've got to have a date certain," Herb Stover, CEO of Carpenter replied,"when we can finalize documents and get onto the site. We have deadlines on the options to surrounding property, you know. So, no later than October 15. Preliminary grading and some survey-ing for street layout has to be done before freeze-up. It's pretty damned late already, if you ask me."

Jim recognized hard bargaining when he heard it.

"Put it in the contract, then," he'd replied. "I can assure you that everything will be ready on my end."

"Good." Stover snapped. "We'll have the final agreement to you by next week, reflecting what we've discussed here. We agreed there must be some local investors to keep community interest focussed. And there will have to be an agreement with the County on the five years of tax forgiveness."

"No big problem. I've talked to the commissioners in a prelimi-nary way. Two plants in Hamilton got five years, but the taxes were phased in—nothing the first two years, then one-fourth, then one-half, and the fifth year three-fourths."

"Do better than that," Mark suggested. "But it's not a stopper," he added quickly. "But the local investors are pretty key. We figure we'll need the assurance of at least a quarter million of local money. That about right, Herb?"

"It will do." Stover was not one to give much leeway. Jim could tell that they wanted the Henslow place bad, it and the Chautauqua res-ervoir shoreline.

As the plane was making its descent into Sioux Falls, Jim Henslow was feeling warm satisfaction that he had negotiated each provision with confidence, that he had stood up to the big operators. For one thing, he had the deal well in mind and it showed in the discussions. What he could not admit to Herb Stover was that his discussions with Pettigrew and the other money in Hamilton at Andy's Restaurant had not yet borne fruit. He also could not convey the feeling he had that his law partners seemed tentative, wary of investment, as if nothing of this magnitude could possibly come to the county.

Then there were the details of local arrangements for the site. The question of utility service was pretty well set these days with electric service territorial laws in place, but he'd have to talk to the Dakota Gas and Electric Company to see if Prairie Electric could be kept out. That way the project could avoid having to deal with a manager operating under a part-time board of directors consisting of local farmers. He didn't particularly like the co-op bunch anyway.

As he went down the list of things he had to do. The forged trust agreement had to become less bogus and the deal more of a reality by the old man's actual agreement to turn the property over to him as promised. Except for that stolid old man, little by little the deal was moving forward. But he was under pressure now. Horst had to come around and sign the legitimate document this week, otherwise the negotiations had a soft bottom, likely to collapse in an instant should Peterson discover what he had been negotiating on. Henslow had a vague sense of discomfort that the he might face being sued by the Carpenter Group if he couldn't come up with a valid trust agreement after all the promises he'd made. He shoved the thought aside.

The drive to Hamilton from the airport was calming. Interstate 29 north had little traffic at eight in the evening, the two lanes rising and falling over the rolling countryside. This was the corridor on which commuters would travel to and from Chautauqua Village, a gated community for the upwardly mobile who were able to invest in quarter million dollar homes. He imagined the shot of economic adrenaline the development would give Hamilton. Like twin cities, the old and new would grow, contribute to the life of each other, and prosper. It would be clear to all that Jim Henslow had been the force that transformed the city and the county. A proven leader.

Cottonwood Acres was quiet as he negotiated the winding streets. Arriving at his house he was irritated to see that the picture window had not yet been repaired, the sheet of plywood a wound on the meticulous order of the neighborhood. Art Rogers would have to pay for this. Henslow was resolved that Rogers' skills would yield more useful results when applied to the Henslow farm.

Sheri's Lincoln was not in the garage when the motorized, overhead door rose to reveal an empty garage. Jim pulled into the garage and got out the Explorer with his briefcase. Entering the house he called out, thinking perhaps the Lincoln was being serviced at Perry's Auto World and had not yet been returned. Lights were on in the kitchen and dining room. There was no answer. It was disconcerting to Jim. He'd expected to report to Sheri on the success of his meeting. On the refrigerator was the note: "Will be late. Dinner with Louise W. at SFCC after shopping."

Louise Wilson, wife of Dr. Olin Wilson was a sure prospect for a shopping trip, Jim knew from past experience. Sheri liked Louise because she was mousy, and admired Sheri's rough and ready opinions as worldly. She'd giggle whenever Sheri used coarse language. It was not their first "Day in Sioux Falls." They both loved and often repeated the cliché, "Shop 'til you drop."

Jim put his briefcase on the desk in his bedroom, took off his suit and dressed in chinos and a cotton plaid shirt. In the kitchen he poured half a glass of Scotch whisky over ice and returned to his desk. On a legal pad he began to list what needed to be done, and put beside each a date. These were deadlines by which he must resolve issues: trust sig., electric power, investors. Horst was at the top of the list. He'd have that problem resolved by Saturday. The key to everything, his own political future, was now in the simple gesture of this old man writing his name on the agreement. Resisting as Horst had been, it did not seem possible that he would refuse the argument he, Jim, was prepared to make. If it came down to a final 'no' from Horst, he would have to make it clear to the old man that the trust agreement would either be executed or the farm would be tied up in the suit he would file to recover his mother's estate and what was rightfully his share. It was flimsy on the surface of it, he knew, but the threat would be real enough to Horst who hated legal entanglements. That much he knew for sure.

When he heard the garage door rise, he went to the bedroom door, glass in hand, waiting for Sheri to appear at the door down the hall which led to the garage. The overhead door shut. The hall door opened and two large shopping bags came through the doorway first. One was printed large with the name of Sheri's favorite store, "Silverton's." Sheri followed, dressed in a tweed suit, a bright red scarf at the neck. Sharp as ever, he thought. And she knows it, too, he thought to himself.

"What have we got here," he greeted, tuning his voice lightly, approvingly. It was not a time to argue about expenses.

"Trifles. Mere trifles." She smiled her stage smile. "You aren't bankrupted yet, my dear."

"Let me fix you a drink while you put that stuff away. What'll it be?"

"Scotch and soda. Light on the booze. Little Louise and I had wine with dinner. A little too much for her, I might say. Chatted away the whole time during dinner. And what news I have for you."

She spoke in her sarcastic, all-knowing tone.

"What's that?"

"In a minute. Let me get comfy before I dump the whole horrible mess in your lap."

What, he thought, could Louise Wilson have to say that could interest him. He mixed Sheri's drink, adding a twist of lemon he knew she liked. He refreshed his own drink with a double shot.

In the living room Sheri reclined on the broad, curving sofa, stretching her long, attractive legs in front of her as she sat upright against the armrest. She liked that pose, he thought, dressing gown open in a deep V between her breasts, and thrown back to reveal her legs to mid thigh. She would often strike that pose, imagining what, he could not guess. It was a conscious pose, as if she were mimicking some actress she had in mind. She held her drink before her, as if ready to make an offering, which indeed she did.

"Louise was full of news from the hospital. If you think doctor-patient relations are sacred don't go to Doctor Olin Wilson. He's been treating Gloria Miller, for depression, according to Louise. Which isn't so surprising when you consider…"

"Wait a minute," Jim interrupted. "Is that the woman Mrs. Rienhart has at her place? Has a kid, but not married? The one Dan Morris talked about?"

"There is only one Gloria Miller in town, and," she said, pausing for emphasis, "and she is not living with Thelma Reinhart any longer. You'll be delighted to know she is living with your old man. Now isn't that just the sweetest damned thing you've ever heard?"

Sheri's tone was as much accusatory as sarcastic, and touched with anger. What Jim heard was Sheri's opinion that he had failed to control events, that a stranger had slipped into his plan and he had done nothing to prevent it.

"When? What the hell did Louise actually say?"

"Today. This morning. Olin told Louise at lunch before we left for Sioux Falls. Gloria told him she wouldn't need to see him any more. That she had a job at the Henslow farm as housekeeper. I bet! She'll be in bed with that old fart before the week is out, and you know who'll be in his will as sole heir by next week—just out of geriatric gratitude."

She downed a third of her drink.

"Damn it to hell," Jim said. He rose out of his chair and was standing in the middle of the room. "You'd think Dan Morris would mind his own business. He did that, you know. Mentioned the Miller woman to Horst and me when he was out investigating the swastikas spray painted by someone on Horst's place. Gloria needed a job, he said." Jim's voice shifted to a mocking tone. "Poor, neglected broad got in trouble and had a baby. Wouldn't it be nice if Horst had someone to keep house. Damn it all."

"And you should have put a stop to it right then." Sheri raised her voice, disgust pinching her brows as she gestured toward him with her glass. "What the hell is the spray painting about?" she continued. "You get that done?"

"Of course not. I haven't the foggiest who did it."

"Looks to me you're thoroughly screwing up the deal for the farm," she continued. "If you had any guts you'd get the old man off that place one way or the other."

The rest of the evening at Jim and Sheri Henslow's new house in Cottonwood Acres was spent cursing, first Horst Henslow, then Dan Morris. Jim Henslow swore again and again at the wild card introduced into the deck—Gloria Miller.

Sheri got in her share of criticism of her husband. "Bungling the whole deal," she muttered. "Fat chance you have of getting that old buzzard to sign over the place now."

"And you could do better, I suppose?" he replied, feebly.

"Well, you might think of just getting him out of the way."

"I have. But he won't go to Arizona."

"I was thinking of Arizona in the sky, dimwit."

She finished off her third scotch.

He looked at her without reply. Sheri had deep inside her a capacity for cold hate he had never completely fathomed and with which he could not argue. There was a calculated fierceness she brought from her family, members of which had been constantly at war with one another throughout her childhood. Her own survival might require severe means, she seemed to say, and no matter what the circumstance, she would survive. It was that very energy which had made her a daring photographer when she chose to use it.

After he'd related the developments in Minneapolis and admitted to Sheri that he did not have much time to get the farm, Jim Henslow spent a sleepless night trying to fit Gloria Miller into, or totally out of the plan for development of Chautauqua Village. It was time for more and sharper warnings to Horst about his past. And if that didn't work, the threat of the law suit. He couldn't think of what else to do. If he only knew who had done the spray painting. An unknown player had entered the game. But it was time for Art Rogers to use his barn-burning talents, and soon. But Sheri's anger spread a cloud of doubt and confusion over Jim Henslow. She had given final expression to her disgust with a backward wave of her hand as she went to her room and closed the door. He had followed, intending to take her in his arms, to make her understand that everything would be all right. They would work it out together. But her door was locked.

❦   ❦   ❦

The third press run of double page sheets of "The Tenured Heart" was complete. Jack Traid lifted the type form from the Chandler and Price press and laid it on the imposing stone work table. The heavy sheets of handmade paper, the type impressions in deep black having made slight impressions into the texture of the paper, were beautiful in the morning sunlight that poured in from the southeast windows. Since early morning, after a forty-five minute run at the college track, he had been in the studio, eager to complete the printing phase on Roger Faregold's book. The day before United Parcel had delivered a five yard long roll of Japanese cover material, a deep blue fabric with tiny carmine florets woven in a disciplined pattern. The project was beginning to reveal itself in actual components as it progressed. It was satisfying to Jack Traid to see the book emerging he had imagined in his mind months before. But it would not do to hurry. He was relearning the patience this craft demanded. There were still nine sheets to be printed on the reverse side of those already done. The sheets would then be folded into signatures for sewing. He still had time, but he'd promised Roger that the fifty copies of the book would be finished by Thanksgiving. They were to be Christmas gifts from Roger to his family.

The ringing phone awakened him to the present. Wiping his hands on a rag, he went to his desk and picked up the hand set.

"Traid," he announced.

"Are you the nice detective who solves mathematical problems?" Ellie's voice asked.

"No, mam. There are no cops here," he replied, playing her game.

"Well, I'm looking for the nice guy who has a birthday on Saturday. Is he anywhere around there?"

"Just a minute, lady. I'll have to look." Jack held the phone at arm's length. "Hey, old man, there's some lady want's to talk to you."

Bringing the phone back to his ear he said in a quavering voice, "Old Jack Traid, here. Who's speaking, please?"

"Okay, buddy. We know how old you are. And we're going to have a party Saturday night for you, here."

"Whoa. That's too much!"

"Nope. We're going to tell the world how ancient you've become. A few guests will be there to help get the message out. A gift or two will be presented. And a special cake covered all over with candles will be presented. Wanna come?"

"How could I resist? But no candles."

"Oh, there will be candles. How about one a decade?"

"That's better. What time?"

"Better be here by six so you don't miss any of the fun."

"Ellie! You shouldn't make a big deal of my birthday, you know," he said, meaning it.

"Wanted to. You deserve it," Ellie said. "So be here at six; that's an order."

"Yes, ma'am."

After he hung up he paused at the south window and stared out across the side yard of his lot. A few leaves were beginning to fall onto the grass. His birthday in early fall, and the beginning of school, had always meant new beginnings. This season was like the start of a new year. It had often been a time for renewal, as it had been the year he had driven for the first time from Dallas to Iowa City, Iowa, in a Model A Ford. He had been accepted at Iowa earlier in the year and spent most of his time explaining to parents and friends why he was not going to the University of Texas instead of Iowa.

"The Writers Workshop," he explained. "Iowa has one of the best programs in poetry and fiction writing."

He ignored the looks of surprise. He had told few people of his interest in writing fiction. Although he had worked on the high school newspaper writing feature stories about community events and historic places. He had not talked about wanting to write fiction. He had dreamed of writing a novel. It seemed as if it were the only way to express oneself, and show independence. But that beginning at Iowa had been a diversion, lasting only into the second semester when he wearied of the carnivorous shredding of his stories by undergraduate intellectuals fresh from reading Beat Generation writers. There was a more ordered, sensible world in mathematics, and he switched his major. That was a new beginning that had eventually led, after a tour of duty in Vietnam, followed by a year of graduate school, to investigative work on the Dallas police force.

Half an hour later it was Dan Morris who called.

"You were right about barzel meaning iron. I've figured out why it was sprayed on Henslow's house."

"Let me guess," Jack replied. "A revenge message."

"You could call it that. Remember your telling me about the Dallas incident and the Jewish cemetery? You mentioned a group of protesters, young guys from the Jewish Defense League. Well, I looked them up. There is a group in Minneapolis that has a phone number. They preach just what their name says. Defense of their Jewishness. I called them."

Jack felt his guard going up.

"So?"

"Oh, nothing wrong about that, I guess, unless they have gone on the offensive, like spraying threats."

"So what's the connection with the word barzel?"

"The JDL, according to the guy I talked to in Minneapolis, is based on five principles, one of which is barzel, iron. Meaning they will not accept the image of the Jew as a weakling. They mean barzel to represent their determination to be strong, physically as well as psychologically, against the attacks made upon them."

"So why Horst Henslow?"

"Not sure yet. The League person I spoke to said his organization did not condone vandalism. He said no member of JDL would spray paint such a message on the house of anyone, not even an ex-Nazi. He said something to the effect they didn't go out looking for trouble. They're just ready to meet trouble when it was directed against them."

"And where does that leave you?"

"As you said last Sunday about the Henslow's window being shot out and the tractor boiler pipe leak. There is a confusion of attacks. The spray painting seems a lot different to me. A threat, to be sure, but not a direct bodily attack. I can't put them together in any logical way."

"Maybe the publicity about the tractor business just got Horst Henslow into the spotlight. You know, that bit about his being a guard at a German concentration camp. Some rogue member of the League decides to make a statement. Harassment."

"Sure, something like that. But there is no organized group in Sioux Falls, or in South Dakota as far as I know. The Minneapolis guy said they make mailings from time to time to South Dakota addresses. He said there weren't many but but he wouldn't give out any names over the phone and won't send us the mailing list. That's why I'm calling you."

"Why's that?"

"Well, there is no way I can get away from the county, what with Sheriff Taylor away on his so-called research. Taylor and I thought you might have time during your semester break to do a little errand for us."

"Go to Minneapolis?"

"Yeah. Taylor said he could deputize you and that would let us pay your expenses, up to a point, of course. Could you give me a hand? We really need to get closer to the League to see if there are some connections with them and some group in the state. I figure you could use some of your Dallas talents to persuade them to give us some names."

"I'll have to think about that Dan," Jack replied, wondering if Dan included his ethnic background as part of his 'Dallas talents.' "I wasn't planning on leaving town during break. Got all kinds of projects. Like a birthday party I can't miss on Saturday."

"Yeah, I know. I'll be there."

"Really. Well, that Ellie. Anyway. Let me think about it. I might not be very convincing."

"Well, you can think about that. Maybe just a direct 'this is police work' approach. Just appealing to the guy's civic duty might work."

"Well, maybe a couple days next week out of my plans won't hurt. But I'm not anxious to play cops and robbers again."

"Whoever is threatening Mr.Henslow may be a lot more serious than robbers, Jack. I have a gut feeling we better put a stop to what is going on with him or it could turn ugly."

"Guess I have to agree," Traid replied.

Hanging up the phone, Jack turned back to the quiet of his shop. The call had been an unwelcome intrusion. Yet, he owed Dan, after all that Elliot and Minnie had done for him. And, of course, Dan was the best trombonist in the region. But Minneapolis? If he went would he dare go to see Mildred? Maybe Minneapolis was not a safe place for him.

❧   ❧   ❧

The weather front that had moved through the region setting off showers was followed by colder air from the northeast, a huge cyclonic system curling about Minnesota and into the Dakotas, siphoning in sub-artic Canadian air. Friday morning, September 1 turned crisp and cool in bright sunlight. Fall was in the air and the citizens of Hamilton moved with quicker steps and were more animated in speech. August's heat and humidity were gone. Harvest was in the air. The Labor Day weekend promised a parade, last picnics of the season, speeches from the courthouse steps on Monday. Those who were not aware of the angry call from Professor Riemer to the sheriff's office, might believe that God was in his heaven and all was right with the world, at least in the environs of Hamilton.

"Dumped in the ditch, right at the corner of my property," Riemer explained. "That's six miles south of town on County 19. Heavy oil. Must be three or four inches deep in places."

Professor John Riemer and and his wife Martha lived on a farmstead abandoned when the original one hundred sixty acres had been incorporated into the Alex Johnson operation, a corporate operation of more than five thousand acres. The Riemer place consisted of the four acres fenced off from cultivated land, house and outbuildings no longer of use in the aggressive farming practices of the Johnson company. City people from the east coast, the Riemers prided themselves in the large gardens of vegetables and flowers they tended with meticulous care. "Organic gardening methods," they boasted. They thought of the place as their 'back to nature' move.

"Don't touch that stuff," Dan Morris warned. "We're getting other reports that someone's been dumping PCB oil in different parts of the state. EPA considers it very toxic. If it is PCBs, we'll need to get a toxic waste clean-up going out there."

"Well, it's a damned shame. Whoever did this ought to go to prison."

"They will, if we catch them. Big fine too. I'll be out to talk to you as soon as I can get away."

When he got to the Riemer place, it was clear to Dan Morris that the site for the dumping had been chosen because of the clump of trees at the corner of the property, hiding anyone on the road from being seen from the Riemer house. The intersection was at the crest of a hill, affording a long view of the roads in all directions. A quiet place in the early morning hours.

The Riemers were standing in the front yard at the edge of the ditch when Dan arrived. Both were in their sixties, their hair beginning to gray. Short, and of the same height, they seemed like twins. They were agitated and it showed in John Riemer's strained voice.

"I didn't notice anything last night," Riemer reported. "There was the usual traffic after supper, the occasional pickup or car."

"Didn't see a truck stop?"

Both John and Martha shook their heads 'no.'

"What about our well? Is that oil going to seep into the water table?"

"Well, it could eventually, but we've notified Prairie Rural Electric to give us a hand on clean-up. They have trained people. They'll get all the oil picked up and will have to take whatever soil has been contaminated. Looks like another big expense for the county to have it disposed."

"Is that why someone's dumping it?" John Riemer asked.

"Sure is. There are dozens of reclaimed electric transformer operations around the country. Costs them a lot to get rid of PCB oil properly, so they pay independent operators who say they'll take care of the problem—if no records are made. But don't worry about your well. This oil moves through the soil pretty slowly. Prairie Electric will have it out of there by tomorrow."

Reassured, the Riemer's started back toward their house.

"If you're talking with neighbors," Dan added, "ask them if they might have seen something in the middle of the night. That's when these guys usually operate, when there is less chance of being spotted."

The Riemers promised to phone neighbors.

Before he prepared to return to Hamilton, Dan placed yellow police line ribbons around the spill. Carla Garza, the *Times* reporter had arrived by then and took pictures of Dan looking into the ditch where a black puddle of glistening oil covered grass and stood in pools between clumps of weeds. On the side of the ditch where gravel had been bladed by a maintainer, Dan could see tire marks. It was clear that it had been a truck, probably one of the larger pickups, for there were tracks of double rear tires where it had backed up to put the truck bed over the edge of the ditch. But in the loose gravel there were no clear signs of footprints. Nothing else had been left behind to serve as a clue.

Carla approached Dan after taking pictures of the spill. Dressed in Levis and a bright red western shirt, she moved like an athlete, sure footed and graceful. Her olive toned skin and angular features spoke of her Spanish ancestry. Carla Garza, Dan remarked to himself, was a dark beauty uncommon in these northern plains. She was deserving of close attention, he decided.

"Since this isn't the first case of oil dumping from what I hear, has the Sheriff's department any suspects by now?"

Her question was challenging him, and the department.

"Like you, I'm new to the job. This is my first oil spill."

Carla's dark eyes narrowed just perceptibly.

"Yes, but they tell me at the paper that at least one other oil dumping has been reported in Chautauqua County in the past six months. Hasn't your boss any ideas yet?"

It was an interesting situation, Dan thought. This employee of his father's newspaper was doing her job going after a sluggish sheriff's department while he the rookie was put in the position of defending Tom Taylor, absentee law enforcer. But it wasn't the time to undercut his unfocused boss.

"I believe we'll find out who did this, Carla." He said her name in friendship, thinking to shift the tone of the interrogation. "With a two-man department and a crime wave centered on the Henslow family, we've gotten spread a bit thin."

"Yes, I can see that," Carla replied, her tone softened.

"The County Commission has refused to add personnel as other counties have. They say its the smallest county in the state and can't be compared to any of the others. It has been a two-man operation since the 1930s, despite the fact that the county's population has doubled since then. That might make an interesting story about local government."

"Yes it should. I'll have to work on that."

"You sure are busy enough yourself," Dan continued, deciding that Carla was a more interesting subject. "I read your by-lined stories. You're really good."

"Thanks. It's pretty neat to have so much excitement during my first months working for your father. Certainly gives me a chance to show what I can do."

"Where'd you go to college?"

"U. of Missouri. Columbia School of Journalism."

"And home?"

"San Antonio. I know what you're thinking. What's a nice Hispanic girl doing in the infamously cold Dakotas instead of returning to sunny Texas to work her trade."

"Well, yeah. Something like that, even if I think my dad got a good deal." Dan offered the compliment with a smile.

"Horizons," Carla replied. "I felt I had to experience a lot of the country if I wanted to work for a major daily, like the St. Louis *Post-Dispatch*, or someday the Washington *Post*. I want to learn the business from the ground up and the *Times* offers a beginning journalist wider scope than say going directly to a paper like the San Antonio *Express-News*. There I'd probably be writing up traffic accidents and obits."

"I see," Dan replied. "Well, best of luck. Maybe the sheriff's department will have to try a little harder to solve these crimes before you go on to bigger stories."

He had commented without sarcasm, but noticed that Carla's eyebrows lift slightly. She was alert to nuance.

"I mean," he added, "we'll be aware that a serious reporter is watching our performance—just as it should be."

"I'll be around for a while," Carla said, smiling, "but that doesn't mean the *Times* won't be on your case for answers to the threats against the Henslows, and," she added, nodding toward the oil-stained ditch, "another oil dumping."

"I'm glad," Dan replied, matching her smile. "It will be my pleasure to have you on my case." He was pleased that Carla was smiling, her perfect bright teeth gleaming as she turned and went to her flaming red Camero.

During his lunch hour on Friday, Jim Henslow gave Art Rogers instructions on the telephone, straining to keep the urgency out of his voice.

"The shed's got to go tomorrow night, for sure. Maybe before ten. That's just before the old man goes to bed. I want him wide awake when the shed goes up in flames."

He sat in his Ford Explorer next to the roadside phone booth at the Mobil station at east city limits. He was on his way to the farm and this was the safest phone from which to call Chesterton.

"Whatever you say, Henslow," Art Rogers replied. "I drove by there the other night. There might be too much traffic moving on forty-three before ten."

"There's a grove of trees behind the barn with a gate that is unlocked. You can hide your car in there. Won't be seen from the highway."

"Yeah. I saw that gate."

"You'll figure it out, Rogers. But a nice little fire on a Saturday evening will cause all the more stir in town than if you torch it after midnight. The volunteer fire department guys will be all over town at nine or nine-thirty."

"So what?"

"So a little drama will bring out the crowds and will impress the old man that someone is serious about his past and that the whole town is wondering why."

"You want me to do the white shed south of the barn, right?"

"That's right. Make sure it looks deliberate. And while you're at it, since someone painted swastikas on his house, why don't you just paint one on the gas can you'll leave. Maybe that will really convince him he can't escape his past."

"You sure are a son-of-a-bitch. He's yer own old man."

"He isn't, and don't trouble yourself about my character or gene-alogy."

"Don't worry. But if I do this, you better get your ass in gear with the parole board to spring my brother."

"I've already talked to my friend the warden," Jim lied. "The board meeting is a month away yet."

"I'm risking my ass dealing with you, Henslow. But for Clarence that's okay. I'd just like to be convinced you were really working on getting him out."

"Look, Rogers. The warden and I are friends and I know two members of that board pretty well. I think that speaks for itself. We'll work on the idea that he deserves another chance to go straight, laughable as that will seem to everyone in the county."

"Don't be a smartass, Henslow. I'm serious. You screw me in this deal and you'll regret it. It won't be a window you'll have to worry about."

"You can quit making threats Rogers. Your brother will go free in less than two months, even if I have to have him paroled to me personally." It was another promise he was not sure he could or would deliver on.

"Okay. Saturday," Rogers said. "Before ten o'clock, if I can get in there then. And swastika on the gas can, right?"

When he hung up Jim Henslow sat for a moment staring down state highway forty three toward the Henslow farm five miles away. He had to go out there today and get the Miller woman out of that house before she got settled in, and before the old man took a liking to the arrangement. As he thought of the situation on the farm, Sheri's word replayed in his mind. "Just get him out of the way. Arizona in the sky." He wondered if it would come to that. Would he be able to engineer that scenario?

It was just after twelve noon when he pulled into the farmyard, parking next to the house on the driveway leading to the garage at the rear of the house. In front of the garage doors was a beat-up Chevrolet sedan, its fenders rusted and the once dark blue paint faded to a dull, spotty silver. Doubtless the Miller woman's car, Jim thought. As he went around to the front door, which seemed strange to him, for he would ordinarily go in at the back door, he felt he now approached as a stranger, an unwelcome intruder. Or, he amended the thought, at least like a salesman filled with the pitch he had to make one more time.

On the front stoop he opened the screen door, rapped on the door and then opened it a crack. It was, after all, nearly his house.

"Anyone home?" he called.

There was no answer for a moment, then a women's voice from the kitchen answered.

"Just a minute."

Another pause. Jim edged the door open another foot.

"It's me, Jim Henslow."

"Oh, Mr. Henslow," Gloria Miller exclaimed. She stood in the dining room at the far side of the table, a dishtowel in hand.

"I didn't hear you drive up. I was tidying up the kitchen."

"Yes. Well…" he didn't know where to begin. Gloria Miller was an attractive if unkempt young woman in her middle twenties. Her flowered dress covered with a white apron could not hide her generous shape, overweight by thirty pounds. With care, he thought, she could be very attractive.

"Well, I came to see my Dad. Is he around?"

"He went over to the Village, Mr. Henslow. He said he wanted to take a walk this morning. He also said he wanted to get the leak welded on his tractor so he could be in the parade on Labor Day. I expect him for lunch anytime."

Jim entered the living room and stood next to Horst's recliner chair opposite the television. It irritated him that he was face to face with Gloria. He had expected to deal with Horst, convince him that it was not wise to have this young woman in the house with him.

"I heard that he was considering asking you to help him out here. Do you plan to drive out each day?"

"Oh, no. Your dad says I can have one of the upstairs rooms. He's really a very nice man, your dad."

"He's hired you, then?"

· "Oh yes. He said I need only make his lunch and dinner and keep the house clean. I can have most of the afternoons to myself."

"And what about your baby? I heard you had a baby."

"My mom's taking care of him now. Maybe later I can bring him out, when Mr. Henslow thinks my being housekeeper is okay with him. Kinda more permanent like."

"Well, that is why I'm here, miss Miller."

His tone changed to the courtroom mode, filling it with authority and certainty of purpose.

"I realize this arrangement probably is very nice for you, but it just won't do. My wife and I are very worried about my Dad. You no doubt heard about the accident with his tractor and then someone painting threats on the house."

"Oh, yeah," Gloria interrupted, her tone cold, hardening as she spoke. "Some bastard is trying to scare your dad. He told me about that. Just because of the war all those years ago. But I'm not afraid, Mr. Henslow. This job is too important to me. I really need the work."

"I realize that. Maybe we can find you something in town when my dad moves into an apartment. I'm sure I can help you."

"That's nice. I sure appreciate it. But I want to stay out here for now, just as long as your dad says he needs me. It's so nice here in the country."

"It just won't do. In fact, it would be wise if you packed your things right now and left. I'll deal with my…"

"No, Mr. Henslow. I can't leave. I just have to stay. And your dad needs me. He said so."

"And he isn't in his right mind just now with all these threats against him. No, it's not safe out here for him, or for you. Both of you better understand that."

"Well, I'm not afraid…"

Horst filled the frame of the kitchen door, straw hat in hand. He said nothing for a moment. Jim wondered how much he had heard.

"Afraid? We're not afraid out here, Jimmy," he said, nodding toward Gloria who turned quickly to him, startled by his quiet entrance.

"Oh," she uttered.

"We were just talking about the danger to you, Papa," Jim said. "I don't think it is safe for Miss Miller to be out here, or you for that matter."

"I told you, Jimmy. I'm not afraid of any of them. If they think they can scare Horst off his place, they better have plenty of guns."

Gloria stepped back as Horst came through the dining room and stood under the archway between the dining and living rooms. She backed toward the kitchen door, seeking the security of her inter-rupted work. As Jim began to speak, she slipped into the kitchen and could not be seen from where he stood. But it didn't matter. She could hear what he had to say.

"It just is not a good idea for you to have that woman out here, Papa."

"Vhy not? Two days now she has been a good housekeeper. I told her she could move into a room upstairs."

"There will be talk."

"Talk? Talk? I don't care about talk. Gloria is a good Vorker. She is going to earn her pay for keeping this old place clean and cooking for an old man."

"But consider the threats against you," Jim argued. "Someone is trying to hurt you. Maybe you're putting your's and Gloria's lives in danger by being out here."

"I wonder who wants me off my farm the most?" Horst looked straight into the eyes of his stepson.

"Since you won't listen to reason, Papa, I have to tell you that if you and I can't agree on how I get my promised share of my mother's estate, I may have to take you to court. After all, it was her farm in Pennsylvania that got you…"

He was impossible. Immovable. He really did not care what anyone in Chautauqua County might say about this young woman living in his house. Just as Cheri said. Ending up in bed. And, Jim thought, the old man probably enjoyed thinking of the innuendoes that the gossips would work around to, what with Gloria Miller's reputation. 'Old geezer's got himself a bed warmer.' The subject would work through every iteration, but Horst Henslow would live out of earshot of it all. But there was another card to play. The physical threats were one thing, but Horst would hate it far more going to court to defend his property.

"Your mother and I vorked together." The words came with a hard edge. "It was not some hers, some mine. We took dat little bit she had in Pennsylvania and made it grow. We vork together all doze years to make dis place vhat it is. Ya, you get yours vhen I go. It's in the bank. Money enough for you. But dis farm place is vhere I stay. It is vhere I die, too. You can't have it for any fancy development."

The anger had risen in him, his voice swelling, taking on the guttural sounds of his native tounge. It was the voice Jim heard in the barn years before, when Horst had brought the leather rein down on his back. He half expected this rigid block of a man to raise his fist again, but he did not. He stood staring at his stepson, controlling his anger.

"Damn it to hell," Jim shouted. "You never cared for me and now you're not listening to what I have to offer. You just want to get even. Well, okay. Have it your way. I'll see you in court and I'll tie up this property in a way that will take you years to unravel. It's as much mine as anyone's."

"It's not yours. Never vas yours. And, Jimmy, it never vill be yours," Horst said, his voice firm, patient. "Now, please leave me in peace. Don't come back here if it's wit crazy plans to take my farm." He was pointing toward the door, commanding.

"You'll regret this. You go back on your promise to my mother and, and I'll…"

He stifled what might have sounded like a threat against Horst's life which he almost spoke, realizing that Gloria Miller was listening in the kitchen.

Jim turned and rushed out to his car. In the Explorer, he gunned the engine and spun around in the drive. Lunging in anger toward the front gateway, he skidded to a stop at the highway. 'Burn the whole damned place down,' he thought. Maybe he'd ought to tell Art to get the barn too. But no, a little at a time would be more effective.

CHAPTER 8

Saturday Jack Traid took his time going to his print shop. He awoke from a dream to the fact of his fifty-fourth birthday, and lay in bed gazing at the window which the rising sun tinted pink. In the dream he was walking with difficulty down a country road through a wasteland. It was a landscape of war, of this century, where bombed-out huts with missing walls lined the rutted road, just as seen again and again on movie screens and television. In the landscape of his dream there was no humans. Yet, danger lurked behind each crumbling hovel. In the illogic imagery of dreams, he was wearing a police uniform, the pants legs splattered with mud. With urgency he had hurried forward. The straps of a backpack seemed to pull him down into the muddy road. The going was slow. A woman was sobbing in the distance. He'd awakened catching his breath.

As he watched the changing hues of sunrise on the bedroom window, he had the feeling he had been letting past experience suffocate his present life, that he had lived more than half a century without a real sense of himself, of what his life was meant to be for others. The memory of his service on the Dallas police force remained as a bitter residue. Although the daily stress was only half remembered, there remained the vivid sense of the explosive anger he felt over and over at officialdom, at the chaotic slums where he practiced his trade. Nothing he did could put it to rights. And there was Alice, dear careless, flighty Alice who never understood the filth and violence he waded through most days, and who was unable to fathom the anger he brought home to her at night. How many nights had his rage made love-making impossible? How many times had he told himself that however much he was recognized as an effective cop, he had to get out of the force and do something else. What he had deprived his and Alice's marriage of remained in his mind as a daily accusation. He had failed her, finally. Their marriage could have been more meaningful. Alice might have wanted a child. But, she was not the source of his frustration. Maybe it could have been, he thought, a committed partnership if he had tried harder, had not hidden in the routine of the crimes he investigated each day. He could not shake the feeling of emptiness which was more like an open wound than like the scar across the back of his left shoulder and upper arm.

If he were to face facts, he thought, maybe he had not yet gotten out of the wasteland of himself here in Hamilton. Maybe he was still avoiding true personal commitment and his teaching routine welcomed only as palliative. And tonight he was going to be honored by the woman with whom he had begun to feel comfortable but to whom he knew he was not yet ready to make a commitment.

Ellie was attractive, and outwardly affectionate, but Traid knew that she was holding herself back too. If she had sought him as the man she needed now for love and as the man with whom she would resolve her denial of sex since Ralph's death, he would have responded, he thought, with delight. That would have been a mutual basis to build on. But their being together had taken on an implied and potential commitment to her farm, her dream, her world of Gordy and Ralph. Most certainly Ralph was still central to her life. It was probably Ralph's ghost that detained him most, as if it moved across the county like the albino stag revealed in moonlight. Away from Ellie and the warmth of the farm house, he did not feel up to competing with the perfected image of the dead husband. What had he to give to the relationship? Rasputin offered no answer, circling around the pillow, his throat rumbling the message that it was time to be fed.

"No doubt, Rasp, the trouble is with me," he said, sitting up in bed.

The cat went to the foot of the bed and turned to await the next move.

"Not like you, old friend. You were really betrayed. Maybe the problem here is that I keep betraying myself."

He got out of bed, pulled on a bathrobe, descended the narrow stairway into the front entry, and turned down the hall to the kitchen being lead all the way by Rasputin just a step ahead.

"Fish or beef?" Jack asked.

He selected tuna, Rasputin's favorite.

"Let's pretend it's your birthday too. There'll be treats after the main course."

Rasputin purred his answer, circling Jack's legs as he moved slowly from pantry to sink.

Once the cat was fed, the coffee percolator charged with water and coffee, he mixed frozen orange juice in a plastic pitcher, smashing the pulp with a wooden spoon. He needed the coffee, he thought to himself, to get out of the mood of his dream. It was as if he still carried a heavy backpack and was half suspended in that other confused world of war and city filth. His day refused to get into the rhythm of the minutes ticking away on the stove clock.

So it was for most of the morning. He allowed nostalgia to wrap itself about him, and took the dangerous path of taking photo albums down from the top shelf of the bookcase where they gathered dust, real prairie dust and the mental dust of his own forgetting.

He allowed himself to start with the most recent photos, Hamilton college events, Mildred at her exhibit of paintings, which reminded him he had a decision to make about going to Minneapolis for Dan Morris. Beautiful Mildred smiled brightly, girl-like in the picture, her Dakota landscape stretching out behind her in hues of tan and brown, an autumn piece reflecting a modicum of peace she had found years after her divorce. Turning the page he found the one photo of Rasputin, curled up on the back porch. It was a rare shot of a cat which dared not venture beyond the security of the house. As he got to the last page of the most recent album, he realized that in the past year neither he nor Ellie had taken a picture of each other, or of having someone take a picture of them together.

Deeper into the past there were pictures of his first wife, Mary. The setting was graduate school, the two room apartment over the downtown theater. Serious Mary Geats, soon to be a social worker and his wife, soon to tire of his endless hours of duties in Dallas. Three years and the marriage was over. Memories of Mary had dimmed in the years following, the bachelor years before Alice had rescued him, jockeying him into a proposal of marriage. She of another world was here pictured—beautiful, joyful Alice in front of her parents' suburban ranch house in Arlington, the Dallas suburb. Both Alice and the house were expressions of satisfaction, of self-assurance and ease of wealth. Another picture of Alice and him had been taken in Rocky Mountain National Park, arms around each other in front of a range of snow-capped peaks. A stranger had offered to take the picture of them together. It had been one of those brief interludes they had managed to find together, far from Dallas crime, far from suburbia's yearning for more possessions. Theirs was a pose like millions of others taken at a lookout spot along the road with the wilderness far in the background. But the pictured embrace, he thought, was like a promise that was never realized.

In the back of the album was a single page of photos taken in Vietnam. He and Lieutenant Colonel Vance Bannier stood next to a jeep, both looking confident. Another was a Polaroid shot which a nurse had taken of him in the army hospital bed, his left arm and shoulder bandaged and held raised and ridged in a brace. There were several photos on following pages of Dallas police department ceremonies. They showed men in uniform standing in rows behind a smiling commissioner, or perhaps the mayor of Dallas. He could not remember his name. He could remember the names of only a few of the officers. Except for the fact of his own stern but young face staring out from the group, it was as if it were a picture of no place he had been.

A deeper nostalgia settled upon him as he opened the older album of photos his parents had kept and which came to him after their deaths. He and his sister Margo—he twelve, she nine—standing on the front steps of a bungalow. It was the only picture he had of her. She died the next year from polio. His parents' silence and grief the following year, and his own grief, were remembered as a kind of paralysis, as if taken on from the dead child. There was a certain coldness with his parents after Margo had died, as if they did not dare invest more love in a child, or that they would suffer some guilt if they expressed love they could no longer give to the dead daughter. The modest house in the photograph seemed to him faintly pathetic, not up to what Margo should have had for a life. The photo showed a clump of carefully trimmed pyrocantha bushes just to the right of where the two children stood. The bushes were planted under a picture window which had a narrow view of a front yard thirty by fifty feet, like every yard in the housing development.

Pictures of his parents taken when they were younger than he was on this his fifty-fourth birthday seemed quaint, as if their nineteen forties clothes were period costumes selected for the occasion. What had that time in their lives meant to them, he wondered. His father and mother had kept the printing business going. They had that together, he thought. That was an achievement of mutual commitment which they had given each other. Certainly, he thought, that was at least part of the meaning of their lives.

At ten in the morning he shook off the sadness of the past, showered and dressed for working in the print shop the rest of the day. Once he was in the shop the smell of ink, the feel of the handmade paper, revived him. Roger Fargold's book was purpose enough for him at this hour. The rest would have to work itself out, he decided. He did not feel he had that much of life to control. Besides, he sighed to himself, classes would begin in one week, beginning algebra and business math would create their little urgencies of purpose for him. But first, he thought, he had to get through the ceremony of passage, a birthday party celebrating what he could not yet believe deserved celebration. But he would be at the Easton farm as promised.

❧   ❧   ❧

Sheri Henslow avoided speaking to her husband as much as was possible Saturday morning. A residual irritation showed itself in her voice when she did speak. Again Jim Henslow had had to report failure. He came home yesterday from the farm full of anger, cursing: "That Kraut s.o.b. That slut Miller woman." As he drank, glaring about his living room as if looking for something to destroy, as if the blank plywood had set a mood for their day, his each word implied a curse on her too. She felt that, felt the anger directed at her, the easy target. But she wouldn't take it, not from this man she once thought had backbone, and was committed to something better for both of them. How great he'd been when he won the election six years ago. It was to have been their release from Hamilton. But after six years in office, he still had not broken free of this town and the dullness of endless dinner parties with his law partners and their bovine wives. It had been all promise and no avenue of escape. The five years of scrimping had at first seemed to be worth what was finally going to come into their lives. Now he could report only that the Miller woman had moved into the Henslow place, and had become just another obstacle to making an escape from this place.

She watched Jim fume. How was he going to make good on the promises he'd made in Minneapolis to the developers but couldn't keep? The forged trust agreement, how was he going to explain that he didn't have an original? And as far as she could tell there was no Hamilton money being bet on his project. Because of his bungling, the Chautauqua project looked like a flimsy get rich quick scheme any prudent investor would shun.

"Pettigrew? Did he make a commitment yet to invest?" she asked, accusing as well as asking. She knew he had not by the way Andy Pettigrew acted a week ago at Andy's Restaurant when Jim had shown them all the drawings of the Chautauqua housing project. Pettigrew seemed to look down on this real estate enterprise as unworthy of any serious commitment.

"Not yet. But once it's moving down the track, they'll all want to get aboard."

"Sure. But as far as I can see, you have no commitments, nothing but what you've made up in your head. It's going to take more than a forged agreement to get that farm."

He did not answer. He glowered at her and sipped his drink. She could see his anger rising. She left the room and went into the kitchen thinking it was one hellova way to spend a bright Saturday morning. It was a bitch of a way to spend a life. It was already ten o'clock. The day was going to hell, filled with Jim's anger. It struck her then as an absolute certainty that there would never be a Chautauqua housing development if it were left to Jim Henslow. It was clear as the morning sky, the future foretold. It was all coming down around this fool's ears. Then where would they be? What would happen to her? Sure as hell, she said to herself, not in the state legislature or any other legislature. Jim Henslow was not going to be the people's choice, not now, not ever. It had come as a revelation to her and it was time to act upon this certainty.

There was one avenue of escape, at least for today and maybe for her future, and that was to go to Sioux Falls to get an assignment from Derrick Holmes at the *Argus Leader*. It would not be the first time she had sought quiet companionship with Derrick, journalist, editor, lover. His was an inventive conversation. His flirtations were those of a man who did not have to make excuses for his success. Derrick had poise and self confidence. Early on he had made his desire clear through each casual touch of her knee, her hand held softly. Derrick's marriage had been no barrier to their affair, not until his wife found out about them. He had ended the arrangement abruptly, apologizing for what he liked to call his stupidity. But, she reasoned, he still owed her something. She'd get a new assignment, whatever it might be, and enjoy whatever else Derrick Holmes might have on his agenda these days.

Once decided, she went to her room and changed into a light gray, linen suit and chose a bright orange scarf to wear about her neck. The tight skirt came to just above her knees and showed her long legs to advantage. She saw herself through Derrick's eyes as she stood before the full-length mirror on her closet door, remembering his intense manner when he had touched her. She recalled his sure hands as she smoothed the skirt about her slender hips.

Making sure she had her car keys in her purse, she left her room, waved goodbye to her husband as she went down the hallway to the door to the garage.

"Where in hell are you going?" Jim demanded.

"I can't stand to stew in your juices all day. I've going to talk to my editor at the Argus about an assignment he promised," she lied.

"What the hell? See that creep Holmes? Sure, abandon ship when it gets a little rough here."

"Don't get all shit for confusion. I haven't forgotten the deal at Andy's Restaurant tonight. You're going to try once again to talk Pettigrew and Johnson into investing in your deal. Okay, maybe I'll be back by six. But don't count on it. If I were you I'd start to figure out how to save your ass, and soon."

With that she went into the garage, pressed the button on the wall to open the overhead door, and got into the Lincoln. The smell of new upholstery, the quiet of the interior enveloped her once again with calm. It was, she thought, what she deserved. What she did not deserve, she was sure, was the screwed-up, two-bit real estate deal meant to finance an iffy political future.

Left to himself and the solid, blank wall Horst Henslow had raised before him, Jim Henslow mixed another scotch and water. Let her go. She'd have spent the day bitching at him anyway. The deal wasn't over yet even if his marriage seemed to be. He would bide his time. See what a fire on the Henslow place would do to the old bastard's resolve. His own resolve, bolstered by the second scotch, was that the final confrontation between stepfather and stepson was yet to take place—in or out of court.

Art Rogers knew there were precautions to be taken if he was going to torch the machine shed on the Henslow farm and leave evidence of a threatening act. The gasoline cans he would leave behind were the two new ones he had purchased in Sioux Falls four days earlier when he had gone to Roman Industries to pick up six fifty-five gallon drums of PCB oil which he trucked to the Sioux City disposal site. He'd used Clarence's Ford 350, which he kept in the garage at the farm. Used to haul cattle trailers, the 350 could carry heavier loads than his Ford 150 pickup.

From the gasoline storage tank behind his welding shop he pumped fuel into the one-gallon cans. He'd decided it would take two cans of gasoline to start the fire in more than one place in the shed. He remembered Henslow instructing him to paint a swastika on a can, so he painted both cans for good measure. He had to admire Henslow for thinking of details. The funny part, he thought, Jim Henslow was probably one of the guys who'd painted swastikas on the front of the old man's house.

While in Sioux Falls he had also visited Clarence in the State Penitentiary and brought him up to date on the deal he had with Henslow. The guards were sitting close by so he avoided using Jim Henslow's name, referring to him as "your special lawyer friend."

Clarence warned him. "Be careful of that ambitious s.o.b. He'll turn on you if he thinks he can get something by it. He's as crooked as any of the guys in the joint."

"I figured as much. Don't worry about me. I'll do the deal I promised and then put the heat on him to get you out. Just for insurance, I got me a little tape recorder that works on the telephone. Got him twice. Once when he told me to hold off on torching the shed and once again when he told me to go ahead next Saturday. He'll love the sound of his voice."

"You better make a copy for me to keep here. For insurance. No telling what that bastard will try to do. Just let him know there is more than one copy."

"Yeah, sure. Good idea. I'll bring it to you next week."

They had both enjoyed the imagined scene when Jim Henslow would first hear the tape and learn there was more than one copy.

"Maybe Henslow can really do something with the parole board," Clarence said, "but in any case put the screws to him real good."

In the welding shop Art stood back to admire the swastikas in fast-drying, black enamel spray paint glistening on the new cans. He hid them behind a workbench in the shop until he needed them that night.

❦   ❦   ❦

Dan Morris spent Saturday morning on the telephone. In the counties surrounding Sioux Falls and Minnehaha Country, there were three electric transformer renovating plants: Acme Electric located east of Interstate 29 and ten miles north of Sioux Falls, Roman Industries located west of Sioux Falls five miles, and Samuelson Electric Supply, a one-man operation located near Lennox, south of Sioux Falls. The only other entity handling PCB oil was the rural electric cooperative. Prairie Electric shipped PCB oil in its own tanker truck to the Dakota Electric Company generating plant near Big Stone City, Minnesota. It was burned in the boilers there at temperatures that assured destruction of the toxic material. There was little chance that oil could be diverted from the co-op's system.

When questioned, Acme's man was less than forthcoming. He said he had read about the oil spill south of Hamilton but couldn't think of who would do such a thing. Sure, they were required to keep records for the Environment Protection Agency. He told Dan that Taylor had checked them out just a week ago.

Carla Garza, the *Times* reporter stepped into Dan's office mid-morning asking for more details about the oil spill. She brightened the barren sheriff's office, he thought, pleased that she thought she needed more information from him. He repeated what he knew about the spill, adding that he was checking the transformer plants for their records. He wondered to himself if asking an employee of his dad's for a date was going to complicate things for both of them. He decided to hold off. If this olive-skinned beauty was coming into his life, there was time enough. He told Carla he'd call her if he got any new information.

"Call any time," she said. It was an invitation.

Dan's other calls had produced little. The receptionist at Roman Industries said her boss was not in on Saturday mornings. No, she didn't know the names of any of the people who trucked oil for them. It all went to Sioux City. Her boss would be in Monday or Tuesday. Could she take a message? Dan left his telephone number for the owner to call.

Samuelson Metals was located south of Sioux Falls and two miles east of Lennox. It was a small one-man operation. Greg Samuelson dealt in scrap of all kinds and had taken on electric transformers when the Environmental Protection Agency had ordered utilities to get PCB oil out of their systems. Mostly, he told Dan, he dealt with the municipally-owned electric systems in his area. The distribution cooperatives, he said, were all in a deal with Prairie Electric, so they weren't a good source. Trucking the oil? Two or three local guys had taken a barrel or two to Sioux City when they had something else to do there. Mostly he hauled his own. Names of those who hauled for him? Sure. And he named three men, all of whom lived in his county. Dan thanked him and filed the names in the case folder. Maybe Taylor could look into their activities on one of his trips to Sioux Falls.

Maybe Samuelson's operation was the source of the oil that was being dumped in ditches around the country, but Acme's was the place that needed a closer follow up. He'd have to ask Sheriff Taylor what Acme's records he had and what they showed, and maybe Taylor would also go to Roman Industries next time he went to Sioux Falls. They just needed to get some names to follow up on there too. Taylor had said not to worry, he'd take care of Acme, but there were no records on file in the office as yet. In any event, Dan thought, he had to keep the pressure on to get the names of truckers.

Iowa Disposal Systems in Sioux City assured him that every delivery was documented, exact number of gallons and fractions of gallons, date delivered and by whom and the source of the oil. "Our books are open anytime you want to look them over," he was told. The plant manager then agreed to photo copy the records of the past month and send them to him. The records would provide names of truckers who brought oil in for disposal.

*   *   *

Mail was delivered to the Henslow farm at two o'clock in the afternoon on Saturdays. Horst had waved to Chick Swanson as the latter pulled up to the mail box on the other side of state highway 43. Horst had finished painting over the gray smudges under the front windows of the house where the spray paint had been removed with rags and turpentine. Putting the paint bucket and brush next to the front stoop, he walked slowly down the driveway. The afternoon was cool, the sun showing in and out of slowly moving clouds. It was fall-like and refreshing. The quiet of his farm, the well-ordered yard and bright red barn spoke to him of his success. His and Marie's success, he thought to himself. Even if Jimmy tried to pry all this away from him and kept on fighting him, it was his and Marie's work that made this place the model farm it was. He knew he was going to stay here for the rest of his life.

And, he was thinking, there was comfort in having young Gloria Miller in his house. Even after two days he had begun to feel cared for, looked after. She picked up the newspapers he'd left in the living room. The evening meals she fixed were good. As good, he thought, as Marie's cooking. It was strange that he could make that comparison without feeling guilty. It was no betrayal of Marie to be enjoying this young woman's care.

In the mail box were two letters and the Friday edition of the Hamilton *Times*. One of the letters was an advertisement for insurance being offered by a local bank. The other letter had no return address. The postmark was Sioux Falls. As he walked back into his yard, he tore open the end of the envelope and removed the triple-fold sheet. He stopped still in the middle of the driveway. The message was short, a single scrawled line of capital letters under the printed letterhead of the Jewish Defense League.

"Nazis pay for their crimes. Hadar!"

The crudely written threat was like a child's printing. He swore to himself, anger rising. Maybe, he thought to himself, it was Ludwig Krainer come out of the past to get revenge for his uncle Mathison's death. Maybe it was Jimmy doing this. The sadness of the thought filtered into his anger. Would Jimmy hate so much that he would try to scare him off the farm? What would be next? This message meant something else was going to happen. There would be some kind of attack. He had to be ready for it. And he would be. His resolve hardened.

Shoving the threatening letter back into its envelope and putting it his back pocket, he moved with deliberation as he retrieved the paint can and brush. He took them to the tool shed where he cleaned the brush and put a lid on the paint. He closed the machine shed door behind him and walked with purpose into the house.

Gloria Miller had been watching him from the window and was standing in the living room when he entered.

"Is something wrong, Mr. Henslow? You seem upset."

He pulled the letter from his pocket and handed it to Gloria.

"This letter. Someone tinks dey can scare Horst Henslow. Vell, dey can't."

He went to the gun case and took out the twelve gauge Remington automatic he'd put there after shooting at the masked intruders early Wednesday morning. From the drawer at the bottom of the cabinet he took three shells and shoved them into the magazine.

"If they come again, I'll be ready."

"I can shoot too, Mr. Henslow. My dad use to take me hunting. If you want me to have a gun too, I can handle one."

"Vell, ya. If dey come in here you take dis 20 gauge to them. Here." And he took the single barrel shotgun from the cabinet and handed it to her. From the drawer he took a handful of shells and put them in her outstretched hand. "Good goose hunting gun with this steel shot."

There was tension in the room. Gloria felt it. Arming against the unknown. Still, she felt no panic. For the moment she was glad she had not brought her baby out to the farm. Here she was having to defend the old man and farm which had seemed to offer security to her just two days ago. She carried the gun into the kitchen and propped it in the corner near the back door. Horst sat in the living room. He was talking to her and to himself at the same time and

Gloria could not be sure if she was supposed to respond. The poor old man was frightened.

"Never locked doors before. Not here. Not vhere everything is safe."

He paused to think about what he'd said.

"Vell, we lock up. If dey come tonight we vill be all locked up. Padlocks on the shed, on the garage."

He told her he would make the rounds before dark and check all the locks. Armed, he would stand guard all night. After dark he would go out and walk guard around the farm buildings.

"Maybe I surprise them before dey know it. But don't you vorry," he said, raising his voice and turning half way toward the kitchen door. "You stay in the house here and you'll be okay."

Gloria didn't reply. It wasn't necessary. She listened to Horst prepare his defenses.

By eleven thirty Sheri Henslow had ordered her second Scotch mist in the Sioux Falls Country Club lounge, seated in a corner just at the left edge of a wide picture window overlooking the tee box for the first hole. The cool, bright day found late morning golfers eager to move forward at the starter's command. On the putting green off to the left a foursome bent over their putting games. Despite the lingering irritation with a day already gone wrong, Sheri enjoyed the muted sounds and colors of the lounge, the smell of liquor, the wide view of the ritual movements of golfers on the putting green. They were well outfitted men in their thirties and forties. One of the younger men wore light chino trousers and a Ralph Lauren polo shirt. His older partner wearing a plaid cap and beltless acrylic trousers with sharp creases, sported a rich yellow sweater Sheri was certain was cashmere wool. These were successful men, she thought.

They moved with assurance, certain of their right to independence from family on this Saturday morning. Here they were absorbed in the safe camaraderie of their game, their class, their club. There were no women in the line-up. Saturday mornings at the club were understood to be reserved for male members. A recurring wish drifted through Sheri's mind. She should have been a man, privileged on Saturday mornings, making decisions that counted all week long and able to create a life of wealth and comfort. Today, she reflected, she and Jim were sinking deeper into the confusion of his indecision, as if he didn't have the conviction of what he said was his ambition. She didn't know where their finances were. He was already late with August's payment on the Lincoln. She knew that. And she was left to worry about it.

She tried to work her way around the morning's frustration with her husband. The image in her mind was of Jim stuttering away as he tried to explain how he was going to get the Henslow farm. And it was just like him to fumble the development deal, afraid to deal forcefully with the old man about the farm. It was as if his anger at his step-father had paralyzed him. Like a child he was still intimidated by that uncouth old farmer. The image of Horst which Sheri retained in memory was of a dour and arrogant man who could think only of his land. He always seemed to disdain her, and never spoke directly to her that she could remember. It was as if he felt protected by the hundreds of acres he owned and needed no one. Jim should be able to see that and have the guts to get him out of the way. There were all kinds of ways. There had to be. Maybe have him committed, judged incompetent. That could be engineered. If Jim had the courage he wouldn't fool around with threats of a law suit.

As her mind searched for solutions to Horst Henslow, Derrick Holmes appeared in the lounge doorway, saw her and started toward her. As he moved through the room he greeted club members who were beginning to take tables for the lunch hour. Derrick was well known at the club and served on its board of directors. As assistant editor of the *Argus Leader,* he was one of the movers and shakers.

Sheri envied the deference shown Derrick as he greeted people. She envied the fiftish woman he bent over and kissed on the cheek. Five years ago he had done that often when he met her here, when they were in the midst of their affair. She admired the assured movements of this successful man, his nearly six foot, trim body moving with ease between tables. Jim Henslow always came into such a room on the defensive, unsure of where he ranked and worried about where to put others in some hierarchy of his imagination. Derrick knew where he belonged and, she knew, felt no such quandary about why he deserved what he had.

Reaching her table he took her hand, holding it briefly in greeting. It was not a hand shake. It suggested familiar friendship, but was reserved. He did not bend over to kiss her but instead seated himself opposite her and facing the window. It was, Sheri thought, as if his wife were watching, ready to threaten divorce once again if he got any closer to Sheri Henslow.

"Got your message on my answering machine at work this morning. I'm sorry I can't stay for lunch as you suggested, but since you sounded so eager to come out of retirement, as you called it, I thought I'd better talk to you."

Sheri detected the wariness in his voice. As he spoke there was an implied question, or questions. She remembered that in the past his voice had soft edges, was suggestive. Today he was impatient, carrying out an old obligation and restless to be on to other subjects in other places.

"I need to get back to work, Derrick. That hick town is driving me nuts."

"Hasn't changed for you, has it?"

"It's worse. And it will never change."

She stopped herself from bringing Jim into the conversation. She would do this solo. It was her future and it was on her reputation that she was banking to get Derrick to hire her. She was not just the wife of a third-rate lawyer with low-level political ambitions and she didn't need to plead for escape to a job. She needed no sympathy. Her photographic work, both of them knew, had been too good to require begging.

She leaned forward and reached out to touch Derrick's hand. He responded with a quick squeeze of her fingers, then removed his hand as a cocktail waitress placed a lime-topped cocktail between them.

"Your usual, Mr. Holmes," the young girl said sweetly. Sheri recognized the voice, her own simpering voice of seventeen years ago. She waited for Derrick as he thanked the waitress, tested his drink, and prepared to talk business. He blinked. She had never noticed Derrick blink. He was not certain about what he was to say. She waited.

"Well, Sheri," he started, slowly. "If you haven't lost your touch with a camera, I do have one assignment right now that I need covered badly. You might like it. That is if you're willing to go to Aberdeen today, pronto."

"Sure. I'll go. What's the deal?"

It disappointed her that their conversation was now all business. Today there were none of his solicitous questions, no sharing of gripes, no wandering hand to caress her knee. Yet, she knew, she had not expected more from Derrick since their break-up. The assignments in those days included the best motel suite in town where they dared to meet and where photography was not the principal subject. No such offer was on the table today and Aberdeen was a hundred sixty miles north, far from the comforts of the Country Club and the Ramada Inn.

"It's a farm protest," he explained. "A tractorcade is supposed to form in Aberdeen tomorrow morning and start for the Canadian border. This bunch of wheat farmers are joining others in North Dakota. They threaten to blockade the roads to prevent Canadian wheat from being brought into the States."

"Sounds like it could get nasty," Sheri said.

"Maybe. That's possible. I need some pix, though. Close-up stuff. Angry farmer faces. Lines of tractors on the road. Get in close. Get their story. Their words too. And they'll be eager to tell you."

"Okay. Sure. I can do it. And when I get back, what then?"

"What about?" he asked, a flickering embarrassment crossed his face.

"A job," she said. "I want a job, Derrick. I need to get back into my photography, and on my own."

"It's none of my business, but are you and Jim…"

"Not yet," she interrupted, "But I can't just sit around being a wife of a States Attorney. I've got to get on to something of my own."

"Sure. I understand." He put on his thoughtful, executive expression. "Well, things have changed at the paper. Tightened up. Maybe something can be worked out, but I'd hate to make any promises right on the spot."

"Even steady part-time work," she said, trying not to make it sound pleading.

"Yes. Well maybe if the Aberdeen story impresses the editorial board, and old Alfeson, of course. He's still publisher and right in the midst of decisions even at eighty-four."

"Try, Derrick," Sheri urged. "I can be as good as I ever was," she said, leaving it for him to interpret as broadly as he might choose.

"I bet you can,' he said, pushing his chair back from the table. As he stood he reached over and patted her hand. She hated the condescending gesture.

"Two hundred bucks a day and expenses. See how good you can make the protest story," he said. "Get your stuff back to me by Tuesday a.m. Contact our stringer Matt Singleton when you get there. He's on the story, and can fill you in. We're going to do a mid-week news bit and then a full page feature for the Sunday edition. We need plenty of color."

"You'll get it," she promised, both hands wrapped about her cocktail glass for security.

"Good. See you then, Sheri. Good luck."

He left, his drink nearly untouched, and hurried out of the lounge. And that was it, she thought. The assignment but not the man. Maybe not a job. She wondered if Derrick's marriage had been repaired or whether there was another, younger reporter.

"To hell with it," she muttered aloud. She didn't need Derrick in bed anymore. She needed him to want her photographs. It was through the lenses of her cameras that she would escape and find a way to be on her own. Leaving Jim Henslow, States Attorney of Chautauqua County for a real life, she thought, was becoming an altogether more attractive decision unless things changed. But freedom would require more than a six hundred dollar assignment. She had to manage to arrange for more security than that.

❧   ❧   ❧

When Jack Traid arrived at the Easton farm at ten after six there were already several cars parked in the farm yard. The house was bright with lights, warm and inviting, he thought, like home port. He entered at the back entry, stepping up into the kitchen where he was greeted by Ann Faregold first, who gave him a firm hug and looked up at him with a broad smile.

"The birthday boy has arrived," she announced over her shoulder.

Ellie turned from the refrigerator and reached her hand out to Jack. They squeezed each other's hands, then embraced briefly.

"Happy Birthday, Jack," Ellie said softly.

Ann picked up a tray and went into the other rooms.

Professor Riemer was helping himself to a glass of wine at a side table under the kitchen window. He stepped next to Jack and in a stage voice said, "Take care Jack. When they begin to show affection they have their own agenda."

Martha Riemer came into the kitchen carrying a tray nearly empty of the hors d'oeuvres she had carried into the living room.

"Mind your tongue, John," she said cheerily.

"Just a warning. Fair warning for this young man."

Jack smiled. "Better fortify myself then." At the side table near the window Ellie had provided a self-serve bar. Jack helped himself to Jack Daniels over ice.

Patty Reinhart stood at the stove supervising the evening's dinner. Ellie's closest friend and unmarried at thirty-five, she had earned the reputation of guardian angel for Hamilton kids because of her dedication to her job as a junior high teacher of English. Ellie had told Jack about how Patty had befriended Gordy right after his father was killed, helping him get through classes during the worst of his grief. Like her mother Thelma, Patty was a care giver.

"Hi Jack," she said as she half turned to the room, a floral apron covering her ample body. "Have a birthday, okay?" she said, keeping the cliché to a minimum.

"Thanks Patty," he replied, reaching his arm around her neck and squeezing her shoulder. Patty was not a hugger, he knew, and it amused him to threaten her with demonstrated affection.

"Better see who's here," Ellie said, taking his arm and leading him through the dining room into the living room. "I hoped Reverend Masters could have come but he's been in Rochester all week. Charlene is reported to be failing."

"Serious?"

"Very. They had to put her on life support. No telling when poor Clyde will be able to get back."

"That's sad. Such a young woman, too," Jack said.

The dining room was festive. Red, white and blue streamers converged on the chandelier over the table from the corners of the room. Balloons hung from the archway between the dining room and living room. At a quick glance he saw that the dining table was set for twelve and with a set of china he had not seen before. The silverware was brightly polished. Ellie had gone all out. As they passed through the dining room she whispered, "This is my first big dinner in three years. I'm glad it's for your birthday."

"It's too much, Ellie. But I love it." He tightened his grip around her waist. He wondered at the doubts that had haunted him that morning. Ellie and the party with friends seemed to put him where he ought to be.

They walked together through the archway of balloons into the living room.

"Happy birthday, Jack," Mike Wilkins called out as he saw Ellie and Jack come into the room. The others turned from talking with each other. Mike stood with Roger Faregold and Minnie Morris in the center of the living room, each with a drink in hand. Elliot and Dan Morris were at the front window with Gordy who was explaining about the salt lick he'd put out to attract the albino deer.

"Happy birthday, Jack," Roger and Minnie called out in unison.

Seeing Jack come into the room, Elliot came into the group at the center of the room. He held his hand out to Jack and they shook warmly.

"A bit more of an elegant party than the one we had at the U some hundred years ago," he said smiling.

"What I remember of it," Jack replied. "Mostly spent being athletic with beer at the Airliner. We did get back to South Quad on our own, though."

"You've forgotten how long that took."

"I try."

"Happy Birthday, Jack," Gordy said, standing to one side of Elliot, hands dangling at his side, undecided.

"How about a shake on that," Jack replied. "Did you tell these folks about seeing the albino deer?"

"Yeah. Mr. Morris wants to go out and watch for a while after dinner, don't you, Mr. Morris?"

"Sure do." Elliot replied, "I've heard stories about the albino buck. It would be great to see it before someone claims Andy Anderson's reward. We need to do a story about it."

Mike Wilkins, journeyman printer, and Elliot Morris, publisher and Mike's employer, and Gordy Easton, high school track star, were huddled together on the subject of the reward offered for killing the rare animal. It was interesting, Jack thought, that here in small town USA the three of them seemed unaware, or at least relaxed about employee-employer relationship, and the adult-teenager age difference. There was, it appeared, an ease with which they were able to share the subject. How different this was from the dinners Alice would supervise for her suburban friends. As out of place he felt there, he felt at ease here.

"Andy's upped the prize," Mike was saying. "Offering a thousand bucks,"

Jack's attention was averted at the approach of Randy Spies. Jack turned and the two shook hands.

Randy smiled sheepishly as he greeted Jack.

"Some party Ellie's thrown for you," he said.

Randy had been Mildred Singer's office mate in the art department before she left. He was a tall and skinny thirty year old and had a delicate demeanor which some interpreted as effeminate, if not signaling that Randy was gay. Jack had learned from Mildred that Randy was profoundly shy about other people. It was a shyness about the demands others made upon his attention. The more aggressive an individual, the more Randy would shrink from them. Groups of more than three made him nervous, as if he could not fit himself into any assembly. Mildred had been Randy's protector while she was at Hamilton State. She claimed he showed great promise as a printmaker. His lithographs showed depth and sensitivity deserving wider circulation than the shows at the college and in a Sioux Falls gallery. Even this limited exposure had to be mounted at Mildred's urging. Randy resisted merchandising his own work and, Jack was certain, felt the loss of Mildred almost as much as he did. Randy was at the party, Jack knew, because Ellie, turning match-maker, thought that maybe a spark of interest might arise between him and Patty Rinehart. Jack noted over the past several months that they were friendly with each other but they had resisted the most obvious of hints by the matchmakers that they had something to share, both being teachers.

"Haven't seen you on campus lately," Randy said.

"I've been working in my print shop at home during semester break. You ought to stop by to see the progress on Roger's book. You'll like the handmade paper I got from Indiana."

"Yeah. Roger told me you were doing that for him."

"Well, give me a call to see if I'm home. I'd like to show you. In fact, we ought to do a limited edition with some of your works, something like Leonard Baskin's 'Othello.'"

"You've seen that?"

"Just an off-print promoting it."

"Monumental," Randy said. "I saw a copy in the Fine Arts Museum in Minneapolis last month when I went to visit Mildred. She asked about you, incidentally."

"Yes. I got a note from her. About her Canada trip."

"She'd like it if you would visit her sometime. Maybe even answer her letters."

"She said that?"

The argument for his going to Minneapolis for Dan Morris took on strength, and disturbed his present sense of well-being created by this house and this party in his honor.

"Not in so many words," Randy was saying, "But I could tell she misses you—a lot."

Ellie stood in the archway between the living and dining rooms, festooned balloons shifting on either side of her.

"Soup's on, everyone. Place cards will tell you where to sit."

The roast beef dinner was served by Ellie and Patty, both of whom were helped by Mike Wilkins, a bachelor whose talents beyond the print shop were in the kitchen. As he helped serve he bragged about being trained as a waiter years before when he was in Minneapolis working his way through Dunwoody Institute learning printing. Jack marveled at Mike. A craftsman, satisfied to live in a small town, Mike was widely read and had a reputation as the best chef in the region. Jack had heard that a few years ago one of the country clubs in Sioux Falls had tried to hire him for their kitchen. Mike liked being what he was and where he was. There wasn't a restless bone in his body. Maybe that attitude, Jack thought, would rub off on him as he and Mike worked together at Pioneer Village.

Conversation at the table turned to the front page stories about the oil spill out at the Riemer place and the spray painting on the Henslow house.

"It's just terrible, a regular crime wave around here," Martha Riemer opined, and went on to describe how they had discovered the spill when going out to their mail box.

Roger explained to the group how PCB oil had to be treated to meet Environmental Protection Agency regulations.

Elliot Morris commented on Martha's description of the 'crime wave' in Chautauqua County.

"It happens like that. Sometimes not much news, and then we have more stories than we can cover adequately. Like what's behind the swastika painted on the Henslow house?"

He turned to his son across the table.

"Seems that the spray painting might be the work of a rogue element of the Jewish Defense League," Dan explained

"How can you be sure of that?" his father asked.

"Well, I can't. But we know that the word 'barzel' sprayed next to the swastika stands for one of the four principles of the JDL. Means 'iron.' But the guy in the Minnesota office of JDL says that none of his members would take that kind of action. They exist in defense of Jews and not to commit violent acts. He insisted that they aren't Nazi hunters. So, we'll see. It doesn't change the fact that the apparent threat against Henslow is very strange. Especially following the boiler pipe incident."

"Yes, and a little scary," Ann Faregold commented. "For old Henslow, at least."

"Well, he was in the German army, or Hilter Youth as a kid," Dan continued. "The swastika has to be directed at that."

"Why would anyone do that," Ellie asked, "after all these years?"

"If I can convince Jack to give me a hand, we might be able to get a connection between the JDL and South Dakota."

"How's that?" Ellie asked.

"Sheriff Taylor and I have asked Jack to go to Minneapolis to do a little investigation. Be a deputy for a few days. How's that for a promotion from the Dallas force!"

Ellie looked down the table from her end at Jack seated at the far end. She was frowning.

"I haven't decided whether or not I want to get back in the business," Jack said, answering the frown. "Maybe I could help. Maybe not."

He wanted to drop the subject, but the talk continued about Horst Henslow, the tractor incident, Jim Henslow's window and tires, and now the spray painting.

"You'd think Jim Henslow would be raising all kinds of hell about this," Mike commented.

"Well, I saw him on television," Patty said. "He said he would find out who did it, as if he was going to solve it all by himself. He always sounds a little pompus when he gives out with his 'prosecute the perpetrators to the fullest.'"

Patty did not disguise the sarcasm in her voice. Jim Henslow, thought by some to be one of the rising stars of the state Republican party, was not a favorite of Patty's, but she suppressed open partisanship here at Ellie's party for Jack.

It was eight forty-five when dessert was served. Dishes had been removed from the table and everyone was seated again. Ellie brought the cake from the kitchen, five candles flickering as she placed it before Jack at his end of the table. Someone began singing "Happy Birthday," and all joined in. When they had finished Elliot Morris sang out, "Stand up, stand up and tell us how old you are." There was applause which continued until Jack stood.

"Come on. You are all just great and you make my being fifty-four seem like a thing a guy likes to be. And thanks to Ellie for all this attention. I just…"

He was interrupted by Mike's and Dan's pagers buzzing at the same time.

"Something's up," Dan said, rising from the table and hurrying to the telephone in the kitchen. Jack seated himself and waited with the others.

Mike had left the table and was at the kitchen door. He turned to say, "Fire department call. Sorry Ellie. Gotta go."

He left the room and could be heard rushing out the back door. The remaining members of the party could seen through the double windows of the dining room a blue flashing emergency light on top of his pickup. The local radio station would tell him where the fire was. The headlights of his truck come on, swung across the house and pointed down the drive. Dan stepped back into the room.

"Fire. At the Henslow farm."

"Oh my," Martha Reimer exhaled.

Dan was out the back door and into his cruiser before anyone could comment further. The flashing red and blue lights on the roof of the car reflected into the dining room as Dan left the farm yard. Out of habit, Jack looked at his watch. 8:55.

The interrupted party sat quietly for a few moments. Then through the east-facing dining room window they could see a growing orange glow reflecting on low clouds to the east. They all went out into the farm yard and walked past the barn that obscured part of the horizon. Roger and Ann Faregold stood together. Martha and Professor Riemer, Gordy and his mother were in front of the others. Jack and the Morrises were to one side. The light in the east became brighter, more yellow. As they stared at the shifting light in the sky it was the Morrises who were the first to see the swift movement of white in the shelter belt, a ghostly blurr bolting from the salt lick.

"There," Elliot said, pointing.

"The albino," Gordy nearly shouted."I saw it too!"

Then it was gone, deeper into the trees.

The birthday party stood silently for a moment.

"How strange," Ellie said as if to herself.

"Might as well go in and enjoy the cake," Patty said. "We'll get a report when Dan gets back."

Inside Ellie cut the chocolate cake and placed pieces on dessert plates, passing them to each side as she did so. Gordy talked excitedly to Elliot Morris.

"It was there. You got to see it Mr. Morris."

"Yes. At least a glimpse of it."

For Jack the interruption carried a foreboding message. The warm comfort of this evening and this group of friends had been compromised by the continuing assault. Whatever was happening out at the Henslow farm was being moved with a vicious intent. A kernel of anger simmered in his mind. The rural peace was again threatened, ruptured by someone's hate, by anger or envy that infected the community. Was he responsible for helping with a solution? He'd been asked directly by Dan for help. He knew he would have to wait until everyone had left so he and Ellie could talk about his going to Minneapolis.

❦   ❦   ❦

After eating a hurried lunch alone at the Country Club and signing the tab to Jim's account, Sheri Henslow went to Harvey's Photos for film, then went through a drive-through ATM and withdrew two hundred dollars, after which she started for Hamilton. She felt a wave of confidence as she realized that she was declaring independence from the role as dutiful wife of an ambitious politician. It was well, she reasoned, that Derrick wasn't interested in rekindling their old flame. She was free of him too. Feeling energy like that she had the day she got the story at the prison, she knew she could do anything.

There was no hurry, she thought, as the Lincoln glided smoothly north on Interstate 29. She had time to think, now that she was committed to getting free of the role Jim insisted she play at his side. She began to create in her mind the person she would recapture, the person she really was. She was a woman who acted, made things happen. She would prove it once again. The Aberdeen assignment was exhilarating. She reviewed her options of how to break the news to Jim that their marriage was about to change. She could ease into the announcement by saying she had this assignment but would be coming back as a different person, one with her own career. She was going to let him know right off that after this story, she expected to have others and that if he objected to her taking steady assignments, she would move out of Hamilton. He had better realize that he had an obligation to her after all these years. Given enough time maybe he would figure that out. On the other hand, she thought, he would erect barriers. The truth was, she had to admit, he was the barrier.

Her neighborhood and her house with its blind-eye piece of plywood still covering the window were disturbingly familiar. Old man Procter was mowing his front yard. Melissa Cronk next door was just rolling her bicycle into her garage. She waved to Sheri. Sheri waved back, smiling. She never liked Melissa because she played the sweet little housewife but blathered women's rights clichés, as she lived her little satisfied housewife existence. Despite her dislike for Melissa, Sheri had to fight off the feeling that she, herself, was returning to a safe haven, to her home. But it was too late for feelings of security that depended only on Jim's career.

When she drove into the garage it was four forty-five in the afternoon. Jim's Explorer was not in the garage. That made leaving for Aberdeen easier. She had more time to think about how she would announce their new relationship. For now, a note saying she had an assignment would be enough. It might do him good to worry a little about her, and about them.

She hurried to pack her Nikon camera equipment in two cases, one camera with a long lens for close-ups, and another for wide angle work. She then started to pack an overnight bag with a simple black dress, a change of underclothes, a jewelry pouch. The two hundred dollars she'd gotten from an ATM in Sioux Falls would be adequate, she thought.

She went to Jim's room and scribbled on a sticky note, "Assignment for Argus in Aberdeen. Back Tuesday." She stuck the note on the computer monitor on Jim's desk. As she turned to leave the room she remembered that Jim said he had bought a revolver to keep in the house after the window was shot out. He said it was to protect them. She remembered that he said he'd had put it in his top dresser drawer. It was amazing, she thought, what the long-term benefits could be from a simple little revolver, if Jim only had the guts to use it. The idea formed slowly. The gun, that little persuader, might be the only effective answer to the stubborn old man—at least warn him what could happen. The daydream played out in her mind. If Jim just had the guts to use it. The pistol, she realized, could be the way of keeping the Chautauqua deal from crumbling into dust. She wondered if Jim knew that, or could even think that deeply into the disgust he felt for his step-father.

The fascination with what the gun looked like drew her to Jim's dresser. She opened the top drawer. He would think his socks would hide the gun from burglars. The drawer was a mess. Among old receipts, an unopened package of gum, was a jewelry box for cuff links with a cup for change at one end. Rolled up socks filled the right half of the drawer. She pulled the drawer out further and pushed aside some of the socks. Sure enough, the gun was there—bright metal new, polished and still in its open box at the back of the drawer. An open box of shells was next to it. Sheri realized that Jim must have already loaded the revolver. She took the pistol from its box and broke it open. The cylinder had six shells in it. There was a strange but comfortable feel to the gun. She put it back in its box and rearranged the socks. Next to the box was the switch blade knife Jim said he'd found in the tire of her car. It was Art Roger's knife that Jim had kept. As she returned to her room she wondered if Jim would be smart enough to make use of the knife and the gun. They were in her mind parts one and two of a three part answer to Jim's problems.

Back in her room she changed into dungarees, a flannel shirt over which she put on her favorite World War Two aviator's leather jacket. She had worn the jacket years before on assignments and it had brought her luck. She finished packing the overnight bag with panty hose and pumps to go with the black dress. She just might want to dress up while in Aberdeen, she thought to herself. Who knew what might come up? She then put on hiking boots. She was in her working uniform and ready to get at the story as soon as she reached Aberdeen.

As she packed she couldn't get the knife and gun out of her mind. If Jim only had the guts to use them to get the old man out of the way the development deal would just fall into place. Maybe, she thought, that was the reason he had bought the gun after all. Maybe she wasn't giving him enough credit. If only they could work on the solution together. There were risk-free ways to get a solution if they just put their minds to it. That would make something meaningful in their marriage.

By the time she had fixed herself a sandwich for the trip north, sipping on a glass of Chablis as she worked, it had gotten to nearly six o'clock. She realized she was lingering, still undecided, wondering if Jim might be about to come into the house before she left. Maybe, she thought, his anger would have cooled and they could plan the solution to their problems together. Maybe he would say he was sorry for the row and was ready to accept the change that had to come in their marriage. Maybe he would finally agree with her that there was only one way to make sure the Chautauqua housing development was going to happen. But when he had not come home by six she gave up on thoughts of their solving the big problem together that night. It depended on her, she thought as she went back into Jim's room for the gun and Art Rogers's knife. She had to be the person of action, to be decisive. It was time for her to take charge of her life and her future. That meant a visit to the Henslow farm.

It was nearly seven thirty before she finally left Hamilton. She saw no one in Cottonwood Acres as she moved slowly through the streets. Tonight she had begun the journey into a new life. She was certain of it and Jim Henslow better appreciate all she had done for him. And he had to realize that she was not going to give up on a revived profession as news photographer. She shivered with the excitement of the risks she was taking that night. Already she was feeling what it was like to be an equal with her husband, putting her own hand on destiny. She was, she thought to herself, a pretty clever woman when one got right down to it.

Sheri Henslow listened to the tires of the Lincoln hum softly to her as she sped north on Interstate 29. Exhilarated with her freedom, with the daring of her actions this night, she accelerated to ninety miles an hour. Since she had taken more time than expected to leave Hamilton, she revised her plans and decided to stay overnight in Watertown, just sixty miles away. The highway rushed toward her in the bright headlights of her car. She needed to rest. The excitement of the afternoon and evening had exhausted her. She would get an early start in the morning for the remainder of the trip to Aberdeen. The Coyote Inn was a familiar motel where she had stayed before. Today had been long and memorable.

※   ※   ※

Andrew Pettigrew and Tommy Johnson sat at the circular table inside the Duck Blind at Andy's Restaurant. Jim Henslow had just arrived and stood before the table where dishes had been pushed aside, unrolling the Chautauqua Acres site plan before them once again. Pat Pettigrew and Delores Johnson had excused themselves to go to the restroom when he arrived. Sheri Henslow had not returned from Sioux Falls.

"She said she had some shopping to do," Jim explained lamely. He now faced the two lawyers, his partners, with a sense of urgency.

"We went ahead and ate without you," Tommy explained.

More than an hour late for the seven o'clock dinner date, Jim invented the excuse that he'd been on the phone with the Carpenter Group. In fact he had driven to Sioux Falls mid-afternoon looking for Sheri. The bartender at the Country Club said she'd left about noon. He wouldn't say if she'd been with anyone. Jim had driven through the parking lots of both the Holiday Inn and Ramada to see if her Lincoln was parked there. He then drove to the Empire Mall and walked through Silverton's Department Store, but Sheri was not to be found. It was a futile search.

By six o'clock the effects of three double Scotch drinks had worn off and left him with a nagging headache. Jim's anger had shifted into resolve. As he drove eighty miles an hour in the gathering dusk back to Hamilton, he told himself that it was the last time she was going to do this to him. If she wanted to live in Sioux Falls she could do it on her own. If she was sleeping with that creep Holmes, so be it. He wondered how much she would take with her in the divorce. It was, he thought, turning out to be as much her idea as his, this boredom with each other and her frustration with being stuck in Hamilton. When he got back to town there was not time to go home to shower so he drove directly to Andy's Restaurant. It was eight twenty.

As he spoke to Pettigrew and Johnson, the anger of the afternoon simmered in his mind. He forced himself to press on about the project, to argue his case. As he described potentials, the hoped-fors, he heard himself pleading for some of the success which the two partners before him so confidently showed. Their expressions reflected the self-assurance of the secure, he thought. It was a self-approval he had never felt.

"It would be a damned shame for Hamilton and the county to lose this project," he was explaining, "but if we can't get local investment, the Carpenter Groups says it'll go elsewhere."

"What other projects have they done?" Tommy asked.

"Three or four I know of. Two in the Minneapolis area. One in Iowa. They're first rate developers."

"Well, I might be interested," Andrew Pettigrew began, giving the first glimmer of hope to Jim, "if, and it is a big if, I could be convinced that your dad's place is going to be the site and that the Carpenter bunch wasn't just fishing for the best deal they can get on taxes and land costs."

"I suppose they are," Jim said. "As I told you they are looking at North Sioux City too, but I think we have a leg up on that location."

"What about your dad?" Tommy asked. "Is he ready to go with the deal?"

Jim noticed that both Andrew and Tommy looked at each other as they waited for his answer. He had to be cautious, not hint at having shown the bogus trust agreement to the Carpenter people.

"I think he'll come around. Frankly, he's not too hot on the idea, but I think he recognizes that I ought to inherit the farm just as my mother had him promise. But we're still talking to each other about the final arrangement."

"I tell you what, Jim," Pettigrew offered, his voice full of the decision he'd just made, "when you and your dad have a definite deal that you can show me, I'll be glad to invest. And I think there will be others too. But right now, nice as the drawings are, the whole idea, and the material facts of the deal are still too sketchy for me."

"I think you'll have to put me in that column too, Jim," Tommy added. "And you'll forgive me for saying it, don't get too tied up in this project. You might erode a promising political future with too much enterprising. The '96 primary season will be upon us soon. If you're going to run for state senate, you'll be too busy for a development project."

Some partners, Jim thought to himself.

"Fair, enough," he answered. "I'll have the agreement with Dad by next week," he heard himself promise. They had eased him into a corner from which there was but one exit. And the gate-keeper on that exit was his step-father.

"But something's going on about Horst." Tommy was saying. "I'm concerned about the tractor boiler pipe, the spray painting. And for that matter, what about the tires of your car being slashed last week, and before that the window of your house shot out? That's rough stuff. What do you make of these attacks? Clearly, someone is threatening the Henslows."

"Don't worry about it. The tires and window, at least. I have a pretty good lead on who did it and with a little more proof I'll nail him. Dan Morris is working on the spray painting. When someone read in the *Times* that Dad had been a guard at Bergen-Belsen concentration camp, it must have triggered some kind of revenge. Maybe whoever it is thinks he is a war criminal."

"Do you think his life is threatened?" Tommy asked.

"Oh, I don't think so. Seems like pranks. Unless, of course, there is more to his past than we know, and there is still more to come. He hates to talk about those times."

It was useful, Jim thought, to leave the impression that Horst Henslow might deserve what was happening to him. It occurred to him at that moment that should Horst Henslow, ex-Nazi, die because of his past, a great many of Jim Henslow's problems would evaporate.

The wives returned to the table and Jim rolled up the Chautauqua Acres plans.

"Sorry about Sheri not being able to be here," Patricia Pettigrew said. There was a critical edge to her tone.

"You know Sheri," Jim replied. "She's got to check on the latest sales at the mall in Sioux Falls."

As they began to order after dinner drinks, they heard several beepers sounding throughout the restaurant. Three men quickly got up from their tables and hurried out the front door.

"Volunteer firemen," Tommy remarked.

Jim Henslow looked at his watch. Eight forty-five. Art Rogers had made an early appearance as instructed.

Andy's restaurant was too far west from the center of town for anyone there to hear the fire siren on city hall. But as the fire fighters drove toward Hamilton they could see an orange glow tinting clouds in the eastern sky.

Jim Henslow sat down at the table and began to sip a scotch and soda. No one in Andy's Restaurant knew or had yet said there was a fire at the Henslow farm. But Jim felt certain that Art Rogers had carried out his assignment. His law partners and their wives seemed to be intent upon his words as he expanded on his stepfather's stories of what it was like being a guard at the notorious Bergen-Belsen concentration camp. He needed to leave the impression with this jury that ex-Nazi Horst Henslow believed that past had come back to haunt him.

❀   ❀   ❀

The pumper was nearly to the Henslow place when Dan caught up to it and followed it into the farm yard. Flames enveloped the interior and back half of the machine shed. Part of the roof had collapsed and flames stabbed eight and ten feet into the night sky. A black, roiling cloud rose from the structure. The smell of burning oil and paint greeted the fire fighters as they attached hoses to the pumper and began to play water against the side of the barn where paint was already scorched. Another stream of water was trained on the interior of the shed. The pumping engine roared and men shouted over its din. The intense heat of the fire kept the firefighters at bay.

"Check inside the barn. Make sure nothing's started inside," Chief Henderson was yelling.

Dan was out of his cruiser and about to help with a hose when he saw Gloria Miller standing on the front stoop of the house, a shot gun held at the ready. He ran across the drive and yard to where she stood.

"I called 911. But it's too late," she was yelling to him.

"Are you all right?" Dan shouted.

"Sure. But where is Mr. Henslow? He was guarding the place after dark. I don't know where he is."

"Better give me that gun and get inside," Dan ordered.

Gloria did not move at first, but stood as if in shock and held the shotgun as if guarding the entrance to the house.

"I shot him," she said said to Dan.

"Who?"

"I shot the guy running away from the shed. I could see his back as he was running away from the flames. I think I hit him."

"Go inside now, please. And give me that gun," Dan ordered again, reaching out for the gun. Gloria gave it up and went inside. Behind them as they went through the front door were the flashing lights of Dan's cruiser and the fire trucks, joined by the blue flashing of removable lights volunteer fire fighters had put on the roofs of their vehicles. Three more pickups and two sedans of volunteer fire fighters shot into the farmyard.

In the living room of the house Dan questioned Gloria who sat in the recliner, hugging herself. She had begun to shake and was shaking her head from side to side. Dan did not have to ask her to tell him what happened. She began talking in a stream of words, nearly breaking into sobs as she told about how she and Horst had been on guard.

"He got a letter that scared him. This afternoon. In the mail. He took the twelve gauge and loaded it. He gave me the twenty gauge there and told me to stay in the house. He went out about six o'clock. He said he was going to patrol the farm. He didn't come back. Then I got a telephone call. About seven. A woman said she was a nurse at the hospital and that my baby had an emergency. I drove in as fast as I could. But when I got there no one at the hospital knew anything. When I went to my mom's everything was all right with my baby. I knew something was fishy then and hurried back here and came inside for the gun."

"What time was it when you got back," Dan asked.

"I don't think it was eight thirty. Maybe eight fifteen or so. I walked around inside the house. The shotgun was loaded. I kept looking out the windows for Mr. Henslow. I did that for maybe twenty minutes when I saw someone moving out by the machine shed. At first I thought it was Mr. Henslow. But the guy was hunched over, kinda running, and then disappeared behind the shed. He was carrying something. I could see that plain as anything."

Gloria stopped and caught her breath.

"Mr. Henslow told me not to go outside, but when I didn't see him and then saw this man sneaking around the shed, I took the gun and went out onto the porch. Then I started to walk toward the shed and barn. That's when the flames exploded. The whole back of the shed, all at once. Then I saw this guy was running along the front of the big barn. I shot at him just before he went around the end of the barn."

She was crying when she stopped. Dan put his hand on her shoulder.

"You're okay now. I'll have to take this gun until we clear this up."

He began to tell her she might be better off going back into town with her mother when Chief Henderson stepped into the doorway, holding the door open.

"Dan. You better come with me. Something serious." Henderson was looking at Gloria.

"Okay," Dan replied, then turned to Gloria. "Why don't you stay inside until I can get back to you. I'll leave this gun here by the door."

Gloria nodded in response, wiping her eyes with the back of her hand.

Outside Clyde Henderson stopped below the front steps and turned to Dan.

"It's old man Henslow. The boys found him dead inside the barn. Shot."

"Jesus," Dan exclaimed.

They broke into a run toward the barn. Three men in yellow slickers and fire helmets with visers up stood at the flung open double doors. Dan saw that Mike Wilkins was one of the three.

"Where is he?" Dan yelled to Mike.

"Down on the right side, just outside the last stall. I checked for pulse. Nothing. He's been shot."

Dan and Henderson walked into the barn. Smoke had seeped into the interior and hung heavy in the still air. The dying fires sent intermittent flashes of light through the small windows to their right.

They approached the hunched over body cautiously. Dan could see that the Horst Henslow lay on the shotgun he'd thought would protect him and his farm. His face was half buried in straw. A single bullet hole in is kaki shirt was apparent between the shoulder blades, another at the top of his skull. There was a small blood stain on the shirt, and evidence of oozing blood from the head wound.

"Don't touch him," Dan said to Henderson. "We'll have to leave him like this until the coroner comes. Keep everyone out of the barn."

He and Henderson retreated to the open doors. On the cruiser's radio Dan ordered the dispatcher to send Don White, the coroner, to the Henslow farm. From the trunk of the cruiser Dan got a roll of yellow police line ribbon. He fastened the strip across the open doors. He felt inadequate, not ready for murder. He heard Henderson order everyone away from the barn. Dan knew he had to find Sheriff Tom Taylor. He knew too that he would have to call Jack Traid. This would be old stuff for him.

The fire had cooled and the volunteer firefighters had moved in closer to the smoldering machine shed. From behind the collapsed structure Mike Wilkins came carrying two one-gallon gasoline cans. He was holding the cans up so all could see the swastikas painted on their sides.

CHAPTER 9

※

$\mathcal{E}$llie and Patty Reinhart were putting the kitchen in order and loading into the dishwasher those dishes Jack and Gordy had cleared from the table. The other guests had left the party after dessert, Eliot Morris saying he had better make sure his reporter Carla Garza, was covering the fire. He intended to go to the Henslow farm and take pictures himself.

Jack Traid was anxious to leave, feeling himself already involved in the Henslow matter, but Ellie's look when she heard Dan Morris tell about Jack being deputized to go to Minneapolis told him they had better have a talk before he left the farm that night. In the kitchen he volunteered to wash pans that would not fit into the dishwasher.

"With all the help you have here," Patty said to Ellie, "I guess I can leave you three to finish up. Hope you appreciated all the excitement arranged for your party, Jack."

"Nice planning," he replied.

"I can see you're straining at the leash," Patty offered. "Old instinct, needing to be at the center of the action?"

"A little bit, sure," Jack mused. "I'm just very curious about what's going on out at the Henslow place. You know that I was with Dan when he first investigated the boiler pipe explosion."

"Well, goodnight to the three of you. I've got to get on home before mother begins to worry that the fire siren means I'm in trouble."

Patty dried her hands and found her purse at the end of the kitchen counter. She waved goodbye to Jack as she went out the back door. Ellie followed her out into the yard.

"Thanks for your help, Patty. I couldn't have done it without you."

"It was a great party. I can tell that Jack loved it. And, dear one, don't be too hard about his wanting to go to Minneapolis for Dan."

"Don't worry about me, Patty. I've got no chains on Jack."

"But you care and you're worried. So don't kid me. Mildred Singer is in Minneapolis and that is enough for you to worry about."

"She's the very reason Jack has to go, and I'm going to tell him so. Besides, he can really be of help to Dan and Sheriff Taylor. And as far as we are concerned, he better find out what Mildred means to him these days."

Patty eased her ample self under the steering wheel of her Pontiac sedan. She was smiling her 'sweet understanding' smile.

"Thata girl. Put him to the test."

"Goodnight, Patty," Ellie replied flatly.

As Patty's car went down the driveway Ellie turned to look east. The eerie glow of half an hour ago no longer showed on the clouds. From the farmyard she was unable to see State Highway 43 but imagined that by now a stream of cars were headed for the Henslow farm. The location of the fire would have been broadcast on the radio fire alert and the curious would be gathered at this, a community event nearly as important as a high school athletic contest. After all, the volunteer fire department had won many state competitions between volunteer units. The department was the pride of Hamilton.

When Ellie walked into the kitchen Jack and Gordy were working at the sink, Jack washing, Gordy drying. It was a pleasing sight in her eyes and she felt a vague yearning that it could remain undisturbed. This good man was searching for the peace offered by dishwashing, by grading math papers, but she was well aware that he was not yet at ease in his mind with such a private life. She knew that much about Jack Traid. He had not yet learned, she thought, that he could not live in both worlds. He seemed balanced tonight between returning to the intensity of police work and the comforting obscurity of the college classroom. And his restlessness included thoughts of Mildred Singer, she was sure of that. It was no secret that they had been nearly inseparable the year before Mildred left town. Whatever Mildred had to offer Jack Traid, Ellie thought, it had no resemblance to what she, Ellie, had in her son and in what this farm was in her life. She had succeeded in holding on to this fragment of her dream. It was a full life which Ralph had left her to confront and she did not intend to bargain it away for an uncertain attachment.

"Well, that's about it, Gordy," Jack said. "Ellie and I'll finish up."

"Sure. Okay. I've got stuff to do in my room."

Ellie and Jack said nothing until they heard Gordy reach the top of the stairs.

"I hadn't really made up my mind," Jack offered, jumping into the middle of both of their thoughts. "Dan had asked me, but I wasn't sure I wanted to get involved."

"It's okay with me, Jack."

"You were frowning when Dan mentioned my being involved."

"I was surprised, that's all. You hadn't said anything to me about it. And I guess I didn't think you were much interested in police work after all this time."

"I know. I didn't either. I don't need it, but when Elliot suggested and Dan asked for help, I just didn't feel I could say 'no' right off."

"And Minneapolis and Mildred?"

Jack paused before answering. Was there a challenge in her voice?

"That is involved. Sure. If I'm going to be honest about it, the fact that Mildred is in Minneapolis and told Randy she'd like to see me made me think I'd better not go."

"No, Jack. I think you should go. You owe it to yourself. If you don't find out what you want, how can you be sure that Hamilton is right for you? Or that we are..." She didn't complete the thought, not having the word she needed.

"That we are right for each other, isn't that what we are about?"

"It seemed that way to me," Ellie said, looking down to avoid his eyes.

Jack put his arms around her, pressing her head to his chest. She fought back tears, then backed away from his embrace, holding both his hands in hers.

"I care very much for you Jack. That ought to be clear by now. But I can't take a chance that you aren't sure about us, or about you and Mildred. So, don't you see? You have to go because you are afraid to go. I want you to. When you come back you'll know. We'll both know."

The telephone next to the doorway to the dining room interrupted their reading each other's expressions. Ellie picked the phone out of its cradle before the second ring.

"Eastons," she said. After a pause, added, "Sure, he's right here."

She handed the phone to Jack. "It's Dan."

Jack listened for a moment.

"Henslow? That's terrible."

He shook his head as he listened to Dan, frowning at Ellie who watched.

"Okay. I'll be out in a few minutes. Just be sure to secure the area. Don't let anyone in there. Not the barn or house. Has Taylor shown up yet?"

Finished with his conversation, Jack hung the phone back in its wall set and turned to Ellie.

"They found Horst Henslow shot to death. And one of the out buildings has been burned down. Obvious arson. Swastikas again."

Ellie gasped, hand to her mouth.

"Dan feels over his head and Sheriff Taylor isn't to be found. He wants me to help him out. To look over the scene."

"You must," Ellie said, touching his arm. "What has been happening to that poor Mr. Henslow?"

"Well, it appears now that the tractor incident and spray painting might have been meant as more than just pranks. Henslow has been a serious target all along. And now Chautauqua County may have a murder on its hands."

As he started for the door Ellie stopped him.

"Just a minute Jack. Before you go, I have your birthday present."

She handed him a book-sized box wrapped in bright red paper with white ribbons.

"You can look at it later. I wrote you a note too. Let me know what you think."

❦   ❦   ❦

When Jack reached the Henslow place in his Toyota, its windows rolled down, he could smell burnt asphalt shingles and wood. Cars were parked along the highway and traffic was slowed as some of the curious drove by without stopping. Two state highway patrolmen were directing traffic. Jack edged past a car nearly blocking the front driveway, and pulled into the farmyard. A crowd of people stood on the lawn among parked pickups and cars to the right of the driveway, directed to stay out of the way by Chief Henderson. Both Elliot Morris and the Carla Garza were taking pictures of the burned out structure and of the gas cans with swastikas painted on them which Mike Wilkins was holding for them. Firefighters were rolling up hoses and stowing them in the pumper unit. The machine shed's roof had collapsed. Wisps of steam rose from the center of the pile of charred two by fours and remnants of wood siding. Emergency lights on the fire truck and Dan's cruiser continued to send sweeping beams of light across the barn, garage, house, and faces of onlookers. Jack saw Dan standing at the barn door talking with Donald White, mortician and Chautauqua County Coroner. Easing his car to the left of the driveway, Jack parked against the fence out of the way of the other vehicles. The three men turned to him as he approached the barn.

"Jack, you know Don White, don't you?" Dan said.

"Sure. We're neighbors at the Village."

"Don just got here." Dan explained. "Should we go in and take a look?"

The three men ducked under the yellow tape and entered the dim interior of the barn which was lighted by three ceiling lights arranged down the center corridor between the stalls on either side. A haze of smoke remained in the still interior. The smell of burned wood, rags and oil hung heavily in the quiet of the barn.

At the far end of the aisle, in front of the open door of a horse stall, Horst Henslow's body lay as if in a sleeping position, his head upon his right arm, his face in the straw and dirt of the floor. The tip of the barrel of a shotgun showed under his head, pressed into an ashen cheek. His left arm was flung out from his side.

The three men looked down at the body. Dan and Jack waited for White to make his examination. A powder-smudged, single bullet hole showed clearly in the light khaki shirt. The wound was almost precisely between the victim's shoulder blades. There was a small blood stain surrounding the hole. Above the edge of the fringe of hair around his bald head was another entry wound. A small amount of blood, now dried, had seeped from the wound.

"Two shots, from the looks of it," White offered. "Two entry holes are clear enough." He was putting on rubber gloves from the satchel he'd been carrying. Kneeling next to the body he gently lifted and turned Horst's jaw. There was no exit wound in the face. White moved the outflung left arm.

"Been dead for hours," he said quietly to the others.

Dan looked at Jack for comment.

"Looks like the first shot might have been in the back," Jack said, hesitating. He crouched down next to White. "Then the second one was to make sure. Fired from close up. See where the muzzle blast struck around the entry hole. But something's strange here. There isn't much of a blood stain on the shirt. Or what you'd expect at the head wound. Entered the skull at a downward angle. Not straight through, back to face. Can't remember seeing a gunshot wound just like this."

"I noticed that," White offered quickly. "Well, I'm going to write it up as an obvious homicide. When you've finished looking him over, I'll have my guys remove the body."

Don White felt the dead man's body again and moved the stiffened left arm once more. He then stood up and stepped aside for Dan and Jack to examine the body and clothing.

"I'd say he was shot maybe two, three hours ago. Maybe longer," White said.

"Before the fire, then?" Dan said.

"I think you're safe in thinking that," White replied.

"Looks like he didn't get to use his gun against his assailant," Jack said. "Fell on it."

He touched the inside of the barrel of the shotgun with his index finger, which he brought to his nose. "Been fired. But I don't think tonight, anyway."

The corpse bothered him. It didn't look right.

"It looks like he might have been ambushed from this stall. You probably should go over the inside of it carefully, Dan. Any fabric or threads caught on the wood, or anything dropped. The straw out here on the floor won't tell us much. Too many people have walked in here tonight."

White took off his rubber gloves, put them in his bag and closed it.

"I'll go back in town for the hearse. Get Elmer and Harlan to help me with the body. You fellas can look things over now."

With that the Chautauqua County Coronor, elected to the office in the past six elections, left the barn feeling that this case would assure him another term. 'On top of the job,' were the words that came to his mind. The voters would be pleased.

As White left the barn, Dan bent over the body. He could see the edge of a folded envelope poked out of the back pocket of the victim's dungarees.

"Might be the letter Gloria Miller said Henslow got today," Dan said. "She told me it came in today's mail. It scared him. I'll get some evidence bags from my unit. And I'll try to make radio contact with Sheriff Taylor again."

"Right," Jack replied. "The letter might have fingerprints. Incidentally, who does the forensic work for the County?"

"Have to send it to Pierre. The State Crime Lab. That's where Taylor had me send the can of spray paint we found. Lab says no prints on it."

Jack studied the posture of the corpse. From the appearance of the straw and dirt on the floor beyond the body, it looked as if Henslow had crawled a foot or so. But if he had, he would not have been in position to be shot from the stall. It appeared he had been crawling while he was shot. But the scene didn't look like there had been a struggle.

Dan returned from the cruiser with a briefcase.

"Taylor is on his way. He's about five miles down the Interstate, coming from Sioux Falls."

Dan pulled on rubber gloves and with his right hand removed the envelope from Horst's pants pocket. Unfolding the envelope he was able to slip out the letter from inside. He opened it and tilted it to the overhead light above them. They both read the hand-scrawled message under the letterhead of the Jewish Defense League, c/o Levy's Book Shop, Box 87, Appleton Center, Minnesota.

"'Nazis pay for their crimes. Hadar.'" Dan read aloud.

"That's not a signature," Dan explained. "Its another of the Defense League's words. One of their principles according to the guy in Minneapolis."

"Yeah," Jack replied, "I think this means 'dignity.' Clearly meant as a threat."

Jack paused, looking more closely at the letter.

"There is something curious about the letterhead."

"What's that?"

"It isn't printed. It's a photo copy of printed stationery," Jack said. "All black, tones different where color was copied."

"Yeah, I can see that."

"Pretty crude copying job too. You can see the shadow line where the letterhead was cut and pasted on to another piece of paper before being copied."

"Yeah," Dan said.

"Whoever sent Henslow this wanted him to believe the League was after him, like the Nazi hunters."

"But that's not what the League is about," Dan said. "At least that what Mr. Levy said."

"Henslow wouldn't know that. Or it's a ploy to implicate the League and mislead us. Why would anyone send the victim such an obvious clue," Jack said. "Especially if you planned to kill him?"

"If you've seen enough," Dan said, "I'll bag the letter."

"Sure. Make sure Sheriff Taylor, or anyone in your office, leaves it untouched. You'll want to have it analyzed by the lab. The toner, the ink used to write the threat. Fingerprints."

"Gotcha."

"First, let me make a note of that bookshop telephone number. I'll need to phone to get a street address when I go to Minneapolis."

"You'll do it, then?" Dan exclaimed. "Great. Sheriff'll be glad to hear that."

Putting the evidence in his brief case, Dan knelt down next to the body and moved Horst Henslow's head carefully, feeling that rigor mortis was already evident.

Jack knelt down next to Dan.

"Look at the shirt again, Dan. The muzzle of the gun must have been only inches away. That's strange. Couldn't have been fired from the stall."

"How so? Someone shot him from the back but not from the stall?"

"Both shots were from very close? If you look carefully there are powder burns around both entry holes. And just a little blood. I can't believe he began to crawl after those two shots, or either one of them. Tell you what Dan. Insist on a thorough autopsy no matter what anyone says. This is a very confused picture in my book."

From behind them came the booming voice of the Sheriff.

"What in hell happened here?"

He stopped when he saw the body. Taylor was five feet six, a rotund belly reaching over his belt. He had a pinched face that seemed fixed in an angry grimace. To Jack the man's eyes seemed too close together, as if nature had decided this man would look down narrow tunnels all his life, certain that what he saw was all there was to know. It was his voice, Jack decided, which got him elected sheriff, for it was incongruously melodious, in the lower reaches of the tenor range.

"Jeez. You didn't say, Dan."

"I didn't want to broadcast it. Scanners. If everyone knew there was a body out here we'd really have a crowd. Most still think it's only a fire."

Taylor shook hands with Jack as he spoke.

"White was out, was he?"

"Sure was," Dan replied. "Says he's writing it up as a homicide."

"Yeah, seems obvious enough," the sheriff replied.

Taylor merely glanced at the body, as if it held little interest to him, or that death was too profound a fact for him to ponder at the moment. He had a deputy here to see to that.

"Glad to see you here, Jack. Looks like we're going to need your big city experience. Don't get many of these," he nodded toward the body. "Last time we had a killing, it was a suicide. That must have been in '88 or '89."

There was an upbeat lilt to Taylor's voice as he spoke, as if the body lying just beyond them was a new asset of the Sheriff's Department, which was now elevated to dealing with the most serious of community business.

"Jack's agreed to go to Minneapolis for us," Dan said.

"That's great. We'll get you deputized Monday morning. Really be a help. Commission thinks two of us is one too many for the sheriff's office in the state's smallest county. But I got enough in the budget to pay for your expenses if you're willing to volunteer your time."

"No problem," Jack replied.

"In the meantime," Taylor declared, "I better get hold of Jim Henslow. About his old man."

❧   ❧   ❧

KOLO's television crew had waited at the Chautauqua County Courthouse since eight o'clock Sunday morning for the arrival of Sheriff Tom Taylor, who did not arrive until fifteen minutes after the agreed-upon time. Standing with newscaster Jerry Holt was Carla Garza from the Hamilton *Times*. It was she who had phoned Holt with the story of the fire and apparent murder.

Holt injected urgency into his interrogation, his voice on edge, a nervous accusatory tone pushing against Taylor's obvious reluctance to be pulled away from Sunday morning's domestic routine.

"Can you give us a quick run-down on what happened last night Sheriff?"

"A shed was torched at the Henslow place. We found Mr. Henslow's body in the barn adjacent to the shed. Had two bullet wounds, one to the head, one in the back. Obvious homicide. Execution style, I'd say. Body's at White's Funeral Home right now. The state medical examiner will be up here to do an autopsy. Probably tomorrow."

"Henslow wasn't in the shed, then?" Holt asked.

"Oh no. Found him on the floor of the barn."

"What kind of gunshot?" Hold continued.

"Small caliber pistol."

"Sheriff, you said it looked execution style. Do you think Henslow's death is the result of a vendetta being waged against him because he was a former Nazi?" Carla Garza asked.

"Vendetta?" Taylor questioned, not sure of the implications of what the young woman was getting at. "Well," he went on, "I'd have to say probably."

"There were swastikas on the gasoline cans that were found and I understand that a threatening letter was found on the body. Don't you think they are connected with the threat painted on Henslow's house last Wednesday morning?"

Dan Morris was standing behind Taylor and to one side. Taylor turned to him.

"What do we have on that, Dan?" Taylor asked.

"Too early to tell if there is an actual connection. We'll have the paint analyzed. There is some confusion about the swastikas."

"In what way?" Holt asked.

"The swastika painted on Mr. Henslow's house was the Nazi sign, but those painted on the gasoline cans found at the scene of the fire were in reverse, like the American Indian use of that symbol."

"But isn't it obvious, Sheriff, there has been a campaign of threats going on?" Holt asked, ignoring Morris and pursuing the person he believed to be in charge. He moved the microphone an inch closer to Taylor's chin in a jabbing motion.

"Appears that might be," Taylor offered lamely.

"I understand that even his own son admitted that his father had been a guard at one of the Nazi concentration camps," Holt said, expanding the question of motives. "Doesn't that suggest that whoever is behind this wanted to get revenge?"

"Possibly. We'll work on that angle. But right now we don't know. It's too early to know," Taylor replied.

"Do you think Mr. Henslow's son, States Attorney Jim Henslow's life is threatened?" Carla Garza asked. Dan watched her eyes rivet Taylor with her demand for an answer.

"Can't say."

Taylor felt the interview wasn't helping him. The Sheriff's office was under attack by this kid reporter from out of town.

"But Jim Henslow's window being shot out," Garza persisted, "and the tires of his car slashed last Saturday. Don't you think that those acts suggest he's under threat too?"

"Possibly. We've talked to Jim Henslow about that. Have his complete cooperation," Taylor explained, making up his mind that this should be obvious to anyone, even if he had hardly spoken to Jim Henslow early that morning over the body of his step-father. Henslow had come to White's from Andy's Restaurant. They hadn't talked about any threat against him. Fact was, Taylor thought, it was all just a formality and little had been said by anyone there at White's Funeral Home.

"When do you expect a report on the autopsy?" Holt asked, still recording Taylor's responses.

"Can't be sure. Mid-week if the state medical examiner ain't too busy down to Sioux Falls."

"But what have you found out about Wednesday's attack on the Henslow place?" Garza asked, persisting in an attempt to get some kind of definite answer. "Weren't there two men reported running from the scene?"

Taylor looked over his shoulder for Dan's help.

"That is correct," Dan answered. "Mr. Henslow reported to us that he saw two men in ski masks."

Carla pounced on the answer.

"So there was a conspiracy involved. More than one person."

"Clearly so. At least in the case of the paint on Henslow's house. We are trying to tie the evidence together, but it is too early to really know for sure."

Dan watched Carla Garza's eyes narrow. She was good at her job, he thought. She wasn't going to be put off by vague answers. The sheriff's office had better perform or the world, this corner of it anyway, would know about its fumbling.

Taylor was feeling that the attack was overcoming his defenses.

"Look," he said, just able to surpress his irritation at this brat of a female digging at him. "The investigation is proceeding. We have evidence from the painting incident, like the spray can, and we are…"

Carla interrupted again.

"What about the word painted on the house? What did you find out about that?"

Taylor had forgotten what Dan told him. Once again he turned to Morris for help.

It wasn't necessary at this point, Dan was thinking, for them to tell the media everything they knew. Whoever did these things didn't need to know how much they knew or didn't know. But Carla wasn't going to be off their case until she had something she felt she could print as central to the story. Dan stepped forward and stood next to Taylor, a head taller, athletic, calm.

"The word means 'iron' in Hebrew. We aren't sure why it was painted on Henslow's house. You can assume that it was someone from an anti-Nazi group making a statement. Maybe a Jewish organization, maybe not. We can't be sure. But you can report that the word is Hebrew and has a connection with an organization we are checking out."

"Which would be?" Carla shot back.

"Which could be one of dozens. We'll let you know when we've made a definite connection."

"But," Holt said, interrupting, pushing the mike toward Dan, beginning to understand who was actually in charge of the investigation, "don't you agree that these events look like a conspiracy was involved."

It was then that Dan figured out what the media wanted. Holt wanted to report a 'conspiracy.' The word was hot, and would inform his report beyond any actual facts he had to report. He figured he could give them both that. A story tag.

"Sure. You can say there was a conspiracy. But there may be much more to it than that. As soon as we have the autopsy report, and the reports on other evidence we sent to the Crime Lab, we'll let you know."

Dan had taken charge, Taylor began to feel. It was too late for him to change the appearance of the deputy taking over. What the hell, he thought.

Dan was continuing.

"What we know is that there have been threats against both Jim Henslow, Chautauqua County States Attorney, and his step-father Horst Henslow. We aren't sure how they may be connected. The fact is that the elder Henslow is dead, apparently from two shots from close range. It might turn out that whoever did the painting was involved in the fire and death of Mr. Henslow, but we must make a definite connection based on evidence which has yet to be followed up on."

Dan paused, looking down at the reporters, a faint but friendly smile on his face.

"Sheriff Taylor and I have a lot of work to do today, so we'll be getting back to you as soon as we have something more definite."

With that Dan touched Taylor's arm and indicated a retreat into the courthouse. They left the media reporters dissatisfied that they had not helped solve the crime that very morning.

❧   ❧   ❧

It was one o'clock Sunday morning when Jim Henslow returned home from White's Funeral Home where he officially identified his step-father's body. His mind raced with conjecture, waves of fear pushing at the questions in his mind. Rogers had gone too far. He'd done the fire, as they had agreed. But killing the old man? Why would Art shoot him? The gas cans had the swastikas on them, as he'd told him. But Rogers had gotten him mixed up in murder. He hadn't figured that Art was capable of killing. He had to go to Chesterton first thing Sunday and get Art out of the country.

Although the Lincoln was gone from the garage, Jim went to the closed door to Sheri's bedroom. His confused thoughts offered the possibility that her car was in the auto agency garage, that she'd gotten a ride home somehow. He rapped lightly and called out. "Sheri, get up. Something's happened."

There was no answer and he knocked again and turned the door knob. The room was empty. A dresser drawer had been left partly open.

"Bitch," he said aloud.

In his own room he saw the yellow note stuck to the computer monitor. Reading it he swore again.

"Damn it all to hell."

He was well rid of her, he thought.

He did not sleep the rest of Sunday morning. At first light in the east he dressed and went to the kitchen. The stove clock read six thirty-eight. In the refrigerator he found orange juice, and poured himself a full glass. After brewing coffee he drank a cup hurriedly, standing at the counter. The cherry wood cabinets and counter tops of Corion were of the best quality. Sheri had insisted on that. So was the carpet and furniture in the living room. They had bought the best of everything for the house, he thought. They were in hock to the limit. She'd even spent six hundred for a mirror for the hallway. But he had taken some pleasure in their having the best materials and furniture in the house. They had both made a big thing of it when showing it off at the housewarming they had given themselves. But for what? Well now, he thought, for getting top price for the house when he sold it. He certainly didn't want it. Sheri would be moving to Sioux Falls, no doubt, leaving him. He saw it coming. And in the midst of this he had to confront Art Rogers. Find out what went wrong that he had to kill the old man. It was time to look out for his own skin.

The thermometer outside the window read fifty-five. Chilly but not yet cold. Fall weather was beginning to refresh the town, the season changing the pace of school and community activities. Family vacations were over. School was about to start next week after Labor Day. In the midst of those routine memories, and the pleasant nostalgia surrounding them, he had to confront a dangerous man this very Sunday morning.

Returning to his room he pulled on a sweater and chose a tweed sports jacket from the closet. In the top drawer of the dresser he found his revolver lying in its box. Taking it out of the drawer, he opened the cylinder. Six bullets. From the box of shells he took six more, just in case. His hand pushed among the rolled socks, searching for Roger's knife. A wave of panic swept over him. He was sure he left it there with the gun. The evidence that would point to Rogers.

He sat on the edge of the bed, the revolver still in his hand. What was he going to do about Rogers. Maybe he'd have to pay him to get out of the state. He did not finish the sequence of possible events. Daydreaming was not going to settle the dilemma.

"Damn it all. Maybe I left the knife in the office," he thought to himself, but no memory confirmed what he hoped.

Jim tried to calm himself. There was time yet, before anyone could figure out that Rogers had killed Horst. Somehow he had to make the killing fit in with the threats against him, the tires being slashed, the broken window shot out. Rogers went from harassment of the Henslow family to killing the old man. Maybe it was believable, but it wouldn't stick together for him. Not just yet.

He put the gun and loose shells in his right jacket pocket and closed the dresser drawer. Just in case Rogers threatened him, he was prepared. The more difficult assignment was to get Rogers out of the country. Convince him that he had nothing to worry about from the State's Attorney's office. Not for a few days anyway. As far as he could tell from their talking to him last night, neither the sheriff or Dan Morris had a clue about how the fire started, or why the old man was killed. But why had Rogers carried a gun when he went out to set the fire? If Art Rogers was running around the countryside armed, that was reason enough to carry his own revolver.

The logic of the plan was simple. He'd promise to give Art a few days to run and then put out a statement that he had his suspicions based on what he'd already told Taylor and Morris. It made sense. Rogers slashed the tires on his Lincoln. Then he threatened the old man to get at Sheri and him. All because his brother got sent up. He had motive enough. Give him a few days to disappear and then lead Dan Morris to the scent. For one thing, convincing Sheriff Taylor wouldn't be a problem. He'd had enough troubles with the Roger brothers to believe they were capable of any kind of mayhem.

It was just past seven on Sunday morning as a light fog sifted among the houses in Cottonwood Acres. He backed the Explorer down the drive and onto the street. Half way down the block he saw Eric Procter, optometrist who had been a bomber pilot in World War

II. Procter was a certified hero. This morning he was retrieving the Sunday paper thrown in his driveway. He was in his dressing gown, pajama pants showing beneath. The two waved to each other. To a casual observer it would appear to be a gesture of domestic tranquility, the rhythm of this day just beginning, the people stirring themselves for a day of rest, a day of worship, the peaceful certainties of a small prairie town in place. In the turmoil of his marriage and the crisis created for him by the murder of his step-father, Jim Henslow had no feeling of peace which this quiet street suggested.

Out of town on west forty-three the fog was heavier in the gullies between rolling hills. He drove carefully, without hurry. It was a simple thing he had to accomplish—warn Art Rogers he had four or five days to disappear. Let it drop on him like a judgment.

When he reached Chesterton he drove slowly down the nearly empty main street. The sun was poking through the low hanging clouds, breaking up the fog. Two pickups were parked in front of Sally's Place. An old man with a cane had nearly reached the front door of the restaurant. Jim drove to the end of the next block and turned left to the side street where Rogers' Welding shop was located.

The shop doors were closed. There were no vehicles to be seen near the building. Getting out of his car, Jim felt the revolver in his jacket pocket. The office door was locked. A padlock secured the double doors of the workshop. He walked around to the side of the building. In an iron rack were lengths of angle iron, pipe, flat iron. In the weeds were stacks of rusted tire rims and three fifty-five gallon drums with black paint peeling away from their sides. At the back of the building he found the doors locked. Several other oil drums were stacked against the wall of the workshop. Maybe Art Rogers had already left the country. But to make sure he would have to find the Clarence Rogers place. Art might hide there for awhile.

Jim drove to the main street and Sally's Place. He took the revolver from his pocket and put it in the glove compartment and locked it. He then went into the cafe. Two men wearing green caps advertising

John Deere were seated in a booth opposite the lunch counter. They were finishing breakfasts of eggs and pancakes. The old man Jim had seen walking into the restaurant with a cane sat at the counter, a cup of coffee in front of him. Sally was just placing a plate of scrambled eggs before him. They all looked at Jim. He knew they would know who he was.

"Good morning," he said to the room, to include all four of them. "Looks like fall coming on."

The men in the booth nodded toward him but said nothing. The old man was into his breakfast.

"Get you a cup?" Sally asked as Jim seated himself at the counter, leaving a seat between him and the old man who had propped his cane against the intervening stool.

"Sure. Black please. And those eggs and bacon look good. With wheat toast."

"Sure thing," she replied, placing a cup before him and filling it from a Silex pot now nearly empty.

"Be another fresh pot in a minute," she explained, then went into the kitchen.

Sipping his coffee carefully, he waited for the old man to acknowledge his being there. Finally the grizzled oldster looked up at Jim.

"You're the lawyer fellow we elected. That right?"

"You got it right."

"Hmmm," the old man hummed. "Figured you were."

After a pause the old man wondered aloud, "Out here on official business then, on a Sunday?"

"You might say that. And maybe you could help me."

"How's that?"

"Well, the district court wants me to look into Mr. Roger's place. Clarence Rogers."

"Oh, ya. Stole some cows. Got hard time, too, didn't he?"

"Sure did. We put him away for five years. I wonder if you could you give me directions to his place? I've forgotten exactly where his farm is located."

The two men in the booth, apparently father and son, were finishing their coffee and listening to the conversation at the counter. They were big men, huge hands nearly concealing their coffee cups.

"South of town," the younger of the two finally said. "Take County 13 where it cuts off from 43 at the city limits."

"Three miles. You'll recognize it," the older one added. "Looks like a junk yard."

"Thanks," Jim replied. "Much obliged."

Sally placed his breakfast on the counter and turned to the coffee maker. The gurgling and wheezing signaled a new pot nearly ready. As Jim began to eat his breakfast the two men rose from the booth and the younger one took a bill from his billfold. Sally went forward to the cash register and made change.

"I'd be careful out there," the younger one offered. "Since Clarence went up, Art Rogers has put no trespassing signs all over the place. Chased a couple of hunters off with a rifle a couple weeks ago. They were just trying to ask about a lease. Sioux Falls guys. Scared hell outa them."

"Yeah," Jim assured them. "I know about Art Rogers."

"Ask me," the older man offered, "he ought to be in the pen with his brother."

With that the two left the restaurant.

"He's out there now," the old man said quietly.

"What was that?" Jim asked.

"Said Art was out there now. Saw him at midnight. Walking my old dog Sam 'cus I can't sleep nights. And here he come down Main Street here. Like a bat outa hell. Pick up nearly skidded when he came around the corner."

"You saw him then?"

"Sure, I saw him. I know that s.o.b. And he had his left arm in a sling too. Was driving with one hand." The old man expressed satisfaction with his observation. "Must have got in another fight out to the Frontier Bar."

"How can you be sure he went out to Clarence's place?"

"He was driving Clarence's Ford 350. He keeps that out to the farm most of the time when he ain't hauling for one of them transformer outfits. There weren't any barrels in the truck, so I figure he'd done his delivery and was going back to Clarence's to get his own pickup."

"That right? Why doesn't he use his own pick up."

"Not his little 150. For heavy loads he needs the bigger rig. Duals on it."

"I didn't know he was in the trucking business as well as the welding," Jim added.

"Oh, yeah. Heard him brag about it right here in the cafe. 'Easy money,' he said. Said he takes them oil drums to Sioux City."

"That is interesting. Or maybe he doesn't take them that far. Have you heard about the oil spill south of Hamilton?"

"Yup. Read about it the paper. Probably Art. He'd do a thing like that."

Jim was finishing the last of the toast and eggs.

"Looks like I have a lot to talk Art Rogers, about."

"Well, like I said, he's more'n likely out to Clarence's place," the old man said, not looking up from the last of his eggs.

Jim got up from the counter and went to the entrance where the cash register sat on a glass case. Showing through were advertisements for cigarettes and a poster of an auction sale scheduled for the next Saturday.

"Three eighty-five," Sally said, "with the coffee."

"Good breakfast," Jim said, handing her a five dollar bill. "The change is for the good service."

"Well, thank you. Don't get that many tips, you know."

County road 13 was paved for two blocks in town and then became gravel. The road was damp from fog and rain of the past few days and there was no dust raised behind the Explorer as he accelerated to fifty miles an hour. Art Rogers seemed to have more than one reason to get out of the country, Jim thought. But as far as threatening to turn Art in, he thought, the oil spill didn't measure up to what he'd done at the Henslow place.

Jim noted the number of country roads between sections, slowing as he approached the third. There on the right, beyond the road going west, was an overgrown shelter belt, the underbrush choking the spaces between evergreens. A quarter mile further he came to the entrance to the Rogers farm, designated with certainty by an over-sized rural mail box clearly lettered 'ROGERS.' A metal gate was closed across the driveway. Jim pulled up to the gate on the drive over the culvert. For a moment he sat quietly surveying the farm-yard. He could see no vehicles. Rusted farm machinery lay on either side of the narrow drive. Weeds and brush grew up among abandoned tractors, a manure spreader, unusable rakes. Other pieces of equipment were so overgrown with weeds Henslow could not make out what they had been.

Jim rolled down the window. He could hear cattle lowing in the feedlot beyond the farmyard. Sparrows were chirping in the bushes along the fence line. The small cottage of the house appeared dark, its grimy paint peeled from nearly a third of its surface. From the road Jim could not see all of the house because of the bushes and trees to the right of the driveway. If he were to confront Art Rogers, he was going to have to climb over the gate and walk down that drive. It was a menacing scene. For a moment he considered giving up his mission. Let the sheriff pick him up. No one would believe he'd been hired by the State's Attorney. But it would be safer to have him out of the country.

Resolved to get the confrontation over with, he took the revolver from the glove compartment and put it back in the right pocket of his jacket with the loose shells. He got out of the Explorer and went to the gate, in the center of which was a large 'No Trespassing" sign. He paused, listening again. A chain and huge padlock secured the end of the gate to a steel post. Jim mounted the gate carefully, keeping his balance as it swayed under his weight. It occurred to him that he made an easy target poised at the top of the gate. But then, he knew, Rogers wouldn't want a dead body at his front gate. And he might remember too that the warrant for his arrest for slashing tires was still in Jim Henslow's desk. Henslow felt he had enough insurance for today.

He walked slowly up the rutted drive, keeping to the center hump. He could see freshly made tire tracks in the damp earth. The old man in the cafe had guessed pretty well. Jim did not hurry. It was better to appear casual, as if there was no urgency in this visit on a Sunday morning. Ten yards from the screened front porch he stopped and surveyed the neglected cottage. The wooden steps to the porch slumped to one side. Here and there the screens had rusted and broken open. He could not see clearly the downstairs windows beyond the dark screens. The two second story windows in the gable end had shades drawn. He watched for movement but saw none.

"Rogers," he shouted. "I want to talk to you."

There was no answer.

To the left of the house beyond a rutted farm yard were the outbuildings, a metal building of recent vintage to the right of what appeared to have been a chicken house long since abandoned. The double doors to the thirty by fifty foot Butler building were closed, but truck tracks showed that it was being used as a garage. Beyond the buildings was a feed lot with a dozen cattle in it.

Jim shouted again and started to walk closer to the house.

The voice from the porch startled him. Because of the sunlight coming from behind him and shining on the rusted screen, he had not seen the seated figure of Art Rogers until he was within five feet of the house.

"I wouldn't come any closer, lawyer," Rogers warned.

When he got his eyes focussed on him, Jim could see that Art held a rifle across his chest, cradled in the crook of a bandaged left arm and shoulder. His right hand was on the pistol grip.

"I just need to give you a little advice, Art. Looks like you're in big trouble."

"That so," was the reply, nearly growled. "And I suppose you think you aren't too."

"We'll see about that. But I'd just like to know why you thought you had to kill the old man."

"Bull shit. What are you talking about?"

"When they went out to fight the fire you set, they found my old man shot—dead."

"If he's the one that winged me with the shot gun, he deserved it, the bastard."

"So he caught you and you had to shoot him?"

"No way. I set the fire and was running for it. I got hit from the back just as I was going round the end of the barn."

"That story isn't going to fly in court, Art. You killed Horst and then set the fire. Sheriff says the old man was dead when the fire was set."

As they talked, the dark screen between them, it occurred to Jim that he ought to be hearing a confession. The image amused him. He was prepared to pardon this sinner who had taken care of a detail he himself had not accomplished. Horst was dead. Art's penance would be to hide out in Texas. For himself, he thought, the way was open for Chautauqua Acres development.

"I never saw your old man. I did the fire at the back of the shed, away from the house, just like you wanted. But I had to go out into the open and around the front of the barn because of the cattle yard. Someone winged me as I was going around the corner."

"That was Miss Gloria Miller, according to the sheriff. Horst had armed her to help guard the place."

"You said to do the fire before too late."

"Turns out that was not too smart an idea. But what about the threatening letter? Was that your idea of being cute?"

"What letter? I didn't send no letter."

"But you painted the swastikas on the gas cans, like I suggested."

"Sure. But I didn't kill the old bastard."

"You might have a hard time convincing a jury of that. And thinking of your welfare, I came out here to tell you that I'll cover for you for four or five days. Get the hell out of the state and when our dim-witted sheriff figures out who torched the shed and shot my old man, you'll be long gone."

"Like I guessed. You think you've set me up, don't you. Well, smart ass, I think you got it wrong."

Art Rogers spoke firmly, his tone threatening. He had not moved from the seated position, but took his right hand off the trigger guard.

"Like it or not, Rogers, if you stick around, you'll be rooming with your brother before snow fall. And it won't be for thieving cattle."

"I don't think so, Henslow. Let me play you my little recorder here."

Jim could see Art manipulate something in his lap. Then he heard his own voice, instructing Art to go out to the farm to set the shed on fire. Then there was a break, followed by his voice telling Art not to set the fire on that night. A pause again and then his voice instructing Art to go out early Saturday night. His voice explained that the timing would make sure that the fire would be noticed more by the town. Paint a swastika on a gas can. The instructions were all clear.

"This is just my insurance policy, lawyer. And I made a copy of this tape for my brother to keep, just in case you think you can get this one."

"You bastard," Jim yelled.

"Aren't we both," Art scoffed. "A couple of bastards, partners in crime, as they say. I like the sound of that. And as far as you're concerned it better be the perfect crime or one hellova lot of people are going to know who paid for torching his old man's place. Probably make them think you had the motive to do the old man in, too."

Jim Henslow stood facing the shadowy figure of Art Rogers, rising now from his chair, the rifle back at the ready. Jim felt himself riveted to where he stood. His right arm was against his body and he could feel the pistol against the inside of his forearm. But he did not dare put his hand in his pocket. A long moment passed. The sound of a car on the gravel road behind him was the only hint of the ordinary calm of the Sunday countryside.

"So," Jim started. "So we have a little deal here. You have a recording of someone who sounds like me talking about a fire someplace…"

"Forget it, Henslow. It's your voice. No way you can talk your way out of it. All I want from you is cover, see. It's going to be up to you to throw the sheriff off the trail. As far as you're concerned, Art Rogers was no where near your old man's place at any time. Got that."

Jim waited to reply. For now there was nothing to do but agree. But the tape. He had to make a deal about the tape.

"Okay. So we have to make a little arrangement, then. I think I can handle Taylor. That young Morris might be a problem. Too eager for my taste, but I'll take care of him too. But when do I get the tape from you? What about my insurance?"

"Easy. You get it when Clarence is on the outside and the fuss about your old man's fire and his going dead on us are all figured out, settled. That is, without Art Rogers having anything to do with it. Then you get the tapes, this one and the one Clarence has up to the pen. Now a smart lawyer like you ought to be able to handle that."

"Okay," Jim heard himself say. "We can manage that. But how will I know how many more copies of the tape you've made?"

"You'll have to trust me, now won't you."

Jim Henslow did not answer. He backed away from the house and after three steps turned his back on Art.

"I'll be in touch," he said over his shoulder.

"You sure will," he heard Rogers say.

❧   ❧   ❧

After the interview with KOLO and Carla Garza, Dan knew it was urgent that he get back to the Henslow place Sunday morning. Jack Traid was still out at the farm. He had been nervous about leaving the scene unguarded until the next morning and volunteered to stay on the place until Dan could get back. Dan arranged for Mike Wilkins to take Gloria Miller to her mother's in town. He left the front gate closed but not locked before going to White's Funeral Home with Taylor.

"Take your time to go over the scene tomorrow morning, when all the excitement is over." Jack had advised him. "Get your head into the scene the way it was before the fire, before Henslow was shot. What was happening out here? See if you can find anything that will begin to answer that question."

The old detective's advice turned over in Dan's mind as he observed an emotionless Jim Henslow view the body of his step-father. What was he thinking? The bad blood between the step father and son was well known.

It was seven in the morning by the time Dan was able to get back to the farm to join Traid who was sitting in his car. Together they had returned to the barn where the dimly lit interior challenged them to discover its time-covered history. Dan imagined he could smell death, a faint odor of decay that reason told him must come from old straw and manure which had sifted into hidden corners, not the body that had been trundled out on a gurney only ten hours earlier. They had walked up to the spot where the body had been.

"Too many people have been in here," Jack told him, "but don't forget a detail we saw when we first looked at Henslow. Up to the spot where he lay, from the opposite direction he was heading, the straw and dirt on the floor seem to have been disturbed, as if he had been crawling. After he was shot? I doubt it. Was he on his knees, begging his assailant? And the wounds. Not like any I've seen. Too little blood. But some. Strange angle of entry."

The half door to the stall next to which Henslow had fallen stood ajar. Inside was a layer of fresh straw, as if it were being prepared for an animal. The overhead lights were too dim to show any detail. Dan shone his flashlight across the straw-covered floor.

"Looks like someone cracked open that bale in the corner and pulled straw out onto the floor," Dan observed.

"Curious. Rather obvious way to try covering up something. Like leaving a signal," Jack observed.

"I'll sift through it in a little while," Dan had said, then added, "I'll have time this morning to do the fine tooth comb bit. But I got to tell you what happened at White's funeral home. After Jim Henslow left and Taylor and I were talking with Don White, Tommy Johnson came in, just before I was headed back here. He'd heard the news about Horst when Taylor went out to Andy's and got Jim Henslow. Johnson said he hadn't wanted to bother us out at the Henslow place but thought we ought to know something important. Turns out that Horst Henslow made a will this past week leaving the entire farm to Pioneer Village. The whole eight hundred acres."

"No kidding! Who else did Johnson tell?"

"He said he's told no one, but thought we ought to know."

"Yeah. Who else knew? Maybe someone knowing the place was going to be the Village's created a motive."

Jack paused a moment, considering what he had just said.

"Look Dan. Get back to Johnson today. Get him to agree to have the Village board and Jim Henslow come to a meeting. Let him spring it on them at the same time. See what happens. A little tree shaking."

"Okay. I guess I can get him to do that. You probably want to get home now and get some rest."

"Yeah. I promised Ellie I'd fix dinner today after church. Guess I'll have to beg off. I'm not used to this all-night business any more."

As he prepared to leave. Jack went over with Dan what he had thought through while sitting in his car during the night.

"There was a conspiracy, Dan. No doubt about it now as far as the painting on the house goes. But this final attack on Henslow was a lot different. But also well planned. Someone called Gloria Miller to get her off the place, then moved in on Henslow. But then an hour or two later, the fire. Why? Not to cover up the murder. Clearly not an attempt to destroy the body. I think the arsonist didn't know the body was in the barn. That's what you're going to find out."

"Yeah. Okay. If you say so."

"I'll check in with you when I get to Minneapolis tomorrow," Jack said as he turned to leave the barn.

As he heard Jack's car accelerate onto the highway Dan got to his knees in the stall, carefully clearing away straw. It was fifteen minutes before he found a switch blade knife. On the horn handled was neatly carved the initials A.R.

CHAPTER 10

*J*ack Traid left for Minneapolis at ten in the morning on Labor Day. Before he left Hamilton he had phoned the number on the letter in Horst Henslow's pocket for the Jewish Defense League in Appleton in the Minneapolis area. The voice on the other end of the line acknowledged he was Jacob Levy. Jack explained what he wanted to discuss. Levy's reply was a cheery "As I told Mr. Morris from your sheriff's office, that's no problem. We've nothing to hide here. I just can't send out our mailing list."

He wasn't sure why, but Traid expected truculence, or at least a sullen reluctance to talk. The League, he recalled, was known for its militancy. But Levy gave him his street address without hesitation. They agreed to meet Tuesday morning.

"We're not rich. So we do League business out of my bookshop," Levy said. "Easy to find us."

Jack hoped that the drive to Minneapolis would give him time to think about what he'd gotten himself into by promising to help Sheriff Taylor and Dan Morris. During the five hour drive he would be alone. The solitude of driving state highways, idling through small country towns, would maybe help him sort out what was happening to his life. Without seeing it coming he had reached a crisis with Ellie. He had called her Sunday morning when he got home from guarding the Henslow place and begged off preparing Sunday dinner as he had promised.

"I've been up all night watching over the Henslow farm until Dan could get back to it. Would a rain check for Sunday dinner be okay?"

Ellie understood. Jack welcomed the excuse to miss going to church with her that morning, pondering instead her birthday gift of a leather bound Holy Bible. He admitted to himself that Sunday at church with Ellie had become an uncomfortable interruption in his life. Although he acceded to her wish to attend church, while there he played a mental game in which he translated Pastor Clyde Masters's certitudes into his own quandries. Until Saturday's birthday party, and Ellie's gift to him of the Bible, he had thought he was on neutral ground, even in church, where his doubts would not be questioned and his silence accepted by Ellie as the reservation of a friend. But the gift revealed another dimension of his relationship with her. It annoyed him that he had not anticipated Ellie's desire, her question. Her note in the birthday card was simple: "Maybe we can share this someday." Clearly it was a new provision of an unspoken draft contract they had been working on these past months. The gift and note said more than Ellie had ventured to express directly. What would she consider to be an adequate response? He had not decided on how to answer as he drove east out of Hamilton toward Minnesota. On the phone with Ellie he had feared to say anything about her gift. That would have to come later.

Now he found himself driving toward Minneapolis, into the midst of the investigation of Horst Henslow's death, reluctantly going back into life as a detective. What he could not be sure of was if he was going back into his and Mildred's lives. Perhaps, he thought, agreeing to help Dan was a mere pretense on his part, a showing off for his friend Elliot Morris. But here he had none of the apparatus of the Dallas police force to back his investigation. What made him think he could actually help solve the murder of Horst Henslow? It was as if he were acting without intention, as if he were letting events determine his future. Agreeing to help Dan Morris was also leading him to Mildred. He drove slowly hoping a long day would offer solutions.

The events on the Henslow farm had no logic to them, no clear signature, as did most scenes of violence. The scene on Henslow's farmstead was like a field where competing forces sought recognition, a chorus of conspiracies. Typical of the confused scene were the swastikas. Those painted on the house and those found on the gas cans at the fire were much different, not made by the same hand or emotion. Sabotage of Horst's tractor was a carefully planned, deliberate act. So were the gun shots which killed the old man.

As he had told Dan, by Sunday night as he packed for his trip to Minnesota, he was sure that the fire and the murder were unrelated. And if so, why the fire? It would have been more convincing and logical if remains of Horst Henslow's body had been found in the burned-out shed, an attempt to cover up murder. But no. They were separate events. Henslow had been shot in the head and the back from less than a foot away. And it had happened hours before the fire. And how did the assailant get that close to Henslow in the first place when he was armed and probably on guard, alert to possible attack? And what about the disturbed debris on the floor? It appeared as if the old man had tried to crawl. That certainly had not happened after he'd been shot twice. Was he begging his assailant and then shot?

There were other clues to consider. Dan had phoned him at eleven o'clock Sunday morning, awakening him from sleep. He had explained that after Jack left the farm he'd finished his search of the barn. He explained that he had found a switch blade knife under the fresh straw in the stall. Initials AR.

"As in Art Rogers?" Jack asked.

"Maybe. Jim Henslow has claimed all along that it is Rogers who has been harassing him, but said he had no real evidence. I plan to go to Chesterton sometime today to see where Rogers was Saturday night."

"Be kinda clumsy of him to drop an initialed knife at the scene, don't you think?"

"Sure seems that way to me," Dan replied. "But I found something else that might be just as important—a small bit of hide snagged on a protruding nail on the side of the stall door. It's only a quarter inch piece. I can't be sure what it is, but I thought I better preserve it because Henslow hasn't kept animals in that barn for years."

"Forensic ought to be able to tell us what kind of animal its from. And how long it's been there."

The question in Jack's mind was how he and Dan would get the evidence properly evaluated? In Dallas there had been the entire apparatus of a well-equipped city police force, and people he knew. They were forensic specialists he could bring into a case whenever he needed them, and from whom he could get quick answers when he was hot on a scent. He knew nothing of the South Dakota set up. He had to trust that the people in the State Crime Lab were capable of careful analysis. Otherwise, he thought, he was on his own. Dan was depending on him to give him direction. Taylor seemed to have little interest in the Henslow matter, having turned his attention to the oil spills.

"Insist on the autopsy," he'd told Dan as they talked.

"White is saying it's too obviously a homicide. Why bother?"

"Well you've got to get it because White doesn't know anything about how Henslow was killed. He's guessing. And you at least have to retrieve the slugs to get a ballistics test. And for all White knows Henslow may have been clubbed and knocked unconscious before he was shot. Question is, are there any other marks on the body? And how come hardly any blood from the wounds?"

"Yes. I see what you mean. White said Jim Henslow was reluctant to give his okay."

"Tell him that it isn't up to the States Attorney to make that decision. It's your and Taylor's investigation."

As he crossed the Minnesota state line thoughts of Mildred intruded again upon his review of Dan's call. What did she want with him, anyway? She had left him and Hamilton just when he thought they were inseparable. Here he was headed toward meeting her and he did not know his own mind. He admitted to himself, he who hated indecision, that he didn't know what to think about the two women in his life. "Trap. Trap-Traid," he recalled was one nickname he'd left behind at the Dallas force. It had been hung on him by fellow detectives. They kidded him about making up his mind decisively after sorting through evidence. As useful as the certainty of his mind had been on the job, it was the trait that caused most of his conflict with Alice. He knew that. Once made up, his mind was like a bulwark of certitude. "Bull headed," she'd say and would rage against it.

"You think you know everything. But you don't know how I feel."

Feeling. That great female mystery, he thought. It had been like a curse on his marriage—not her feelings but his failure to fathom them. Alice's feelings were shrouded in dark thoughts, cloaked in imponderables that he was expected to discern with no evidence to go on. She was actually grinning when she repeated to him what she had said at the dinner party about her abortion. It was her outward mask of gaiety that enraged him and had momentarily blinded him. But he knew he had operated on the surface of things. The outcome of the emotions of hate and rage he had experienced in plenitude, for they were the foundations of most of the scenes of violence he waded through. But he had not understood a thing about the subtleties of Alice's mind, certainly not what she was feeling as she told him she was not ready to have a child. Her feelings, the firmness of her conviction that she should not bear his child even after five years of marriage, escaped any logic he could bring to bear on it. His parentage? Did she hold some deep prejudice he had never suspected? Or was it that she could not think of him as a father? He was always to be the trophy husband? In her eyes maybe he was meant only to play the hard-nosed detective who broke the smooth symmetry of the dinner parties where the other husbands were successful lawyers and businessmen with hard purpose in their eyes, and whose wives moved and talked with crafted manners. Alice referred to them as the "dull, well-behaved crowd." He had not figured out Alice's true feelings about them. They were her people and she could not leave them. Disdaining their predictability, she nevertheless felt secure in her clan membership.

At the dinner party, she had actually bragged about the abortion. His rage in the car on the way home that night ended in his never being able to penetrate her feelings, never to understand. He knew that he had not yet got it straight in his mind, this rejection of him somewhere deep in her soul. And now she was gone. Until Mildred and Ellie entered his life, he had hidden his anger and confusion about Alice in the monk-like refuge offered by Hamilton State College. Now he was about to confront Mildred, the woman with whom he had experienced love and companionship he had never before known. But was her move to Minneapolis another rejection? And Ellie, his affection for whom had filled the sense of loss after Mildred left, had placed a firm marker in their relationship with her birthday gift.

Cool September air rushed in at the open window of the Toyota, its fresh eddies enveloping him in the smells of maturing corn stalks and the rich black top soil. He crested a hill and began a gentle descent to the city limits of Pipestone, Minnesota. He slowed to the thirty-mile an hour speed limit. The cleanly swept streets and well-kept houses and yards declared a community of satisfied conformity. Lawns were raked. Bushes were trimmed. The sense of certainty and contentment reflected by these neighborhoods was attractive to him on this bright fall day. Those were feelings that seemed to escape his life. During the hours, the days growing into years on end of his unsettled life on the Dallas police force, he had never felt secure, properly in his place. The crimes he investigated were easier to read, he thought, than what his life was about, where he and Alice had been headed. And now, he thought, he was being challenged by Ellie's feelings, the test she was putting him through. That was clear enough. Her birthday gift and her insistence that he go to Minneapolis and respond to Mildred's oblique invitation by way of Randy Spies was a challenge he had no choice but to accept. He had better solve the mystery of his own feelings too.

His mission on behalf of Dan and Sheriff Taylor was simple enough. Properly deputized as an official of Chautauqua County, he was to go out to Appleton to confront Mr. Levy at the Jewish Defense League with the problem of the threatening letter and swastika painted on Henslow's house. He would just ask for Levy's help, straight out. Who in South Dakota was a member of the organization, or was getting information from them? If Levy would not send copies of their mailing list, maybe he would at least let him go through it. If so, the JDL investigation would take but an hour, at most, he thought.

As he visualized the Henslow farm, the image of old Horst patrolling under the security light on the barn, shot gun at the ready, the image of the model farm loomed in his mind. It was the product of years of labor, of that immigrant pride that something special had been made by supreme effort. The known discord on the Henslow farm arose from father and step-son. The hints of a development deal that had circulated at Pioneer Village focussed on Jim Henslow. The hot argument between Horst and Jim the day before the murder which Gloria Miller reported warranted something more than a casual check with the Carpenter Group about the extent of their interest in the Henslow farm. That might take longer than interviewing Mr. Levy, he reasoned.

The real mission for himself, he admitted, was Mildred. He had to face up to his own feelings about her. When he phoned Sunday afternoon to tell her he was coming to Minneapolis the sound of her voice triggered a casual, warm familiarity he'd always felt near her.

He thought he had gotten over the longing he had felt during the months after she left Hamilton. He knew that the question of her staying in Hamilton because of him had been a secondary consideration in her mind. Her frustration with the small town and the college was well expressed. She hid no feelings, he thought. If she was angry, all those around her knew it. Irritation she expressed with a wide vocabulary of words and gestures. Affection did not frighten her, and she showed her feeling with clear words and body gestures. Her supple body pressed unashamedly against those she chose to hug in greetings. How unlike she was from cautious Ellie who balanced all her cares on each word. It was, he thought, as if Ellie's feelings for him were filtered through her calculated concerns for Gordy, weighed against the financial status of the farm. It was clear that her thoughts about him were in the context of her devotion to her church, the thoughts of its minister, and her memory of a dead husband. Her entire demeanor certainly held to the undimmed memory of Ralph Easton. And yet. And yet, he thought, Ellie had seemed to promise unwavering affection and commitment once the tests had been passed. He felt sure of that. But he was not sure he was able to pass the tests.

Mildred had invited him stay overnight in her apartment.

"Let me give you directions to my place," she'd said.

"Okay, but I've got a reservation at the Super Eight near the airport. That might be better."

"Oh. Well, that's up to you," was her reply, which he read as saying 'you fool.'

"It's best, Mildred. But I'll pick you up at seven and we can have dinner. We'll talk," he had added lamely.

She gave him directions from the airport and said she knew of a dinner club, Jazz Cats, that he would enjoy. And he knew he would.

＊   ＊   ＊

When she called Jim early Monday morning from Aberdeen, Sheri Henslow had turned sweet. Her voice sounded bright and energetic.

"I tried to phone you yesterday afternoon," she explained, "but you weren't home. Where were you?"

He did not reply. He wasn't going to tell her about confronting Rogers, certainly not about the tapes.

She continued quickly when there was no response, explaining her assignment for the Argus to cover the farmer demonstration.

"Did you lose any sleep about my being gone?" she asked, seeming to tease him.

"Slept like a baby," he lied, the irritation in his tone levelled at her.

Sunday morning after returning from White's funeral home where he identified Horst's body, he had slept only two hours from exhaustion, turning over and over in his mind Art Rogers's threat about the tapes. All day Sunday he'd stayed in the house, going over and over what had happened to his plans. They had been undermined, even if the farm was now nearly his. He was standing on a house of cards under which Rogers had planted a bomb, recordings that clearly implicated him. He had to get the tapes. And because Rogers had been wounded, he reasoned, it would not be long before he was questioned. And when he is arrested and confesses to setting the fire on his, States Attorney Jim Henslow's orders, their conspiracy about the fire will be made clear by the tapes. There would be little doubt in the Sheriff's mind that the plan also included the hired murder of his step-father. He wasn't prepared to share these worries with Sheri. She would enjoy too much knowing he had stumbled into being trapped by Art Rogers's tapes.

"What's the matter?" she was asking.

"You didn't hear about the fire and the old man being murdered?"

"Oh sure," she replied casually, "It was on Watertown radio when I got up yesterday morning. So old Horst got himself killed. That's why I'm phoning, Jim. "

"What do you mean?" be replied slowly.

"Oh, I thought maybe you might tell me what happened out there. When did you get up the courage?"

"For God's sake, Sheri, I was with Johnson and Pettigrew at Andy's. I didn't know what happened until Dan Morris called me at the restaurant."

"Well, then you have nothing to worry about, do you? Air-tight alibi."

She seemed to be taunting him, her tone playful, as if not willing to let him know what she was actually thinking.

Cheri continued with conjectures.

"Do you suppose that Rogers did it? Getting at us by setting a fire and doing away with our beloved father?"

"Don't be cute, Sheri. It's a damned serious deal. He probably did. And there is no doubt that he shot out our window and did the tire slashing. All aimed at us," he continued, attempting to sound convinced. "They were warnings, I guess. I told Taylor and Dan Morris I thought it was him who did the tires and window. So we're already connected to Rogers. But killing the old man? Had to be he got surprised by Horst, killed him and dragged the body into the barn."

As he reviewed the story in his mind, the tire and window incidents seemed glaring at him as pointers. What had happened at the Henslow farm was connected to what happened at the Henslow residence in town. And it would unravel. Would people believe Rogers's acts of vandalism were prelude to murder? As he talked to Sheri, Jim struggled with the flimsy logic that Art Rogers's spasm of revenge had escalated into murder. Could it be made believeable.

"Well then," she said happily, "isn't it nice that Rogers did in the old man for us?" Sheri's voice was full of conviction.

"Who'll believe it?"

"It figures, doesn't it? Like you said, he went out to the farm to do some more mischief to get back at you," she answered. "Like setting the fire. He was probably hiding in the barn, just as you said, and Horst caught him and got himself shot."

"Maybe, but it isn't that easy to pin it on Rogers. The Coronor says Horst was dead a couple hours before the fire was set. Maybe Rogers was out there that long before the fire, but maybe he wasnt. What if the Sheriff thinks I did it?"

"Well, think of the positive side. Your problems are over, Jim. The old man's out of the way. Art Rogers will eventually be found out and sent to prison and you'll inherit the farm just as you were promised."

Sheri made it seem simple. But it wasn't simple. Here he was having to cast doubt on Rogers's involvement for his own protection. It meant that he had to protect Art Rogers to save himself. And he had to get Art out of the country.

"It's not that simple, Sheri," Jim repeated.

"Well, I still think it's clear as can be that Rogers killed your old man. You said all along that it was him who was doing all this stuff. I figure he should be credited with the big one, too."

Maybe he had to tell her everything about his and Art's deal. He needed her help. Especially now, he thought, now the farm was within his reach, provided no one found out about his hiring Rogers. He decided that he could tell Sheri part of the story now. Then maybe she could help get the tapes back, somehow. Her charms, he thought.

"I don't suppose Rogers knew that you and Horst hated each other," Sheri was saying.

Her persistence about motives irritated Jim.

"Maybe he thought the farm was already partly yours. Makes a good story, at any rate. We have to protect you by being sure everything points to Rogers."

"What do you mean by that?"

"Oh, you know. When Sheriff Taylor begins to interrogate people, that Miller woman is going to tell him you were out there threatening Horst. After all you have the strongest motive of all to kill your old man."

"Jesus, Sheri. I didn't threaten to kill the old man when I went out there Friday. I just said I'd take him to court for my share of my mother's property."

"It might not come out that way when Gloria Miller tells it. She's going to be big trouble."

Sheri was taunting him.

"When she starts blabbing it'll look like you had to remove the old geezer to get the Chautauqua deal. Either that or someone might think you arranged to have Rogers do it. Wouldn't that figure?"

"Stop it, will you? Whatever story the sheriff comes up with has to include the fact that I was with Tommy Johnson and Pettigrew Saturday night when it all happened. Sure, I can tell you that I happen to know that Art Rogers was out at the farm Saturday night. We had a little deal, and that is the problem. And Dan Morris told me that Gloria Miller shot whoever was running away from the fire. So they got themselves a wounded guy. They don't know for sure that it was Rogers. Not yet, anyway"

"But you do, don't you hon? So you can give them a little helping hand in finding him."

"Okay, Sheri. You gotta know that the situation is a lot more complicated than that. I know where Rogers is. We had a deal about the fire, Rogers and me. I figured we could scare the old bastard off the place."

"So maybe that bright young Morris will figure out that it was you and Rogers who did the painting on the house, too. A couple of fine characters."

"Bullshit. That wasn't part of my plan. I don't know how the hell that happened. Or who did it."

The tone of her voice remained cheery, as if spinning amusing tales. It was as if she couldn't get it through her head that the trail from Art Rogers led right back to him.

"I could always testify," she went on happily, "that you were at home with me Saturday night when I packed. You know, before I left after dark for Watertown. That is if the situation gets all the way to where they accuse you. By the way, where were you Saturday? I phoned Andy's before I left town and you weren't there yet."

"Working in my office on the Chautauqua deal," he said, trying to bring the inquiry to an end.

"Not when I called your office you weren't."

She was building her own story and was circling him with what she knew. Maybe, he thought, she knew that he had gone to Sioux Falls to look for her and had never got to their house until late Saturday night, after the fire, after Sheriff Taylor phoned him at Andy's Restaurant and had him go White's Funeral Home to view the body.

"But you were in Sioux Falls," he said with irritation, "so how could you testify to where I was?"

"Well, I wasn't in Sioux Falls by supper time. I was at home getting ready to go to Aberdeen. And waiting for you, dear. But I'll lie for you. That's what a wife is supposed to do, isn't it?"

"What the hell does that mean?"

She talked pleasantly enough, he thought, but the insincerity of her tone threatened him. It was too wild, uncontrolled. The rancor of their Saturday morning fight had not entirely dissolved. The ironic glee in her voice signalled that she was on the attack.

"I guess I could testify that I saw Rogers sneak into the barn when I was driving east to Interstate twenty-nine on my way to Watertown."

"Oh for Christ's sake Sheri. What in hell are you talking about? Things are messed up enough without you being involved."

"Calm down, honey. You'll figure it out. But now you can have your farm and the big development project and I can have my job back as a photographer. Won't we both be happy now? That is, if you figure a way to get Rogers set up."

He stopped speaking because he could not think what he was going to do about Sheri.

"Don't say anything to anyone," he growled into the phone. "And get back here pronto."

"When I've finished my assignment, dear."

Trying to calm himself he reminded her that today, Monday, was Labor Day and that he couldn't do anything about Rogers until he was done with his part of the morning ceremonies on the Court-house steps following the parade. She said she knew that and was sorry she wouldn't be there to accompany him. She did not sound convincing.

"Probably best you're not anywhere around here," he reasoned aloud. "After the speech at the courthouse I've got to go out to the farm and look things over. Dan Morris told me he had Gloria Miller taken to her mother's place Saturday night after the fire. He's put the whole place off limits until he's finished investigating. But I've got to find the old man's copy of his will. You know that Tommy Johnson is his lawyer. There is no way I dare get at his files in Tommy's office."

"Maybe there isn't a will. Then what?"

"Be better for me, being the only heir."

"And the one with the clearest motive to get him out of the way."

"Jesus, will you stop saying that."

"Well, face it. You have to work out a fool-proof motive. Dan Morris and old fat-ass sheriff will be looking you over pretty closely. Of course, I was out of town, on my way to Aberdeen, so I can only testify that you were with me until the time I left town."

"Do we have to go over this again and again? I was with Johnson and Pettigrew at Andy's when all that happened. Can't you get that through your head?"

"I believe you. But you have to make sure that every thing points to Rogers."

She had to know, he thought. Otherwise she wouldn't understand his problem.

"What I didn't tell you is that Rogers has made a recording of my calls to him about setting the fire. He's blackmailing me with them to get his brother out of stir."

"Kill the son of a bitch, then," she spit out.

"Quit saying those things, Sheri."

"But you got to fix the evidence so that Rogers did it. Went out there to set a fire, got caught and shot the old man with the pistol he stole from you. That would be believable. It's that simple."

"Aren't you the smart one," he said with disgust. "It wasn't my gun that killed the old man. It's right here in the house."

His breath was coming in short bursts, as if he had just sprinted a hundred yards. In his exasperation and confusion, he could think of no more to say.

"Well, hon, I've got to be getting on my way to the demonstration," Sheri said, closing their discussion. "See you Tuesday night. Get the story straight by then about Rogers and we'll talk about it. Maybe I can help."

Story straight? He repeated the phrase in his mind as he hung up. Now she knew too much.

The telephone rang almost immediately. It was Tommy Johnson.

Jim remained standing at the kitchen counter as he talked.

"Hi, Tommy. What can I do for you?" He tried to get the tension out of his voice.

"I've been trying to get you for the past fifteen minutes," Tommy complained.

"On the phone with Sheri. She's doing a photo story in Aberdeen."

Johnson ignored the explanation and went on to say that he was having a meeting with some of the Pioneer Village people in his office in the afternoon, after the Labor Day parade.

"It's urgent that you be there, Jim. It has to do with Horst?"

"In what way?"

"It better wait. All I can say is that I have some papers we have to go over in view of Horst's death. Sheriff Taylor will be there too."

Tommy's tone was distant, business-like. To Jim's ears he did not speak with the familiarity of a law partner he'd been a friend with all these years. How much did he really know?

CHAPTER 11

❀

Rachel Bickerson was in her kitchen at 10:45 Monday morning when the phone call came. Jonah and Sarah had left to take part in the Labor Day parade, both in their high school band uniforms. Jake was in the barn working on a combine.

She dreaded telephone calls. When she was alone in the house, the dread ran deeper. Fear that one of her children was hurt, or some fate-driven bad news was about to emerge that would take their farm from them, made each ring of the telephone startle her.

"Yes, this is the Bickerson farm," she answered tentatively.

"Mrs. Bickerson, my name is Tommy Johnson, I'm an attorney in Hamilton. I wonder if I might speak with Jake."

He explained that Jake knew him through his work with the Pioneer Village Board.

Attorneys meant trouble. Rachel's voice tightened as she explained that her husband was out in the barn. She could call him in.

"That won't be necessary. Would you tell him there is an important meeting in my office this afternoon at one o'clock, Mrs. Bickerson. I realize it's a holiday, but it's Pioneer Village business that can't wait."

He gave her his telephone number should Jake wish to call back. She promised to give her husband the message. She hung up the phone and hurried from the kitchen. Getting a sweater off a hook in the back entryway, she went out into the cool, bright September morning. It was the investigation about the tractor accident. That was her fear. Jake had said that Sheriff Taylor acted as if all the Pioneer Village board members were suspected, Even Jake, who would never hurt anyone. And now the horrible news over the radio that Mr. Henslow had been murdered. The announcer said that Mr. Henslow's being burned by the steam leak last week was very likely connected to his death Saturday night. People get accused of crimes they had nothing to do with, she thought. She hurried out into the farmyard.

Jake was bent over the combine, wrench in hand. He looked up when he heard the screen door of the house slam shut. Seeing Rachel's agitated running-walk, he put down the wrench and went to the wide open double barn doors and into the sunlight.

"You got to go to town. The lawyer Johnson just called."

She was breathless.

"Calm down, Rachel. What did he say he wanted?"

"Village business, he said. There is a meeting at one o'clock in his office."

"Well, I wonder what that could be. Today, on Labor Day."

"Maybe it's about the tractor business and Mr. Henslow being killed. You said the Sheriff suspected everyone, maybe even you."

"That was about the boiler, Rachel, not about Horst being killed. And I don't think they really suspect me. They know I wouldn't do anything like sabotaging a tractor, not even as a joke. It must be about Horst's plans for the Village that Johnson wants to talk about. The board knew Mr. Henslow was planning a big announcement during Pioneer Days."

"But you can never tell," she said, not reassured.

"It will be all right, Rachel. So, I better quit here and clean up. How about a fresh cup of coffee and we talk over lunch?"

Jake put his arm around his wife's shoulder as they walked back to the house. He attempted to calm her. She was a worrier. And now the murder and fire following the boiler incident made it all seem connected with Pioneer Village. And her worry was that because he was Chairman of the Village board, he was involved in some terrible way. Maybe she was right to fear that the violence was coming too close to their lives.

"Don't be so concerned, Rachel dear. Nothing is going to happen to us."

"I don't know. The news is so bad about poor Mr. Henslow. And I worry about Jonah, too. He's so quiet lately. Won't talk to any of us. Staying out late, him and the Marritz boy. When they are together here they keep to Jonah's room."

"Boys do that when they're that age. Probably talking about girls."

"I know, I know. I just wish Jonah was more open with us. Everything seems to be changing. Jonah going away next year to college, wanting to be free of us. Sarah wanting to date already. I don't know what to think some days."

"It's all right, Rachel. It's what life is all about."

"But something bad is happening in town."

"Well, it's not concerning us," he assured her.

Led by Hamilton Chief of Police Albert Ford in his new Chevrolet patrol car, its red and blue rack of lights flashing across its spotless white roof, the Labor Day parade turned onto Main Street from Highway 43 where it had formed an hour earlier. Like every celebration and parade in Hamilton, the preparations and route disrupted traffic passing through town as well as that on Main Street. The confusion surrounding the clearing of the celebrated main street added to the festivities, seeming to certify their importance. Several clutches of people had arrived early, some having brought folding chairs and claiming choice curb-side spots.

Marching behind the police car, The American Legion and Veterans of Foreign Wars had joined in an eight man color guard, the younger Vietnam vets now outnumbering the old men of the Korean War and World War II. Along the curb the older men took off caps and hats and with the others put their hands over their hearts, their gestures as much a part of this town's communal belief system as attendance on the day before in its churches.

Mayor Herman Olson rode in the back seat of a convertible with his wife Alma. He smiled and waved in the manner expected of a town father, both of them appearing embarassed at being momentary celebrities. Here and there he called out names, "Hey, George. Hi there Luke."

Since it was Labor Day, the Chamber of Commerce, which was in charge of such affairs, had to concede a place for the representatives of the workers, those who would be recognized on this day as the backbone of the country and eulogized for making this country what it had gloriously become. It was for this reason, and the fact that local telephone company employees were members of the union, that the Communications Workers union had been invited to be represented by its state president out of Sioux Falls. On both sides of the Buick sedan a banner displayed the union's logo and name. Its representative leaned out of the window to be better seen by those at curb-side. One or two of the telephone company employees recognized him and called out; most of the others watched silently, wondering about the meaning of unionized workers in Hamilton.

Hamilton's pride, the high school's senior band followed, emerging onto Main street with smartly executed turning movements, marching as a phalanx of well-trained, in-step performers. When the entire band had made the turn and was headed south down Main Street, they struck up a Sousa march which had been transformed by a Latin beat. Cheers went up from the curbs where parents, brothers, and sisters watched as the bright red and blue uniforms passed, instruments glinting in the September sunlight. A sea of red plumes fluttered above the bright white vinyl shako helmets worn by its members, giving the band the appearance of a single living creature.

After the band came the floats representing the various clubs. There was the Future Farmers of America float with a teenager holding tight to a calf tethered to a stanchion built into the platform. Then came the Sons of Norway on a miniature replica of a Viking ship able to hold eight of the waving members. Two of them wore helmets with horns. One of the old men kept asking the crowd, "Are we to America yet?"

Next in line were fifteen aged Knights of Columbus members marching out of step in two columns, their sword scabbards flashing in the sunlight. The Cub Scouts were the most numerous, not marching so much as being herded by their leaders behind a banner carried by two of the older boys announcing they were part of the Big Sioux District. The Boy Scouts, then the Girls Scouts followed, both making serious attempts at marching in time to both the band ahead of them and the visiting Rutland High School band which followed them.

Sorenson's Implements contributed to the parade's length by including two mammoth International Harvester tractors. Close behind was Harvey's Farm Machinery Company running three John Deere tractors, painted the familiar green. The rival tractor manufacturers rolling down the street in tandem incited comments from partisan farmers at the curbs.

Pioneer Village was represented by Hank Severson driving a Hart Parr steam tractor. A banner rigged on top of the cab touted Pioneer Village Days, October 5-6-7. As the steel-wheeled tractor screeched and rumbled into its turn down Main Street, Severson let go with a blast of the steam whistle. The piercing sound made on-lookers jump and then burst into cheers. The prolonged blast echoed down the brick buildings of the Main Street.

Following the tractors was the Pioneer Village Saddle Club, a dozen riders with Sheriff Tom Taylor mounted at their head. The riders struggled to keep their mounts calm at each blast of Severson's steam whistle. Gaylord Piper, public relations man for Prairie Electric, was close behind the horses. He was dressed as a clown and pushed a barrel on wheels equipped with a broom and scoop. The crowd knew that the horses and Gaylord signaled the end of the parade and began to step into the street to follow the parade to the courthouse for Labor Day ceremonies.

In front of the Chautauqua Country Court House the high school band marched off the street in single file, up the steps and onto the lawn where chairs had been arranged for it to the right of the raised platform. A line of United State's flags stretched out on either side of the permanent stage, their blue fields and red and white stripes undulating in the soft breeze. The east-facing platform was bathed in sunlight. Dignitaries waited for the end of the parade to pass. Mayor Olson, followed by his wife, had made his way from the parking lot in back of the court house to the podium. Jim Henslow was already in his place. He rose to shake hands with the Mayor.

"Where's the wife?" Olson asked.

"On assignment for the Argus. That farm protest in Aberdeen."

The mayor had expected to sit next to Sheri Henslow, as in past years. He enjoyed getting a close look at her long, thin legs crossed and revealed to mid thigh. His disappointment today was sincere.

"Damned shame, Henslow." Olson said, trying out his gallant tone. "That woman of yours gives this place some class."

Alma nudged him from behind.

"Where do we sit?" she demanded.

Olson indicated two seats next to Jim Henslow to the right of the podium.

The Communications Worker's president was introduced to Henslow and Olson, but neither of them caught his Polish name.

The speeches skirted the theme of the day, except for the union representative who urged this rural town to think of the problems of the working man. The workers' right to organize, he argued, was the very breath of a free, democratic life. There was a scattering of applause from a handful of telephone company employees.

Jim Henslow, Chautauqua County State's Attorney, spoke for only three minutes, explaining that a crime-free community was a safe community where all workers had a chance live in peace. He was careful not to suggest that a union was necessarily the way in which workers would find advancement or contentment. But he was emphatic about his duty to uphold the law, for, he explained, the rule of law was of paramount importance in a great country and in Chautauqua County. General applause greeted his blissfully short remarks.

Mayor Olson launched into a history of Chautauqua County, once named Hamilton County. He mentioned earlier mayors whose names most of those in attendance had forgotten, or never knew. It was the opportunities provided workers by the enterprising men and women who had built and maintained businesses up and down main street that all could celebrate on this day. They too were workers, these men and women of integrity, not the buffoons depicted in some novels, like *Main Street*, a book he had not read. Olson went on to say, "Our magnificent Main Street is a symbol of the broad street of freedom, the street of opportunity, and the great wide street of free enterprise."

He gestured widely toward Main Street.

"It is a day when," he read from notes he had prepared, "the fruits of our honest labors produce the peace which our town enjoys and the dear friendships that flourish among our citizens."

At the end of the Mayor's ten minutes of oratory, the Hamilton High School Senior Band played the national anthem. Heads were bared once again, and hands were held over hearts.

Mayor Olson looked across at Jim Henslow. Thin and handsome, this young man had a great future, he thought, feeling a tinge of envy. Jim was the kind of ambitious young man that the community needed but so often lost to larger arenas. Henslow not only was building a reputation as an effective prosecutor, but it was rumored that he was kingpin in a big real estate deal that was coming to Chautauqua County. Herman Olson suppressed his envy. After all, he thought, he'd gotten elected mayor by a large majority, even if he had not finished his degree at Hamilton State's predecessor, Hamilton Teachers College.

※   ※   ※

For Tommy Johnson the practice of law was the cement of justice that held a community together. It was true, he would admit, that the continued need for wills, contracts, and estate planning assured him and his firm comfortable incomes. Seldom had he defended anyone in a criminal action. That was the realm of his partner and State Senator Andrew Pettigrew III, grandson of the founder of the firm. They shared civil cases, one farmer suing another over a disputed boundary, or bankruptcy litigation. But it was Andy, and Jim Henslow before he became State's Attorney, who handled criminal matters. Johnson was uneasy with the role Dan Morris had asked him to play this afternoon.

Pettigrew, Pettigrew, Johnson law offices had taken over the Hamilton State Bank building when it was left empty after the state-chartered bank had been bought out by Banco corporation of Minneapolis, which had then built a new building. The firm's conference room was paneled in mahogany plywood. It had large windows looking south across First Street to the front yard and entrance of the court house where workmen were removing the podium and chairs.

To the assembled group, the nervous, business-like demeanor of Johnson underscored the seriousness of the meeting.

"I apologize for intruding on your holiday," Johnson began, looking down the conference table at members of the Pioneer Village board of directors, and Jim Henslow, Sheriff Taylor and Dan Morris, "but there is urgency in revealing to everyone immediately concerned with Pioneer Village what the wishes were of Horst Henslow before he was killed."

Johnson paused, deepening the anticipation in the room.

"There has been talk in town about what has been going on out at the Henslow place this past week or so. I'll leave that to the sheriff to sort out. Nevertheless I felt it my duty to let the sheriff as well as the Village board, and you Jim," he said directing his gaze at Henslow, "know what Horst Henslow's will provides. As some of you may or may not know, I have represented Horst Henslow for a number of years."

Dan Morris watched the expressions on the faces around the table. He noticed that Jake Bickerson smiled faintly, as if knowing what was coming next. Jim Henslow raised his eyebrows in an expression of anticipation, conscious that Johnson was watching his reaction. Sheriff Taylor was staring at members of the Village board, seeming to find in their expressions something he should know.

"Horst has willed all of his farm to the Village," Johnson said abruptly, watching the expression on Jim Henslow's face.

Frowning, and staring back at his partner, Jim Henslow said nothing.

"There are some conditions to the bequest," Johnson went on, "to which the Village board will have to agree, but, I believe, are not serious ones. The will stipulates that some appropriate memorial, a monument, be placed in the Village commemorating Mr. Henslow's love of the Village. The bequest also requires the preservation by Pioneer Village of his farmstead for at least the next fifty years as a model farm."

All members of the board but Hank Severson were nodding agreement. Jake spoke up at this point.

"Some of us knew from Horst that he was thinking about making the will in favor of the Village to some degree. Most of us agreed that to repay such generosity we would elect him chairman next year. Wasn't unanimous, but we agreed because of his intended generosity."

"So," George Carter interjected, "putting up an appropriate monument is no problem for us. That right, Hank?"

Hank Severson was caught off guard, not expecting to be called on. His opposition to the deal Horst wanted was known to all the board members, but he had decided to keep his mouth shut.

While the dialogue was going on among board members, Jim Henslow noticed Dan Morris watching him. He had not taken his eyes off him during the last ten minutes.

"Guess not," Hank replied. "Not now, anyway." Hank did not look at the others but was staring at the middle of the conference table.

Johnson continued with his explanation, turning to Jim Henslow.

"Jim, I realize that this is probably a big disappointment for you in view of your plans for a housing development. But Horst provided for you in the will, which I will go over with you later in private. Horst talked to me about this for more than a month now and when he made up his mind last week he swore the board and me to secrecy until after opening day at the Village in October. So I couldn't say anything to you until now."

Johnson looked around the table, signaling that he had completed what he wanted to say to the group.

"Are we free to make all this public now?" Jake Bickerson asked.

"I see no reason why not," Johnson replied. "Sheriff Taylor, do you have any reason to try to keep this under wraps?"

"Nope," Taylor replied, getting up from his chair. "Won't change the fact that we're still looking for Horst's killer."

Taylor scanned the table. Jim Henslow thought he was being too dramatic in the implications of the look.

"After the Crime Lab in Pierre gets done with the forensics," Taylor went on, "we'll have more to go on. Now it's all a matter of who was harassing the Henslows. Who wanted Horst dead?"

The meeting broke up slowly and some members of the Village board huddled at the end of the table opposite Johnson. Jake Bickerson, one of the group, spoke up.

"We're not sure from what you said Mr. Johnson, when the Village will actually take possession of the property."

"The will has to be probated and that will take some time. I would say at least six months to a year, if there are no challenges. Incidentally, the will provides that anyone who challenges it is to be removed as a beneficiary. So, hopefully there will be no delay because of the investigation into Horst's death. That could possibly change things."

Dan was watching Jim Henslow's stony reaction as Johnson replied to Jake. As Jack Traid had suggested, a tree had been shaken, Dan thought to himself. Although Johnson had been reluctant to hold the meeting, the tension in the room seemed to promise that hidden motives might boil over from the leaders of Pioneer Village.

Sheriff Taylor, a message in hand from his office, was the first out the door. As the rest of the group began to leave Johnson's office, Morris stepped next to Jim Henslow and spoke quietly to him.

"If you don't mind, Mr. Henslow, I'd like to go over some details about Saturday night with you. Would you mind coming over to the courthouse in about thirty minutes?"

"I'll be in my office, if you want me. You can come up there." Henslow's unblinking stare challenged Dan.

"Okay with me," Dan replied.

Hank Severson hurried to catch up to Sheriff Taylor as he left the law offices. Taylor had crossed the street and was in the courthouse parking lot where his new Ford 350 diesel pickup was parked. Attached to the pickup was a horse trailer with his favorite quarter horse shifting about inside. The parking lot space was marked "Sheriff Taylor." His assigned patrol car was parked in the next space, but for the past month Taylor had chosen to use his own pickup for official as well as private business. "Not so conspicuous," he incongruously explained to Dan on the first day he bought the big pickup. "Still have some leads in Minnehaha County on the car thefts," he'd added.

As Hank caught up to him, Taylor was preparing to heft his short, rotund body up onto the driver's seat of the pickup.

"Have a minute, Sheriff?"

Taylor was clearly impatient with being stopped. He shifted on his feet, waiting for Severson to begin. Taylor's uniform was freshly pressed, the creases of the trouser legs and shirt sleeves sharp. His cowboy boots, leather holster and belt were shining from recent neat's-foot oil treatment. As the six-foot Severson approached him, Taylor unconsciously straightened his five foot six height to its fullest.

"What can I do for you Hank? I'm in a bit of a hurry this afternoon. Gotta get this animal back to my place."

Severson paused and thought a moment.

"Well, maybe in that case I'd better talk to you another time," he replied, the edge of irritation clear in his voice.

"No, no. It's okay."

"It's about Horst Henslow. When I heard over the radio he'd been killed Saturday night, I begin to think I better talk to you. Johnson's meeting just now made me decide."

"You know something about his being shot?"

"Oh no. Not the shooting. I just thought I better tell you about the Avery steam line leak. How I pulled a little trick on him."

"You mean the tractor accident."

"Ya. A couple of us thought we…"

"Look," Taylor interrupted, "I'm on a tight schedule here. Why don't you catch Dan Morris? He just went into the office. I've got him following up on the tractor business."

Taylor sensed immediately that in his eagerness to leave he'd made a mistake handing Severson off to Dan. Hank had influence of a kind, especially with the Village bunch, and some of the veterans in town. Most of them were votes he figured he could count on but one had to be careful.

"Sorry you can't handle it," Hank said coldly. "I'll go talk with young Morris then."

"I'd appreciate that, Hank. You understand. After I get rid of my horse, I gotta keep an appointment in Sioux Falls and deal with Mr. Henslow's murder," Taylor explained lamely.

As Taylor's diesel truck engine pounded and clattered on start up, Severson turned from him without another word. He entered the door at the rear of the court house resolutely and descended the back stairway to the Sheriff's Department offices. Located in one quarter of the basement, the three offices were connected by a barred door to three jail cells. The smells of food, the faint odor of vomit from a drunk picked up the night before, flavored the poorly circulated basement air. Plans for a separate Sheriff's Department building had been approved by the County Commissioners but no action had yet been taken on the bonds necessary to finance construction.

Sally Edwards, receptionist and department dispatcher greeted Severson with practiced enthusiasm. She knew his name and enjoyed the familiarity she urged on elders she met.

"Hi Hank. What have we done to deserve your visit?"

"Morris in?"

That Hank was not in a jolly mood was obvious to Sally.

"Sure is. Dan," she called toward the far office. "Someone to see you."

Dan Morris appeared in the doorway of the eight by ten foot office he shared with the copying machine and storage shelves.

"Well, hi Hank. Some surprise announcement Tommy made just now. The Village ought to really be able to develop."

Hank made no comment, waiting for Dan's direction.

"Come on in," Dan said, stepping aside and motioning to the chair at the front of his desk. Sensing Hank's need to talk in private, Dan closed the door behind him.

"I need to report something to you. The sheriff was too busy to listen just now in the parking lot."

Dan did not comment. It was not the first complaint he had been hearing about the absentee sheriff. Maybe he thought, he had a responsibility to say something to Taylor.

Severson's anger was not lost on Dan. Hank was a man who was daily conscious that he had served his country in time of war and as a result was recognized by fellow veterans who had chosen him Commander of the VFW post on six different occasions. A moderately successful farmer, he was considered an important player in county affairs and not to be ignored. Taylor would be reminded of that, Dan thought, as he watched Hank gather his thoughts.

"What's with Taylor, anyway," he blurted out. "I just wanted a minute of his goddam time about a very important matter. He brushed me off as if I had a complaint about stray dogs."

"I'm sorry, Hank. He's got some emergency in Sioux Falls. He says its something about Horst's murder, but he wouldn't say. Said he was taking over that investigation, first hand."

"Sure, and I suppose Minnehaha County pays to run that fancy new pickup of his, too."

"How about a cup of coffee while we talk," Dan offered.

Severson calmed down as he mixed sugar into the cup Dan set before him.

"What did you want to report, Hank?"

"Sunday when I heard on the radio that Horst was shot dead out to his place, I started to think. I've been worried ever since. They said it looks like murder."

"Appears that way. We'll have to wait for the autopsy report to make it official."

"You don't know for sure, then."

"Not officially. Don White has the body at the funeral home until the state medical officer can come to do the autopsy. What with the weekend and the holiday, I don't suppose we'll have anything from him until Thursday, or maybe as late as Friday. Sure looks like homicide, though, because Horst sure didn't shoot himself twice."

"Well, as you and that ex-cop were guessing when you came out to talk to me at the Village, the steam line leak on Horst's Avery wasn't an accident, either. I fixed it. We were getting tired of hearing the Kraut brag about how much better his tractors were, how the rest of us didn't know how to keep ours up properly. So, we thought we needed to teach him a little lesson."

"You're saying 'we.' Who are the others?"

"Oh, no one else rigged the tractor. I did that. It was just talk by the others. I drilled the hole, filled it with solder. Worked the way I thought it would, but I didn't plan on the steam hitting the Nazi bastard any more than a hot foot."

"You couldn't get over his being a German, could you?"

"It would have been all right if he hadn't acted like the war was some kind of joke, or a mistake that the Krauts lost. His attitude. Drove me nuts some days. Especially during Village board meetings. Talked all the time. Interrupted other members. He was intent on taking over Pioneer Village."

"Well, he didn't, did he?" Dan interjected.

"No he didn't. And I don't know who killed him. The tractor thing was meant as a joke, a practical joke to maybe make him a little humble."

"And then you and one of the other guys went out there at night and painted the front of his house with the swastikas and…"

"No we didn't. Now you listen, Dan Morris. I come in here to tell my story straight because what I did was wrong, but it wasn't meant to hurt Henslow. And I didn't have anything to do with that other stuff."

"Okay," Dan said, speaking calmly to quiet Hank. "You were just involved in fixing the tractor. Is that what you are saying?"

"Yeah. That's all I did. That's why I come in because I don't want you guys to think I'd do anything more serious just because I hated that man's guts."

"Are you willing to make a formal statement, then?"

"You mean sign something?"

"Yes. Just a short statement saying what you did, and that it was intended as a prank. Say when you did it, and so on. Or you might want to get a lawyer before we go any further. That's your right, you know. To remain silent."

"Don't need no lawyer. I come in to own up to the steam leak. I'll sign a paper saying I did that. Take the consequences."

Dan typed a paragraph himself, thinking he didn't need Sally to spread the news of Hank's confession just yet. He got details from Severson as he typed. The wording, he made certain, was factual and avoided judgment words. Hank read the sheet slowly and without a word took a pen from Dan's desk and signed it.

"Mind writing the date too, Hank. September 4, 1995."

Hank scribbled the date below his signature.

"You were right to do this Hank," Dan said. "To admit the prank helps us a lot. It had us confused all right, what with the swastikas on the house and gas cans. Do you think some of the other guys out at the Village might have been involved in those threats?"

"I don't know. I know what I did and that's all."

Dan realized he was not going to get much further with Severson.

"I'm sorry about all this," Hank continued, his voice softening. "Old Henslow really believed in the Village. He worked hard to make it better. Guess his giving us all the land says it all about what he felt. Bet his son got a big disappointment just now."

"How do you mean?"

"Oh, we've been hearing about that housing development across the lake from the Village. Jim Henslow's idea. Guess he figured he was going to inherit the place."

"I suppose," Dan said.

"Look," Hank said, his a frown spreading across his brow. "Is this statement going to get in the newspaper?"

"Not until something official happens, Hank. I have to talk to Taylor, then Jim Henslow. He's State's Attorney, after all. Might be some charge filed against you. Misdemeanor mischief. But for now I'll keep it here in my desk until some other things are cleared up."

"Appreciate that," Hank said, standing. He then reached out his hand. "Thanks for your time, Danny. You'll make a good sheriff one of these days."

Dan let the promise of promotion pass. Being sheriff of Chautauqua County was not on his agenda just yet. He shook Hank's hand and then opened the door for him. He followed Hank to the office entrance and the stairway to the back entrance.

"Stick around, Hank. Okay."

"Yeah. I ain't going no place."

"Right. I'll give you a call later."

When Dan returned to the reception area Sally pounced on him.

"What was that all about? Closed door and you typing?"

"Hank had some ideas about what happened out at the Village. Trying to be helpful. But more interesting to me right now is what happened to Taylor that made him light out of town like he was on fire. We were supposed to talk to Jim Henslow together."

"He's up to something about the oil spill. I got a call this morning from Rich Arnold who owns that transformer outfit you've been having me call. Acme. Well, he called just before the parade started and wanted to talk to Taylor. Urgent, he said. I told him the parade was going on and the sheriff was in it. I did what I promised and sent a note over to Johnson's law office while you were all there in the meeting. I figure he had some follow up on the oil spill."

"I suppose." Dan replied. "But it's strange he didn't say anything about it to me at Johnson's office. Since I hadn't made much of a report to him on the PCB oil dumping, I talked to him before the meeting. I told him I hadn't made any progress in the investigation of Acme. I told him I thought they were stonewalling us."

"Well, the owner sure wanted to talk to Taylor himself."

"I saw him read your note. Seemed to irritate him. But that explains it. When the meeting was over he told me he was taking over the oil dumping investigation himself. He said he had a lead he couldn't discuss. He told me I better concentrate on the Henslow murder and report to him once a day on how it was going. If he's around, that is."

"I know. We don't see much of him here since you got hired."

"Has he filed a report on the auto thefts yet?"

"Not for my files. He did tell me he was on to something in Sioux Falls, but that was it."

"Well, I'll stick to the Henslow matter. Right now I've got to go upstairs and get some details from Jim Henslow about Saturday night, and all the harrassment stuff. Did Taylor say anything about talking to Jim Henslow?"

"Well, the sheriff sure didn't tell me anything, as usual," Sally complained.

"Look, I'll be gone for awhile this afternoon. After I talk to Jim Henslow, I've got to interview Gloria Miller again. Maybe she can remember something about the guy who set the fire. She thinks she hit him when she shot at him with the 20 gauge. She's at her mother's place."

As he was about to leave the basement office and go to the first floor where the State's Attorney's office was located, the phone rang. Sally answered and said "He's right here," and handed the phone to Dan. It was Jim Henslow.

"I'll have to put off talking to you this afternoon, Dan," Henslow said. "Something's come up that I have to take care of right away. Can we put off our little meeting until tomorrow sometime?"

"Sure, I've got some other interviews I have to do today." Dan replied. "How about tomorrow morning?"

"Make it eleven a.m. I have to be in court until about then."

When Dan hung up he looked at Sally and shrugged.

"Seems like our State's Attorney is too busy to talk to the sheriff's office while the trail is still hot."

Sally shook her head.

"Way it is most days," she said.

CHAPTER 12

The Jazz Cat Club proved to be what Jack Traid needed after the long, brooding drive from Hamilton. Listening to accomplished jazz musicians and having a relaxed dinner with Mildred was like the best of times they'd had together. He had nearly forgotten how beautiful she was—Mildred the natural, who wore little makeup because her skin had a natural rosiness. She was attentive and enthusiastic at the same time, asking about the Henslow matter, then shifting to a story about a gallery show she'd done three months before. It was, he thought, as if they had not been apart these many months, and the thought disarmed him. He caught himself touching her arm and feeling a twinge of guilt, as if even this innocent gesture was a betrayal of Ellie. But then, he reminded himself, he had not made any commitment to her. Probably, he thought, revising, not even to himself.

They ordered pasta and a bottle of Chianti as a quintet was warming up. The club was only half occupied when the band opened the first set, playing ballads to accompany the diners being served: "Dancing in the Dark," "All of Me," "April in Paris." Finally after forty minutes of the romantic and quiet, the band tore into "Tiger Rag," ending the set to enthusiastic applause.

"Okay, so you're here playing detective," Mildred said. "That surprises me, Jack. I got the impression from what you said long ago that hunting criminals was something you did in another incarnation. You said you'd left that forever."

"I thought I had. But we've got a new Deputy Sheriff, Dan Morris, who's one of the best trombonists I've heard in a long time. He's now a member of the Dixieland Ramblers. I'm here mostly as a favor to his dad Elliot. You remember we went to graduate school together."

"Sure. But the case interests you. Right?"

"I have to plead guilty. It starts out with what looks like a deliberate prank with one of Horst Henslow's old steam tractors at Pioneer Village a week ago Friday. Boiler pipe breeches on the tractor and burns him on the arm. Not seriously, but with implications that it could have been worse. And it might have been meant to be worse. Then his son Jim, who is State's Attorney, as you may remember, has the picture window in his house shot out on the same day, followed the next evening with all the tires of his car slashed."

"In quiet little Hamilton?"

"Yeah. But it doesn't stop there. It started to get worse when at two o'clock in the morning of the next Wednesday old Horst is awakened by two men painting swastikas on the front of his house. Two men, mind you. He shoots over their heads as they're running away to scare them but doesn't recognize anything about them. Painted on the white clapboard siding with the swastika is the word "Barzel," which means "iron" in Hebrew. That leads us to the Jewish Defense League here because it's one of the four words in their proclamation of principles. So I'm here to find out who in South Dakota might be active in the JDL. The JDL office in Appleton is the nearest one to South Dakota in the region. I'll check it out tomorrow."

"You said it started to get worse with the painting. Then what happened?"

"Then Horst Henslow is found dead in his barn last Saturday night when the fire department goes to put out the fire which destroys the machine shed right next to the barn. Obvious arson. His housekeeper Gloria Miller shoots at one guy running from the fire.

Thinks she winged him. We find swastikas again on the gas cans deliberately left where they can be found. But they look nothing like the one painted on the house. When the fire fighters go into the barn they find Old Henslow with two bullet holes in him. One was in the middle of his back, one nearly at the top of his skull. At first glance it looks like an execution, but the appearance of the body and the wounds looked strange to me. But Henslow's death raises the question of his Nazi past during World War II. Did some Nazi-hunting group come after him? The whole scene, the attitude of the body, all the obvious clues, makes the crime as confused as any I've ever seen. It's a mess. Another word, "hadar" meaning pride or dignity comes from the same JDL declaration and it shows up in a threatening letter we found on Henslow's body."

"How do you mean, it's a mess?"

"It's too complicated. Most murder scenes, even the gory ones, are not very complex. Straight on evidence that fits together, even when there is not very much of it. Not the Henslow matter. It's as if we have too much evidence."

"Dan appealed to you for your help and you couldn't refuse the challenge, right?"

"Mostly. But to change the subject and get that stuff out of my mind, it turns out I had another motive for coming to Minneapolis. It seemed a better way to answer your Christmas card and your note about the Canada trip. I liked that."

"Liked what?"

"Your writing. Remembering."

"I didn't think you cared. You didn't write back."

"I couldn't decide what your letters meant. Did you really think about us?"

"Oh yes. I spend a lot of time remembering our being together in my apartment. I even liked remembering the times you took me to Sioux Falls to that ratty restaurant where we listened to that funky trio of old guys playing umpah music."

"They're called 'Ole and the two Swedes.' I love them. And you tried to teach me to polka."

"I miss that, Jack. Our being together."

"But not Hamilton?"

"Not Hamilton. Not Hamilton State. I know it was a case of desertion, but I felt my art was being suffocated there. And me. Now I have better students with lots of talent. And for me there are far more opportunities for shows."

"Do I hear some reservation? Despite all the benefits?"

"It's lonelier. Sometimes I think I made a mistake."

"You, lonely? You who can make friends across an aisle in a restaurant?"

"Sure. There are lots of those friends. And there are great people in the art department here. Young, inventive. Fierce at times."

"Hmmm."

"Yes. Youngsters. Doing stuff with their art that I don't dig, frankly, but haven't the energy to argue about. I do my thing. There's a gallery that shows my work. I know I'm not going to change the art world with my stuff, so I just try to get better at what I do. And I do get to show here a lot more. But I have to admit that I miss the intimacy of Hamilton State. By the way, who's taking care of Randy Spies since I left?"

"No one. And it tells. He misses you almost as much as I do."

"Sure you do. Randy tells me your new steady has a son and owns a nice farm. A very homey set up. Ready made."

"That might be one way to put it. Ellie Easton. You might remember reading about her husband being killed in a tractor accident three years ago. And there is their son Gordy. Yeah, we have become good friends. We three. But it is complicated."

"Not surprising, knowing you?"

"What does that mean?"

"It means, dear one, you don't know what you really want for the last half of your life. I know you well enough to know that. Still running from those bad dreams and anger about Viet Nam. Still guilty about Alice's death. That's about right, isn't it?"

"Yeah, you'd know that," he replied. "But you ran too, so I lost what I thought I could hold on to. Someone I had come to love. I'll probably be a sour-ass bachelor until I'm one hundred and four, still grading freshmen math papers, doing an odd gumshoe job, missing the big chance at love."

"You brush it off, Jack, but I sometimes think that by finding others who are guilty you avoid your own true feelings. And even more important, I think you are wasting a great talent."

"Which is?"

"Your books. Admit it. Your life changed. After you gave up the police force and after Alice's death, you escaped to what was deepest within you."

"You mean my print shop?"

"Sure. You say its only a hobby but I saw the change that took place in you when you got that shop together and began to print and bind books. You began to relax, almost know what serenity is all about. I know the feeling. I get it when I'm taken up by painting. It becomes what is really important in my life. And in my opinion if you were really serious about your books you would be as good as any of the limited edition book designers and printers around here. That and teaching ought to be fulfilling enough."

"Just a hobby."

"Not really. And it wouldn't be if you are ever able to shake off the past. Your guilt, and anger, too, immobilizes you. Maybe that was another reason I had to leave Hamilton. I couldn't live with your ghosts. I had enough of my own to deal with."

"Your divorce."

"And a child lost who was too delicate for this world."

"Amy. You told me. She was how old?"

"Six. After that Bruce and I seemed to have nothing left. All I had was painting and teaching."

"And since you moved to the metropolis life has become more fulfilling. And there is a man in your life?"

She looked him in the eye and smiled as she reached across the table and touched his hand.

"Sitting right here at this table."

Her eyes begin to fill with tears and she looked down. Jack reached across the table and took both of her hands in his.

As the band began the next set with a slow number he got up from his chair and pulled Mildred to him. He guided them onto the tiny dance floor, holding her tightly.

"Green grass?" he whispered in her ear.

"Yes. I didn't figure on the weeds that are here too. I've missed you so much Jack."

Their feet stopped dancing and they stood at the edge of the dance floor, other couples gliding past them as they held on to each other.

"Musicians and cops are lousy dancers," he whispered.

Taking his hand she led him back to the table. With a wan smile she raised her glass in a toast.

"To old loves," she said.

"To you Mildred."

"Me?"

"For not being afraid of your feelings. I wish you had never left Hamilton. You're needed there."

"Oh, sure."

"No, I mean it. The college needs you. Certainly Randy needs you. And if he hadn't been so damned afraid to say it, there's one broken down old cop who needs you the most."

"I'll drink to that," she said, raising her glass. "In fact, let's drink to the retirement of the cop and the rebirth of an artist."

They sat quietly, listening to the band rollick through another Dixieland piece.

It was a matter of loyalty, Jack thought to himself. This woman, the first he had cared about since Alice's death had left him for the city, for the excitement of a larger art department. What had seemed solid and promising, had changed suddenly because she could not abide the small town. They had not dealt with his uncertainty about them, or hers for that matter. He wondered: had geographical place, their need for different environments, separated them for good?

In his thoughts the questions before them ricocheted off the secure feelings he had at the Easton farm. What were those feelings for Ellie he now tried to hold tightly in his mind? What ghosts had he been pursuing through the domestic order and commitment Ellie had made on that place? And there was the birthday gift of a Bible from Ellie. She had put down an immovable boundary marker and it was up to him to decide if he could find his way into Ellie's territory of the secure and committed.

Mildred's pushing the subject to the fore made him realize that he had been playing a role based on his own needs, and that he had not considered over the months that Ellie might have requirements of her own. That explained the steady view that seemed to govern her reservations about the two of them.

As he held Mildred's hand, it seemed that the comfort he had felt in the presence of Ellie, on her farm, with her son, had all been a borrowing, second-hand emotions borrowed from the effort and commitments of others. His imagination had not had compass enough to grasp the wide reach of those commitments. He had to see that clearly, somehow.

As they danced again it was as if they had never been separated. She pressed closer to him. As they turned his leg pressed against the inside of her thigh. They paused, holding on to the sensation of their bodies entwining. Mildred's apartment in Hamilton filled his mind, the smell of oil paints, the incense she would burn, the sweet scent of her body as he would kiss her breasts. The mood held both of them as they hurried back to her apartment. Inside, the faint glimmer of street lights filtering through blinds, like candle light, caught them clutching at each other, dancing to the music in their hearts, shedding clothes, helping each other tear away the fabric holding back their need. Falling into bed as in a furious fight, they went at each other's bodies with a hunger nearly forgotten. Straddling his legs, she sat upright, her taut body displayed and given generously. It was a calm of purpose which directed them, a *pas de duex*, rising together into the timeless crash of resolution. They had found each other, finally, Jack thought.

＊   ＊   ＊

It was eight-ten Tuesday morning when Dan got Jack Traid's call from Minneapolis. Taylor had come in earlier than usual and asked for all of Dan's paper work on the oil spills. It was then that Dan also handed him Hank Severson's statement confessing to the tractor sabotage. Without a word Taylor snatched the statement and Dan's notes on the transformer oil outfits and hurried into his office.

"How did Johnson's meeting go?" Jack asked.

"Big news is that Horst's will leaves the entire farm to Pioneer Village."

"No kidding. That is news. Nothing for Jim Henslow?"

"Something, I guess. Johnson said he was going over that with Jim in private."

"Henslow's reaction?"

"Didn't blink an eye. Fish stare, like he hadn't heard. But the meeting did produce results as you suspected," Dan went on. "The boiler business is cleared up, if what Hank says is true."

"What's that?"

"He said he fixed Horst's tractor. A prank."

"You mean you think he might be lying?" Jack asked.

"Not exactly. He might be covering up for others. He claims he wasn't one of the two men involved in painting a swastika on the front of Henslow's house. But maybe that was just a prank too, and one of the others was out there with him. That's a possibility. Hank hated Horst, as much for his past as for his pushiness on the Village board. And it was pretty clear from what Bickerson and the others said that Horst was buying his way into chairman of the Pioneer Village board with a promise of the farm. Although it was really obvious, Jake Bickerson seemed to resent that, something like Severson's reaction."

"So maybe Severson and Bickerson were in on it together," Jack offered. "Jake appears to be a nice guy but he was the one who was getting all the pressure from Hank, maybe others, to keep Henslow from taking over the Village board. On the other hand, he also knew what Horst had done for the Village and would very likely do for it in the future."

"Sure," Dan replied. "It's just possible the two of them figured they could scare him off from being chairman."

"Possible. But complicated."

"What do you mean?" Dan asked.

"It's such a complicated way for them to deal with it. Maybe the prank with the tractor, but why the middle of the night painting of his house? Or the threatening letter? It just seems too much, even if Hank has confessed to fixing the tractor. What would they have expected Horst to do?"

"Yeah. I see what you mean."

"What about Jim Henslow? What did he tell you when you talked to him Monday afternoon?"

"Didn't talk to him. He put me off. Said he couldn't talk until today. Eleven thirty."

"He had motive enough, provided he didn't know about the will," Jack said.

"Well, I guess he did have a motive and it's my bet he didn't know about the will. As I said, he hardly reacted when Johnson told the meeting that the farm had been willed to the Village. Didn't say a word to anyone but that dead stare of his meant something. Shock maybe."

"I think you haven't concentrated enough on our State's Attorney. What about his motives?"

"As you say, he had motive enough," Dan replied. "From one angle he does seem to be a target of harassment too. It certainly looks as if all the Henslow family was being threatened. On the other hand, the fact that Jim has been working on a housing development deal to go on the Henslow farm property has become well known among the Village crowd. And Tommy Johnson told me that Saturday night at Andy's Jim Henslow was especially anxious to get financial support from his partners and from Elliot Morris, but no one would make a commitment until Jim had Horst's agreement. Of course, Johnson knew about the will. He knew there just wasn't going to be any Henslow farm land for the housing deal. But if Jim didn't know about the will he probably expected to inherit the property eventually?"

"Yes, I was thinking that, too. I thought I'd check out the development outfit in Minneapolis he's been dealing with."

"You mean the Carpenter Group."

"Right. I'll stop by there for a chat while I'm here," Jack promised. "We better see how far along the deal really has gotten. But back to what we have. It's possible, you know, that the window and tire slashings aren't connected in any way to what happened out at the Henslow farm. After all, they are much different actions. Different style."

"Jim Henslow has said all along that he thinks Art Rogers is responsible because of the threat he made when his brother Clarence was sent to the pen," Dan replied. "But Sunday morning at the mortuary when I brought up Art Rogers name as maybe being connected to the murder, he told me not to move on him just yet. He said he thinks he has some conclusive evidence he can get his hands on if Rogers isn't alerted. Not clear to me what he's talking about. But I can wait a bit, and Sheriff Taylor hasn't told me what he thinks. He just agreed with Henslow that I should wait before questioning Rogers. What Jim Henslow doesn't know, of course, is that later on that morning I found the knife with Rogers' initials on it at the scene of the murder."

"What did Taylor think about the knife?"

"He says it could be a whole bunch of guys with the initials A.R. He told me to send the knife to the state lab for fingerprints."

"Sure. In the meantime I think what you have to find out is exactly where Jim Henslow was the night of the fire and Horst's murder," Jack said. "Hour by hour, maybe minute by minute."

"He says he was at Andy's Resturant. At least part of the evening. With his partners, Pettigrew and Johnson. Johnson verified that he got there for the planned dinner, but an hour late."

"Pin down the exact time."

"According to Johnson's story, Jim Henslow was late for the seven o'clock dinner meeting, a meeting he himself set up to promote the development deal. Didn't get there until eight or so. He was still at the restaurant when Taylor found him to tell him about his father."

"So there is a window of opportunity. Couldn't Henslow have gotten to the old man's farm before going to Andy's?"

"Sure. I think so. At any rate, I'm meeting with him at eleven-thirty today. I feel a little awkward about questioning him, since he's the State's Attorney and kinda already involved in the investigation. I was hoping the sheriff would handle him since they've worked together for a number of years."

"Don't wait on Taylor. At first just act like you need to review the case with Henslow. You need his help. Ask him what he thinks happened. Don't be afraid to appear obvious. Peel it back little by little. Play dumb, as if you haven't a clue what went on out at Horst Henslow's farm and that maybe he can help you out. He might tell you more about his relationship with his step-father than he intends to tell. And work around to the fact that it was Jim Henslow who got that stuff in the Times about Horst being a prison guard. You might ask him why he did that."

"Carla Garza told me Jim just volunteered the information about the old man being a guard at Bergen-Belsen. She hadn't asked any such questions. Not a thing most people would broadcast about their father—even a step-father."

"Unless it was part of Jim Henslow's agenda."

"It's well known that the two didn't get on. The old man was involved in the Village but Jim Henslow had nothing to do with it or him. And as you know, they had a confrontation the day before the Horst was killed, according to Gloria Miller."

"The young woman housekeeper, right?"

"Yes. The morning after his house was vandalized, I suggested to Horst Henslow that he might hire her, and he did. She moved out there right away. When I talked to her again yesterday, she confirmed having overheard the two of them arguing Friday afternoon. She said Jim Henslow had come out to the farm to try to get her to leave the farm. But the old man intervened, ordered Jim off the farm. According to her, Jim then threatened the old man, but, with a law suit. She said Jim Henslow was furious."

"Interesting. What about the anonymous phone call to the Miller woman?"

"I questioned her about that. She said a nurse, or someone saying she was a nurse, called her Saturday about five thirty in the afternoon and told her baby was desperately ill and had been brought to the hospital. When she got there, no one knew anything about a phone call. The baby was with Gloria's mother. Nothing had happened to it. The deal was a set up."

"Right," Jack said, "meaning that Horst wasn't killed because he caught someone in the barn. It means someone intended that he be alone on the farm. Horst was being pursued."

"It was a woman's voice. But I suppose Hank, or for that matter Jim Henslow or Art Rogers could have arranged for such a call. I still think Rogers is up to his hips in the Henslow killing."

"Maybe," Jack replied. "But dropping a switch blade knife while he's hiding in a stall seems strange and unlikely. What would he be doing in there with a knife? Especially if he was waiting with a gun to ambush old Henslow."

"Yeah. I see what you mean."

"If I were you, Dan, after you quiz Jim Henslow, I'd put a lot of pressure on Rogers, whether or not Taylor wants you to get at him. Just act like you know a lot more than we do. A murder rap might scare hell out of a guy with a reputation for petty crap. But the longer you wait for Henslow's go ahead the more time Rogers has to arrange for alibis."

"Okay. I guess it's clear that Taylor isn't going to question Rogers. He told me I was to concentrate on the Henslow murder. He said something about my having the big city detective to help me."

"Did that make him nervous?"

"I don't think so. He says he'll be too busy with the oil spill matter. He is almost relieved that you are in on the murder investigation. That all seems turned around, but he's the boss."

"I guess. Then it's up to you to decide on when to question Rogers. By the way, who's doing the autopsy on Henslow?"

"State medical examiner will be coming here from Sioux Falls. After I insisted on a careful job, Don White said he'd rather have the state do it. He admitted that the ME had more experience. We expect a report by Thursday."

"While I think of it, it would be a good idea for you to check out Jim Henslow's neighborhood. The window being shot out is strange. Seems aimed at young Henslow. Like the tire slashing. But why the same week as the fire and murder of the old man? Just a coincidence or part of the same story? Maybe one of the neighbors saw something. I'd go door to door. What do the neighbors say has been seen going on during the past week?"

"I'll do that. As I said, Henslow says those things were done by Art Rogers. But when I checked him out right after the business with the tires he had an alibi. Two of his drinking buddies said he was with them that night at the time the tires were cut. As I said, Sunday morning Henslow didn't seem to want to push that any further, so I haven't done any more looking into Rogers. Even if Taylor told me to drop the oil investigations and to concentrate on the Henslow matter, he better turn up something pretty soon or that new reporter, Carla Garza, is really going to get on our backs about no progress on these cases."

"It's just as well you can focus on Henslow's murder. I get the strange impression that our Sheriff is only mildly interested in the biggest case of the decade. Preoccupied."

"Well, he sure hasn't questioned anyone about it. He was at Tommy's meeting about Horst's will, but took off right afterwards with some vague explanation about following up a lead. But he didn't say what. Told me to talk to Jim Henslow. And when he got in this morning, I told him about Hank's confession. He's sitting in his office right now reading it over, probably wondering what to do. Maybe after you check out the JDL we'll have something more to go on."

"Hope so. I see Mr. Levy at ten this morning. I'll give you a call this afternoon. Maybe I'll have something from the Carpenter Group."

Dan hung up the phone and stared across the tiny office at the calendar over the copying machine. Although the events concerning the Henslows had come in rapid succession, Jack was right. They didn't add up to a coherent picture. So Severson pulled a trick with the tractor. But he wouldn't have come forward if that attack had been prelude to a murder he was planning. It was Horst's death that scared him into confessing to the sabotage. But it didn't make sense to think that Hank was harassing Jim Henslow. And Jim Henslow suspected that Art Rogers shot out his window and slashed the tires of his Lincoln. That made sense if Rogers had really made a threat to Henslow the day his brother was convicted. Maybe Art was involved in the shooting. But why would he want to kill Horst Henslow? And why was Jim Henslow now reluctant to have Rogers picked up for questioning? As Dan reviewed the case in his mind he realized that Jack Traid was right. He would just have to do the grunt work himself. The question right now was, what did Jim Henslow really know and where was he Saturday evening before the dinner at Andy's?

And what about Bickerson, he thought. Maybe he had to bear down on him, too. That man's sweet manner might be covering up a lot more than he's telling. It's possible he and Hank were involved in painting the swastika on the old man's house. Maybe the two of them thought they could scare Horst Henslow out of trying to run things at Pioneer Village. It was getting clear to Dan Morris that he hadn't begun to get to the meat of the investigation. Carla was calling it Hamilton's crime wave. And the Sheriff's Department was looking like dopes. He knew for certain that he had to confront Art Rogers on his own, despite Jim Henslow's hesitation, and despite Taylor's absorption in the oil spill leads.

The twenty-foot wide Aurora Bookstore was squeezed in between the Koffee Klach cafe on the right and Perfect Cleaners on the left. A signboard in the shape of an open book hung from a wrought-iron bracket over the doorway. Below the name of the store was the printed "New and Used Books—Jacob Levy, Prop."

Jack Traid stepped into the quiet of the shop, announced by the tinkling of a small bell attached to the top of the door. At ten in the morning no customers were in evidence. Along both walls were eight foot high, home-made and unfinished pine book shelves marked with hand printed cards tacked along the top: Politics, Science, Social Studies, Travel, New Age, Mystery, Poetry.

"Hello?" Jack called out.

From the rear of the store the sound of boxes being moved ceased and a male voice responded.

"Be a minute. Just look around."

Jack was next to the counter at the entrance. A vintage cash register sat to one side. On the sides of the counter were posted meeting notices: "Meditation Made Easy," announced one; one outdated poster sought to rally the people, "Protest Tree Cutting on Third Avenue, Mass Meeting September 1." He wondered if it had been a mass meeting. On the first set of shelves marked "Recent Releases" were novels, autobiographies, a well-known figure's essay on morality in America. Jack was thinking he wasn't keeping up with his reading when a tall, slender man in his sixties came forward from the back, walking briskly, smiling broadly.

"You must be the Mr. Traid who called me. Right on time."

They shook hands. Levy was relaxed, Jack observed, not appearing to be on guard or defensive. It was a good sign.

"Traid?" Levy began, "now what ethnic tribe came up with that?"

"Would you believe the Traidovsky clan. Once a part of your tribe."

"Ah. I stumbled onto it."

"Like so many, my grandfather shortened the name when he moved to Texas in 1904."

"You kosher, then?"

"Oh no. Long history before we get to me. Grandfather Vladamir escaped the Czar's pogroms, came to the State's and became Vernon Traid. Then he married his first love, a Texas girl of German descent. From there you can guess the permutations."

"So you don't go to temple?"

"No. And it's been years since I've been to the Unitarian church my parents loved."

"Ah-ha. One of those. Out on a limb!" Levy laughed, patted Jack's arm in friendship.

He was irresistible, Jack thought. All questions, interests.

"Now I get to ask questions," he said to Levy.

"Certainly. I can tell you my family was New Jersey. I talk New Jersey even now, after thirty years here in Minneapolis."

"I appreciate that, Mr. Levy. But I need your help about a matter in our little town in South Dakota."

"You said on the telephone. Someone doing mischief and using our principles."

"Yes. I finally figured that out, remembering a case in Dallas where a group from the League protested the desecration of a Jewish cemetery. I remembered 'barzel' from then."

"Yes. Iron. We don't have to shrink from the challenge. Steel in our backbones, okay?"

"I understand. What has happened in Hamilton appears to be a case of vandalism on the farm house of a man who was once a guard at a Nazi concentration camp."

"One of the animals, then."

"Well, in this case he was a kid of thirteen. Hitler Youth in the last few days of the war and made to guard Bergen-Belsen."

"That terrible place."

"After all these years that fact came out in our town's newspaper. The man, a Mr. Horst Henslow, said he was just thirteen, hadn't been there but a week and was taken prisoner by the British. That seems to check out considering his age. But Saturday evening Mr. Henslow was found dead, shot twice. Our coroner is calling it a homicide and we are awaiting the state medical examiner's autopsy report. But on Henslow's body was found a threatening letter scrawled on a copy, a photo copy I might stress, of the League's letterhead. The threat ended with the word 'hadar.'"

"Pride. Our dignity to protect, yes? Have we any less right to be proud of our painful history, or of our beliefs?"

"No. I certainly don't think so. But the question for us is, who did these things?"

"The League does not go after Nazis. We are not a Nazi-hunting group, much as that might be a pleasure. Most of us Jews have enough troubles without going out and making more for ourselves. We are what we say, a defense league. We stand up for Jews. And for the rights of others, too, to be free of persecution, I might add. We don't go after other people, not even a poor old man who it seems couldn't escape his past."

"There has to be someone in Hamilton, or somewhere in eastern South Dakota, who learned about Mr. Henslow from the paper, someone with connections to the League. Otherwise, why the explicit use of principles of the league? And that person must have had a letter from the League from which was made a photo copy to construct a threatening letter."

"Yes, I understand your logic."

"And I have been deputized by local South Dakota authorities to undertake an official investigation, if that isn't putting it too heavily."

"You said on the telephone."

"And the mailing list?"

"I refused to send a copy to you because we have a by-law provision saying we can't sell or give away the list of people who get our materials, members or non-members. There are ugly people out there who'd use it to get at individuals."

"But you might let me read through it to look for South Dakota addressees? I am only interested in South Dakota names right now."

"I talked to the other members of our board. We wish to cooperate. We won't make photo copies of any part of the list, but I'm allowed to let you look at that part with South Dakota zip codes. Make notes if you must."

"That will be very helpful, I think. And could I also have a copy of your letterhead which might have been copied by whoever sent the threatening letter?"

"No problem. Come on back here with me," Levy said, turning and leading him toward the back room. From a battered roll-top desk drawer he took a sheaf of paper, thumbed through the pages and handed Traid a single page.

"Our list of South Dakota addresses," he said.

The task was simple. The South Dakota zip code list was short, sixteen names.

"It is a short list," Levy said. "I know you are thinking we could have just as well mailed it and saved you a trip."

"Don't apologize Mr. Levy. I understand. And I had other business in the city."

"That is well, then."

The name popped out immediately as Jack focussed on the names. "J. Bickerson." The address was a rural route in Hamilton.

"Here it is," Jack said, pointing.

"So?"

"One of the men directly involved in what is happening is a Mr. Bickerson. A Mr. Jacob Bickerson."

"My name. Jacob."

"Yes. And as pleasant a man as you, too. This is a surprise."

Jack noted several names with Sioux Falls addresses. Two in Rapid City. He jotted down names, indicating SF or RC behind each, but he didn't believe he needed any more from the list. Bickerson. It could be that as chairman under pressure from the rest of the Pioneer Village board, and influenced by Severson's disdain for Horst Henslow, he helped harass the old man, despite Horst's promises of land for the Village. But murder? The scene he imagined in Horst Henslow's barn went out of focus. Bickerson and Severson stalking Henslow? How could he believe that there was such deadly competition for power over a make-believe village? He'd seen jealousy lead to murder. But control of an amateur, rural museum being motive enough for sabotage and murder? That was a new one, he thought.

"Is he a member of the League?"

Leavy took the list back and studied the numbers above Bickerson's name.

"No. He's not a member. After a year we'll write to him and ask if he wishes to become at least an associate member in order to continue getting our newsletter. If not, the name comes off the list. Membership is twenty dollars."

"So how long have you had his name on your list?"

Levy looked at the numbers again.

"According to the code we first put Mr. Bickerson on our list in April of this year."

"And what kind of correspondence would you have in your files from him?"

"Well, if he just requested general information I wouldn't have saved it. But let me check."

Next to his desk was a four-drawer file case. Levy opened the the top drawer and fingered through a file of papers.

"Nothing. Nothing from Mr. Bickerson in March or April. He must have just asked for information."

"You would have sent him a letter?"

"Sure. One of these form letters explaining how to become a member, asking for a contribution. And this brochure."

Jacob Levy handed him a printed brochure which was a single sheet folded twice to fit in a number ten envelop. It was printed in two colors. Not an expensive print job, Jack remarked to himself. Levy also handed him copy of the form letter which was printed on JDL letterhead. Jack reached out his left hand to take the brochure and letter and his right hand to shake Levy's hand.

"I appreciate your cooperation, Mr. Levy. I'm not sure what I just found out makes things any clearer, but it might just break things open at home."

"We're good citizens, too," Levy said.

"Yes. And you helped me a lot, even if I'm not attending temple," Jack said, smiling.

"Certainly. But I think you'll be okay."

"Is that a blessing, rabbi?"

"Maybe it is."

When Dan Morris went upstairs to the State's Attorney's office, Mary Pettigrew, Jim Henslow's secretary, informed him that her boss had not yet returned from the courtroom. Dan seated himself in an ancient maple arm chair opposite Mary. The little office was sterile, he thought, bereft of any personal touch except for a small framed photograph near the telephone on Ms. Pettigrew's desk.

"Who's the picture of?" he asked, breaking the silence.

"Oh. That? My neice. It was taken when she was confirmed. She's in college now at Augustana."

"Oh yes," Dan said. "Got a good reputation. The college I mean."

"Yes it has," Mary said emphatically.

There was silence again. Dan was about to introduce the subject of the changes in the weather when Jim Henslow pushed through the door.

"Sorry I'm late. You'd think we could dispose of a simple assault case in less than two hours. Come on in," he said to Dan, hurrying forward into his office. Over his shoulder he instructed Mary Pettigrew to hold all calls.

"We have lots to clear up, don't we Dan?"

Morris did not reply but quietly pulled the door closed after himself. Henslow sat down in his high-backed leather chair behind the desk, indicating to Dan to take another maple arm chair that had been permanent furniture of the office since the nineteen twenties.

Dan sat down and faced Henslow who was avoiding looking directly at him, seeming to stare out the high south windows at a bright southern sky.

"We need your help," Dan began. "The picture of what has been happening to the Henslows is pretty confusing."

"To understate the case, to be sure," Jim replied.

"What do you think has been going on at your father's place? Before the murder, for example."

"The steam leak that burned him?"

"Well, that for starters," Dan replied. Only Taylor, Traid and he knew of the Hank's confession. Jim Henslow didn't need to know that just yet.

"Probably a threat. Like the swastika painted on his house in the middle of the week. Must be someone from his past, from the looks of it."

"Just out of the blue? No warning, so far as anyone knows."

"I guess."

"But you told Carla Garza about Horst being a guard at a Nazi concentration camp. That got in the paper. Do you suppose someone was reacting to that? Ex-Nazi revealed?"

Jim Henslow straightened up, shifting in his chair. He was frowning.

"Well, I'll be damned if I know why anyone would react that way. I tried to make it seem that he'd overcome lots of obstacles in his life and made a success of farming."

"And Horst appreciated the story Garza did?"

"No. It was a mistake on my part. He hated having people talk about that time. Maybe there was something he wanted to cover up. At least I think so. He just hated getting publicity in the paper."

"You knew that but still told the Times about it?"

"Look, I guessed wrong. I knew he made excuses about being a kid when he was made a guard at the camp. Besides, it was just a casual comment to that reporter."

"Okay," Dan said. "So you think it could be someone from his past?"

"Maybe. But it might be that Rogers thought he could get even with me by working over Horst, too. You know, just another thing like shooting the window out of our house and then the next night cutting up all four of the tires on Sheri's Lincoln."

"You've been saying all along that you think it was Art Rogers who shot out your window and slashed the tires on your car. Mind telling me again why you think he would do that?"

"At first I didn't understand it. You know, I thought it was just his smart aleck remark when the Sheriff took Clarence away after he was found guilty of cattle stealing. Art came up behind me right at that moment and said 'Not too smart.' Something to that effect."

"Nothing more?"

"No. And I didn't react then. I wasn't quite sure what he meant. But I remembered it after our picture window was blasted. It was a threat, pure and simple."

"Why didn't you arrest Rogers?"

"There wasn't any real proof. And you found out the day after the window was shot out that he could arrange to get alibis by just asking his buddies out in that hell hole the Roundup."

"That's right. He did. But then the tires were punctured. And now your father has been murdered. Why shouldn't we pick up Rogers? Or at least question him. You and Taylor both seemed reluctant to act on that suspicion when we talked Sunday morning at White's funeral home."

Henslow straightened up and swiveled to his desk. With hands folded on the desk blotter. He looked directly at Dan.

"You're new on the block, Danny. Maybe with a little experience you'll understand that acting too quickly can spoil a case."

Dan let the put-down pass. Play along with him, Jack had advised.

"Sure. I respect your judgement in this, Jim. That's why I haven't been out to talk to Rogers yet. But he seems to be deeply involved somehow. It seems to me that your suspicions are right. Couldn't he have gone after your father as a way of getting at you?"

"Maybe. It's not too far fetched when you consider his reputation. But wait until you have some solid evidence pointing to him, then get him." Jim sat back in his chair, seeming to relax a moment.

Dan was about to tell him about the knife found in the barn but decided to wait until he had covered a few more points.

"Do you mind telling me about the couple of hours last Saturday before you got to Andy's," Dan asked, changing the subject abruptly. He watched for a reaction, adding, "Before you were late for the dinner you yourself arranged to have with the Johnsons and Petti-grews?"

"What about it?"

"For instance, where were you during the two hours from six to eight, that time just before you showed up for your dinner appointment?"

"Oh, I get it. I'm a suspect, too."

The expression on Henslow's face was intimidating, his eyes narrowing slightly, a flush coming into his face.

"That's putting it too strongly, Jim. It's just that I've got to get straight in my mind where everyone involved was during the time Horst was likely killed."

"A nice way to put it, but it doesn't change the fact that you think I could have killed the old man."

"According to Gloria Miller you had threatened Horst the day before. She said you were very angry when he ordered you off the place."

"Yes, I was. I threatened him with a law suit. What you don't understand, Danny, is that I was promised that farm. My mother, before she died, made that old bastard promise to deed the farm to me. He was only able to build it up because of the place Mother had from her first husband, my real father, in Pennsylvania. When she married Horst he was a penniless ex-Nazi. And if I can find anything she wrote down about that promise, I'm sure as hell going to challenge that phony will that bunch of farmers on the Village board talked him into, if not coerced him to sign. But I sure as hell didn't threaten to harm Horst. If that Miller woman said that, she's lying."

"No, she just said you were angry. It's an obvious detail to follow up on, don't you think?"

"I suppose, but I resent your coming in here and accusing me of murder before you and that lame-brained Taylor have any evidence in hand."

"I haven't accused you of anything. I'm trying to get the story straight, and you still haven't told me what you were doing for the two hours before you showed up at Andys."

"If you're about to arrest me, don't you think you ought to read me my Miranda rights?"

"I didn't come here to arrest you. We have no idea what happened out at the farm and are trying to put it together. Where you were for that very time seems important."

"Okay, if that's so, I was in Sioux Falls looking for my wife. We had a big row that morning and she took off for the city. I figured I could find her in the Empire Mall."

"So she can verify that you were with her at the mall during that time?"

"Well, no. I didn't find her. I looked all over, then hurried back to Andy's without going home when I realized I was going to be late for the dinner. I later found out she'd come home."

"No one saw you at the Mall. Someone who could…"

"No, goddamn it. If you think I killed the son of a bitch, arrest me. But you'll be goddamn sorry. Just remember who's the chief law enforcement officer around here."

"Whoa. I told you I didn't come here to arrest you. Just looking for information that might help us. For example, what do you make of the fact that I found a switch blade knife near where Horst's body was? It has the initials A.R. carved in the bone handle."

Jim Henslow did not speak for a minute. He stared at Dan, his lips tightening.

"A knife?" he asked finally.

"Yeah. Switch blade. With initials A.R. carved in the handle that suggest it might belong to Art Rogers."

"You found it near the body?"

"As I said. It was hidden under loose straw not far from where Horst lay," Dan replied, deciding not to explain exactly where the knife had been found in the stall.

"Hard to think how," Henslow started to say, then paused. "Seems pretty clear, doesn't it. If you can establish that it belongs to Art Rogers, then he has a little explaining to do."

Henslow's tone was conciliatory.

"I thought so too. That's why I'm going out to Chesterton and question Art Rogers this morning. It may be a little early to arrest him on suspicion of murder, but when we get the lab report on any prints found on the knife, that might help pin it down. And I'd like to go through his welding business and Clarence Rogers' place pretty thoroughly. I've asked Judge Nelson for a search warrant for both places. I'm supposed to stop and pick up the warrants this morning at the clerk's office."

"Sure. You planning on going out there today, then?"

"Soon as we're done here and I get the warrants. It would be real helpful, though, if you could remember having talked to someone in the mall Saturday late afternoon. What about your wife? Did you ever catch up to her?"

"No, actually. She got home from Sioux Falls in the afternoon and left for Aberdeen. She got a photo assignment from the *Argus*. We didn't see each other that evening."

"Well, maybe you'll remember seeing someone. Think about it and we can talk later."

"As you say, Danny. But looks like you better see what you can find out at the Rogers' places."

"We'll see," Dan said, getting up and walking to the door. He turned and looked across the room at the State's Attorney who sat leaning back into the soft leather of his new chair. "I'm sorry you think I'm still a kid, Jim. But let me tell you one thing for the record. Whoever killed your old man will pay for it and I'm going to find out who it was, chips fall where they may."

As he went out the door Dan glanced back to see if there was a reaction and saw Jim Henslow lean forward and reach for his telephone. In the hallway Dan stopped at the water fountain for a drink. He felt a weakness in his knees. The tension of the last half hour still had its grip on him.

"Now for Art Rogers," he said aloud to himself. He looked at his watch. Ten to twelve.

❖   ❖   ❖

Carla Garza made Sally Edwards nervous as she stood before her desk, the tone of her voice seeming to demand to see the sheriff. Sally couldn't remember ever meeting a Hispanic person face to face. There were only a few in the state. She'd heard from Dan Morris about how aggressive a reporter Garza was. If he had asked her opinion she would have said that those kinds of news reporters weren't needed in Chautauqua County to snoop into private matters.

"I wonder if I might see the sheriff?" Carla asked.

"I'll see. He's terribly busy." Sally said.

"Won't take but a minute," Carla said, feeling Sally's resistance. "It's for an article I'm doing for tomorrow's *Times*."

"Well, just a minute and let me ask."

Shirley got up from her desk and went to the closed door of the sheriff's office. She knocked softly and waited. He was talking on the telephone, his clear tenor voice penetrating the solid door.

"Come in," she heard him say.

Opening the door wide enough to put her head into the office Shirley spoke just louder than a whisper.

"That reporter's here?"

"What reporter?" Taylor asked, putting down the phone.

"That new girl from the *Times*."

"Oh, the Mexican. Sure. Send her in."

Carla had heard Taylor's "Mexican." It irritated her that the insensitive one's couldn't distinguish between her being native-born American of Hispanic origin or being a Mexican national. But that was another issue she could do nothing about today.

"Come on in, young lady," Taylor said as Carla appeared in his doorway. She wasn't skinny like so many of the young ones, Taylor noted. Fine body. Her bright yellow blouse was tight against shapely breasts. He admired her graceful manner of slipping past Sally and entering his office.

"I'm following up on the story about the oil spill south of town, sheriff. What have you found out about who did it?"

"Well it's nice of you ask. We are doing a thorough check on the transformer outfits in this part of the state. Seems like most of them keep pretty good records."

"Yes, I should think so. EPA regs require that, don't they?"

"Well, yes they do. But some of these small businesses have a tough time with all that federal regulation."

"Meaning what?"

Taylor shifted in his chair. She wasn't just a pretty woman, he thought. He had not asked Garza to sit. He looked up into her dark eyes trying to read her intent. She stared down at him, waiting for his answer. It was damned annoying, he thought, to have this young woman prodding him. She was going to be trouble.

"Meaning that we have a lot more probing to do."

"For tomorrow's paper then I can report that you have made no progress on the latest oil spill south of town?"

Was she trying to make this into an exposé, Taylor thought to himself.

"You might, but that wouldn't be the whole story. Truth is we have our leads and will make an arrest pretty soon. But that ain't for publication yet."

"I can write that you have definite leads, though?"

"Well, sure. There's progress but I can't get into details at this point in the investigation. Might scare off the suspect."

"But this is what, the third oil dumping in or near Chautauqua County this year, according to the *Times* records."

"'Bout right. Maybe they are connected. Maybe not. Lot's of different folks involved in hauling PCB oil from these transformer renovating outfits."

"But each of the companies is supposed to have records of how much oil is shipped and who contracted to take it to a disposal site, is that right?"

"Right. But sometimes the transformer boys get behind in their record-keeping and we have to prod them a bit."

Carla did not like the answer. Notebook in hand, she wrote something. In the pause Taylor began tapping his pencil on the desk.

"Anything else?" he asked.

"When do you expect to have something more on these oil shipment records?"

She didn't want to let him go with the vague answers, feeling he was hiding information behind his authority as the official investigator. He had given her nothing.

"Week or so. I'll let you know when we are ready to make an announcement."

"Seems to me that it has been months since the first oil dumping, and now with this one last week the public would expect that you would have something more definite."

Taylor stood and faced Garza. They were about the same height and he straightened himself. He was tired of this intimidation from a kid reporter.

"Well, I told you what I know for now. You'll have the name of the culprit when we pick him up."

She would not be dismissed, she thought.

"So you have someone in mind?"

"I didn't say that."

"But you did say 'him,' didn't you?"

"That's just a way of saying. Probably is a him, since there ain't many lady truck drivers here abouts."

He was beginning to act irritated, she thought. Better leave it at that.

"Thank you sheriff. I'd sure appreciate it if you'd let us know when you have something definite."

Carla smiled, her perfect white teeth gleaming. Charm the old fool, she thought to herself.

"Count on it," Taylor replied.

As Carla left the Sheriff's Department offices and walked up stairs into the first floor hallway of the courthouse, she found Deputy Dan Morris straightening up from having a drink at the water fountain. She walked over to him as he wiped his mouth with the back of his hand. She looked up at him, remarking in her mind the difference between his cranky boss and this trim, smiling deputy.

"How's the star reporter doing today?" Dan asked as she approached.

"Not very well, considering your boss is stonewalling."

"Really? On the Henslow case?"

"No. I tried to get a follow-up on the oil dumping and he didn't have a thing to tell me. What do you know?"

"Before I handed everything over to Taylor, I'd checked out all the transformer companies. All were pretty straight forward, but there were still some records at Acme over in Worthmore that needed checking. But Taylor's taken over the oil spill investigation. Told me to concentrate on the Henslow case."

"Wow. That's a story. Sheriff leaves murder case to deputy."

"Wait a minute, Carla. It isn't that cut and dried. He's still in charge."

"But he took over the oil spill case and told you to stay out of it?"

"That would be one way of putting it. He has the background on the earlier cases. I don't. So it makes sense."

"Well, to tell you the truth, it seems fishy to me that the Sheriff's Department can't report any progress at all on an environmental crime that has been repeated at least three times in the past year or so. You say there was more to find out about Acme?"

"Sure. But that doesn't necessarily mean anything. Rich Arnold who owns Acme has been out of town over the weekend, so I didn't get to him. I assume Taylor is following up on that."

"He didn't say. Okay. I'll expect the sheriff to make a report on Acme later in the week."

"Yeah, maybe he can."

"You don't think he's stalling, do you?"

"Arnold?"

"No. Your boss."

"What makes you think he would do that?"

"Well, in the first place, he just didn't like being interviewed by the press this morning and he didn't tell me a thing, not even the little bit you just told me about Acme. That kind of hold out is usually an indication of a bigger story. At some point the headline might well be 'Sheriff Stalls Investigation.'"

"Oh, don't make too much of Taylor's claming up on you. He's not used to dealing with female reporters with guts. And you're too beautiful for the job, in his old fashioned opinion."

Carla smiled.

"Don't try to soften me up, Danny. I'll nail both of you if you're holding out on me when there is something important to report."

"I have no doubt about it. In my opinion, if you want it but promise you won't tell him, keep the pressure on Taylor. It just might be healthy for the department."

"What about your investigation? What's the progress on Henslow's murder?"

"There's nothing more than you already know or that I told you this morning for your story for this afternoon's papers. Henslow found shot. Body in the barn. Shed torched. Threatening letter with another Hebrew word meaning 'pride.' That ties it in with the swastika painting on Horst's house last week. Jack Traid is helping us out by checking the Jewish Defense League in Minneapolis because those words are part of the principles of the League. He was deputized to investigate that. Giving us a hand. You knew he was a detective for years in Dallas."

"Yes. So I hear. Convenient for you guys and makes an interesting story."

"More than convenient. He's had experience with this kind of thing. But don't queer the deal by putting anything in the paper about his helping. At least not until it's all over. I promised him."

"Okay, for now. But you haven't a suspect yet, then?"

"Nope, but we have candidates."

"Want to tell me?"

"Well, off the record for now, okay?"

"Don't like off the record, Dan."

"Yeah. I understand. Let's just leave it that I'm going to follow up on a character that may be involved. I'll give you the details later when I have something solid."

It wasn't time to mention Art Rogers, and he didn't dare tell her about the knife found at the scene. Get that in the paper and it would generate speculations all over the place.

"I expect a call as soon as you are ready to move on the killer. Promise?"

"When we arrest someone, you will be among the first to know."

"I take that to mean I can't ride out with you when you are about to make an arrest," Carla said, grinning at Dan's playing cat and mouse.

"Sure would like to have you with me, Carla, but regulations say we can't do that. But I'll give you a call the first thing we lock someone up. Okay?"

"Have to settle for that, I guess. Well, work to do. See you later."

Dan watched as she walked toward the front entrance. My what a beautiful a woman, he thought to himself. It would be easy to forget Cynthia if he could take Carla in his arms. To hell with the fact she worked for his father, or that she was on Taylor's rear end. They had to have a date one of these days soon.

Dan went to the broad staircase near the entrance and climbed to the second floor where the Clerk of Courts office was located next to the court room. Inside two women worked at metal desks behind a high counter. The younger of the two got up and came to the counter where he waited.

"Judge Nelson said he'd have a couple of search warrants ready for me this morning," Dan explained.

"Oh. Yes. The Judge asks for you to go into chambers. He'd like to talk to you about that."

"Okay. Fine," Dan replied, as he was shown past the counter and to the door into the judge's office.

Judge Irving Nelson was a tall, slightly overweight Scandinavian in his early sixties. White hair thinly covered a ruddy bald head. A bushy, white mustache was compensation for the loss of hair. He was smiling welcome.

"Come in Danny," Nelson said, beckoning him to a chair. "I thought I owed you an explanation about those search warrants. Seems I'm getting caught up between two investigations—sheriff's department and the State's Attorney."

"How's that, judge?"

"Well, Jim Henslow just called me and said it was very important to his investigation of his father's death, that you not go out to the Rogers's places just now. What about that?"

"Did he give you any reason?"

"Jim said he didn't want to alert Art Rogers that he was under suspicion until he cleared up a detail in his investigation. Asked me to delay the warrants for a day. That a big problem with you?"

"Well, sir, I guess it wouldn't make much difference if it did. Our State's Attorney seems to think I'm not capable of conducting an investigation."

"Oh, now. I wouldn't be too hard on Jim. He's a hard driver you know. Has a good record of convictions, so he's a bit protective of his record because he's looking for higher public office some day."

"I have evidence, Judge, that points directly to Art Rogers. He ought to be arrested and brought in today."

"Well, I'm going to ask you to wait until tomorrow. In deference to the State's Attorney's investigation. But I'll have the warrants ready for you first thing in the morning."

As Dan Morris descended the stairs to the first floor, and then to the basement and his office in the Sheriff's Department, he tried hard to suppress the anger he felt. What was Henslow's game? Just to skewer him because he asked too many questions? Jim Henslow had a lot more questions to answer, sooner or later.

CHAPTER 13

I t was two minutes to five when the phone rang on Sally Edwards's desk. She was about to leave for the day, turning over dispatcher duties to the part-timer, Elmer Sonderson, retired city cop who liked to keep his hand in, as he put it.

"Sheriff's department," she said wearily.

It was Jack Traid asking for Dan Morris.

"Danny's not in just now. Let me give you the sheriff," she said before Jack could comment. "It's Mr. Triad on the phone, sheriff," she called toward the open door to Taylor's office.

"Okay. I got it," came his answer. "Traid. What did you find out at that Jew outfit?"

"It's called the Jewish Defense League, sheriff," Traid replied, making no attempt to hide his irritation with Taylor's tone. "Mr. Levy of the JDL was cooperative. Very helpful. He let me look at the mailing list for South Dakota and gave me other information." Traid wished he were talking to Dan Morris. There was caution to be taken in what he had found out and Taylor was not a cautious man.

"Well, what the hell did you find out," Taylor asked, irritated that the call was coming late in the day and that he might be late for supper.

"There is one name on the list that is important to you. J. Bickerson."

"What was that again?" Taylor asked, sitting up in his chair.

"J. Bickerson. Hamilton rural route for an address where the JDL material is mailed."

"No kidding. So that's it. Jake must have been in on the tractor deal with Hank, then. Scare the hell out of old Henslow to get him out of the Village. Then they got together to paint up the old man's house to harass him all the more. Then the fire. But they got caught and shot Horst."

"Wait a second, sheriff. That's putting a big load on finding one name."

"Maybe. Maybe not. This ain't a big city deal, you know. We got two guys out to Pioneer Village trying to get that ex-Nazi off their backs. So they try to scare the shit out of him. But they get in trouble when he catches them hiding in the barn before the fire."

"I wouldn't go that far just yet, sheriff. Maybe there were two or three different things going on out there. What about the knife Dan found? A.R. initials. Not likely belonging to either Severson or Bickerson."

"Maybe not connected at all so far as we know. But I can see the motives those two had clear as day. Hank hates Henslow's ass because of the war and his being in the Hitler Youth. Had experience with them when he was overseas. Bickerson hates Horst because he's a Nazi. And not only that, but the old man was trying to take over their precious Pioneer Village. Plenty of motive. Plenty of chances to get at him."

As Taylor was talking Dan Morris came into the doorway of his office. Sally had told him the sheriff was talking to Traid. Dan waited, listening to Taylor's side of the conversation. Taylor was listening to Jack advise caution, for them to do some more questioning before any arrests were made.

"Sure," Taylor said, "and the *Times* is going to be on our rears for not getting any progress on a murder. When you get back you can give us a complete report. Look, Danny just came in. I'll have him get on the other phone with us."

Taylor nodded to Dan to pick up the phone on Sally's desk.

"Dan," Traid said in greeting. "I just told the sheriff I found J. Bickerson's name on the mailing list. But there is one more thing I found out this afternoon that makes me think you ought to be cautious about jumping to conclusions because of Bickerson's name being on a mailing list. It took me an hour and half wait but I finally got to talk to Herb Stover, head of the Carpenter Group, and his development guy, Mark Peterson. You'll be interested to know that they think the Chautauqua Development project is about to begin. Site work is scheduled to start in a few weeks from now, before freeze up. Jim Henslow gave them a copy of a trust agreement with Horst Henslow's signature on it giving him complete authority to deal with Horst's property."

"What was that?" Dan asked. "Signed? Horst's signature?"

"Sure is. I have a photo copy I'll bring back with me tomorrow. That's why I think you ought to let the information about Bickerson stew awhile. Question both those guys separately once again before either knows what we have. But you sure better find out from Jim Henslow and Tommy Johnson why Horst would sign over the farm to Jim at about the same time he's making a will that gives it to the Pioneer Village. Date on the trust agreement is August 30. Something is wrong, for sure."

"Maybe so," Taylor interjected. "We'll go through that when you get back with the document. Tomorrow?"

"Yeah. Late afternoon. I've decided to stay over one more night. No cost to the county. I'll be with a friend."

Neither Taylor or Morris thought about who that might be. The big news was that Traid had made progress. The Henslow case was beginning to break open. They hung up. Dan walked into Taylor's office.

"Well, that's it, then," Taylor exclaimed. "We'll bring Severson and Bickerson in on the charge of murder and…"

"Wait a minute. Like Jack said, we better question Jim Henslow and Tommy Thompson before we go off half cocked." Dan regretted the expression when he saw Taylor's face turn red.

"Look, Danny. Now's our chance to break this thing open. It's obvious as the nose on your face that those two guys were trying to get Henslow. They hated his guts, as almost everyone out at the Village did. And their tricks just went too far. For christsake we have Hank's confession."

"What about the knife I found? AR. Art Rogers needs to answer some questions about that. That is if Jim Henslow will quit protecting him."

"That ain't no proof either. What motive has Rogers got? He was harassing Jim Henslow because of his brother Clarence being sent to prison. I don't believe he got anywhere near Horst Henslow's farm. Hank and Jake are the one's that had motive, means and opportunity. And Hank's admitted fixing the tractor."

"For a prank. But what about the other evidence. Besides the knife, there is the fact that Gloria Miller winged whoever set the fire. Neither Hank nor Jake showed any wound at Johnson's meeting."

"Well, just maybe she didn't hit anyone. We don't know that for sure. But we know Hank fixed the tractor. For God's sake, forget the knife and whatever that broad claims. We better act now."

Taylor sat straight up, holding the edge of his desk. He had made his decision.

"You go out and bring Hank in here. If we aren't going to arrest them, we're at least going to grill these guys about last Saturday night. But make an arrest if he won't come in voluntarily for questioning. I'm going out to get Jake. Those two guys have some explaining to do."

"I don't think…" Dan began.

"Don't!" Taylor snapped back. "Just do like I say."

Taylor got up from his desk, strapped on his thirty-eight caliber service pistol and put on his western cattleman's hat.

"This is more like it," Dan heard Sheriff Taylor say as he led the way out the door of the department. Each got into his own cruiser and left the courthouse parking lot.

Sheri Henslow was still wearing tight-fitting Levis, hiking shoes, and her World War II bomber pilot jacket when she strode through the newsroom into Derrick Holmes's office to deliver six rolls of film. It was pleasing to her that both men and women reporters at their computers looked up as she went to Holmes office door. She had kept herself trim, she thought, and the office was noticing. She knocked on the frame of the open door. Derrick looked up from his desk, smiled, looking her over. Remembering the pleasure, she thought, as she stood straighter, shoulders back.

"How'd it go?" Derrick asked, waving her into the office as he watched her movements.

"Aberdeen was a snap. I was all over that scene. And you'll like what I got," she said, nodding toward the undeveloped rolls of film she held out for him.

"Terrific. And you'll be glad to know that I got another assignment for you, Sheri," Derrick said as she handed him the film. "Another demonstration due day after tomorrow in Pierre. Quieter deal. There will be a couple hundred rural electric folks out there to oppose a bill being considered by a special meeting of a senate committee that would change the territorial laws. Think you can get out there and get me some local color?"

"Sure. That's just great Derrick."

"This assignment will likely be a bit calmer than Aberdeen. Get in touch with Don Fogel when you get there tomorrow. You'll find him in the press office in the capitol building. You remember him. Been reporting for us for years. He's our guy out there during legislative sessions. Incidentally, the name of the person running the state Rural Electric Association is Rodney Chambers. He'll be eager to give you information, like who the major players are in his outfit. Be sure to get their pictures. I also need some crowd shots, serious faces, any kind of confrontation you can catch. You know, one of those old farmer directors button-holing a legislator, especially some young first termer."

"Gotcha," Sheri said. "And Derrick, you're a life-saver. These assignments are just what I needed. It feels great to get behind my cameras again, to make pictures that mean something."

"Wonderful. Give me a call when you get to Pierre. Incidentally, pay will be the same as for Aberdeen and if this works out okay, old man Alfson said you get steady assignments. He remembers the prison riot story."

Sheri stepped forward, put her arms around Derrick, pressed her breasts tight against his chest and kissed him on the cheek.

"Tell Alfson I love him. And I like you too Derrick. You're a prince, really."

She left the *Argus Leader* knowing she was a free woman. Whatever Jim's reaction might be to her going to Aberdeen, the photo assignments had made her life exciting, finally giving it some meaning. Her life in Hamilton was revised from this moment on, she thought. Jim had to understand that.

It was six o'clock when she checked into the Holiday Inn and phoned home. Jim answered after one ring.

"Where'n hell are you?" he demanded.

"I'm in Sioux Falls. I just got back from Aberdeen a couple hours ago and handed in my pictures."

"I've been waiting all afternoon to hear from you. When are you getting home?"

"I won't be home tonight. I've got another assignment. In Pierre. Gotta go out tomorrow for a day or two."

"You and that chief of creeps, Derrick?"

"Don't you worry about Derrick, Jim. He's giving me a chance to get back into my photography. And he isn't in this motel room with me, if that's what you're thinking."

"But we need to talk. Things are getting all screwed up here about the old man's murder."

"What's wrong? You sound like you're about to have a heart attack."

Jim cleared his throat, fighting back the tension.

"Danny Morris told me he found Art Roger' knife in the barn near Horst's body. How in hell did it get there from my dresser drawer?"

"What?"

"The knife, goddamn it. I brought it home and put it in my dresser drawer the night Rogers fixed our tires. But now it shows up at the murder scene."

"Rogers knew you had it, didn't he."

"Sure. It was stuck in the tire when I surprised him and he ran. I figured I'd use it as evidence if I decided to have him arrested. That was before I figured he'd be helpful in scaring the old man off the farm."

"Well, figure it out for yourself, Jim. Rogers knew you had the knife and broke into our house when we were both gone. He knew what you would do with it. That makes sense, doesn't it?"

"There was no evidence of a break in."

"Better report it to the police, anyway. Cover your ass."

"What the hell you talking about?"

"Who's the number one suspect, honey, if it isn't Rogers? It's going to be you. Tell the police you got home and found the back door wide open. Something like that. Say you suspect Rogers because of all that other stuff."

"Forget it, Sheri. Things are more screwed up than that. Dan Morris wanted to go out to arrest Rogers today but I warned him."

"Morris?"

"No, Rogers. I got Judge Nelson to delay giving Morris search warrants until tomorrow. Then I called Rogers and told him Morris would be on the way out to get him tomorrow. Told him to get off Clarence's place and hide out in the old man's house until we can get him out of state. The sheriff will never think to look for him there."

"Aren't you the smart one," Sheri said, laughing.

"If they find Rogers and he talks it's going to be all over for me. And now he's demanding money if he's going to make a run for it. Says he wants two thousand bucks. But I'm not sure he will run. He's blackmailing me. I told you he's got a recording of my making a deal with him about the fire."

"Well, pay him off. You got that much in savings, haven't you? If he doesn't leave town, you can deal with that later. But if he runs, he looks all the more guilty."

She made it seem easy. Except there was only a thousand left in the savings account. And all the credit card balances hadn't been paid.

"Sure, I can see that it would look that way. But he's still got the tape of my telling him to set the fire. And he gave a copy of it to his brother in the pen. And that goddamn knife probably has my finger prints on it. The sheriff will want to know why I didn't turn it in that night."

"Well, honey. I wish I could help you, but you'll just have to deal with it alone. Remember, Art Rogers must have murdered your old man. Horst caught him hiding in the barn and Rogers had to kill him before he set the fire. You don't have to tell anyone you sent him out there to do that. That was after he burglarized our place. If it helps, I'll tell the police that I probably left the back door unlocked when I was in a hurry getting ready to leave for Aberdeen. But right now I need to get some rest. I've got to start out for Pierre early tomorrow morning. Bye, honey."

She hung up. It was, Jim thought, as if Horst's murder had already been solved in her mind. He was dazed by Sheri's recitation of the story of Art's involvement. It was as if she knew his every move. Maybe she was right about Art. But Rogers better not be free to tell everything he knows. As Jim tried to think how that could be prevented, the telephone rang again.

"Taylor here, Jim. You better come down here to the courthouse. I picked up Hank Severson and Jake Bickerson for questioning and I'm about to put them under arrest for the murder of your dad."

"What's that? Hank and Jake?"

"Right. I sent Jack Traid to Minneapolis to find out about that Jew outfit and how it might be connected with the swastikas and all that on Horst's farm. He finds Bickerson's name on the mailing list. And," Taylor emphasized 'and,' "we have Hank Severson's confession to sabotaging Horst's tractor. Clear-cut conspiracy in my book. I'm going to find out if killing Horst was an accident or deliberate. I think you could help me if you got down here pretty quick. These two guys are mad as hornets."

As he hurried to his car in the garage Jim Henslow began to feel himself relax. He didn't have to set up Rogers just yet and expose his role in the fire. Not right away. The gift of diversion had been delivered by the good Sheriff Taylor. It would make sense to Taylor that the whole deal had to do with Pioneer Village politics. Horst was buying the Village out, taking over completely and Jake and Hank hated his guts for moving in on their creation. And who knows, if necessary, one might sell the idea that they got the Village blacksmith Art Rogers to help them. It was a line of investigation the States Attorney's office should open up on its own regardless of what Sheriff Taylor thought. It just might be believable that the Village board harassed the old man into putting them in his will. Long shots, he thought as he backed the Explorer into the street, are better than none at all.

❧   ❧   ❧

Carla Garza decided to investigate a bit deeper on her own when she realized that Tuesday's issue of the *Times* and her story on the oil dumping had been relegated to page three because it contained little that was new. But her write-up of Horst Henslow's murder was the headline story. A four column wide picture of the fire on the Henslow farm was displayed under the eight column headline: CORONOR SAYS HOMICIDE. The subhead read: Threats End in Murder of Local Man.

Related in her by-lined story were the facts that she and Elliot Morris had gleaned that night and on Labor Day. Henslow's body was found by firefighters checking out the barn next to the blazing shed. Coroner White said it was an obvious homicide. Henslow had been shot twice from close up. The fire was an obvious arson, according to Sheriff's Deputy Dan Morris. Gas cans deliberately left at the scene had swastikas painted on them. A picture Elliot Morris had taken that night of Mike Wilkins holding up the two cans was printed at the bottom of the page. Reviewed was the incident of a swastika being painted on Henslow's house the past Wednesday night. The Sheriff's office was connecting that incident to the threatening letter found on Henslow's body because of the Hebrew words "barzel" and "hadar." The article explained their meaning and connection with the Jewish Defense League. The state medical officer had been contacted to come to Hamilton to conduct an autopsy. The South Dakota Crime Lab in Pierre was evaluating other evidence which had been collected, according to the sheriff's office.

It was a sensational story to cover, Carla thought, folding the paper and putting it in her personal file in her desk. It would become part of a résumé she would someday present to a big city newspaper editor. But the oil dumping story troubled her. There was more to it than she was finding out from Sheriff Taylor. She'd driven over to Acme to interview Rich Arnold about his transformer operation after talking to Taylor, but Arnold refused to be interviewed. His secretary told Carla that she could report that Acme Transformers followed all state and federal laws governing the disposal of PCB oil taken from old transformers. That was all she needed to know, he had told his secretary to say. But it wasn't, of course.

She had known that there might have been no way to get past Arnold's secretary but by then she knew being sweet to this guardian of the big executive was likely to be more successful.

"I understand," Carla said as she made as if to leave. "This is a pretty big operation. Must mean lots of reports you have to prepare." She affected a sympathetic tone.

"You can say that again."

"Well, I don't envy you. There must be a whole bunch of different guys coming in here to haul oil. Lot's of reports to prepare about their deliveries?"

"Almost every day. Yeah. Number of different guys."

"Care to give me a name or two?"

"Oh, I couldn't do that." She got defensive. "Mr. Arnold wouldn't want me to give out any such information. You can ask Sheriff Taylor though. He's over here getting information pretty regular. He and Mr. Arnold are friends from way back."

And that had been the tip. "Pretty regular" and "friends" might mean more than a routine investigation by the Sheriff's Department. Taylor was holding out and there had to be a reason. It was after the visit to Acme she decided to drive out to the Taylor farm, a five-acre place where there was room for the sheriff to keep his horses. It had once been a homestead before most of the land had been sold to a corporate farming operation. The original house had been burned to the ground years after it was abandoned. Two barns remained. The land was sold to Taylor as a hobby farm six years ago. The realtor who had made the sale confirmed that for Carla.

It was at dusk Tuesday night that she sat in her Camaro on the side road opposite the Taylor place, surveying the buildings. The house was a new double-wide mobile home which had been placed back from the road about thirty yards. To the right of the house were two shed-roofed barns, one with an exercise yard fenced around it for horses, three of which she could see in the half light. Beyond the horse barn was another smaller barn, not much more than a shed. Probably used to store equipment, she thought to herself. Lights were on in the house and she could see someone moving about inside. Mrs. Taylor.

She got out of her car and crossed the road, flashlight in hand. The thirty-five millimeter Leica hung from its strap about her neck. She steadied it as she walked. The three-strand barbed wire fence was loose and easy to get over. As she approached the corral slowly, one of the horses snorted and all three began to move nervously in the compound. Carla stopped and watched the house. The sound of the horses had not been loud. She moved around behind the horse barn into the dark shadows. In the ten feet of space between the two barns were stacked square bales of hay. She moved through the alley way between piles until she came to the corner of the second barn. In the diffused light from the house she could see that the door to the barn was padlocked. No way in there. Back between the barns she saw the window that was six feet off the ground. Pulling three bales up against the shed, two below and one on top of them, she was able to step up and reach the window. She pushed it up eight inches. Looking toward the quiet house she took her chance and pointed the flashlight through the window.

There they were. Six fifty-five gallon barrels. The PCB labels were clearly visible. With the camera on the window sill, its lens well inside, Carla guessed at the angle it had to be pointed to get the picture. The flash in the dark barn startled her. It was an explosion of light. Quickly she lowered the window sash, dropped to the ground and pulled the bales away from the side of the barn. She moved quickly along the back of the horse barn, going straight for the barbed wire fence. Looking over her right sholder she could see the front door of the house open and a woman stand in the light momentarily. Then the house was quiet again, the soft yellow light spilling out onto the bushes and lawn before it.

Safely in her car Carla took the camera strap from around her neck and lay the camera on the seat next to her. She wondered if she had been seen, or her car. But she had the picture, she said to herself in triumph. Sure, she thought, Taylor was a frequent visitor to Acme. He'd have to explain why he was illegally storing PCB oil in his barn. That is, when the story broke in the *Times.*

❧   ❧   ❧

When he finished his call to Jim Henslow, Sheriff Taylor came out of his office into the reception room where Hank Severson sat fuming, his face red with anger. Jake Bickerson sat in the next chair, hands folded in his lap, waiting. Dan Morris sat at Sally's desk, looking down at the blotter in an attempt to avoid Hank's eyes.

"Betrayed me, you did," Hank was saying to Dan. "I volunteered information to help you out and now you guys are blowing it way out of proportion."

"Cool it, Hank," Taylor said. "I've asked Jim Henslow to come down here to help us determine what we're going to do. As far as I'm concerned, you two had every reason to harass Horst and your little trick turned bad. Now tell me. Ain't that the way it happened?"

"No goddamn way did we kill Horst," Hank growled.

"You two went out to his place the Wednesday before and painted a swastika on his house to scare hell out of him. And when that didn't work you figured you'd do a little barn burning. Escalate it a bit and really get him scared. Sent him a threatening letter. Make him think some Nazi-hunting outfit is out to get him. But he caught you in the barn. He had his shot gun with him, so you had to shoot him first."

Dan wanted to leave the office. It was a terrible exaggeration that Taylor was playing with. He wasn't connecting it to the two close-up shots to Horst's back and head.

"Maybe you could tell us where each of you were Saturday evening," Dan said, trying to keep his voice calm in order to dampen the charged atmosphere in the office. He was keeping notes as best he could as the interview continued.

Hank did not respond. He was sitting upright, hands on his knees and staring at Dan without blinking.

"I was home with Mrs. Bickerson," Jake replied. "She told you that, Sheriff, when you came out for me."

"Of course she would," Taylor said.

"We usually eat late on Saturday," Jake continued. "It's our Sabbath, you know, and when we get back from Sioux Falls after going to temple, and doing a little shopping in the afternoon, it is late."

"You went to Sioux Falls Saturday?" Dan asked.

"Yes. Rachel and me and the two children. Same as always."

"So the whole family can testify where you…"

Taylor interrupted Dan's query.

"That can come out in a trial. He could easily have coached his entire family to say they were together all Saturday night. Being in Sioux Falls most of the day doesn't change the fact that when he got back he could have got out to the Henslow farm with Hank about seven o'clock or so, and gotten back before anyone saw him in town."

"You're an idiot," Hank exploded. "He's got his whole goddamn family to back him up. What in hell do you think you can prove about Jake in a trial?"

"Well, what about you, then?" Taylor shot back.

"What about me?"

"Where were you Saturday about seven o'clock?"

"I was coming home from a VFW state executive committee meeting."

"What time was that?"

"Well, we had a dinner, five to about six thirty after our meeting. Any of the committee can testify I was there."

"But on the way home you stopped off at the Henslow farm to work over Horst a little more."

"I went home. Got home at eight."

"Were you alone, Hank?" Dan broke in. "On the way back from Sioux Falls?"

"Yeah. Sure I was. And I went the back roads to my place and didn't get anywhere near Highway Forty-three. My wife can tell you what time I got home."

Dan pictured the route through Renner that Hank would have taken to his farm south east of Hamilton. It would have been miles out of his way to go to the Henslow farm.

Taylor was about to ask another question when Jim Henslow came down the stairway into the basement office. Jim was thinking to himself that the fates had decided he needed a favor. He couldn't help but smile as he walked into the charged atmosphere of the Department's outer office. The enraged Hank Severson and the docile Bickerson were giving dimensions to the break he needed. Taylor's going off half-cocked was the gift of fate that would buy him time to get Rogers out of the county. In his own mind he was convinced that Art had got some female friend of his to call the Miller woman to clear the way for setting the fire early. Horst came into the barn where Art was hiding before setting the fire. So Art had to kill him. That was the story that included the evidence of the knife with Art Rogers' initials. But tonight it was a different, a more convenient story. After calming this crew, he had to remember to report to Taylor and then the city police about the break-in at his house and how it probably had been Art Rogers who had retrieved the knife he had left stuck in the tire at Andy's restaurant. Now that Art was in hiding, they could all go looking for him.

"Well, what a fine gathering we have here," Jim said, his tone cheery. He was met with stolid looks from all four men.

"We got a little deal here, Jim," Taylor started. "Hank has confessed to sabotaging your dad's tractor, and it turns out that Jack Traid has found out that Bickerson here has been involved with some Jewish outfit out of Minneapolis and..."

"One minute, sheriff," Jake interrupted. "You say I've been involved in what?"

"We know now that you are connected with the Jewish Defense League, Jake. That's where those Hebrew words came from. You have to admit you've been getting their mail at your place."

"We get all kinds of mail. Newsletter from the Sioux Falls temple. Maybe from the League, I suppose. I don't pay too much attention to those things."

"Well, now," Jim Henlsow interrupted, attempting to calm the questioning. "We can check that out, Jake. In the meantime, sheriff, I think we ought to just take down any statements these gentlemen might like to make and send them on home."

"Not arrest them?" Taylor exploded.

"No. I don't think its time for that," Jim replied coolly. "My office is conducting some investigations of its own, you realize, and I think it might be a little premature to jail these gentlemen just yet."

"I hope to hell you're not as crazy as Taylor, here," Hank spit out.

Taylor stiffened at the affront.

"Don't get too relaxed, Hank," Jim said sternly. "I have a theory about what you fellows on the Pioneer Village Board were up to about my Dad's farm."

Jim spoke in the tone usually reserved for a judge and jury.

"You'll hear from me later. But right now I think we can send these fellas home to think about how serious this situation is."

"Jesus!" Hank exclaimed, shaking his head from side to side.

Dan watched Henslow carefully. He was a cool one, now. Unexcited, resolved. Totally different than the reaction he'd gotten when he interviewed him in his office. None of the defensiveness tonight.

"Go ahead and arrest us, goddam it," Hank spit out. "You'll regret it for the rest of your life, Taylor. I come to you Monday on my own, ready to tell you what I did. But you were too damned busy to talk to me so I gave my statement about the tractor to Dan, here. And now you're distorting that into a charge of murder. So arrest me and you'll end up in court on a false…"

"Now, Hank," Henslow said calmly. "No one is going to arrest you. But it is my opinion that you two fellows had been putting pressure on my father for some reason or another. You wanted him to do something or other. Get off the board, maybe, unless he did a deal about the farm? But this isn't the time or place to get into that right now. So, for the time being let's just say for the record here that the sheriff has asked you to come in voluntarily to give us some helpful information."

"Sure doesn't seem like that," Hank shot back.

"Dan tells me that there is an important piece of evidence that hasn't been mentioned here," Henslow continued, ignoring Hank's remark. "A knife that was found at the scene. That right, Dan?"

"That's right. Has the initials A.R. clearly carved into the bone handle."

"And you found it in the barn?"

"Right," Dan replied. "It was near to where we found Horst's body," he explained, deciding not to be too specific about finding it in the stall. Let that come out later. No use giving Henslow any more information for his investigation than was necessary. "It had been covered with fresh straw," he went on. "Deliberately covered, I'd say, the way the straw was bunched up over it."

"So that leads me to tell you, Sheriff, that I had that knife from the night that our tires were all punctured. It was left sticking in one of the tires. Maybe as a threat to us, as dumb as that might seem. So, I took it home. I was going to confront Art Rogers with it at the right time because of the veiled threat he made to me the day his brother was sentenced. But I never got the chance. Saturday afternoon when I went to Sioux Falls to be with my wife Sheri who was shopping at the Empire Mall, our house was broken into. The back door was wide open when I got home that night. The knife was gone. Art knew I had the knife, knew he left it in the tire that night. I'm sure he broke into our place and got it before he went out to burn down dad's shed in retaliation for my sending Clarence Rogers up for stealing cattle."

"Fine time to tell me," Taylor grumbled. Dan made a note as the men talked.

"Sorry. It was a mistake not to let you know right away. And Dan, I should have told you when we had our talk. But I didn't know it was missing until you said you had it. That's why I asked Judge Nelson to hold up on the warrants. I went right home and saw that the knife wasn't in the drawer where I put it. You can guess how surprised I was. I figured I had some more business with Rogers. But no one answered the phone at either place when I called Chesterton."

Dan listened to the story, the one he was sure Jim Henslow was making up.

"If you want a statement," Jake Bickerson said wearily, "I will be glad to make one about the what time we got home from Sioux Falls, when we had our supper, how my daughter Sarah and son Jonah were doing homework and so on."

"You heard what I had to say," Hank said, still angry. "And if you ain't going to arrest me, I'm getting the hell out of here." He stood up and hiked up on his western belt with its large metal buckle. Taylor looked confused.

"Okay," Taylor said. "We'll leave it like that, then, since the States Attorney thinks that's best. But you two better stick around. And you Hank, are going to have to answer to messing with Horst's tractor."

"Said I would. Owned up to it without your help, by god."

Dan stood.

"I'll take you fellows back to your places."

Bickerson stood and followed Hank out the door and up the stairs. Dan paused at the doorway, turning to Henslow.

"I need to talk to you again first thing tomorrow Jim, before I go out to arrest Rogers," he said.

"Sure thing. What about?"

"About the trust agreement your dad signed giving you power over his farm. Appears he signed it about the same time as he signed his will."

With that he climbed the stairway into the cool September night. Two angry farmers waited for him at his cruiser. He felt like a traitor. He thought to himself that he wasn't becoming much of an investigator. But he had left Jim Henslow with something to think about overnight. If the Sheriff's Department didn't get a break soon, Carla Garza was going to have a great time picking this fiasco apart.

CHAPTER 14

$\mathcal{M}$ ildred was dressed and ready for her Wednesday classes.

"Monday, Wednesday, Friday's its the eight o'clock 'Introduction to Western Art,'" she said coming back into the bedroom. She knelt on the edge of the bed and leaned over Jack who was not yet fully awake. The smell the coffee being brewed had begun to rouse him from the labors of deep dreaming, an interminable trek across war-torn wastes where horizons disintegrated into dark mists. He had been aware of her moving about in the kitchen. He now opened his eyes wide as she loomed over him. She kissed his forehead.

"There, old lover, for everything."

"You have to leave?"

"Eight o'clock class," she replied brightly.

"You were lovely last night."

"And you! My, a man starved for the best thing in life."

"About which you are most artful."

"Stop it. We are beginning to sound like an advertisement for vita-mins. Don't forget. We're having lunch before you leave. The address of the restaurant is on the frig. Eleven-thirty. Okay?"

"Okay. I'll just make a few calls from here and I'll be there before you."

He reached up and pulled her down upon him, kissing her on freshly made-up lips.

"Oh, dear," Mildred said, pushing away, getting up and standing next to the bed. "I just loved that. But don't you know you're not suppose to muss a lady after she's all painted up for the world?"

"Sorry. I couldn't help it. It was just something you said last night."

"About that wonderful member you displayed so proudly?"

"Yeah! No. Afterward, when you were running your fingers along the scar on the back of my arm and shoulder. You said that I had scars that had healed and scars that weren't yet healed."

"Yes, I did say that. I believe it to be true, Mr. Traid."

"And you are right. And you know too that festering sores cause senseless distractions, and lead to one making poor judgments. Maybe seek easy answers. You said that too."

"Yes I did. And I meant it, too. But I didn't mean to hurt your feelings."

"You didn't. I was finally listening as well as just hearing. I lay there afterward as you were sleeping and thought about all the years I had accused myself of Alice's death. For years I've felt guilty about our marriage, how lousy it was for her. For years before you and I met, I figured that women and permanence were not a mixture I could manage. Then I began to think I was responsible for your leaving Hamilton, because I failed to tell you that I loved you. I hadn't even tried to know my own mind. I hadn't focussed on the pain you had gone through with your divorce and losing Amy. I could have tried to understand you better and how those things affected our relationship. But I was all self-pity, turned in. All ego."

"Don't be too hard on yourself, Jack. I didn't make it easy for you. Oh, those cozy afternoons making love in my little apartment were thrilling. We were playing hooky from the campus. Remember? We called it 'hooky nooky.' You gave me reason to live again. You might not have known it, but you did. I should have been fairer about why I had to leave."

"Hamilton was too small."

"Only partly right. I was afraid we were getting serious before either of us was ready for a long-term commitment. Me as well as you. Cheez. I was forty-three. You had turned fifty and were fleeing from your past. It scared me, like it was 'last chance for a life, last chance for love,' and you didn't seem ready. And I was afraid to face it. No. I wanted to face it but I was afraid I'd screw up our wonderful world of escape from both our pasts."

"Don't blame yourself, Mildred. Look, we both just turned twenty last night. There is a whole different life ahead of us if we just want to make it happen."

"I think so too, Jack. 'Just turned twenty.' I like that and I do believe it's so. Give us a little more time and we can make it happen our way."

"We *will* make it happen," Jack said.

He had just proposed to her, he thought. It was some kind of proposal. Marriage? Living together? Whatever it was, he had made it. A commitment.

Mildred pulled on a light coat and went to the bedroom door. She blew him a kiss as she left. He heard the front door to the apartment close. He lay back submerged in the smell and colors of Mildred's bedroom. It was hard to believe that he had thought she was gone from his life. But his unconscious knew better. He had had to come to Minneapolis.

With a start he realized it was already seven-thirty and that he might catch Dan Morris at his apartment before he left for the court-house. Sitting on the edge of the bed, still naked, he dialed Dan's number. Two rings and Dan answered.

"Glad I caught you before you got to the department," he explained. "Taylor answered when I called yesterday afternoon. He seemed excited about my news. What happened after I told him about the League and Bickerson's name on the mailing list?"

"Taylor thought Bickerson being on the JDL list was proof enough of a conspiracy. Right away he ordered me to bring in Hank Severson and he went out and got Jake. Taylor was going to arrest both of them on a murder charge."

"Christ, that's crazy."

"I thought so, but he ordered me to go out and get Hank. He backed off on the arrest, but kept both of them in town a couple hours for questioning. He figured he could scare them into confessing something. Something more, at least, than what Hank already admitted about sabotaging the steam line on Horst's tractor. Then he called in Henslow to help him out with some kind of charges."

"And?"

"Henslow backed him off. Both Hank and Jake seem to have pretty good alibis for Saturday night. But Taylor thought that because they are both implicated by Hank's confession and Bickerson's name on that mailing list, that it proved a conspiracy."

"Maybe. but there's a lot more to it than that."

"Yeah, it sure looks that way to me. The interesting development is that Jim Henslow delayed my getting search warrants to go through the Rogers's places."

"How do you mean, 'delayed?'"

"He got Judge Nelson to hold up for a day on the warrants—on Henslow's saying he was doing his own investigation."

"What about the trust agreement I got from the Carpenter bunch? Did you ask Henslow about that?"

"The last thing I said to him last night was that I'd be by his office today to have him explain why Horst signed a will and a trust agreement concerning his farm at about the same time. I just left it like that. Didn't wait for his answer."

"Dan, you don't have to take my advice, but on the way over here I kept getting a hunch about what was happening to Horst Henslow.

I've boiled it down to what I think is inescapable. The attacks on Henslow were coming from three different quarters, maybe from perpetrators who didn't even know what the others were up to."

"How do you mean?"

"First, we now know that Hank Severson did the tractor. As we guessed, but were not sure. It was a prank that got a bit more serious than Hank had figured. Bickerson might be connected with that, but I don't think Art Rogers had anything to do with Severson."

"I think you're right. Rogers runs that blacksmith shop at Pioneer Village, but from what I learned from the regulars, he doesn't have much to do with the others. But Jim Henslow is certain that it was Rogers who vandalized his house and car tires. But he seems uncertain that Rogers is involved with what's been happening at his old man's place. It's almost as if he's protecting Rogers."

"If Henslow thinks it's Art Rogers who is threatening him, why hasn't he arrested him himself?"

"Good question. He didn't want me to pick up Rogers Sunday morning after I talked to him once he'd viewed the old man's body. Henslow said then that his office was conducting its own investigation and yesterday when I wanted to go out and arrest Rogers, he delayed it. But I'm going out there today."

"So Jim Henslow is trying to make it seem that Rogers is separate from what had been going on at Horst's farm."

"Sure seems that way, but then there's the knife I found with the initials AR. That did startle Henslow when I was questioning him yesterday. Did I tell you he couldn't believe it for a second when I told him?"

"It's a strange piece of evidence."

"Yeah. Isn't it. And Henslow admitted last night to Taylor and me that he took it to his house after finding it stuck in one of his car's tires. He claims Rogers burglarized his house Saturday night in order to retrieve the knife. You believe that?"

"And if Rogers did get it back, why would he take it out to the old man's farm? I have a hard time trying to imagine Art hiding in the barn and accidentally dropping a big knife like that without knowing it. And being there hours before the fire."

"Seems pretty clumsy or careless, or both."

"So maybe it was a plant by Henslow himself. He just hasn't figured out how to connect Rogers to Bickerson and Severson. But go back over the sequence. Right after the steam tractor accident there is a newspaper report about Horst getting hurt and included in the story is the interesting fact of his being at Bergen-Belsen camp at the end of World War Two. That bit of information was supplied by Jim Henslow. He must have had some motive other than filial loyalty to bring up Horst's Nazi background at just that moment."

"So?"

"So, the next thing that happens is swastikas begin to show up and are associated with words from the Jewish Defense League principles. The message targets a former Nazi. Whoever did that may have just learned about Horst's past from the newspaper article. There was no swastika painted on the tractor. The coincidence of their showing up after the newspaper story is too strong to be ignored and I think pretty much rules out some international, Nazi-hunting outfit having just shown up in town. It's a local deal. But the two men that Horst described running away from his house after the spray painting were nothing like two guys in their sixties—not Severson and Bickerson. So, we have an attack coming from another quarter, whether or not Severson and Bickerson were both involved in messing with Horst's tractor. But we know JDL material has been mailed to the Bickerson address for the past six months or so. So maybe Jake isn't telling everything he knows."

"Jim Henslow would agree with you there. Although he told Taylor to send them home last night, he half accused Jake and Hank Severson of coercing Horst into willing the property to Pioneer Village. Didn't quite go that far, but suggested they were putting the heat on

Horst. My bet is we're going to hear more from Jim Henslow about challenging that will."

"When I get back in town I'd like to help you check out Bickerson a little closer. If he's been getting the League literature it might have suggested to him a reason to threaten Horst. Maybe Jim Henslow is partly right about Bickerson and Severson putting some kind of pressure on Horst. Maybe not to get the farm land, but to get him off their backs on the Village board. From everything we've learned, Horst was pushing pretty hard to take over the chairmanship of the Village. Neither Jake or Hank liked that."

"That seems clear enough," Dan agreed.

"Don't say anything to Taylor just yet. I don't think we should encourage him in believing Jake is involved any more than he already thinks. But while we are at it we ought to try to find out what the States Attorney knows about the Jewish Defense League. After all, it was Jim Henslow who started all the business about Horst being a guard at the concentration camp. Could it have been Jim and Art out there that night painting the side of Horst's house?"

"Henslow and Rogers?"

"It may be far fetched. But I keep asking myself why the vandalism directed at Jim Henslow suddenly stops and attacks become concentrated on Horst Henslow? It was after the newspaper article that Horst becomes the target. The nature of the attacks on Horst are entirely different than the tractor incident. They are specifically aimed at his being a Nazi. And you have to remember, there were no more attacks directed at Jim Henslow."

"You're saying that the newspaper article brought on the acts against old Henslow?"

"It would seem that way. And I feel certain of one thing. Hank didn't murder Horst. Hank's confession of sabotaging the tractor is proof that he wasn't out to kill Henslow. That was just a prank, clear and simple. But the spray painting is more sinister. It was meant to send a clear message of revenge."

"Okay. I can see that."

"But the key evidence when taken all together is confusing. The spray painting on the house was entirely different from that on the gas cans left at the scene. Two different hands involved. I'm certain of it. The sprayed lettering on the house was in that same kind of over-dramatic style as the wording in the letter we found on Horst. They both have to come from the same source. Cryptic use of Hebrew words. They were words Henslow didn't even understand. So the message was for a larger audience than one old man. Like it was an initiation of some kind. If there was revenge going on with the painting, it was ideological, not blood sport. Besides, a killer intent on icing someone doesn't go to the trouble of spreading evidence all over the place days ahead of time, sending messages about Jewish dignity. And that's our problem, you know. Too much evidence. "

"And where does that leave us?"

"With Art Rogers and Jim Henslow. Why does it seem that Henslow is shielding Rogers? Delaying your investigation. Was there more going on there than Art just threatening the younger Henslow? It gets tougher though. If Jim had been given control of the farm by the trust agreement, which Horst apparently signed, why would Jim need to put the old man away? Maybe there is something to the theory that Art Rogers was involved, that he knew Jim was about to get the farm and decided that he was going to get at Jim Henslow one more time by torching the shed. It's possible he was in the barn, waiting to do the fire when old Henslow found him there. The way Horst was found, the dirt and straw disturbed on the floor, suggests there may have been a struggle and then Horst was shot from close up. I'm convinced you're going to have to put the screws to Art Rogers. Too damned bad that's been delayed. It's a murder charge, after all. And if Rogers isn't an intentional killer, and its my guess he isn't, he'll be scared as hell. Put pressure on him and he'll talk and tell us what his part has been. Beyond the window and tires, I mean."

"Right. I'm going out to his place first thing this morning. Judge Nelson promised me the search warrants would be ready this morning and I could go through both Art's welding shop and Clarence's farm. He never did argue that the evidence I have didn't warrant a search. He just said he wanted to defer to Jim Henslow's investigation by delaying me a day."

"Good luck. Be cautious of Rogers, though. Guys like him may be petty criminals, but under pressure they can be dangerous. Just a thought."

"I hear you."

When he hung up, Jack went into the bathroom and took a shower. In the quiet of Mildred's apartment, her presence all about him, he felt a million miles from Hamilton. It was time to begin to rehearse what he had to tell Ellie. He had to admit that he was going to regret giving up the sense of security and peace he had begun to feel with Ellie on the Easton farm. He hoped he was not about to abandon the friendship he had with Gordy, the son he had never had. But Ellie's requirements of him were clear. Her definition of what hers and Gordy's life had to be. He would have had to step all the way into the mold he had already begun to try on. If affection for Ellie were to grow into something more serious, he would have had to honor what she wished for her life. It was time to admit he was unable to fit the part she wished he would play. The gift of the Bible was the clear message of the nature of the commitment which had to come from him in order to confirm a serious relationship. The Bible was just a symbol of the certainties in Ellie's life, what she needed, and which he could not embrace. Somehow he had to explain to her that his commitment to Mildred was all on account of his coming to the surface of his own life and being able to breath once again. It was time for him to admit that it was possible for him to love Mildred, the woman who like himself did not need defined structures and for whom color, light, inspiration, beauty were like the food of life. There was no underlying dogma. Mildred's was a limitless horizon in the midst of creation where he too was free to roam. Life with Mildred would be full of adventure which they both would understand.

♦   ♦   ♦

Dan Morris got to the State's Attorney's office at ten minutes after eight Wednesday morning and learned from Mary Pettigrew that Jim Henslow had phoned moments before telling her he'd be gone all morning. There would be no explanation, Dan realized, from the State's Attorney about why Horst Henslow would sign two totally conflicting documents on the same day. Tommy Johnson had confirmed the fact that Horst's will was signed August 30, the same date Jack Traid said was on the trust agreement.

After picking up the search warrants from the Clerk of Courts office, Dan drove to Chesterton. The welding shop was locked when he went to look for Art. He was reluctant to use a bolt cutter to break the padlocks on the front and back doors of the garage-workshop until he had found Art and handed him the search warrant. Downtown he learned from Sally at the cafe that as far as anyone in town knew, Art Rogers was still out at his brother's farm south of town.

"He hasn't been living at his place over his shop since Clarence went to the pen," Sally explained. "Stays out there all the time now. 'Spose he takes care of the cattle. I seen him late Monday afternoon at Mac's Grocery. He was stocking up on groceries. Three or four boxes full."

"Did you notice if his left arm was bandaged?"

"Not particularly. He was wearing a denim jacket. But come to think of it, he seemed to be favoring it some. But old Henry Potter said he saw him early Sunday morning tearing out of town all bandaged up. I found out that Pete Brasley the veterinarian had treated him. Made a joke about it in here yesterday during lunchtime."

"Brasley has his clinic on the north city limits, that right?" Dan asked.

"Yes, that's right. He was in for lunch and backed Henry's story. Nobody in town is surprised that Art got himself shot. You don't suppose he had anything to do with that killing over to Hamilton?"

It was dawning on Sally that Dan had a purpose in coming to her restaurant.

"Might have," Dan replied. "That's what we'd like to know."

He paid for his coffee and went back to the cruiser. At Brasley Veterinary Clinic he found Pete outside talking with a farmer by the side of a hog trailer pulled into the parking lot.

"Sorry to interrupt you fellows, but I need a little help about a shooting, Doc. I was told at Sally's that you treated Art Rogers last Saturday for a gunshot wound. That right?"

"Sure did. He came to my house sometime past ten. I was watching the ten o'clock news on TV. He had on a leather biker's jacket, you know with Harley Davidson wings on the back, and holding his left arm. He said one of his drinking pals accidentally shot him. I brought him over here to the clinic where I have disinfectants and bandages."

"Why do you suppose he didn't go to a medical doctor?"

"Well, there isn't a doctor in Chesterton. He said he didn't think it was serious enough to go all the way over to Hamilton."

"How bad was it? The wound, I mean."

"He's lucky he had on that jacket. Even at that it was a nasty looking wound. Maybe half a dozen steel shot ripped through the leather and penetrated his triceps. I didn't try to take out all the shot. Couple appeared to be pretty deep in the muscle. Cleaned the wound up and put a bandage on it for him. Made a sling for him too because it hurt him to move his arm much. I told him to get on over to the Hamilton Hospital for treatment first thing in the morning."

"I guess you might have told us about the gun-shot wound, Doc."

"Well, I should of, but I half forgot about it Sunday. Went to church like usual and when I did think about it, I figured he'd gone to the hospital by then. I figured they'd have to report it. But I saved the two steel shot I took from his arm. Want them?"

"Sure do."

"They're in the clinic."

Doc Brasley excused himself to the farmer waiting to have his hog treated and went into the clinic. Dan followed him into the bright white interior of the reception room and waited while Doc went into one of the small animal examination rooms. The smells of animals, disinfectants, salves were strong in the room.

"Here they are."

"Appreciate your keeping them, Doc. They might turn out to be pretty important evidence."

"Art involved in the Henslow murder? Is that what you're investigating?"

"He just might be. The guy who set the fire Saturday night on the Henslow place was shot at by the housekeeper staying with Mr. Henslow. She thought she hit the person running from the fire. Looks like we might have the man."

"About time."

"How's that?"

"Well, in the past couple years we've had two barns torched out around here. Art was suspected because in both cases he had been in a drunken fight with the owners sometime before. Got beat up both times. Everyone figured he got back at them with the fires."

"If he was on the Henslow place Saturday he'll have a hellova lot more to answer for than arson," Dan replied.

"Incidentally," Brasely said, "I helped Art because he and Clarence have hired me from time to time to treat their cattle. I wasn't trying to practice medicine, you know."

"No problem, Doc," Dan replied. "I appreciate your cooperation."

Dan carried the shot to his cruiser where he opened the trunk and put them in a plastic evidence bag.

When Dan reached the Clarence Rogers farm the three-slat metal gate was closed and padlocked. He parked the cruiser on the driveway over the ditch and got out. The countryside was quiet except for the sound of sparrows among the bushes and weeds, the bawling of a calf in the distance. Dan adjusted the thirty-eight caliber service revolver in his holster, checked the search warrants he carried in his back, left pocket.

Over the fence, Dan walked quickly toward the house. He watched for movement in the farmyard, looked up at the twin windows in the end gable of the house. It was dead quiet. Tire tracks lead to the steel Butler building. Equipment storage, he thought, mentally checking off the scene. At the screened porch he found the door unlatched and stepped in. He knocked on the door, peering in at its upper half which was an etched glass window in the pattern of lace. The interior was dark. He knocked again and then tried the door. It was unlocked.

Just how dangerous was Art Rogers, he wondered. The police training he's taken in Pierre had laid out procedures for entering a building with unclear dangers. Secure backup. Determine where occupants were in the house before entering. None of that seemed to apply now. He was on his own.

"Rogers? Art Rogers," he called out.

The living room where he stood was sparsely furnished. An overstuff couch was along the wall to the right beneath an open stairway. A small television set was across the room on a table, next to which was a chair which matched the couch. Both chair and couch were worn and soiled. The room smelled of fried food. The air was stale as if the windows had not been opened for months.

"Anyone at home?" Dan called again.

Dan ran up the stairs and into the upstairs hallway. Three small rooms, and a bathroom were off the hall. One of the rooms was a bedroom with an unmade bed, a dresser with a drawer left half open. Shirts, socks and underwear were in a jumble. The house was empty and it was clear that Art Rogers had left in a hurry.

Downstairs, Dan went through the dining room into a small kitchen at the back where he found unwashed dishes piled in the sink. An open cereal box lay on its side on the counter. On a table against the opposite wall were two boxes packed with groceries that had not yet been put away. Change in plans, Dan thought.

A door to his left lead into a back entryway, a glass door and windows straight ahead, windows to the right. Next to the entry door were two pairs of mud-spattered rubber boots. Two Mackinaw jackets, a rain coat, two worn felt hats hung in a row on the left wall. An empty gun rack was just inside the back door. Through the window in the storm door Dan could see the farm yard and the metal storage building. The door was ajar. He pushed the door open and went into the fresh afternoon air.

The sliding door to the metal building had not been pulled entirely closed, nor locked. A padlock hung open in the hasp. Pushing the door aside, Dan stepped into the half-light of the interior. A Ford pickup with dual rear wheels was parked against the far wall. To the left was a John Deere tractor. Dried mud on the concrete floor showed where another vehicle had been parked.

Dan inspected the pickup, walking around it slowly, noting the mud caked on the sidewalls of the tires. The doors were unlocked, and he was able to feel under the seat. Nothing except an oil rag and flashlight. The crew seats behind the front seat were empty. He admitted to himself that he didn't know what he was looking for. It was when he closed the driver-side door that he saw what appeared to be a heap of grain sacks hanging from a hook on the side wall near the back corner of the building. Lifting the sack aside he found a jacket, the left half of a Harley Davidson insignia visible, the upper left arm and shoulder torn by shot. Taking the jacket off the hook he went outside into the bright sunlight.

He started to walk to the cruiser, then stopped to look over the cattle yard behind the building where half a dozen yearling calves milled about nervously. Dan went to the fence. There was still feed in the bunkers and a roll of hay bundle was broken open at the center of the lot. He made a mental note to see that someone cared for these animals if Art was detained, once he was found.

Back at the cruiser he put the leather jacket in a large plastic bag and shut the trunk lid. In the car he radioed Sally at the Sheriff's Department.

"Tell Taylor that I have enough evidence from Rogers' place to justify our putting out an all points bulletin to have Art Rogers picked up."

"Sheriff left for Sioux Falls right after lunch," Sally said.

"Okay. Then I'm asking you to do it on my authority. You'll find a description of Rogers on the top of my desk, at least what we had in the files from his past arrest records. Make sure you indicate that he may be armed."

"Okay. I'll put the bulletin on the state net right now."

"Good. I'm coming back to the office after I've gone through Rogers' welding shop. If Taylor calls in, tell him what I've done about putting out the bulletin and that I'll be back in the office in an hour or so."

The drive back to the Chesterton and the Rogers Welding shop took less than five minutes. From the trunk of the cruiser, Dan took a bolt cutter and went to the garage door. The four-dollar padlock yielded easily to the cutter. Dan pulled both doors wide open to reveal a workshop cluttered with metal bars, a power hack saw, welding tanks, a workbench where a half-finished metal rack lay on its side. The heavy odors of grease, paint, and raw metal filled the still air. On the workbench he found a quart can of enamel paint which had been opened and then sealed again. Next to the can was a coffee can half full of kerosene with a half-inch paint brush standing in it. If this paint matched the enamel paint on the gas cans, Art Rogers

would be found guilty not only of arson, but certainly of gross carelessness about implicating himself. It was as if he believed there was
no likelihood of his being suspected of burning Henslow's shed.

Dan put the can of paint and brush in a small cardboard box he
found on the floor of the shop, and returned to his cruiser, putting
the evidence in the truck.

As he drove back toward Hamilton, he wondered how far Rogers
had run. What had caused him to light out today after the apparent
casualness with which he had prepared for the arson? Dan recalled
the remark in Sally's Cafe that Art had been in Chesterton Monday
afternoon shopping for groceries, apparently for many days. He
must have thought then that he had no reason to disappear. Yesterday or early today, Dan thought to himself, Art Rogers had had a
sudden change of heart.

❀   ❀   ❀

It was dark and overcast as Jim Henslow drove east from Hamilton on State Highway Forty-three. He slowed the Explorer as he
approached the Henslow farm. There were no lights in the house,
which was a good sign that Rogers was being careful. He felt pleased
with himself for instructing Art to hide at the old man's farm where
no one would think to look for him.

Across the front of the barn he could see the yellow police line
tape that remained, hanging limply. His approach to the house had
to be from the rear where there would be no chance of his being
observed, just as he had instructed Art. His memory of the fields
behind the buildings, the stretch of shelter belt west of the house, the
coulee lying east to west where spring runoff made its way to the reservoir, were all mapped in his mind. How many times, he thought,
had he wandered alone across those acres? Sometimes he would hike
along the perimeter fence line at night to avoid having to stay in the

house with his step-father. He knew this farm land like his own back yard, land that was meant to be his. But first Art Rogers had to be gotten out of the state to avoid being arrested for arson and murder—and telling all.

The Hamilton *Times* lay open on the seat beside him, the eight-column headline punctuating the urgency of his mission tonight: LOCAL MAN SOUGHT FOR ARSON. The subhead declared, "Art Rogers Also Wanted for Questioning about Henslow Murder." The five-thirty newscast from KOLO in Sioux Falls had broadcast the story from the Chautauqua County sheriff's office. Deputy Dan Morris was quoted as saying there was positive evidence tying Rogers to the arson committed Saturday night on the Henslow farm east of Hamilton. There was also reason to believe, Morris had said, that Rogers was connected to the murder of Horst Henslow.

Too well known in the community and among Pioneer Village regulars, Rogers would have to make his escape at night, Jim reasoned. The thousand dollars he had in tens and twenties in the left pocket of his jacket had better satisfy Art, even if it was only half of what he had demanded. As Jim approached the interstate highway, he touched the revolver in his right jacket pocket. There was also the issue of his own escape from a dangerous situation.

On Interstate 29 Henslow headed south, the eastern edge of the Henslow farm on his right. In another mile he left the interstate and got on the county road going west, a road marked "Dead End" because of the construction of the Chautauqua dam and reservoir. He had circled the farm, remembering that it surrounded a small farmstead of a few acres that Horst had been unable to bargain for at his price. Jim slowed the car as he watched for the driveway into the abandoned farmstead which adjoined the Henslow land on the south. The entrance over the ditch was narrow and just visible in the Explorer's headlights. Jim turned onto the drive over the culvert. The clock on the dashboard read eight thirty-five. He turned off the headlights. It was a pitch black sky and no moon or starlight to light his way. It was fortunate, he thought, there was little light. For a moment he sat quietly waiting for his eyes to adjust to the dark. Hamilton's lights glowed dimly on the overcast to the west. From this slightly raised hillock he could see part of Chautauqua Reservoir that made the western side of a thirty-acre pasture that defined the southwest corner of the Henslow farm. Beyond the lake on the opposite hillside a mile away he could see Pioneer Village under the half dozen security lights placed throughout the invented town. Jim was familiar with the nearly abandoned county road on which he had just traveled. It led to the reservoir's dam which, when a steel gate was opened, had a road on its crest which entered the village just south of the tractor barns. For years the Henslow pasture had been used to line up antique tractors for the Pioneer Days grand parade. From the pasture and across the dam the giant machines made a grand entrance into the Village, steam whistles piercing the air as they turned up the main street.

There were no buildings left on the abandoned farm where Jim Henslow was parked. A few foundation blocks lay scattered in the clearing. Jim got out of the car and lifted the wire loop that secured the sagging gate to a post. Driving through and getting out again to close the gate, he recalled the fall days he had walked this very fence line hunting pheasants. Those peaceful days were gone, he thought, and he had to face up to what had gone wrong with his plan. Now he had to confront the man who had got them both into the depths of an unintended killing.

Back in the Explorer he eased down the driveway which ended at the empty farmyard. From there he was able to follow the weed-covered pathway once used to move equipment from the farmyard into the fields. He could just make out the faint tracks of another vehicle which had preceded him. Ahead was a neglected tangle of the remains of a shelter belt that had been partially removed. He was relieved to find that Art had found the patch, for his pickup was well hidden in the head-high brush. There was still enough cover for the

Explorer. Jim leaned forward over the steering wheel, watching for fallen branches and eased the car into the brush between four of the larger trees, stopping just behind the pickup.

The tension of his mission made him unsteady. When he turned off the engine and waited before opening the car door, he saw in the diffused light from the Village a bright shape shift in the weeds at the far west edge of the woods; then a white deer rose, turned his antlered head toward him, paused and then bounded out into the cleared field and made toward the reservoir. Jim watched the buck as it circled back toward the road when it was halfway to the lake. The grace of its bounding movements, the ghostly white form gliding across the stubble field fixed his attention. He did not move until he saw the stag cross the road and disappear into brush below the dam.

It was just over half a mile from the vehicles to the Henslow farmstead. He had planned his approach carefully, just as he had told Rogers to keep from being seen. A short jog across the stubble field got him to the dry stream bed in the cut that ran across the north end of the field. From there, moving in a crouched run, he was able to get to the edge of the windbreak that ran back to State Highway Forty-three and the house. Once in the trees Jim stopped to catch his breath. His legs were shaking from the exertion; he needed to get hold of himself, he thought. And how dangerous was Rogers?

He approached the darkened house slowly, keeping back in the shelter belt, between pines and the shorter Russian olive trees, which had been planted as the first row. Once parallel with the house he could see the highway clearly and waited when he saw traffic coming from the east. Three cars and a delivery truck whined past, going toward Hamilton. When the road was dark again he hurried to the back of the house and made his way to the breezeway between the garage and house. The storm door was unlocked. The familiar interior of this mud room still had Horst's mackinaw hanging on a hook next to the back door to the house. A pair of rubber boots were on the floor below.

Jim eased open the back door and entered the kitchen. The faint smell of bacon greeted him. He wondered if Rogers had cooked himself a meal or if the odor was left over from last week of Horst's life. His own voice startled him as he called out hoarsely, "Rogers?"

"In here," he heard the reply, the gruff voice loud in the dark.

Seated in Horst's recliner, Rogers held a rifle across his legs. The chair was swiveled half way around to the dining room. He did not get up. A diffused yellow light from the sodium vapor security light at the barn filtered into the room through the curtains over the front windows. Jim noticed that Rogers had not shaved for several days.

"Fine fucking mess you got us into," Rogers swore.

"You mean that you got us into. Why the hell did you have to kill the old man?"

"I told you, goddam it, I didn't kill him. I did the fire and ran for it. Then that broad winged me, just like it said in the paper."

"And because you got yourself hit, the sheriff's office found out it was the vet who treated you in Chesterton. Danny Morris told the *Times* he has your jacket, too, which was shot up. Found on Clarence's farm. Here, read it for yourself," Jim said, tossing the paper on the dining room table, wary about getting too close to the rifle that was close to being pointed at him.

"Shit. I didn't figure anyone would find it in the barn. I thought I might get it repaired."

"Okay, so you're stupid. Fact is, that's all behind you now."

"Sure, you can say that. But after I got the vet in Chesterton to fix my arm it started to get infected. I had to go to Sioux Falls to the clinic there."

"So the medics there will report they treated you. The important thing is for you to get the hell out of state. I brought you some money, like you asked. For the tape, remember?"

"Two thousand?"

"No. I couldn't get my hands on that much. Here's a thousand in tens and twenties," Jim replied, taking the bills from his left coat pocket but not handing them over.

"Bullshit. That can't get me much further than Kansas City."

"If you don't want to room with your brother, you better go a lot further than that. Maybe I can get…"

"Just wait a goddam minute. I said two thousand. You ain't got it, I'm not giving you this tape," Rogers said, tapping his shirt pocket, "and I ain't going to make a run for it. Besides, lawyer, I got me some insurance you ought to know about when I was in Sioux Falls."

"What's that?"

"This recording of your telephone calls? I made a copy of it and left it with Clarence at the pen. I told him that if something happened to me, he was to make it public. Big ass state's attorney's a crook. What a nice headline."

"So. Why should I believe you did that?"

"You don't have to. Believe what you want, but if I don't call him or write him after two weeks, he's to turn it over to the warden. Now who's stupid?"

"Okay. So we both go to prison. You for murder and arson. Me for conspiracy to harass an old man. Is that what you want?"

"You know, Henslow, I was a goddam fool to get involved with you. I thought you might get Clarence out, but you're an idiot, far as I can tell. Now we're both in deep shit."

"If you'd calm down a bit, we can figure it out," Jim said, his tone tuned to persuade the jury. "If you hadn't killed Horst, it wouldn't be so bad. I could figure a way to protect you."

"Well, I didn't kill him, and you better believe it."

"Okay. Say you didn't. But for sure, then, you have to get scarce until they find out who did. Maybe one of those guys at the Village. They got pulled in by the sheriff. Hank Severson, old Bickerson. Sheriff thinks they did it."

"No shit?"

"Sent home, though. They both had alibis that will probably check out. But if it wasn't you, maybe with a little investigation I can show how they were involved. In the meantime you've got to get the hell out of the country for awhile."

"Not on a thousand bucks."

"Okay, okay. If I get you another thousand and bring it out here, you'll make a run for it?"

"Have to be another two thousand."

"Jesus. I just don't have that much in my account just now."

"Get a loan. Guy like you must have good credit."

In exasperation, Jim did not reply. If Rogers didn't have the rifle, he thought. He forced himself to be calm. Reason with him, he thought. There was one way out of Rogers' trap and he had to go with it.

"Okay. I'll get another two thousand and bring it out here day after tomorrow night. Okay?"

"Better be tomorrow night. Someone might begin to poke around here. It's spookier than hell out here all day."

"All right. Midnight tomorrow at your truck. Two thousand, and you hand over the tape."

"Ain't you afraid of what Clarence will do with his copy?"

"Nothings going to happen to you, Rogers, so he'll keep it safe until you're in the clear. That okay with you?"

"I guess it'll have to do. Midnight, then. At my truck?"

"Yeah. That's where I'm parked tonight. No one uses that old county road. Cars can't be seen in what's left of that old shelter belt. You'll be able to make it to the Minnesota state line in an hour, then head south through Iowa."

"Don't worry about me, Henslow. I know how I'll get out of here."

"Good. Tomorrow night, then," Jim said, backing away toward the kitchen.

"The thousand bucks," Rogers commanded. "Leave it on the table there."

"Okay. Sure," Jim said, putting the wad of bills held by a rubber band on the end of the table.

"Just in case you don't come back," Rogers said.

"I'll be back. I've got too much invested in you to lose interest at this late date."

"I'm glad you got that figured out."

Jim Henslow hurried through the kitchen, went out through the breezeway and into the night. Hurrying along the back of the house, he broke into a run for the shelter belt's security. Once in among the trees he stopped, breathing hard. The noose Art Rogers had put about his neck was yet to be untied. There was much to be done by midnight tomorrow.

He retraced his route, speeding back on the Interstate to State Highway 43 and back to Hamilton. Back in Hamilton and in the driveway to his house, he pressed the remote to open the garage door and slowly brought the car into the quiet of the garage. Both his legs were trembling. Pressing the remote once again, he closed the garage door and got out of the car. He held on to the door as he steadied himself. It was nine forty-five by his watch. The house was empty. He was by himself to work his way through the entangled circumstances that had sprung unbidden from his simple plan.

CHAPTER 15

$\mathcal{D}$ an Morris had agreed on the phone Wednesday afternoon to go with Carla Garza on her "mission" as she called it. She didn't say where she wanted to take him, but the prospect of a break from the Henslow matter and a date of sorts with beautiful Carla was motive enough to say "yes." But she insisted that he be in uniform, saying there was official county business to conduct. She picked him up at his apartment at nine o'clock that evening.

"It must be something pretty interesting you want me to see, what with all this mystery," Dan said as Carla backed into Main Street and then headed south. The faint floral perfume in her car pleased him, nearly as much as watching her confident movements. Her slender legs in dark slacks suggested to him that she was on the job, that they were not on their way to a party. She wore dark running shoes. Over a red blouse she wore a dark blue windbreaker, a thin red line down the sleeves. She was all business tonight.

"You might find what I have discovered very interesting," she replied.

"Certainly secret enough a mission," he said. "Why did you want me to wear my uniform? I was suppose to be off duty tonight."

"To be revealed soon enough," she said, chuckling.

They continued south out of town. The sky was overcast. Powered by rural electric cooperatives, security lights on scattered farmsteads gave evidence of the sparse habitation among the rolling hills of the Dakota prairie. Three miles south of town Carla turned east on an even narrower gravel road. After driving slowly for less than a mile Carla stopped and backed into the driveway of a vacant farm yard. Carefully she pulled along side a weather-beaten chicken house which had not been occupied in ten years.

My god, Dan thought, has she brought me out here to get on with an affair we haven't even decided to start? The idea of pulling her into his arms stirred him and he shifted in his seat, facing her.

"What's up?" he asked, his voice stressed.

"Not to worry," she replied, smiling. She could feel the tension in his body as he moved. "Just watch the road to the east. I'm expecting a new Ford 350 to come this way before long."

"You know exactly what you're looking for, don't you?"

"I do, and it will help you solve one of your little crime wave problems."

"Which is?"

"Just be patient."

They sat in silence. Dan thought he would reach over for her hand, just in case this was an invitation and he was being too stupid to know that Carla had decided to make the first move.

"Whatever this mission is," Dan ventured, "I could wish that I was getting a signal to reach over and touch you. To get started with what I have been feeling."

"Not tonight, Deputy. October 4th, maybe, after you take me to hear Sammy Gail's big band in Sioux Falls."

"Yeah. I know Sammy. Sat in with him a couple times."

"I know that. Did the research. And I got the tickets for the October 4th benefit, too."

In the diffused light of the overcast night, Dan saw Carla smile, her eyes still intent on the road in front of them.

"Great!" was all he could think to say.

It was then that the excitement of being alone with Carla shifted to abrupt recognition. The pickup speeding down the road before them, a rolling cloud of dust behind it, was Sheriff Tom Taylor's new Ford 350.

"There he goes," Carla said flatly.

"Taylor?"

"De sheriff hisself," she said in a cartoon voice. In her own serious tone she continued, saying "We'll follow him from a safe distance."

She started the Camaro, eased down the driveway with the lights still out, and turned west into the settling dust. Over the rise in the road they could see Taylor turn south on the county road they had taken out of town. Carla sped forward, lights still out, straining forward to see the roadway in the darkness. At the county road she turned south and with lights on accelerated enough to keep a mile behind Taylor.

"Did you notice what was in the back of his truck?" she asked.

"No. He was going like a bat out of hell."

"Barrels. Fifty-five gallon barrels of PCB oil."

"Jeez. What…"

"What is the good sheriff doing with PCB in the middle of the night? A very good question, Mr. Deputy. And if we don't get too close to him, I think we'll catch him either dumping their contents in a ditch, or moving them to another illegal hiding place."

"What do you mean, another?"

"Taylor has been storing barrels of PCB oil in one of his barns. I have pictures of them. Six barrels as far as I can make out. He must have been alerted by his wife that someone like a *Times* reporter was checking out his barn, so he's moving them, or dumping them like he did the others."

"My god. How did you find out all this."

"Nose for news, Dan. When I was snooping around for the story on the oil dumping, I found out that he was an all too familiar figure at Acme Transformer. The secretary there let that slip. So I've been watching Taylor and his farm. The night he was going to arrest Severson and Bickerson I was out at his place taking pictures. I brought these prints along for you."

Carla handed Dan an envelope as she slowed down at the crest of a hill. They watched the pickup turn east again. The road Taylor was taking ran along a ridge and they could see the lights of his truck speed along the horizon.

Since it was too dark to look at the photos, Dan put the envelope on the inside pocket of his uniform jacket.

"Better give him a little time," Carla remarked, slowing even more as she approached the side road. She turned slowly, putting out the headlights as she edged up the ridge. They could see the red tail lights of Taylor's pickup blink and he braked. He was slowing down. They watched as he turned into a drive and stopped. Carla pulled over and stopped. They could see Taylor get out of the truck and go into the light from his headlights to the gate to open it. Once back in the pickup he drove through the gate without bothering to close it and continued along a fence. From their position on the ridge they could see Taylor approach a barn that stood alone a hundred yards from the road. The sweep of his headlights crossed the front of the barn as he turned around, then backed to the doorway. The pickup's lights went out.

"We'll give him a little time to get on with his job," Carla said. Dan marveled at her coolness. There wasn't a flutter in her voice. They sat silently for what seemed an hour but not more than five minutes had passed when she asked, "Want to go now?"

"Kinda tough, don't you think? My moving in on my boss?"

"Sure as hell is. For Taylor. He has a lot of explaining to do."

"You're right. Let's go for it."

Carla sped forward, headlights still out. In the distance to the northeast they could see the security lights of Pioneer Village casting a dim glow upon the low hanging clouds. It was a closed-in, dark prairie night and he had a duty unlike any he had had to face before.

Swinging into the driveway and accelerating as they passed through the gate, Carla switched on the car's high beams, floodlighting the Ford pickup and open barn doors where Taylor stood, legs apart, his belly protruding over his holster belt. Dan saw his hand drop to his gun.

"Stop here," he ordered Carla. "And stay in the car."

"Be careful, Danny," Carla said.

Jumping out, Dan yelled, "Taylor. It's me. Dan."

"Jesus H Christ, what the hell are you doing here?" Taylor yelled back at him. "Get your ass out of here."

"'Fraid not, Sheriff. Why don't you just quit what you're doing there and listen to me."

Taylor had not moved. One fifty-five gallon drum was in a chain harness of the lift attached to the back of the pickup, ready to be lowered onto a dolly he had brought out from the barn. Three other barrels remained in the truck bed.

"Just what the hell do you think you're going to do now?" Taylor challenged.

"I guess the best thing is for you to put that barrel back in the bed of the pickup and then the two of us will ride back to town together."

"You and who else is going to get that done?"

"I think I can handle it alone, Tom. Besides, Carla here has photographs of what you had in your barn. She has the story, so you better be thinking about putting the best face on it."

A flash bulb went off. Taylor and Morris jumped.

"Goddam it, what the hell do you think you're doing," Taylor shouted at Garza.

"Wrapping up a story, sheriff."

"Carla, dammit," Dan snapped over his shoulder, "No more of that. Back off now while I get the sheriff into town. I'll talk to you later."

The door to the Camaro slammed shut but the car did not move, its lights still flooding the scene. Dan did not move, waiting for her to leave. But she was waiting. A witness, he thought, and was pleased with her caution.

"Tom, I'm going to have to ask you to put that barrel back into the truck. But before you do, I'd like you to hand over your gun."

"No goddam way."

"Be best for you," Dan said, moving forward. The Camaro's headlights were like a spotlight on Taylor. Dan put out his hand toward Taylor, waiting for the sheriff to move.

"Are you arresting me?" Taylor asked.

"Whatever you want to call it," Dan said. "I just know that you will have to go to town with me and explain to the County Commission and State's Attorney what all this means."

"There's a simple explanation, Danny. I was just helping out my friend Rich Arnold over to Acme."

"Okay. You can tell that to Henslow. But give me your gun so we'll both feel safer."

Dan was five feet away from Taylor, standing within arm's reach of the oil drum hanging from the crane. Carla still had not moved her car. It was a good thing, Dan thought.

"The gun," Dan demanded. "I mean it, Tom."

"Goddammit to hell," Taylor said, pulling the revolver from its holster, his hand upon the grip. He paused a moment as if considering what his next move would be. Dan watched his eyes, blinking in the bright beams of Garza's headlights. Slowly Taylor took the barrel of the gun in his left hand and then thrust it forward, handle first toward Dan.

"Good," Dan said, thrusting the pistol under his belt. He stood back while Taylor swung the dangling barrel back over the truck bed. He was moving slowly, considering, Dan thought. Tom Taylor was awkward in his movements as he climbed into the back of the pickup and shifted the drum back against the others. He fastened them with a strap to the front of the bed.

When the oil drums were secure in the truck, Taylor jumped down and closed the endgate.

"You drive," Dan said as he went around to the passenger side.

As both men got into the pickup, Carla backed the Camaro around and went slowly toward the gate as if waiting to see if they were following. Taylor started the truck and turned on the headlights. They could see Carla's low-slung, red car accelerate, turn west on the gravel road and speed away. Taylor drove slowly through the gate.

"Want to close the gate?" Dan asked.

"No need, I guess. No cattle in there."

They rode west in silence until they reached the county road.

"I need a break," Taylor said finally, not turning toward Dan but eyes fixed on the road ahead as they headed toward Hamilton. He drove thirty miles an hour, delaying their arrival in town.

"Maybe you can understand Danny. Man to man. It was just a little extra money. Arnold said he'd pay me top dollar for taking care of the oil, no questions asked. Stuff that wasn't documented too good with records."

Taylor hesitated, as if composing his story.

"I ain't proud of any of it, but I got this girl friend, see. You know how it is. Younger woman. Lives in Sioux Falls and…" Taylor choked up. Dan could see in the dash lights that his eyes were tearing up.

"I know it was wrong," Taylor continued, "but, well, I just got involved and began spending money on her, you know."

There was nothing to say, Dan thought. Let him talk it out.

"So can't you understand? If you arrest me and turn me in, my life is ruined. After all those years in the department. Getting elected, and everything. My wife will leave me for certain. It's one hellova mess."

Taylor was pleading, his voice strained.

"Just a little break, Dan. I'll make everything right. Take the oil back to Acme and…"

"What about the oil that got dumped?" Dan asked.

"I don't know anything about that," Taylor snapped, his voice hardening, defensive.

"Maybe so. But it would appear that you are the one handling oil illegally."

"Art Rogers," Taylor snapped back. "It has to be Rogers who's doing the dumping. He's been picking up oil from Acme for months. Records there will show that. Far as I can tell he never delivers it to the incinerator in Iowa."

"The records I had of all the other places showed every shipment Art picked up he delivered to Iowa the same day. Every barrel accounted for."

"Not Acme's oil," Taylor shot back.

"Well, I guess we'll just have to go over the records with Rogers after we pick him up for arson."

"Pick him up?" Taylor asked.

"I put out a bulletin this morning for his arrest. There is ample evidence that he was responsible for torching Henslow's shed, maybe responsible for Henslow's murder."

"You didn't say anything to me about that."

"Tom, you were the hell away from the office again," Dan replied sharply. "It was pretty obvious to me that you were too busy to worry about Rogers, or anyone else connected to the Henslow murder."

"Now wait a goddam minute."

"No, Tom," Dan shot back, anger rising in his voice. "You are in no position to complain about what has been going on in the office. It's bad enough to have Jim Henslow blocking my investigation. But one way or the other I'm going to have Rogers picked up as soon as he can be found. Then maybe we'll get to the bottom of the Henslow killing. In the meantime, you'll have to face the State's Attorney and the County Commission about storing this oil."

"I'm sorry I got pissed there, Danny. It's just that everything is going to hell. Can't you just forget this oil stuff. I'll get the barrels back to Acme tomorrow, and then everything will be okay."

"I'm afraid it's too late Tom. Carla Garza has pictures of the clearly marked PCB oil drums in your barn. She has a picture of you tonight. You can bet she's doing a story for the *Times*. How you going to explain that away?"

"She works for your old man, doesn't she? Can't you do something about that through your old man? Maybe put a little pressure on her to forget about the story? For a little while, anyway, until I get it all straightened out."

"No chance. She can't be bought or threatened. Nor can my dad."

They were at the outskirts of Hamilton. Taylor slowed as they went up Main Street toward the courthouse.

"So you aren't going to help me?" Taylor pleaded again.

"You know I can't, Tom. Why don't we just park this truck in the parking lot and go into the office."

"You going to put me under arrest?"

"I want to call George Carter, he's Commission chairman. Then I'll call Jim Henslow. I'll ask both of them to come down here tonight because I'm not quite sure what I should do."

As he thought about what he had to do, Dan noticed by the clock on the dash that it was ten forty-five. It was not too late to call either of the two men.

"Be easier to let this business cool off overnight, wouldn't it?" Taylor said, continuing to bargain.

"It would be easier, Tom, but that wouldn't be right. I'm sorry, but you've got to face up to the Commission. Maybe they will decide that no crime has been committed. Just a temporary misunderstanding. But I can't make that judgment."

Taylor pulled into the parking place next to his cruiser behind the courthouse. The two men got out and went into the courthouse and down the stairway to the Sheriff's Department.

❧   ❧   ❧

On his drive back to Hamilton from Minneapolis on Wednesday afternoon Jack Traid carried with him a list of names to which the Jewish Defense League was sending material, including Chautauqua County's own J. Bickerson. He also had in his brief case a copy of the three-page trust agreement signed by Horst Henslow. It was the keystone to the Carpenter Group plans to begin site preparation that fall for the housing development. The drawings Mark Peterson and Herb Stover showed him of the layout along the eastern shore of the Chautauqua Reservoir were impressive. Winding streets, half-acre lots, a community center with shops and a theater all added up to months of planning. Within easy commuting distance to a burgeoning Sioux Falls, Chautauqua Acres was conceived as a planned town for a growing population of upper income professionals and affluent retirees. Peterson and Stover were full of the statistics about their expected clientele, and recited in detail the demographics for Sioux Falls and Minnehaha County. It seemed clear to Jack that their plans were based on careful research. Jim Henslow, it appeared, had found a way to convert the old home place into a gold mine. What would this document look like placed next to Horst Henslow's will which Tommy Johnson had revealed to the Pioneer Village Board of Directors and to Jim Henlsow during the Labor Day meeting in his office? Both bore the date August 30, 1995.

Jack Traid was also carrying back to Hamilton the promises he and Mildred at made to each other at lunch, and afterward when he delayed his departure. She had no afternoon classes and they returned to her apartment. They helped each other undress, entering into a timeless zone of warmth, and the rising excitement of discovering each other all over again.

At three in the afternoon Mildred poured them each a glass of wine. They said nothing, gazing over their wine glasses at each other with a kind of amazement at what was happening. Then both sought words with which they tried to say what these two days had meant. They agreed they would find a place where they could live together, all other details to be settled later. Where? How soon? Mildred to South Dakota? Jack to Minnesota? They would work it out.

"I can quit trying to avoid the obvious. We're not going to waste these days on memories," Jack said.

"Not ever," Mildred had replied.

"I'll be back in two weeks, after I get through fall registration and class schedules. We'll make our plans."

"When you have solved the murder?" she asked.

"When I've finished this little errand for Dan Morris, I'm out of it. I'll get back to my classes and get the semester going. Then you and I are going to deal with the problem of geography and all these miles that separate us."

All the way back to Hamilton the settled commitment of living with Mildred interrupted his thoughts about housing developments, the JDL principals, a dead ex-Nazi at the center of a struggle to control Pioneer Village. Taylor and Morris could figure out what happened to the promise that the Henslow farm was to be Jim Henslow's. The entire Henslow matter faded in his mind. He had more important problems to solve. Maybe he would have to leave Hamilton State, move out of the comfort of his retreat at the city limits of Hamilton and find something in Minneapolis. If that was what he had to do, that is what he would do. Mildred was his chance for a life, finally, without the ghosts of the past to remind him how he'd failed. Mildred and her love made a future he once would never have risked.

Traid arrived at his house at nine-thirty in the evening. Entering through the back entryway-gallery, he stopped a moment to look at Mildred's painting. "Love's Splendor" was all the clearer, he thought.

Rasputin greeted him in the kitchen, complaining at being left alone with dry food and water.

"Guess I owe you a tuna supper. Think that will do?"

Jack reached down and rubbed the cat's head over the missing eye. A deep rumble responded to his touch.

After putting a dish of tuna before the impatient cat, Jack took the phone hanging next to the doorway to the front hall and called Dan Morris's apartment. No answer. He then called the Sheriff's Department and reached Elmer Sonderson, night dispatcher. In case Sonderson didn't know him, Jack identified himself.

"Dan's off duty tonight. Did you try him at home?" Sonderson offered.

"I did. Would you tell him that I got back from Minnesota and have some things for him."

"Sure. I heard from Sally that you were doing some work for us in the cities."

"Got all over town, I suppose."

"What's that?"

"Oh nothing. When he checks in, please be sure to tell Dan I'm home."

"Sure. No problem."

Jack had delayed as long as he dared. It was ten o'clock when he mustered the courage to phone Ellie. After the third ring Gordy Easton answered.

"Hey, Gordy," Jack said. "Your mother home?"

"Not yet, Jack. She and some of the lady's aid women are getting things ready at the church for Mrs. Masters' funeral Friday. She said the funeral home was bringing the body back from Rochester tomorrow. There will probably be a big crowd at the luncheon after the funeral, Mom says."

"Yes, I suppose. Tell her I called, will you Gordy? I'll talk to her tomorrow, or at least on Friday, probably after the funeral, sometime."

"Sure."

"By the way," Jack continued, "any sign of your white buck?"

"Nope. Not around here."

"Well, keep an eye out for him. See you later, Gordy."

Jack was surprised by the hint of sadness that had entered his voice. It was as if he were saying goodbye to Gordy for ever. It was a farewell he did not want to make. How was Ellie going to understand how he felt about Mildred? About their decision? Was the friendship with the Eastons to dissolve?

❧   ❧   ❧

Don Fogel wasn't exactly handsome, Sheri thought to herself, but he carried himself with an attractive, casual confidence of a man who knew his importance. He was the *Argus Leader's* top reporter and he knew his business at the state capitol. They sat at the Western Bar and Grill five miles south of Pierre. They waited for the steaks they had ordered. Best in the state, Fogel had promised. Sheri sipped on a Jack Daniels on ice. Fogel had given up thirty years of hard drinking five years ago, he explained, after awakening in a corn field stark naked, unable to remember how he got there. He played with the Coke in front of him, watching Sheri carefully, pleased that the people he knew in the restaurant were watching them. Half of the thirty patrons on this slow Wednesday night knew who Fogel was and his reputation as the reporter not afraid to be tough on any state official.

Two state legislators and a reporter for the *Aberdeen American* had come over to their table to greet Don, inquisitive about this stunning woman in slacks, high heels, and flight jacket. They didn't hide their envy at Fogel's good luck tonight. It was common knowledge that Fogel had been divorced years ago and reigned in Pierre as the fiftish bachelor reporter from Sioux Falls who acted ten years younger. The state capitol was both his assignment and his playground. The question among regulars at the Western Bar was which of the clerks from state agencies had he enticed to dinner.

"What'd you think of Rodney Chamber's when we talked to him about the rural electric rally?"

"Not much. Full of himself. Looking for publicity."

"Well, to be expected. It is his job to get their pitch on the front page."

"So will he get as many people out here tomorrow as he says?"

"Maybe. Two hundred directors from the rural electrics aren't all that hard to muster," Fogel mused. "But it will be a quiet crowd. Nothing very dramatic to photograph."

"Just how hot a deal is the legislation the special committee is meeting about? Will the co-ops be really upset?"

"Not this time. Just sullen, is my guess. You'll get nothing like those pix of yours of the prison riot. I remember that the staff photographers at the *Argus* were really pissed that you'd got inside."

"A break, you might say," Sheri replied, remembering Derrick Holmes reluctance at first to even give her the chance.

"So you've come out of retirement?"

"So I've come out of small-town hell."

"Oh? What's that?"

"Hamilton. You know my husband is State's Attorney for Chautauqua County."

"Yeah. I know Jim. Story in Republican circles is that he's going to be coming out here before too long as a Senator. So what's your husband's job got to do with your coming out on the rural electric story?"

"With my being bored senseless? Easy to figure, isn't it? A husband lawyer turned politician, not to mention he's got a big real estate deal going that keeps him occupied. I just decided that I wasn't going to fix meals, clean house, and serve on the hospital auxiliary for the rest of my life. Simple as that."

"Figures. Talent like yours shouldn't be wasted."

Let the innuendo float, Fogel thought. Hers was a talent the *Argus* staff knew had reached beyond the camera, and had embraced for a time their boss Derrick Holmes. And just maybe, Fogel mused, there was some talent left for him tonight.

Sheri didn't miss the implication of the way Fogel said "talent."

"If you think you're going to get me in bed tonight, forget it," she said quietly, looking Fogel in the eye.

"Oh? Too soon to tell, isn't it?"

"Not at all. I've got one reputation I'm going to retrieve and that's as the best goddamn news photographer in the state. That doesn't include spreading my legs for you."

Fogel hesitated, startled by her directness.

"You sure as hell make things pretty clear," he said, finally. "So we'll be all business, okay?

"That's the way it's going to be."

"Okay. Then maybe you can let me in on what's going on in Hamilton. Derrick says we haven't had much of the story for the *Argus* yet. Apparent homicide. Some business about one of those antique steam tractors blowing up out there at Pioneer Village. I thought you might know something I could follow up on. Something your husband thinks about the case."

"I'll tell you what the story is. A guy named Art Rogers killed the old man, my husband's father, step father, that is. I know that because Rogers dropped a knife in a horse stall near where the body was found."

"You know that?" Fogel asked, taking a note pad from his jacket pocket.

"Sure as hell do. The knife has his initials on it. A.R. My husband's investigation turned that up. And if you want my opinion, I think my husband is about to take over the investigation that our rinky-dink Sheriff Taylor is trying to conduct. But sooner or later either the sheriff or the State's Attorney is going to have to put out a warrant for Rogers' arrest."

"Yeah," Fogel interrupted. "Derrick mentioned Rogers. I guess you didn't know that there was a warrant put out today for his arrest. Wire services all have it."

"About time. Evidence all points to him. Did I tell you that the bastard shot out the front window to our house? His little revenge game against my husband went too far when he went after Jim's old man. You can quote me on that when you get the rest of the story."

"Interesting. So your husband is about to start his own investigation?"

"That's my guess. The sheriff's an idiot. Jim won't sit back much longer if those yokels don't bring in Rogers pretty soon."

"Yeah. Well, your husband has the power to do his own investigation, I guess. I'll have to give him a call in the morning. See how things are going. In the meantime, here are our steaks."

A waitress in a tight red t-shirt and Levis shuffled plates before them. Foil wrapped potatoes, slabs of T-bones.

"Western style," she commented, "medium rare just like you like it Donny." She smiled down on Fogel.

CHAPTER 16

"Sheriff Taylor has been suspended with pay for the time being,"
State's Attorney Jim Henslow announced to the gathered
media on the front steps of the Chautauqua County courthouse
Thursday afternoon. The sun was warm on this clear September day.
Leaves of the trees at the corners of the courthouse lawn were beginning to take on color. The air was cool, hinting of fall. Jim Henslow
was feeling energetic and in command. It had been a triumphant
return from the search he'd conducted with the State Penitentiary
warden that morning in Sioux Falls. He had every cassette tape
found in Clarence Rogers' cell safely impounded in the safe in his
office. The unmarked recording found in a Chet Atkins commercial
recording case, now separated from the rest, was secure in the inside
pocket of his suit jacket, next to his heart. Art Rogers' insurance had
been cancelled, he mused.

Before he left for Sioux Falls, he had had his secretary Mary Pettigrew call the Hamilton *Times* and Sioux Falls television stations to
announce a three o'clock news conference regarding the suspension
of Sheriff Taylor and developments in the Henslow murder case.

Set up in the center of the broad portico in front of the county
courthouse, two television crews from Sioux Falls had their cameras
trained on him. He stood behind the rostrum which he'd ordered the
janitor to move outside, in the same place as it had been for the

Labor Day ceremonies. He recognized Carla Garza from the Hamilton *Times* standing to the right of the television cameras, notebook in hand. Henslow suppressed a smile, pleased with being in command and now the focus of attention. Finally he had control of the situation again, he thought. His earlier plan to encourage Horst Henslow to retire may have gone astray, fallen into the chaos of unexplained attacks at the Henslow farm and the old man's murder, but now it was being rescued. He was confident that he could manage the outcome, regardless of the origins of the other attacks. It was time for him to transform Sheriff Taylor's shaky theory of a conspiracy by members of the Pioneer Village board into a believable scenario.

"Mr. Taylor has been released," he explained after noting the reason for calling the news conference. "He is released on his own recognizance until my office has investigated in more detail the facts in the matter of PCB oil spills."

"Is Taylor responsible for dumping oil in ditches?" Jerry Holt from KOLO asked.

"That's yet to be determined. What we have is evidence that the sheriff was illegally storing PCB transformer oil on his property. We'll go from there."

"Will your office or the Sheriff's Department be doing the investigation?" Garza asked.

"In view of the circumstances, the State's Attorney's office will supervise the investigation," Henslow replied.

"What about the Henslow murder?" Carla continued. "Will the Sheriff's suspension affect that investigation?"

"As a matter of fact, it will. My office has new evidence in the case and I expect to bring that evidence to a grand jury within the next week. We will look to the jury to determine, on the basis of the evidence in hand, who's responsible for the harassment and eventual death of my father, Horst Henslow, and to return appropriate indictments."

"It's going on to five days since the body was found," Holt asked. "Have you got an autopsy report yet?"

"State Medical Examiner Ronald Bradford arrived in Hamilton Tuesday. The Labor Day weekend delayed his getting here. But he's expected to have a report for us soon."

"What evidence do you have for the grand jury?" Garza asked.

"You all know there is a warrant out for the arrest of one Art Rogers. We have evidence that ties him to the scene. When he is found and arrested, we can expect an indictment against him on the basis of existing evidence that he committed arson. But the situation is more complex than an act of a single party. My office has other evidence that suggests Art Rogers acted as agent for other parties. Part of a conspiracy, I might say, to harass Horst Henslow because of his position with respect to Pioneer Village."

"Can you be more specific? What do you mean 'his position'?" Holt followed up.

"My office has evidence which gives us reason to believe it warranted, although the grand jury will have to determine whether the facts warrant an indictment of members of the Pioneer Village board. Some of them may have been involved in a conspiracy to harass Mr. Henslow and to take advantage of him because of his position on the Village Board of Directors. Despite his generosity in the past, we believe those involved in the conspiracy improperly induced him, under duress, to make a will that gave all his property to the Village."

"You mean you believe his giving his property to Pioneer Village was because members of that board were forcing him to do it?" Carla asked.

"That may well be part of it. The grand jury will have to evaluate the evidence we have in hand."

It was plausible, he thought. This was not the first time the press had inklings of internal arguments over the management of Pioneer Village. Two years ago there had been a resignation from the board in the midst of complaints of how things were being run. The context was right.

Consciously making a frown, Jim Henslow leaned forward as he replied to Garza, she who would keep the fires burning about the case in Hamilton, she who tracked down Taylor and was hot for an exposé. It was she who in exposing Taylor had made it possible for him to take over the case, he thought, controlling it from now on to convict Art Rogers in the public mind. It had to have been Art, who when caught hiding in the barn, killed the old man, regardless of what he claimed. And it wouldn't matter much, once Rogers was gone. The important thing now was that a grand jury be convinced that Rogers acted on orders from Hank Severson and Bickerson. The investigation of conspiracy would set the machinery of the law in motion for months, buying him time to get Rogers out of the way. He could then move on to proving Horst's will was tainted. The two-birds-with-one-stone theory was too good to pass up. It was also his only choice in the circumstances, he reasoned.

As he talked, speaking with conviction, Jim Henslow saw Tommy Johnson standing at the rear of the small crowd of media representatives and curious onlookers who had drifted up to the courthouse steps from the street. Johnson's expression had no hint of curiosity, no wonderment about the new theory. His eyes and brow were knotted together in rage. He was shaking his head.

"Don't you think you have a conflict of interest," Garza was asking, "since you were the likely heir to Horst Henslow's estate?"

"That is the very reason I will be taking the case to the grand jury. We will present the jury with the evidence we have and it will make the judgment about proper indictments. Not me."

"Does that evidence involve a Mr. Hank Severson and Chairman of the Village board, Mr. Bickerson?" Carla continued. "They were picked up Tuesday by the Sheriff's department, weren't they?"

Carla's probing encouraged the TV crews whose cameras continued to run.

"Yes, it does involve them."

"Involved in the conspiracy you mentioned?"

"That is what the grand jury will have to decide. Was there a conspiracy? And if so, for what purpose?"

"But you think there is a basis to believe that there was a conspiracy."

"I do. We know who sabotaged Horst Henslow's tractor. We also now know that the vandalism on his farm home leads back to Mr. Bickerson and an organization he is a part of."

"Which is?"

"That will come out if the grand jury finds a basis for an indictment."

"And you think there is a reason to indict them."

"There is strong and I believe convincing evidence in this case that demands a grand jury weigh it carefully with a view to bringing the guilty to justice."

Tommy Johnson's eyes were ablaze. Henslow avoided his stare.

"Mr. Henslow," Holt began, "are you suggesting that your office is taking over the case because the sheriff's office has bungled the investigation of the vandalism of your father's place, and then his murder?"

"You can draw your own conclusions about that. Sheriff Taylor picked up both Mr. Severson and Mr. Bickerson earlier this week as was just noted and then did nothing about them. There is clear evidence, including Mr. Severson's confession…"

"He confessed to the murder?" Holt interrupted.

"No, no. We have a signed confession by Mr. Severson admitting he sabotaged Mr. Henslow's tractor. There is every reason to believe that this action was part of a conspiracy involving these men and Mr. Rogers. There is reason to believe that Rogers was at the scene of the crime on the night of September 2. The extent of the conspiracy and who all has been involved is what the grand jury will be looking into."

"Mr. Henslow…" Holt began.

"Sorry. That is all I have for you today. We'll let the media know when the grand jury has made its decision. So, you'll excuse me while I get back to my job."

Henslow turned and walked into the courthouse, briskly in case the cameras were still on him. He avoided looking at Tommy Johnson, who stood off to the right at the edge of the raised entry platform. What a break, Jim thought to himself, that Taylor had been caught. His suspension had undermined the whole effort of the Sheriff's Department. Young Morris, new on the job and inexperienced, would be left high and dry without the elected sheriff in command. That ought to be obvious to anyone. The ball was in the State's Attorney's court, as the public would expect.

As Henslow entered his office he was aware of Tommy hurrying down the hallway behind him from the entrance of the courthouse.

"Jim! Just a minute," Johnson called out, his strained voice echoing in the hall.

Henslow stopped in the doorway and turned. As he watched his furious law partner approach he thought calmly that the difficult task was going to be to keep Johnson from demanding to examine up close his copy of the trust agreement. That moment could be delayed until the challenge to the will had been filed and evidence presented in court. He could always claim that Horst had kept the original, that two originals were not made and that he only had a copy. But before that test, he thought, there would be the considerable delay caused by the Henslow murder case. Buying time, no matter how expensive, was the one and only strategy open to him now. As the evidence piled up in the public media and with Rogers clearly in flight to confirm his guilt, the newspapers and television stations would broadcast to the world that he, State's Attorney Jim Henslow, was now in charge and had evidence justifying a grand jury indictment. He had the breathing room he needed.

Johnson spit out a demand.

"Got to talk to you, now."

"Sure. Come in the office."

As he led the way past Mary Pettigrew and into his corner office, late afternoon sunlight was beaming aslant on the varnished maple floor. Henslow felt a calm he had not known for weeks. It was a powerful conviction of being in command he felt at the moment. His senior law partner could not alter that feeling. Johnson would no longer be allowed to treat him as a junior, a wanting student. With the evidence in Rogers' tape recordings safely destroyed, he could manage the rest of the evidence to make the Pioneer Village conspiracy raise enough doubt in any jury's collective mind to suggest that the Henslow property rightly belonged to him. After all, he was the step-son who had borne the lash of a harsh step-father. It was he, Jim Henslow, who had endured a blunt, unloving ex-Nazi who had wheedled his way into his mother's property. That was a plausible plea that raced through his mind as he prepared to face Tommy. Attorney Johnson, Jim thought, would have the burden of proof laid upon his shoulders.

Jim went around his desk to his chair, still standing, making it clear to Johnson that this was his base of authority. They were not in a partners' meeting in Johnson's office.

Tommy shut the door after himself.

"What in hell are you up to?" Johnson exploded. He did not shout but his voice was hoarse with tension. "You know goddamn well those Village board members didn't put out a contract on Horst."

"As a matter of fact, I don't know that, Tommy. Severson confessed to sabotaging the tractor. That was the start."

"A prank. That's one hellova long way from murder."

"Calm down, Tommy. With Taylor screwing up, I had to take over and it was clear that something was up with Severson and Bickerson. Did you know that Jake Bickerson is part of a Jewish organization that goes after ex-Nazis?"

Johnson was clearly caught by surprise.

"How do you know that?"

"Taylor had Jack Traid go to Minneapolis to check out the outfit on whose letterhead the threatening letter found on Dad's body was printed."

"Traid's the prof at Hamilton State, isn't he?"

"The same. He was a detective in Dallas some years ago. Apparently he's a buddy of the Morris's. Taylor and Danny Morris figured Traid could run an errand for them. Deputized him. He digs out the fact that Bickerson is on the Jewish outfit's mailing list, getting their literature. Put that together with Severson's confession and you have probable cause."

"I doubt that," Johnson blurted out. "It was those fellows giving in to Horst's demands, not making any upon him. Horst was the one who was getting his way because he had promised them more land for the Village. He just wanted to become even more important out there. All he wanted was some kind of monument to himself. And he didn't sign his will under any kind of duress. You know damned well that I wouldn't have allowed it if I thought there was the least pressure put on Horst."

"Maybe you just couldn't tell."

"I could tell that Horst was as calm as anything when he finally made the decision. He was determined to act and in a positive state of mind. He had thought about it for months, talked to me about it at least two months ago and had me draft the will. He then came in after the accident with the tractor and said he'd made up his mind. That was a week ago yesterday. August 30th. It was time, Horst said, to show the Village board he was serious about making a big gift."

"After the accident? Doesn't that suggest to you that he was afraid? He certainly was when I took him home from the hospital. He thought Nazi hunters were after him. Severson knew about his fear. He and Bickerson just worked on that. They could have suggested they would protect him if some outfit came after him."

"Jim, that's far fetched as hell. And I resent the suggestion that I didn't know the state of your father's mind when I prepared that will and then had him sign it. The witnesses in our office will testify that he swore he was signing of his own free will. And if you challenge the will, they will be witnesses to that fact. I'll destroy any claim you make to invalidate the will. I promise you that."

"Look Tommy. I'm sorry if you interpret my actions as being an insult to your professional integrity. That's not intended, but I'm duty bound to find out what happened out at Dad's place. Who was harassing him? Who killed him? All that is one hellova lot more important to me than the will. Right now anyway."

"I'd just like to see the original of the trust agreement you say Horst signed on August 30. You say you'll use it to challenge the will." Johnson's eyes had narrowed, accusing.

"You'll see it in due time, when I file the papers within the time limits of probate. But until then, you can be thinking about how confused that bunch on the Village Board made Dad. He didn't know what he was doing when he came into your office on the spur of the moment to sign over the farm to that bunch. When the grand jury has had its say, maybe its decision about Horst's death will put new light on the curious circumstances under which my father signed that will on the same day he kept his promise to my mother and me by turning the farm over to me."

"I don't believe this." Johnson was shaking his head.

"Well, let's see how it turns out. If I'm wrong, I'll admit it. But Dan Morris is convinced that Art Rogers set the fire, was out there the night Horst was killed. Danny has the evidence. He knows Rogers was shot as he fled the fire. And Dan found his knife in the barn near where Horst's body was found. Rogers didn't go out there to get at me as he had when he shot out our window and flattened our tires. He was working for someone. He was into something more serious than petty revenge. And who hated Horst's guts the most? Severson. And he has admitted it. So put Severson and Rogers together and you have the two guys Horst saw running away the night his house was painted with the Swastika. Like the Swastikas we know Rogers painted on the gas cans when he torched the shed."

It was a convincing argument, Jim thought. But, how ironic. Rogers *was* working for someone. He could say that with conviction to anyone, even if *who* had actually hired him was never going to be known to judge or jury. And now with Art Rogers long gone, he thought, the world would have to believe that it was Art Rogers who was involved in a conspiracy to commit arson that had ended with the murder of Horst Henslow. It was the State's Attorney's job to prove that he did it as part of a conspiracy to get revenge against a pushy ex-Nazi that had become troublesome at Pioneer Village.

"Okay," Johnson began. "You go ahead, if this is what you think you have to do. But you sure as hell are putting a strain on the partnership and, I might add, Pettigrew's and others' interest in supporting you in next year's primary."

"Whoa, Tommy. It's the law we're talking about here. Not your ego. Not the success of a law practice. And certainly not my political future. Maybe Dad really intended the farm to go to the Village. I'll admit that when the facts bear it out. But I'll do that only after I'm damned sure he wasn't forced to hand over what was promised to me."

Believe what you say, Jim thought to himself, pleased with the sincerity of his plea. Convince yourself in order to buy time. Sure, so there was no doubt that Horst wanted the Village to have the farm and not his step-son. That had been clear enough in the showdown with the old man. The admission to himself that he might never get the Henslow farm was the compromise he now had to make. And he would likely have to accept the validity of the old man's will in the long run, he admitted, and give up the Chautauqua housing development. But by that time he would have successfully erased his involvement with Rogers. The grand jury was going to provide the delay he needed. There would be time to repair his reputation with the county Republican committee, even with law partners Tommy Johnson and Andy Pettigrew. The still unknown pieces to the puzzle were the medical examiner's report and the ballistics tests from the Pierre laboratories he had to get from the Sheriff's office. Since Danny Morris hadn't found a weapon in his search of Art's and Clarence's places, it might be necessary to conduct a search of Hank Severson's place. Make a show of it. For now even his law partners could be sacrificed to his need for more time. He would figure out how to conceal the forged trust agreement in due time. Just keep priorities straight, he was thinking to himself.

"Okay. Play out your string," Tommy was saying, interrupting Henslow's train of thought. Turning to go, he said flatly, "But you're going to find out that it was a legitimate will, made by a man in his right mind. He was an old man determined to be known as a good, hard-working American, no matter what he had been as a young boy. He says that in the preamble to his will. He loved Pioneer Village. You know that. And even if he irritated Hank Severson, and maybe others, they all were glad to have him dedicated to the Village. He thought of it as a way to live on in the history of this country. Maybe it was only his fantasy. But it was all he had, wasn't it? His little dream?"

Johnson left and Jim Henslow stood gazing at the door closing behind the man who could have assured his election to the state senate if not higher office. Maybe he had just lost Tommy's support. And maybe his law partnership was about to decay. If those loses were the price of survival, of his escape, so be it. For now he knew it wasn't necessary to look further into the future than convincing the grand jury there was a conspiracy brewed by the Pioneer Village board.

His phone rang, awakening him to the march of minutes on this momentous Thursday in September in the life of Chautauqua County's State's Attorney.

"Mr. Allen from Security Bank is on line one," Mary informed him.

"Yes, Orin," Jim said breezily as he picked up the phone. "Thanks for calling back."

"Sure, Jim. Look, about the signature loan. Nothing serious, but I had to stretch a bit to convince the loan committee. You're a little extended in the credit department."

"I realize. But it's only two thousand, Orin. Small emergency. Six months is all I need."

"I understand. Well, I have the money ready for you. But I thought I needed to tell you there was some reluctance on the part of the senior member of the committee."

Jim knew Orin spoke of his father, Julius Allen, President of Security Bank and Trust of Chautauqua County. Julius was also chairman of the county Republican committee and would be thinking about the suitability of a candidate for senate going to Pierre deeply in debt. Shrewd in the ways of money and power, Julius Allen would have put a question mark after Jim Henslow's name, he was certain of that. Perhaps political success was another sacrifice he had to make on the altar of necessity, but it was a sacrifice he was not ready to make just yet.

In eight hours it would be midnight and the first priority of Mr. Art Rogers' disappearance from Chautauqua County would have to be assured.

❧   ❧   ❧

The Hamilton *Times* had delayed its afternoon deadline until four o'clock because of State's Attorney Jim Henslow's news conference. The eight-column headline declared, CONSPIRACY CHARGED IN MURDER CASE. Under Carla Garza's by-line, details of Henslow's charges were given. Sheriff Thomas Taylor had been suspended with pay until further investigation was made into the charge that he illegally stored PCB transformer oil on his premises; he was not yet charged with dumping oil in ditches in and around Chautauqua County; State's Attorney Henslow had taken over investigation of his step-father's murder because of the failure of the Sheriff's Department to act; the Pioneer Village Board of Directors were to be investigated for conducting a conspiracy to threaten Horst Henslow; it is alleged by the State's Attorney that members of the Village board had hired Art Rogers to carry out threats against the elder Henslow. The case would be put before the grand jury as early as next week, according to Jim Henslow. No arrests had been made as yet. An all-points bulletin had been issued for the arrest of Art Rogers, who was wanted on suspicion of arson and possibly murder.

Elliot Morris, editor and publisher of the *Times,* sitting in the spacious living room of their new house in Cottonwood Acres read his newspaper aloud to his wife Minnie. He was pleased with the coverage, commenting, "That Garza woman is a tiger for news. You know, it was she who found out what Taylor was up to."

"And our Danny is in the midst of this. Do you suppose the Commission will make him acting Sheriff?"

"Logical. Who else? At least for the time being."

"I worry it might be dangerous for Danny. That Rogers sounds like a pretty vicious person."

"Yes. But Danny's got the smarts, remember. He's your son."

"That's no protection, is it?" Minnie said flatly.

"Well, Jim Henslow is front and center on the case now, like the State's Attorney should have been all along. Seems like a pretty nasty situation out at the Village, if what he says is true. You can never tell about envy, even among volunteers. Being a director on that board doesn't seem worth a lot to me. But it apparently does for some. Like Hank Severson."

"Yes, and that Mr. Bickerson. He seems like such a nice man to be getting involved in a thing like that."

"Well, my dear, appearances can be deceiving when it comes to ambition, even for petty power in our own Pioneer Village. And maybe it was more serious. You know, those swastikas on Henslow's house were a message from a terrible past, if you ask me."

Morris returned to the front page with satisfaction. His paper was being quoted by others in the state. The coverage of the story was superb. Maybe the paper would get the Newspaper Association prize for best-covered story this year. That, he thought, was an ambition worth having.

CHAPTER 17

*A*fter the interment of Charlene Masters's body in the Prairie Rest Cemetery northeast of town Friday morning, one hundred twenty relatives, friends, loyal parishioners, and duty-bound city and county officials returned to the Presbyterian parish hall in the church basement for lunch served by the Helping Hands Ladies Aid. The solemn ceremony of the funeral service, the promises of faith eloquently asserted by the robed minister from Sioux Falls, and Clyde Masters's visible grief about which members of the church hovered in consolation, including Ellie Easton, recreated in the mind of Jack Traid the scene he imagined had been at Alice's funeral. But he had not been there. Lying unconscious in the hospital during that whole week after the accident he had been as separated from Alice's funeral as he now felt himself separated from this solemn ritual. Today, at the end of services as the people filed out, he watched from the rear of the church as Ellie consoled Reverend Masters in his grief, holding his hand, leaning over him where he sat in the front pew. Traid knew he was looking upon a part of Ellie's essential life which was rooted deep within the faith of this community of worshipers. He watched with regret, knowing with certainty that it was a world he could not enter. It was a world of assurances his experiences taught him to distrust.

At the end of the funeral service he watched Clyde Masters follow the casket up the center aisle of the church, a daughter and son on either side of him. Traid wondered at the consolation this man found in the sympathy which enveloped him on all sides. It was a cold envy, he admitted to himself, that he felt as he watched these his friends performing at a distance in the common drama unfolding during the morning service and then continuing at lunch in the basement of the church. He imagined how he might have entered into this community, slipped in sideways as it were, accompanied by Ellie, and befriended by Gordy as surrogate son. But that would have required that he become stand-in for Ralph Easton whose commitment to family and his faith remained as bedrock in Ellie's life. It was a part beyond faking. Soon he would confess to Ellie what he had discovered about his own feelings, if, he thought, he was able to find the words that would explain the commitment he had finally made to Mildred and to himself.

Ellie was serving coffee at the end of a buffet table as Jack moved toward her in the serving line, his luncheon plate holding a token sandwich and a carrot stick. Ellie looked up from the urn and held out a small silver tray with a cup of coffee on it. She spoke first.

"You got back all right, I see."

"Yes. Wednesday night. Did Gordy tell you I phoned?"

"He did."

"He told me about the funeral. So sad for Reverend Masters. His family."

"Indeed."

"I would have called you yesterday but I got tied up with registration at school. And I figured you were getting things ready here. Maybe I could come out later this evening so we can talk." The line behind him waited for him to move on.

"Give me a call, will you Jack. I have to help here, maybe until late."

"Okay. Sure. I'll do that."

The truth occurred to him at that instant. She knew what had happened to him in Minneapolis, of course. Maybe she had known all along while they dated that he was tentative toward their relationship because of Mildred. Ellie knew of his and Mildred's year when they had been nearly inseparable. And Ellie had seen Mildred's painting hanging in the gallery-breezeway of his house and commented that its title, "Love's Splendor," was "interesting." Perhaps, he thought, it was his unspoken, even unconscious longing for another woman, signaled by the faintest gesture or tentative tone of voice, which for Ellie had made him seem safe as a companion. In the beginning of their friendship all future options Ellie might imagine had seemed to him open to negotiation, but Ellie's birthday gift of the Bible had made clear her minimum bid requirement.

Distracted by his thoughts about how to explain to Ellie what had happened in Minneapolis, Jack had not noticed Dan Morris in the crowded basement nor behind him as he started up the stairway from the church basement.

"Jack," Dan called. "Got a minute?"

"Dan. Sorry I missed you Wednesday night when I got back, but I was bushed. I left the copy of the trust agreement and the JDL mailing list with Sally in your office yesterday morning. Couldn't wait for you to come in because I had to be at school. Registration."

"Yeah. I understand. Sally gave me the list and agreement. I haven't had a chance to talk to Jim Henslow about them yet, what with all the ruckus about Sheriff Taylor being suspended. What do you think about that? And about Henslow saying he's taking over the homicide investigation?"

"Well, Taylor being caught was reported in the paper last night. So Taylor got himself in big trouble. What's going on about Henslow taking over the investigation? Grand jury and all that? Where does that leave you?"

"He as much as told me I was an incompetent. Both Taylor and me."

"So? What are you going to do?"

"Commissioner George Carter let me know that the County Commission is going to appoint me Acting Sheriff. So as far as I'm concerned we sure as hell will still do our own investigation. But I expect that Henslow is going to make trouble for us. He's already indicated that he wants us to restrict what we do. He keeps suggesting to the press that the Sheriff's Department bungled the investigation, even before we really got started, and before all of the evidence has been evaluated by the Crime Lab in Pierre. It hasn't been a week since we found the body, for crying out loud."

The two men walked down the street toward Dan's cruiser.

"How'd you catch Taylor?" Jack asked.

"Carla Garza got me to follow him Wednesday night. In her car. Boy, is she something." Dan caught the enthusiasm in his voice and then added, "I mean as a reporter. She had discovered that Taylor was storing drums of oil on his place. Then she figured out that he was going to move them because his wife had probably seen Carla's car on the side road near their place. That was on the night Carla got pictures of the oil drums inside of his barn. We caught him trying to move drums of PCB oil from his farm to an old barn south of town."

"You arrested him?"

"I guess you'd have to say that. I brought him back to town and called Jim Henslow since he's the chief law enforcement officer in the county. And I called George Carter. Carter suspended Taylor on the spot. Like I said, the Commission meets this afternoon to decide about my taking over until they figure out what to do."

"Hell of a way to get promoted. Did Taylor do the dumping?"

"Don't know for sure. He says no. Henslow is going to charge him with illegally storing the oil. Henslow said I should see what I could turn up on the spills. But Henslow's trying to wave me off his old man's homicide case. And it bothers me to hell and gone."

"What do you mean?"

"As I said, he as much as told me I wasn't competent to continue the investigation, being right out of law school and police training. Wants our office to turn over all the evidence we have once it comes back from the crime lab, which includes the steel shotgun pellets I got from Doc Brasley in Chesterton, and Art Rogers' jacket, which I got Wednesday. And Henslow got Judge Nelson to delay giving me search warrants Tuesday to go through the Rogers' places. Pisses me off, frankly. The delay gave Rogers a chance to run."

"So what did you tell Henslow when he asked for all the evidence?"

"Well, despite Commissioner Carter suggesting I not tangle with Jim Henslow and sort of hold back on the Department's investigation, I told Henslow we'd be prepared to present what we had in court or before a grand jury, but that I wasn't giving up our investigation."

"Good for you. And what did he say to that?"

"Shrugged it off. Said he'd call on us to present evidence to the grand jury when it was needed. And you should have heard him at the news conference yesterday. He's saying that Art Rogers was hired by Severson and Bickerson to harass Horst Henslow as a way to scare the old man off the Pioneer Village board and, if you can believe it. Then he says that was the way they tried to force his step-father to deed the farm to the Village. He accused Sheriff Taylor of failing to arrest Severson and Bickerson after bringing them in and having evidence to hold them. Completely distorted what happened. And I have my notes of what went on that night."

"Well, in my opinion," Jack said, "the Village board could have wanted to do one or the other, but it doesn't make sense to think they would believe they could do both? Scare him off the board and at the same time get him to give his property to the Village? Doesn't compute."

"They couldn't and wouldn't, if you ask me. There is something fishy as hell, Jack, the way Henslow has moved in. Kind of desperate like. The day after his old man was killed he was telling me to lay off Rogers. He said then he was conducting his own investigation into how Rogers was harassing **him**. But now his theory is that Severson and Bickerson hired Rogers to burn the shed to scare the old man, but that Art got caught in the barn by Henslow and had to kill him."

"But you did find Rogers's knife near the body. Is Jim Henslow using that evidence?"

"Sure. But let me tell you the fishy part. This morning I get a call from Don Fogel, the *Argus Leader* reporter. He's calling from Pierre. He read the Hamilton *Times* story and he's been talking to Jim Henslow's wife Sheri. She's out there on a photo assignment for the *Argus*. He told me that he figured there'd been some pillow talk between Henslow and his wife. He said that Sheri Henslow told him about the knife with the initials AR which, according to her, proved Art Rogers shot the old man. But listen to this, she told him it was found in the stall near the body. Jack, I never told anyone exactly where I found that knife."

"Yeah, that's right. Come to think of it, you didn't. You just said you found it near the body."

"The way it was obviously covered by a heap of straw made it appear to be planted. At least that was the way it seemed to me at the time. So I figure I'd just let it's exact location be my secret until the whole picture got clearer."

"So how did the State's Attorney's wife know exactly where it was found?"

"It's my opinion," Dan said, "that the conspiracy in the Henslow homicide case is a bit more complicated than a bunch of old guys jockeying for position on the Pioneer Village board? The question is, what have Jim and Sheri Henslow been up to?"

"And it fits in with what I've been saying about the scene out there. It wasn't just Art Rogers' signature, like the gas cans. More hands were at work out there than a single hired arsonist. When are the reports from the Crime Lab expected?"

"I got some of them this morning. Special courier from Pierre. Slugs in Henslow were from a .32 caliber pistol. That snag of leather I found on the door of the stall could not have come from Art's leather jacket. The lab says it was an old piece that had been tanned years ago. I sent Art's jacket and the steel pellets into the lab today to confirm that. So the leather bit doesn't add up to anything yet. But there are some connections. The spray paint that was on the house is not the same as the paint on the gas cans. My guess is that when the lab analyzes the paint I found in Rogers' shop, it will turn out to be the same as that on the cans. Rogers' prints are on the knife. His were in the state files because of an arrest a couple years ago. Other prints have not been identified yet. There were no prints on the threatening letter. The steel shot gun pellets Doc. Brasley got out of Rogers will be checked by the lab to compare them with the brand of shells Horst Henslow gave Gloria Miller for the 20 gauge. So, if those bits of evidence prove out, there seems no doubt that Rogers was the guy who was shot as he was fleeing from the shed and, therefore, is the one who set the fire. But was he in the barn? Would he have been there hours earlier with his knife, stalking Henslow, who was shot, not stabbed? It doesn't take alot of experience to know there is something strange about the crime scene."

"Oh yes. As I said, too much evidence. Too many hands in the deal. It would sure help to grill Rogers for a couple hours. No one has seen Rogers since you put out the APB? No sightings?"

"Nope. The warrant has been out on him since Wednesday. Every law enforcement outfit in the country knows we're looking for him."

"Yeah, right, along with a hundred other wanteds," Jack replied.

"Well, he's on the run, which at least helps Henslow's theory that he's the prime suspect."

"Well, it seems pretty clear now that Rogers set the fire," Jack said, starting to enumerate. "and slashed Henslow's tires, and shot out the window. But Rogers and the Jewish Defense League don't fit, not that or a threatening letter. And there is the curious business of the swastikas on gas cans that Rogers must have brought to the scene. Painted backwards, not the Nazi way that was splashed on Henslow's house. Other hands were at work there."

"But, you have to ask yourself," Dan replied, "is there any possibility that Severson and Bickerson hired him and then paid him to disappear?"

"I have a hard time leaping from Severson's prank with the tractor to a deep, dark conspiracy with a hired arsonist. Think about what was going on at the Henslow farm that Saturday night," Jack spoke slowly, threading through events carefully. "We know from Gloria Miller that someone called her to get her off the farm, away from Horst. Female voice. We also know from her that Horst was on guard because of the threats. And he and Jim Henslow had just had a big argument. So there the old man was, armed and patrolling his farm from late afternoon on. But he's not around when Miller returns to the farm and goes right into the house. It's a couple hours past the time she got the phone call. Then we have to remember that Coroner White guessed that Henslow had been dead for several hours before he was found during the fire. So he was probably dead by the time Miller got back to the farm. It was obviously planned that way. Does it make sense that Rogers would get some woman to call Miller to get her off the place and then hide in the barn for hours, shoot Henslow, wait a couple more hours and then set the fire?"

"Not in my book," Dan replied.

"And you'd be right."

"Seems to me," Dan went on, "that if you're going to commit arson, you go to the scene, do the job and get the hell out of there."

"Which leads us back to Sheri Henslow knowing where Art Rogers' knife was found when common sense suggests he wasn't even in the barn. The way it looks to me is that the two suspects which will not be presented to the grand jury are Jim and Sheri Henslow."

"Well, she sure knows something or Fogel wouldn't have known exactly where the knife was found."

"Right. Step back and look at the whole landscape, Dan. In the first instance Jim Henslow doesn't want you to pick up Rogers when its him that Henslow suspects is harassing him—the guy who shot out the living room window, slashed the tires. He was going to take care of that, remember. Then, according to Henslow, in a matter of days Rogers has become the centerpiece in a conspiracy against his old man with two Pioneer Village directors with whom he had little to do, except his occasional appearance as the blacksmith at the Village. Rogers wasn't involved in Village politics. I know that for a fact because I've been out there on a regular basis and have seen Rogers only during Pioneer Days. So what's the real connection between Henslow and Rogers? Why did Henslow have Judge Nelson delay giving you the search warrants? That's what we have to find out."

"We? Are you suggesting you'll still help?"

"I have to tell you Dan, while I was in Minneapolis I found out some things about myself, and about me and Mildred Singer that changes my world. Those days in Minneapolis made me decide to forget about going back to Dallas days and playing detective for you and Taylor. I had decided to give you the stuff I got in Minneapolis and unvolunteer. But I guess Henslow's saying the Sheriff's Department is a bunch of incompetents rubs off onto me too. We can't leave it at that, can we? So, I'm still deputized, aren't I?"

"Far as I'm concerned you are."

"So, what's the delay with the autopsy? I thought the medical examiner was to be in town this last Tuesday."

"He was. Did the autopsy on Horst Henslow Tuesday afternoon, and I guess part of Wednesday. Yesterday he phoned and said he was delaying his report. He said he had some consulting to do with a couple medical experts in Sioux Falls because of a complication. He promised he would be back in town and have a final report this morning."

"So he's in town?"

"At White's Funeral home. He said he released the body to White yesterday. I don't know when Horst's funeral is scheduled."

"Let's go over there, now. Before Henslow gets his hands on his report."

White's was a block west of the church. The two men got in the cruiser and headed back toward the church and turned up the side street. Cars of the funeral goers lined both sides of the street. Dan found an open space and parked in front of the funeral home, a three-story Victorian house that had been converted into a mortuary. As Dan and Jack got out of the cruiser, a White's Funeral Home hearse returning from the cemetery was backing under a logia at the east side of the house. At the same moment Carla Garza's red Camaro pulled up along side Dan's cruiser. Carla was getting out as Dan and Traid hailed Don White.

"Dan," Carla called, "can I see you a sec?"

"Sure." Turning to Traid, Dan said, "See what White knows about the examiner's report while I talk to Carla."

Dan walked over to where Carla stood in the open door on the driver's side of her car. The intense beauty of her dark eyes and the ease of her shapely posture spoke to him once again. The dance she had arranged for them to attend couldn't come any too soon. This official relationship, he thought, would then come to an end. There was a real woman here he had to know better.

"What's up, Carla."

"I just got a tip from inside White's that the M.E. has determined it wasn't a homicide! Henslow died of natural causes."

"What the hell! With two bullets in him?"

"That's why I'm here. What's going on?"

"Besides your having insiders all over the place, Traid and I were just about to talk to the medical examiner. Why don't you wait here awhile. I'll make it official for you, if what you say is true."

"You're pretty nice," Carla said, smiling, "for a cop."

"You're not so bad yourself," he replied, "for a snoop."

Dan hurried over to Traid and White who stood under the loggia at the side door to the mortuary.

"You know what the M.E. found?" Dan asked White.

"Well, he wasn't final about anything last night, just as I was telling Jack here. He told me that it was a strange case. Appears he had some consultation yesterday with other doctors."

"So, what has he concluded?" Traid asked.

"He's questioning my calling it a homicide. But let him tell you himself," White said with irritation. "It seemed clear enough to me, but he's the high powered state examiner and you'll have to take his word for it."

The three entered what was once the front parlor, now set up with fifty some chairs arranged for a service and facing a lectern at the far end of the long room extending into what had once been a dining room.

"My office is over here," White said, leading the two around the ranks of metal chairs. "Dr. Bradford is finishing up his report there."

The three men entered the solarium converted into an office on the west side of the house as Bradford was getting up from White's desk.

"Dr. Bradford," Dan said, holding out his hand, "I'm Dan Morris, Deputy Sheriff, and this is Jack Traid. We understand you have finished your autopsy of Horst Henslow. I'd like to have a copy if you are finished."

"I am that. And let me tell you, I don't think I've ever run into a case just like this."

"In what way?" Dan asked.

"First glance it looks like Mr. Henslow was victim of gunshot. Just like Don White thought. Two shots to be precise. Close up. Small caliber. But not much evidence of bleeding, as you noted in your report. But it wasn't gunshot that killed him. He was dead when he was shot. Massive coronary occlusion. I double checked what I found with my colleagues in Sioux Falls. I have no doubt about the conclusion now. It's in the report."

"Excuse me, doctor," Jack said. "You say you felt it necessary to consult with other doctors before making your decision. That right?"

"Yes. The heart had all the characteristics of a coronary, but was just a little different than one might expect."

"Different in what way?" Jack persisted.

"Indications of fibrillation. But just maybe. But I decided finally that that didn't make much difference. The coronary was clear enough, and my colleagues agreed. It's all in the report."

"May we have a copy now?" Dan asked.

"Soon as Mr. White's secretary has finished at her computer and makes us copies. I'll sign them and the case is all yours."

In ten minutes White's secretary handed three stapled copies of the medical examiner's report to Bradford, who, after scribbling a signature on each, gave one copy to Dan, one to Coroner White, and kept one for himself. Closing his brief case, he prepared to leave.

"According to what I've learned of South Dakota law, no crime has been committed if you pump a few rounds into a dead body. That is, of course, if you weren't doing it to mislead authorities and cover up a real crime."

Bradford was smiling, satisfied with his findings. As he stood in the doorway to leave, he added, "So you folks will have some fun discovering what the real crime was here in Chautauqua County."

Dan and Jack were left alone when Don White accompanied Bradford to the front door.

"You better make the record public before it gets ground up in a grand jury proceeding orchestrated by Jim Henslow," Jack advised. "Despite all the hell you'll catch from him."

"You're right," Dan agreed. "But, Sheri Henslow's knowledge of where the knife was found will be ours alone, for the time being. Okay? That may be the key to a Henslow Pandora's box."

"Jim Henslow won't be the first public official to use the law to protect himself," Jack opined.

"Guess I've got a news reporter waiting for me," Dan said to no one in particular.

❦　　　❦　　　❦

Evening supper finished, the dishes washed, Jack Traid sat opposite Rasputin in the living room, the latter curled up in his chair, his one good eye blinking in recognition of the report being read to him.

"It all seems to be here, Rasp. Except it isn't all here," Jack said over the top of Friday's edition of the *Times.*

Carla's by-lined story about the Henslow matter was printed under the eight-column headline: NO HOMICIDE; ARSONIST SOUGHT. It was clear from the article that Dan had summarized for Carla all the evidence he had except about the location of the knife. There were still Crime Lab evaluations to receive of evidence found on the Rogers' places in Chesterton, Dan had stated, but the evidence pretty clearly indicated that Art Rogers was the prime suspect in the torching of the shed on Henslow's farm. Jack was pleased that Dan had decided to lay the evidence out and ignore the pressure from Jim Henslow to leave the Henslow matter to him. And Dan had guts enough to ignore Commission Chairman George Carter telling him to let Henslow take the lead.

Carla's story reported that the steam tractor accident had been a prank admitted to by Hank Severson who denied any connection with painting a swastika on Horst Henslow's house, or being involved with the burning the tool shed on the Henslow place.

"I was wrong to play a trick on Mr. Henslow," Severson was quoted as saying, "but my friends at the VFW meeting in Sioux Falls and my wife will verify where I was at the time of Horst Henslow's death and the fire on his place."

"Dan Morris," the newspaper article went on, "Deputy Sheriff now in charge of the Department until the suspension of Sheriff Tom Taylor has been resolved, said a region-wide search continues for Art Rogers on the charge of arson." Evidence at the scene, the report said, as well as medical reports of Rogers being treated for a gunshot wound inflicted on him as he allegedly ran from the scene, all point to him as the perpetrator of the arson. Morris also reported that there had been no sightings of Rogers since the warrant was issued, not by members of the public nor law enforcement personnel. The origin of the threatening letter found on Horst Henslow's body had not been determined. No motive for the shooting of Henslow's corpse had been determined by the Sheriff's Department.

"State's Attorney Jim Henslow said," the *Times* article stated, "that he will present evidence to the grand jury to look into the matter of a possible conspiracy by members of the Pioneer Village Board of Directors to intimidate Horst Henslow. Deputy Sheriff Morris said in response to the *Times* reporter questioning, that the Sheriff's Department did not have evidence of such a conspiracy."

The gauntlet thrown down before Jim Henslow by Dan Morris was now public. Traid was pleased. Dan had backbone. And maybe the challenge would be just enough pressure on Henslow to cause him to make a slip. The unfolding of events during the past week saw an abrupt shift in Henslow's tactics with regard to Rogers, first hands-off, then an all-out case of Art Rogers being agent of a grand conspiracy by the Village Board. The change spoke loudly to Traid about Jim Henslow having motives not yet clear.

Traid gazed at the puckered skin over Rasputin's right eye. Sort out the scars, he thought to himself. He reviewed the logic of Henslow's theories about what the Pioneer Village board of directors had allegedly done to Horst Henslow. There were irritations there, between Horst and the other members of the board. But scars that motivated a grand plan? More interesting was the still unresolved problem of two conflicting documents with Horst Henslow's signatures dated the same day. It was there that one found intimation of scars. The mystery to be solved was the one not mentioned in the press. How was it that Horst Henslow signed a trust agreement turning control of the farm over to his adopted son on the very same day that he signed his will giving that same farm to Pioneer Village? It was that mystery that cast a spotlight upon the State's Attorney and explained his need for time. The image of the diligent prosecutor which Jim Henslow had sought to convey to the media at yesterday's news conference was far from the image of Jim Henslow which was developing in Traid's mind.

If Dan's investigation was under implied strictures from a confused and cautious county commission, he, Jack Traid wasn't so confined, and he had nothing to lose.

"Seems to me, Rasp, that I ought to go out and have a word with Mr. Bickerson. Maybe no one has really listened carefully to his story and what really has been going on out at Pioneer Village. What do you think?"

Rasputin blinked his good eye once again, pleased with the quiet of the room, which was broken only with the reassuring sounds of this man's voice.

"Good. I knew you'd agree with that."

Putting down the newspaper, Jack went to the kitchen, looked through the telephone book on the counter until he found Bickerson's number which he dialed.

A young girl answered. "Bickerson residence."

"Hello. My name is Jack Traid. Is Mr. Bickerson at home?"

"Just a minute, please."

Jack could hear voices in the farm house room. "For you daddy." A pause. Someone whispering.

"Yes. This is Jacob Bickerson."

"Mr. Bickerson, this is Jack Traid. We talked at Pioneer Village after the tractor incident."

"Yes, Mr. Traid."

"I'm a friend of Deputy Sheriff Dan Morris, and giving him a little help in the Henslow matter. I wonder if you'd be willing to talk to me again. I'd just like to learn a little more about Pioneer Village. How the board has been run. How decisions are made out there."

"Certainly. I welcome your visit, Mr. Traid. Anytime."

"Even tonight? About eight?"

"Sure. That will be fine with me."

Traid got directions to the Jacob Bickerson farm. It was only a fifteen minute drive from his house. There was time to shower and shave. After all, Jack thought, it might turn out to be a special occasion.

❧   ❧   ❧

Jim Henslow spit epithets toward every wall in his living room, throwing the Friday evening *Times* on the floor. Jumping up from the recliner chair, he hurried into the kitchen to phone Dan Morris. He then changed his mind and went back to the recliner. KOLO's evening news hour was beginning. Holt was re-running Henslow's press conference statement about a possible conspiracy by the Pioneer Village board to harass the elder Henslow which ended in a homicide. Holt stressed the contradiction to that theory posed by today's medical examiner's report that Horst Henslow died a natural death.

"The State Medical Examiner Bradford has found that Horst Henslow died of natural causes, and was apparently shot after he died," Holt announced emphatically. "Chautauqua County State's Attorney Henslow had theorized that harassment of his father by members of the Pioneer Village board had led to murder. But we learn from the state medical examiner that there was no murder committed. The question now is how this information will affect the State's Attorney's call for a grand jury investigation."

"Are you just going to let it hang there, you bastard?" Jim yelled at the television set. "Give me a call and I tell you what the hell is going to happen."

Holt wasn't reporting the reasons he'd given in yesterday's news conference why a reasonable person would suspect the Village board. No mention of Severson's confession. Nothing about the farm being willed to the Village. His theory might be a fiction, but it was a believable one. As Jim Henslow fumed, Holt's report had turned to a traffic fatality south of Sioux Falls on Interstate 29, the television showing the smoldering ruins of an automobile.

Henslow turned again to the *Times* and read once more the statement by Dan Morris that there was no evidence of a conspiracy by the Village board. What the hell did he know? The problem would be to get George Carter to keep Morris busy on oil spills and prevent that worn out cop Traid from meddling any more. The sooner he got to the grand jury the sooner the story would take the focus he needed it to have.

Jim got up again and went to the kitchen to fix a drink. As he poured half a glass of Scotch over ice the telephone rang.

"It's me honey," Sheri said lightly. "Reporting in."

"Did you hear the news?"

"About poor old Horst dying of a heart attack?"

"Yeah. The medical examiner's report today. He decided Horst had been dead when he was shot."

"I knew that honey. Didn't you figure that out when bad ol' Mr. Rogers' knife was missing from your drawer?"

"What are you talking about, Sheri? For christsakes, this isn't some kid's game."

"I know that, Jimmy. Your old man was dead when I found him in the barn that night."

"What the hell. You what?"

"Just in case anyone starts to say different, I found him flat on his face. In the barn. Dead as anything. Least he looked like it."

"You were out there?"

"Why sure honey. I thought you'd figure that out by now."

"For God's sake don't say anything to anyone. And get on home so we can work this out."

"No need to panic, Jimmy. Aren't you looking for that Mr. Rogers who did all that bad stuff? Even if he didn't kill the old bastard."

"They don't know where he is. And they won't. He's long gone."

"I put your pistol right back where I found it before I left for Aberdeen."

"Well, I gave it to Rogers, so no one's going to connect it with the old man. But don't you say anything more, Sheri. Not to anyone. Get back here as soon as you can so we can get our stories straight."

"Okay, Jim," Sheri said, her voice lowered, serious. "I'll be home tomorrow night. I got my pictures here and will drop them off at the *Argus* before coming home. But don't worry, honey. You'll figure your way though this. I really believe you'll still get what's rightfully yours."

When he hung up the phone Jim Henslow was fixed to where he stood in the kitchen, drink in hand. What, he thought, would she have done if Horst had been alive? Had she gone out there with his gun to kill Horst? Premeditated? But right now he had to figure out the reason Art Rogers would shoot a corpse as part of the Pioneer Village conspiracy. Once that fit, then he, Jim Henslow, could relax with the knowledge that Rogers' was no longer around to confess his sins, both real and manufactured. After that he would deal with Cheri, the wild card in the deck.

CHAPTER 18

Two security lights flooded the Bickerson farmyard as Jack Traid turned in from the county road. The newly graveled driveway ran along the fence enclosing a lawn and flower gardens prepared for fall dormancy. To the right of the drive was a double garage, its overhead door closed. Ahead was a steel equipment barn, its wide, sliding door pulled shut. At a glance he could tell that the Bickerson family took pride in its home place.

Getting out of the Toyota, Jack went to the back door of the ranch house and knocked. It opened immediately. Jake Bickerson held the door wide.

"Come in. Come in," Bickerson urged. "Saw you drive in."

"Sorry to bother you at night like this," Jack said, offering his hand. "I just felt that someone ought to listen to your story a little more carefully."

"Yes. I wish Mr. Henslow would, anyway," Jake replied. "Come in the living room. Rachel has made us some coffee and there are freshly baked cookies if you'd like."

The two men went through the modern kitchen, it's oak cabinets gleaming, the counters uncluttered and newly polished. More evidence of care, love of home, Jack thought.

"I want you to meet my wife, Rachel, Mr. Traid. And this is my daughter Sarah."

Jack greeted both, taking Rachel's offered hand as softly as it was given.

"My son is out in the fields somewhere. He's trying to lure that white buck onto our place. Thinks he can get the thousand dollars Andy's restaurant is offering for whoever shoots it and brings it in."

"Yes, I know about that," Jack replied. A fresh memory flashed through his mind, tainted with regret, of Gordy and him sitting against the Easton barn waiting for a glimpse of the albino buck.

"Sarah and I will let you men talk," Rachel explained. "We'll be in the kitchen, Jacob. In case you need us." Woman and girl prepared to leave the room, waiting for husband and father to nod agreement. Observed closely, Jack thought, one could see through the placid appearance and modest voice of this farm woman to a subtle but nervous beauty. Her dark eyes seemed to search for answers in the room before the questions had been raised. Sarah, on the other hand, seemed confident, without worry. She was dressed in a plaid shirt which hung loosely over Levi's. She smiled her braces at Traid. Rachel lead the way into the kitchen.

"Again, I apologize, Mr. Bickerson, for this intrusion."

"Jake. Please call me Jake. Okay? And you are not intruding."

"Thank you. I realized from talking to Dan Morris about the notes he took that no one in the Sheriff's Department, or for that matter the State's Attorney's office, had seriously interviewed you since Horst's death. I understand that during the night Sheriff Taylor brought you into town for questioning the atmosphere was pretty strained. Dan showed me his notes. Both you and Hank offered information about where you were last Saturday night, but I didn't get a complete story from that. Taylor sure wasn't interested in listening, according to Dan. And a lot has happened since Dan and I had talked to you and Hank Severson at Pioneer Village right after the tractor incident. Now we have Hank's statement to Dan about playing a trick on Horst, and I'm willing to believe that it was just that, a prank. But everything that has happened at the Henslow farm since then makes it clear to me there was a conspiracy of some kind to frighten Horst Henslow into believing someone, or some group like the Jewish Defense League was after him because of his past."

"Yes, I know. Sheriff Taylor had Hank's statement about playing a trick on Horst and then jumped into believing that Hank and I were involved in all that business out at Henslow's farm, too. And now Henslow is saying we were forcing Horst to turn over the farm to the Village."

"Well, let me concentrate on you first, Jake. Did you and Hank plan the tractor sabotage together? Did you give him any help or know about what he was going to do ahead of time?"

"No. I wouldn't do anything like that. And I didn't know Hank was going to do something like that. If I had, I would have asked him not to. He has a temper that he let's loose every once in awhile. Horst irritated him a lot. He just couldn't forget that Horst had been in the Hitler Youth, and all that."

"And as a Jew you could?"

"As a Jew I cannot describe the sadness I feel about those times in Germany. But Horst was just a young boy at that time. I don't know what he did back then. Maybe bad things. But I knew he was living in America now, worked hard on his farm, and for Pioneer Village. We got along."

"But he made trouble on the Village Board?"

"Not trouble. He just thought his was the only way. Like the tractor barn. Hank had a plan for how it should be laid out. Horst had another one and because he was paying for most of the lumber, Horst insisted on his way. Hank fumed about that for weeks."

"But the board agreed to make Horst Parade Marshal for Pioneer Days next month. How did that come about when he was so disliked?"

"We all knew being Marshal was what he wanted most. He didn't hide that in any way. He'd say something like, 'If a man contributes enough to the Village, he maybe ought to get some honors.' Hank would nearly explode when he heard Horst say that."

"Hank didn't vote for Horst getting to be Parade Marshal?"

"Oh, no."

"But you did. Why?"

"A good question. I have asked myself that too since Horst died. Maybe if we hadn't made him Marshal, none of this would have happened. I mean Hank doing that trick to his tractor seems to have opened Horst to the rest of those threats. No, I voted to make him Parade Marshal because underneath all his bragging, and his hints that he had more to give to the Village, he was a man wanting to be part of us. He really wanted to be a pioneer, even if he never could be."

"About the hints? Did he offer to will his farm to the Village before the tractor accident, like an exchange for being made Parade Marshal, or elected chairman?"

"Hints, but no bargaining. He told me once that the village was the most important thing in his life after his wife died. He said he wanted to do all he could to make it grow, but he never specifically offered the farm in exchange for anything. The board members knew he was going to make an announcement of some kind at this year's Pioneer Days. He told us that much. That's why I told you to leave some room in the *Village Voice* for a story. But we didn't know about the will until Tommy Johnson had us in to his office on Labor Day, after Horst died."

"Henslow says the board acted together to force Horst into giving the Village his farm, scare him as if you had something on him to reveal if he didn't…"

"Ridiculous," Jake said, interrupting Traid. "In the first place, Horst Henslow was not a man you could scare into anything. He knew what he wanted and didn't care if you didn't agree with him. The important thing is that the board members never got together and made a plan to do something to him. Never."

"But he asserted himself over and over even if it irritated other members of the group?"

"You put it exactly right. But you have to remember that Horst was always giving to the Village. Doing all kinds of things to make it better."

"You've said that he had given up land earlier for the Chautauqua reservoir, and he'd paid for building the tractor sheds. What else did he contribute?"

"Oh, many things. Like moving old buildings onto the Village from surrounding places. Like the Grandview Country School we got a year ago. Horst paid to have that hauled in. Helped do much of the work getting it settled in the Village."

"No one on the board said to him, 'If you give us this, you can be Marshal? And if you don't…'"

"There was no bargaining. No threats. He expected to be recognized. No doubt about it. But you didn't bargain with Horst."

"You didn't object to Horst becoming chairman someday?"

"Why should I? If that was the way a man thought he could prove himself a good American, why should I try to stop him? Especially if the majority of the board agreed."

"What about Art Rogers, Jake? Jim Henslow is saying that you and Hank got Rogers involved in harassing Horst. It is clear from the evidence Dan Morris has that Rogers has been involved in harassing Horst Henslow. Jim is suggesting that you hired Rogers to paint the threat on Horst's house and then to burn down his shed."

"It could never have been like that. Art Rogers had little to do with the board. And the board members certainly didn't associate with him. But he's just the best blacksmith around, and that's why he was asked years ago to run the smithy in the Village during Pioneer Days. He agreed to do it, but was grudging about it. He wasn't out there very many other times. You know that yourself. Art kept the blacksmith barn locked up until the October Pioneer Days celebration because he kept some of his antique forge tools in there. Touchy as could be about his stuff. Fact is, he was the only one with a key to that place. The board agreed that he could lock it with his own padlock. That was the only deal we ever made with Art Rogers."

"Maybe he and Hank had a deal you didn't know about. What about that?"

"Not very likely. No, I don't think so. If Hank disliked Horst, he hated Art Rogers."

"But Rogers was a veteran. Retired from the Army. Didn't that make a difference to Hank?"

"Well, it was the other way around. Hank told me that Rogers made fun of the veterans' organizations. Called the VFW 'very feeble women.' Hank would have nothing to do with him."

"Well, finally Jake, I have to ask you about the literature you have been getting from the Jewish Defense League in Minneapolis. When did you start getting interested in the JDL?"

"I don't know anything about that outfit."

"But your name is on their mailing list. They've been mailing a newsletter to you."

"Someone must have given them my name. Rachel and the kids throw out all that advertising."

"This is a crucial point Jake. Your name is on their mailing list, one of the few in South Dakota. There is a direct tie between Horst's death and that literature because of the threatening letter. Are you saying that nothing from the JDL comes to you in the mail?"

"Our mail comes late in the afternoon. Most of the time Rachel or Sarah, sometimes Jonah, go out to get it. They say that anything from a Jewish League must have been thrown out with the other junk mail."

Voices in the kitchen became noticeable to the two men.

"Must be my son Jonah coming in," Jake said.

"Oh yes. You said he was out looking for the albino deer. I'd be interested if he saw it."

"Well, let's ask him," Jake replied and then raised his voice. "Jonah, come in here and meet Mr. Traid."

As they waited Jake added, "You teach at Hamilton State, don't you? Maybe you could talk Jonah into staying home a year and going there instead of the University. Keep him home a bit longer to make Rachel happy."

"I can give it a try, but the University must be pretty attractive to a young man."

Jonah came into the room casually, looking to his father, then Jack. He had the square, solid body of a varsity football player, was nearly six feet tall and broad shouldered. His full head of dark black hair, which had been ruffled by the evening breeze, emphasized his relaxed, youthful manner.

"This is Mr. Traid, Jonah."

"Jack Traid," Jack said, holding out his hand to the young man.

Jonah shook hands, his grip firm, manly. He looked Jack in the eye as he said, "Glad to meet you Mr. Traid." There was no shyness of youth. In fact, Jack thought to himself, there was a hint of cordial defiance, the accomplished athlete standing on equal ground with his elders. It struck Jack at the moment that up until then no one had notice that there were two J. Bickerson's in this household, and that he may have been interviewing the wrong one, one who had no connection to Pioneer Village politics.

"I have been talking to your dad about what happened out at the Henslow farm. Seems as if Jake is in more trouble than he deserves, in my opinion."

Jack watched for Jonah's reaction. It was Jake's expression that grew into a smile. Jonah's remained unchanged.

"I'm glad to hear you believe me, Mr. Traid," Jake said. "They say you use to be a detective in Dallas before you got into the teaching business."

"Right," Jack replied, still watching for a reaction from Jonah. "If nothing else the experience helped me develop hunches about people much of the time they turn out right, but sometimes not. In your case, Jake, it's clear to me you had nothing to gain personally, either at the Village or in some other manner. From what you've said about your relationship with him, I can see no reason you'd have to harass Horst Henslow. Sheriff Taylor should have figured that out. And Jim Henslow too. The evidence points elsewhere."

Jonah turned to leave the room.

"Jonah, did you happen see the albino deer out there?" Jack asked.

Jonah stopped, then turned to face the two men.

"Not yet. A neighbor saw him a couple nights ago so I put out a salt block and some feed."

"And if it shows up?"

"Well, when deer season opens I might get a shot at the thousand bucks Andy's Restaurant is offering."

"That would help with tuition," Jake said.

"There's going to be a lot of competition," Traid said, and then added, "Since I'm about to leave, do you mind going back out and showing me where you set up the salt lick? Maybe we'll see him tonight."

"Sure. I don't mind," Jonah said.

"This okay with you Jake?" Traid asked the senior Bickerson.

"Oh, fine. You and Jonah go out and have a look."

"After that I'll be leaving," Traid said. "I think I learned all I need from you Jake. I'll put what we talked about in my official report to Dan Morris and the Sheriff's Department. Even if Jim Henslow goes ahead with a grand jury you can be sure that my report will become part of the testimony. I think it will help your case."

Jack saw Jonah frown as he mentioned 'grand jury.'

Jack followed Jonah through the kitchen, remarking to Mrs. Bickerson before going out, "Thank you for the coffee and cookies. And, again, I apologize for coming out here at this time of night."

"No apology. I heard you say you would help prove Jake innocent."

"Well, I don't believe he did anything that either the Sheriff's Department or the State's Attorney should be interested in."

Jonah stood in the open doorway, waiting.

"Well, goodnight," Jack said.

Jake stepped forward and shook Jack's hand.

"Thank you, again, Mr. Traid, for taking the trouble to talk to me."

"No problem."

Outside in the farmyard, Jonah led the way across the well-lighted drive and past the garage. He stopped ten yards beyond it and pointed to a grove of trees at the far end of the corn field they faced.

"Out there in the trees. Other deer have hidden there before, during the day. They come into the corn in the evening. I figure maybe the white buck will too if I put salt and feed out there."

"Could well be. My friend Gordy Easton is doing the same thing. In his case he's hoping the albino will hide there until after hunting season and won't be killed. I was telling Gordy that some Indian tribes thought an albino, like the white buffalo, was a sign of good luck."

"Yeah, I've heard that. Just superstition, though."

"Other cultures see albinism as a curse. It brings bad luck."

"Sure. Like the number 13. Walking under ladders. More superstition."

"What do you suppose this white buck signifies, Jonah? Good luck or bad?"

"What do you mean?"

"Well, in the case of your dad. Is he about to have really bad luck when a grand jury indicts him for conspiracy? Or will the truth about that business out at Henslow's farm be figured out when the jury meets?"

"How should I know?" Jonah shot back, the defiance now in his voice.

"I think you do know, Jonah. You just haven't figured out how much danger, or at least not how much expense and embarrassment your father is in for."

"What are you talking about?" Jonah said, turning and facing Jack. In the light from yard lights, Traid could see in Jonah's strained expression that his questioning had hit the target.

"I'm saying that sometimes grand juries don't get the facts straight and end up indicting innocent people. That makes the innocent person's life a real hell. I think you know that your dad faces that very situation."

"He didn't do anything to old man Henslow."

"I believe that. In fact, I think your dad befriended Horst Henslow. But I don't think you did."

Jonah shifted his position, his legs apart as if ready for the snap of a football. He was tense.

Jack waited, letting the implication sink in. Then it was time to lay it out. What were the motives of this J. Bickerson?

"I was wondering, Jonah, have you decided to join the Jewish Defense League now that you have received their mailings for a couple months, mailings you lied to you father about getting?"

"What's that to you?" Jonah shot back.

"The question is, what is it to Jake Bickerson, your father?"

"Nothing that happened out at Henslow's involved my dad."

"Sure. I told you I believed that. But what you did out there in the middle of the night has gotten him into a heap of trouble."

"There is no evidence that I was out there."

"But one J. Bickerson has been reading up on the JDL, has knowledge of its principles, like 'hadar.' And a Bickerson got at least one letter from the JDL about joining. I figure that the idea of using the JDL to scare Horst Henslow all started when that person read in the newspaper that Henslow had been a guard at a concentration camp. That person decided to send a message to the ex-Nazi, and to the world. Paint a threat on the man's house. Then send another threat on JDL letterhead to make it seem like a whole organization was after him. Is that about right?"

"All those bastards deserve to be punished." Jonah raised his chin, staring back at Jack.

"The guilty do, Jonah. Those found guilty of crimes should be, as many have. But what did you know about Horst Henslow that made you decide to be his judge? Who appointed you judge and jury?"

Jonah did not answer. He did not move, but looked down as if searching for a reply.

"Let me give you a scenario that will help you make up your mind on what you have to do. State's Attorney Jim Henslow, for his own reasons, has decided to promote Sheriff Taylor's far-fetched idea that your dad and Hank Severson were responsible for harassing Horst Henslow. He is saying that they hired Art Rogers to help, and that at least two of them painted that swastika on Horst's house. He's also accusing them of hiring Art Rogers to burn down Mr. Henslow's shed and being involved in Horst's death. He bases all that on the admission by Hank Severson that he sabotaged Horst's steam tractor and the fact that a J.Bickerson is getting JDL material. State's Attorney Henslow will tell the grand jury that your dad and Hank wanted to scare Horst into deeding the farm to the Village, and not to his step-son—him, Jim Henslow. He may even suggest to them that your dad and Hank are responsible for bringing on the heart attack that killed Horst. He might gin-up a manslaughter charge. Then when the grand jury decides to indict your dad, having been confused about the evidence, there will be news stories and then there will be a trial. Your father will have to hire a lawyer and with luck might be able to prove he is innocent."

"Because he is," Jonah interjected.

"Exactly. But he could be saved all that kind of hell if his son owned up to a couple of pretty nasty tricks, like painting a swastika on Mr. Henslow's house, and then mailing him a threatening letter that scared him terribly."

Jack waited, watching Jonah shift on his feet. Jonah turned and walked up the tractor path a few feet, stopped and turned toward him. He raised his voice as he spoke.

"You don't know what it is to be a Jew. All the centuries of persecution. And then the six million those Nazi bastards killed. Do you think that doesn't hang over us every day as we wait for the next son-of-a-bitch bigot to find a 'solution'?"

"I'll tell you something, Jonah," Jack said, beginning to put into words what he had never before articulated. "My grandfather was a Jew driven from Russia for fear of his life. My family has lived their whole lives inside the fear you are just beginning to feel. But let me tell you something else. The curse isn't just upon the Jewish people. It is a curse of bigotry upon all of us. And your deciding that one old man, an ex-Hitler Youth, had to be punished for the sins of his nation is part of that curse. And it damned well isn't what the JDL is about. The word is 'defense,' Jonah, not 'aggression,' not 'retribution.'"

"I'm proud to be a Jew." Jonah nearly shouted the declaration.

"Of course you are. And I don't fault you for that pride. But not you, nor any others, are justified in becoming vigilante, not any more justified than those hate mongers and thugs who ran through the streets of Germany breaking windows on *kristallnacht*, and painting the star of David upon homes and businesses. That was the start of the horror, wasn't it? The question tonight, J. Bickerson, is what kind of man you are to become?"

"We weren't going to hurt him, just give him a reminder. And we didn't set that fire."

"Oh yes. Well, we know who set the fire, but you say there were two of you that Wednesday night—Thursday morning. Who was the other person?"

Jonah did not reply but looked down, avoiding Jack's eyes.

"I tell you what," Jack continued, "I'm going to go into town now, write up my little report of my talk with your dad for Deputy Sheriff

Dan Morris. But I won't say anything to anyone about our little talk. Not just yet any way. You think about your dad tonight and the trouble you've caused him and how it's going to get a lot worse. Maybe you should even talk to him, too."

"What will happen to me if I admit I did the painting?"

"My guess is you'd be found guilty of malicious mischief, pay a fine and maybe some restitution payment to the Henslow family for the damage done. You'll probably be put on probation, considering you haven't got in trouble before."

"Probation? What will that mean? That I can't go to college?"

"No, but you'll probably have to report to a probation officer every so often. Maybe for a year or two."

"Do I have to tell who helped me?"

"What do you think?"

"I don't want to get anyone else in trouble, not like I've done to my dad."

"Don't you think whoever it was will want to share responsibility? Talk to him. See if he doesn't want to own up to it?"

"Yeah. Maybe he will."

"Okay, Jonah. You talk to your dad, then talk to your friend who was with you that night, and come in to see me tomorrow. I'll be in my office at Hamilton State, in the Loomis Building. I'll help you work out a statement if you want."

Jonah had not moved from his position ten feet away from Jack.

"It was a pretty nasty trick you guys pulled, Jonah. But the punishment will be a lot easier to take than what you'll go through when your dad is taken into court, and you knowing you caused him all that grief."

Jack started toward his car. Give him a little room, he thought.

"Mr. Traid?"

Jack stopped and turned toward Jonah.

"Yes?"

"I'll come in to see you tomorrow. About making a statement. Okay?"

"You bet, Jonah. How about shaking on that?"

They moved toward each other. Jack extended his hand first. Jonah was looking him in the eyes and raised his hand to shake.

"Thanks, Mr. Traid."

❦   ❦   ❦

"I guess you know what you're doing," Judge Nelson had said when Jim Henslow phoned him at home Saturday morning. "After you had me hold up a day on it, I gave Dan Morris a search warrant for the Rogers' places in Chesterton just this last Thursday."

"He didn't know what to look for," Jim had replied. "Found a jacket and that was all."

"Well, what is it you think you'll find?"

"First of all, the gun he stole from my house when he broke in to recover his knife that Morris found in the barn later. I found that knife with his initials on it in our tires the night he slashed them at Andy's and he knew he had to get it back."

"What's this about your gun?"

"Sure. I got one for our home after our window was shot out. I told the Sheriff about the burglary. And I think Dan Morris just overlooked details when he went out to search Clarence's place. He's inexperienced, you know."

"Okay. I'll have it ready for you by ten this morning considering Rogers is still on the run and you think there is more evidence to be found."

Jim Henslow had the warrants and was entering Clarence Rogers' house at eleven o'clock Saturday morning. In his mind he replayed his Friday midnight to one a.m. Saturday confrontation with Art. They had stood between Art's pickup and Jim's Explorer in the grove overlooking Pioneer Village, the security lights a half mile away in the Village faintly illuminating their transaction. He had noted especially that Art's rifle was in a rack at the rear window of the pickup. Rogers was for the moment unarmed.

"You got the two thousand?" had been Art's first words.

"Right here," he had replied. "You'll see it when I have that tape recording in my hand."

"Sure. No problem," Art said, smiling as he picked the cassettee from his shirt pocket under his plaid mackinaw. He handed it to Jim.

"Give me the dough and I'm out of here," he then said, his hand still stretched out.

Jim had pulled the envelop out from the inside pocket of his suit coat and handed it to Art, whose defiant smile seemed frozen into his face.

"Just in case you think you can pull something on me," Art said as he handed over the cassettee, "you should remember that I gave my brother a copy of the tape."

"And just so you don't get the idea that I was too stupid to let a bit of evidence like that go wild, the warden and I searched Clarence's cell this morning and I took all his tapes away, including your masterpiece he thought he'd hidden in a Chet Atkin's cassettee case. Easy as could be to find. So, you don't have all the insurance you thought you had."

"Except for those other copies I hid at Clarence's place and in your old man's house."

"You what?"

"Figure it out. I didn't have anything to do sitting out there at Clarence's when I was recovering from being shot. So I made a few copies of our deal. Just in case. And then when I was living in your old man's dump, I made a few more. Hid them all over that place. Kinda like a virus."

Entering Clarence's house, Jim wondered where Art would have hidden a tape, or tapes? Sooner or later Clarence was going to get the word out from the pen that there was a tape with Jim Henslow's voice on it, arranging a crime. No one would believe him unless a tape was actually found.

The defiant image of Art raced through Henslow's mind. Art's voice laughingly repeating the phrase "Kinda like a virus." Henslow could still taste the anger, the rage racing through his brain as he swore at Rogers. The bastard had set a trap—many traps. The condemning phrase repeated itself in Jim's mind as he began his search in the dim and dank interior of Clarence Rogers's farm house, "Kinda like a virus."

Inside the house Jim put his brief case on a chair and ran upstairs to start his search. He ran his hand along the top of door frames inside closets, his fingers gleaning dust. He looked for loose floorboards, but there were none he could find. He threw back mattresses from the two beds to examine the springs beneath. Nothing. It was impossible, he said to himself in desperation. A million hiding places.

He returned to the living room where he found twenty-six tape cassettees in a rack on the top shelf of a bookcase. He opened each, finding only commercially recorded western music tapes but put them into the satchel he carried. Art could have recorded over the music, he thought, desperate to think of every detail. He would have to check them all later. He took each book from the shelves, opening each, and then throwing them to the floor until all he faced was the empty bookcase. Angered at his failure so far, he felt each cushion on the couch, looking for a tear or cut where a cassettee might be slipped into the innards. Standing on a chair under the overhead light fixture, he ran his hand into the diffuser bowl, but there was nothing.

He went to the kitchen with its myriad hiding places. He stood in the center of the room trying to imagine hiding places. Cereal boxes were on the table and he dumped their contents in a heap. Nothing. What would Rogers think was a safe place? A can? A jar? A coffee can seemed too obvious, but he found one on the counter next to the coffee maker and emptied the grounds into the sink. Still nothing. Maybe Art had made up the story about a "virus."

On the other hand, maybe Rogers figured he had to hide a tape in something no one would put their hand into, like a bag of flour, or even syrup or shortening. His eyes searched over the pantry shelf next to the sink. A Crisco can had been shoved to the back of the shelf. Jim flicked open the plastic cover and there was a plastic sandwich bag wrapped around a tape cassette which had been shoved into the center of the grease. He pulled it free, his fingers slippery with the shortening as he fumbled to open the bag. Picking the cassette free he saw the scrap of paper inside the bag. Pulling it out he read the childish printed message, "Tape No. 3." There was a virus after all.

He swore as he pulled cans and cartons from the pantry shelves. He stopped suddenly. Rogers would not have hidden two in the same place, surely. Standing in the center of the kitchen he turned slowly, looking at the walls, the door frames, the light fixtures. He had to take the chance that the other copies, however many there were, were at Art's shop in Chesterton, or at Horst's place, as Art had claimed.

Henslow retreated through the living room where books were piled on the floor next to the bookcase. Outside he realized that it had been in the machine storage barn where Dan Morris had found Art's leather jacket. He walked rapidly, then jogged toward the metal building. Pulling the sliding door open three feet with his free hand, the other carrying his briefcase, he entered. A flutter of wings overhead of frightened pigeons startled him. He was feeling tense. If someone found one of the tapes, it would be fatal. He could hear his own voice being broadcast on radio and TV news programs.

Clarence's 350 pickup was parked on the right, a film of dust having collected on it over the week it had stood idle. Jim opened the door on the passenger side and searched the glove compartment. He ran his hand under the seat. Going around to the driver side, he did the same, his hands searching for what was seeming to be the ever-diminishing size of the vital tape. The search had yielded only one tape. How many could there be? It all seemed futile.

He was ready to give up. Maybe there were copies to be found in Chesterton, in Art's shop. He left the building and hurried down the weed-bordered drive to the gate. He climbed the gate awkwardly, the briefcase impeding his climb. Once in the Explorer, he waited to catch his breath. He felt his body tremble ever so slightly. Calm down, he thought. Use logic. There had to be some pattern to the way Art had decided to hide tapes. One here. One at his shop. Another at Horst's farm. But maybe Art wasn't that methodical. After all, he hadn't mentioned putting any tapes at his place in Chesterton. Maybe he hid only the one copy here and maybe just another at the old man's farm house when he was holed up there for two days.

He had to take the risk, Jim thought, and give up on searching Art's welding shop. It was reasonable to assume that Art wouldn't have gone back there once he got the call that Danny Morris was coming out to arrest him. That was a good bet. So scratch the shop, Jim thought. Horst's was the more likely place he'd hidden more tapes. But it was going to be tricky to get back into his father's home without being seen. After all, the property was now under control of the administrator of the will, Tommy Johnson. Would he sanction a search on some grounds that there was personal property he, Jim had to recover? It certainly wouldn't do to tell him that he, Jim Henslow, knew that Art Rogers had been hiding at the Henslow farm. The search had to be done at night. That was clear. And soon. Tomorrow, Sunday night. Sheri had to help him. She'd understand the stakes for both of them now that she too was involved in some crazy, unexplained way. Shot Horst's body? With the new revolver. Why would she? What deception was going through her quirky mind? Maybe she thought she'd implicate him, her husband. Was she that angry about their argument and about Hamilton? His mind raced over possibilities. No matter what Sheri was thinking, now they both had to clear the slate of any evidence that would pull them into a charge of conspiracy. The only conspiracy that was going to be exposed in court was the one he'd convince the jury had been made between the Village board and Art Rogers. That was the story to be sold. Maybe over and over again until he had time to make sure all tapes were safely destroyed.

CHAPTER 19

The Quarry Restaurant sat on a knoll above the Big Sioux River east of Dell Rapids, its wall of windows overlooking a cut through red granite made by millennia of erosion. Layers of red, moss-covered stone on the opposite bank of the narrows where the Big Sioux River flowed with fall sluggishness were floodlighted for the benefit of evening diners. Time's depth was written in the rock wall on the other side of the river from where Jack and Ellie sat in silence Saturday night at the very same table where they had dined alone for the first time. As he looked at Ellie, her head bowed in thought, silent after the casual talk on their ride to Dell Rapids, Jack was remembering that it had been in this place their friendship had deepened and the possibility of a lasting relationship had presented itself. Prior to that evening nearly a year ago, they had depended on their being a part of a Faregold dinner or picnic, protected against inadvertent intimacy or suggested commitment.

"Was it my gift of a Bible that frightened you away?" Ellie said finally, breaking the silence that had sat heavily between them.

"No," Jack replied, pausing as he searched for careful words to describe what the meaning of the birthday party had actually become for him. "No, and when I thought about it the present didn't surprise me either. I finally began to understand your life. And I finally admitted to myself what was bedrock in yours and Gordy's life."

"Bedrock?"

"You are a very patient person Ellie. Maybe your caring for the sick at the hospital has made you able to understand what had gone wrong in my life. I began to cling to that. Selfishly, it turns out, thinking only of how I could fit into your life, how I would benefit from you. The Bible you gave me said that to me. It didn't scare me away from you, Ellie, but it opened my eyes to the self-pity I had been nursing."

"I don't understand, Jack. How did my gift make you see self-pity in yourself?"

"You and Gordy have been good medicine for me. Sitting with you at Sunday supper, surrounded by the home you and Ralph had built, allowed me to imagine that I could finally, even this late in my life, find something that tied me to the earth, to a place. It was a fiction, of course. For me. Not for you and Gordy. You are where you belong, in the midst of what you believe and know. Your gift told me what was required of me, what I was expected to give in order to enter that world. It was like a pass into your life, but it didn't really have my name on it."

"I didn't think of it in such grand terms, Jack. I just knew you were having trouble with Reverend Masters' sermons, and I thought maybe if you read the Bible you would understand him better. You don't hide irritation very well, you know."

"Yes, I know. And I honor your respect for Clyde Masters and for your commitment to your faith. I would not try to change you because of my own skepticism. That weekend when Horst Henslow's body was found, when his shed had been burned to the ground and more swastikas were found on the gas cans, I began to relate to the selfishness and rage that brought on that scene. By a jump in logic it became clear to me that I had been looking at your life on the farm which you and Ralph had built as some kind of refuge for **me**. But I knew I didn't deserve it, nor could I earn that refuge on your terms. Does that make any sense?"

"Some, I guess. I know we laughed about being 'buddies' when we were among our friends. Even when we were both wondering if there was something more that would develop. We sure were careful about our emotions, weren't we? But you weren't very good at hiding your missing Mildred Singer."

"You noticed?"

"Oh yes. I'd even mentioned it to Ann Faregold. When I asked her how serious you and Mildred had been she made it clear that you two were made for each other. 'Basically free spirits, searching the earth, both of them,' she said. 'Searching, searching,' she said. You are more transparent than you think, Jack. But Ann didn't know what had gone wrong with you and Mildred. And you never offered to tell me."

"That would have been the honest thing to do. I know that now. I owed that to you, Ellie. To admit that I missed Mildred every hour of the day after she left. She wrote me a Christmas note. Then this past summer she sent a letter about vacationing in Canada. I had not replied to either. Still confused, and I guess hurt and a little angry. I wasn't being honest with her either."

"You boil it down to honesty?"

"Yeah. I guess, for want of a better word. Honesty. Responsibility. I had a dose of that last night and this afternoon—owning up to one's own actions."

"This afternoon?"

Jack described how he had waited for Jonah Bickerson that afternoon to come to his office on campus, having confronted him the night before about what had suddenly become obvious to him at the Bickerson home. It had been Jonah who had sent for Jewish Defense League literature. It had been this young man trying to demonstrate his beliefs and confirm his ethnic identity. Jack admitted that in asking a fervent young man with a cause to be honest, he had to require no less of himself.

"It was time for putting confusion, my own confusion, into some kind of operative order," he explained. "I was asking Jonah to be honest, and to recognize that he had done a frightful thing to an old man by making him stand for the crimes of a whole generation."

How could he explain to Jonah, he told Ellie, that painting a swastika on Horst Henslow's house was done in order to satisfy his, Jonah's, own sense of inadequacy in the face of the great horror of the holocaust.

"Does that make sense to you?" Jack asked. "Jonah thought he could right some wrong by branding Horst Henslow, and frightening him. In Jonah's mind he had to cause some payment to be made for the terrible crimes against the Jews and humanity. Deciding that Horst Henslow had to be punished was profoundly unfair. Jonah didn't know that old man, but had made him a symbol. Yes. That's the word that came to my mind, 'symbol,' and if I were to be honest with myself, I had to admit to myself that I had been dishonest in our relationship, Ellie. I had made you a symbol."

"I'm not quite certain what you mean, Jack."

"For me you represented a way of life, a kind of earth-bound permanence. Whether that is actually true or not, doesn't matter. That was the way I thought of you and the Easton farm. You stood for something that I had never had. Faith, acceptance of a given order. It is attractive, but it is like an impossible dream for me. And in the process I had failed to understand you—you as a unique individual with a history, with beliefs, pains and joys. I had looked past you because I sought to heal myself through you. It was a form of using you."

"But you seemed at peace when you were at the farm. I began to believe you were understanding us…me."

"I was. Yours is a special place and you possess it well. I mean, the farm has meaning for you. Few people I've known in my life have that feeling for place that you have. That entranced me, Ellie. It beckoned me, to be sure. And Gordy's friendship and his sharing his excitement about the albino stag took on special meaning. At times I could imagine belonging there with you two, but it was in my imagination, a vagrant wish that clouded over the closer I came to reaching out for your world. And that feeling only abstracted you, Ellie. That wasn't honest. You deserve more. And, I wasn't being honest with you about loving Mildred, and not really having given her up. Under all those layers of wishing for a life at peace, as it appeared to be at the Easton farm, I was wishing for her to return to my life. "

"But you were afraid to make the commitment to her. Or maybe to anyone. Could that be true?"

"Yes. As simple as that may seem. I came to realize that what was thought to be necessary for an authentic life required honesty. And I had failed at that. I'm sorry if I hurt you, Ellie."

"Maybe we both need to admit what was going on between us. Sure, it was great to be courted again. I began to feel that I belonged at the Faregold's dinners, the nights out at Andy's, our concert-going with friends. You did that for me, Jack. I felt safe with you. I guess even though you were tentative, I felt wanted. Yeah, even if there had been no groping for each other's bodies in the dark."

"You thought about that? Our having sex?"

"Oh sure. I wondered. But I wanted to be sure we were right for each other. I sort of waited to find out if I could have a life with someone other than Ralph. It didn't seem possible."

"And I didn't quite make the right move."

"One way to put it. But don't take all the blame on yourself. We were both carrying burdens and looking for someone to share the load. Right?"

"It seems that way."

Their dinners had cooled while they talked. The wine glasses remained half full. Ellie reached across the table and took Jack's hand, holding it firmly as she looked him in the eye.

"Maybe we were just meant to be buddies. Just friends. Okay?"

"Thank you, Ellie. Your friendship has been a great gift. All week as I tried to think how I could explain to you what happened to Mildred and me in Minneapolis, I was afraid I would lose your friendship. You seemed distant and angry at me when we saw each other at Cynthia Masters' funeral. I wondered if I had lost you and Gordy as friends. How would I handle that, I asked myself."

"With care, Jack. Don't worry about it. We both need your friendship, too. And don't you worry about Gordy. He thinks you're great. Friendship works in both directions, remember."

Ellie withdrew her hand. She smiled.

"So what's this about the Bickerson boy?"

Jack explained that Jonah Bickerson and David Marritz had come to his office on campus as agreed the night before. Jonah had talked with his father, who had urged him to do as Jack had suggested. The two young men prepared a statement, explaining that the newspaper article about Horst Henslow made it seem to them that he'd been a concentration camp guard for a long time and responsible for the cruelty and death there. They admitted painting the Henslow house with a swastika and the word from the Jewish Defense League statement—'hadar.' After the publicity about the painted swastika and conjecture about Nazi-hunters, they decided to frighten the old man more with a letter to make him think that the JDL was going to get revenge.

"And you have their statement, then?" Ellie asked.

"Signed by both."

"Now what?"

"That's the strange part for me. After they left my office it occurred to me that I should have warned them a little stronger about their rights. You know, the Miranda rights an officer is supposed to read to a suspect. During the discussion with those boys I was thinking more as an advisor, a teacher, and not as a police officer. Since I was deputized by Taylor, and remain a deputy, it was my duty to tell those boys, and Jake Bickerson, that they should see a lawyer first, before they made any kind of confession to me."

"But you have their admission in writing."

"Yes. But what I'm going to do Monday morning is take it to Tommy Johnson, who is Jake's lawyer, and hand it over to him. I'll let him decide how the admission of guilt should be handled, before Jim Henslow gets a hold of it and twists it out of shape."

"But those boys did a pretty bad thing."

"They sure did."

"Maybe the fright brought on Mr. Henslow's heart attack."

"Maybe. But a lot of other things were going on out there that these boys had nothing to do with. Things we haven't gotten to the bottom of. Just what was Art Rogers really about? We know for pretty certain that he set the fire. But it doesn't make sense to me that he would fire two bullets into Horst's dead body before he torched the shed. Why would he do such a thing? And what was the real reason he was out there with gas cans all prepared with swastikas on them. What message could Art Rogers think he was sending? And why? Or was he just being a copy cat, since the news was all over about the swastika painted on the house? I am convinced that Art Rogers wasn't acting on his own out there at Horst's farm. And he wasn't so clumsy as to drop a heavy switch blade knife near a dead body so the police would think he killed Henslow. Someone else wanted it to appear that Rogers was in that barn and shot Horst Henslow. And when Rogers is arrested and questioned, we may be fairly surprised at the answer."

"So where is he?"

"Good question. It's strange to me that we haven't had any sightings, except for one false alarm from Grand Forks, North Dakota. A gas station attendant reported to the police there that a man who kind of fit Rogers' description had stopped for gas. But it turned out the man was older, had a woman with him who was clearly his wife, and they were pulling a pop-up camper behind a mini van. Not Art Rogers."

"How far could he get?"

"Not all wanted persons are caught, remember. If he's clever, he could assume another identity, settle somewhere permanently. His appearance could be completely changed so no one will recognize him."

"Do you think Dan will be able to trace him?"

"I think Dan feels a bit constrained by the County Commission. George Carter is chairman, but he's also on the Village board of directors. Since Jim Henslow is accusing the board of intimidating Horst, even being in collusion with Art Rogers, I think Carter doesn't want to make any more waves. He's afraid of Jim Henslow. And Jim Henslow's theory about the Pioneer Village board being in collusion to intimidate Horst is just crazy. And it's dead wrong."

"You're sure?"

"I am because the persons who painted the swastika on Horst's house confessed to me this afternoon. It wasn't Jonah's dad, Jake Bickerson or Hank Severson who did it."

"But you said Jonah's confession proves Jim Henslow's charges are wrong. Won't your holding back on the confession just give Henslow more time to muddle the truth."

"Maybe. But I think Tommy Johnson, who was Horst's lawyer too, remember, will be happy to learn how the swastika painting happened, even if he has to figure a way to protect his clients. What it means is that Tommy Johnson will have proof positive that Henslow's cockamamie theory about the Pioneer Village board is pure fiction, a fiction cobbled together to protect the States Attorney himself, if I'm not mistaken."

"Jim Henslow is involved in some way, then. That right?"

"When we find out the true story about a trust agreement signed by Horst Henslow on August 30, giving Jim Henslow complete control of the Henslow farm property. That was the very same day Horst signed his will giving that very property to Pioneer Village."

"Does Dan know all this?

"Sure. But as I said, he feels constrained by the Commission just now. But I think I know how to help Dan. He's been told to concentrate on the oil spill evidence to see if Sheriff Taylor did more than just store PCB oil."

"That seems unfair to Dan, doesn't it?" Ellie asked. "Didn't you say that Dan found the evidence that ties Art Rogers to the arson?"

"It is unfair, and Jim Henslow got that done in order to embarrass Dan and the Sheriff's Department by getting the County Commission to suggest strongly to Dan that the Henslow matter should be left up to State's Attorney. That, in my opinion, is a case of leaving the fox in charge of the hen house. Jim Henslow says he's ready to go before the grand jury but he has no evidence that the Pioneer Village board was involved. Hank Severson has confessed that he acted alone in sabotaging Henslow's tractor. It will be interesting to see how Jim Henslow reacts to Jonah and the Marritz boy's confession admitting they painted the swastika on Horst's house, and sent that threatening letter. Two kids. Not the Village board in a conspiracy."

"You don't trust Jim Henslow, I take it."

"Well, there is plenty of evidence saying I shouldn't. Consider this tidbit that came into Dan's hands yesterday. He got a call from the Sioux Falls *Argus Leader* reporter Don Fogel who wanted an update on the Henslow death. Fogel had been talking with Sheri Henslow who has gotten back into the news photography business and has been in Pierre where she talked to Fogel. She told Fogel she was certain that Art Rogers shot Horst and that his knife with the initials A.R. on it was found in a stall near the body. Dan swears that he told no one exactly where he found that knife. He had said only 'near the body,' and nothing about the stall. Sheri's knowing it was hidden in the stall and not out in the barn indicates specific knowledge."

"Meaning she knows what happened in the barn?"

"Meaning she knows something no one but Dan and I knew. And it suggests strongly that Sheri Henslow is directly involved in some way. It says to me that both she and her husband know what happened in the barn the night Horst died. She was either in that barn that night, or her husband was and told her about it."

"That's pretty serious business, isn't it?"

"Yes. It sure is. It raises the question, 'How is Jim Henslow corrupting his office?' And since nearly everyone has forgotten that I'm still a duly deputized officer of the law, I'm going to quietly go about asking a few more questions of a few key people, like Art Rogers' brother Clarence. He might have an idea where Art has run and just maybe will give me a hint if I go at him right."

"It's not out of your blood yet, is it Jack?"

"What's that?"

"The hunt for the guilty. I think you're a little like Jonah."

❧   ❧   ❧

By Sunday afternoon when Sheri Henslow got to her Cottonwood Acres home in Hamilton, Jim Henslow was into his second double scotch and summing up in anger what she had done to him that past week. He detested almost as much as she prided herself in the casual, macho look she affected dressed in Levi's and the ancient World War II bomber pilot jacket. She appeared to him to actually swagger as she came in from the garage and strode into the living room, tossing her camera case and jacket into a chair before flinging herself onto the sofa.

"What's eating you?" were her first words.

"What the hell do you think? You've been gone a week and I'm up to my ears in crap."

"Don't get on my case," she shot back. "I've worked my rear off all week to prove I can handle their news stories, and by god I did it."

"Sure and you could care less that I'm about to lose everything I've worked for these last eight years."

"Oh, poor boy. Your little plan to get the farm got fucked up."

"Stop that. And tell me, goddam it, why the hell you went out to the farm with my revolver. If you weren't my wife, I'd arrest your ass right now. Just what did you think you were doing? You said on the phone that Horst was dead when you found him in the barn. Was he?"

"He was. Just like the medical examiner said."

"And if he hadn't been?"

"I was going to scare him good. I don't think I was going to kill him, but I was going to tell him that he couldn't steal what your mother promised you and what was rightfully yours, and mine, by the way. I think I would have told him that I would kill him later if he didn't figure a way to turn the farm over to you. What difference does it make now? He's dead as a doornail."

"So you pumped a couple bullets in him with my gun so that once a match was made with my gun, it would look like I killed him. Right?"

"No way. That's not what I was trying to do. Why did I take Art Rogers' knife out there and leave it under the straw? You'd already gotten your rear end in the ringer and didn't know how to get out. I just figured when I found that knife in your dresser drawer with the revolver that I'd leave a little real evidence that Rogers was after Horst and that it was him who shot the old bastard."

"Aren't you the smart one. So you would have killed Horst if he'd been alive? Just to pin it on Rogers."

"Maybe. You didn't have the guts to do it."

"You messed up my deal, you know. I'd sent Rogers out to burn down the shed that night. To scare the hell out of the old man. And you didn't have any idea about that. You just mucked it up all the more by playing your hot shot game."

"Well, it worked, didn't it. The old man is dead. Rogers is wanted and on the run. Isn't that so?"

"The old man is dead but I sure as hell don't have the farm. Not by a long shot. Not until I can break the old man's will. The only good thing right now is that Rogers is far away from here. But goddam it Sheri, you put us in a helluva spot. What if someone figures out you were out there? It's bad enough that I have to find all the tapes Art made and hid around Clarence's place and out at the farm."

"He what?"

"He said he made a bunch of copies of the tape he made of my phone calls to him about his setting the fire on dad's place. I got the warden at the pen to let me search Clarence's cell and recovered the one Art had given to him to keep as insurance. And I found one in Clarence's farm house. But there must be others. If one of those ever gets made public, I'm finished. And now your cute game makes us vulnerable as hell. What if someone saw you out there?"

"No one did. And with one little phone call I got that Miller woman off the place long enough to give me time to confront Horst alone. I thought that was pretty neat planning."

For days Jim Henslow had been wondering about the quirky instability of his wife. Was it **he** who was the target? Was his public disgrace, when everything was revealed, a pleasure she had promised herself? She wanted to be free of him;that was becoming clear enough.

"Well, he wasn't alive, was he," Sheri snapped. "So, now what are you going to do? Can't you get rid of your gun somehow?"

"I already did. I gave it to Rogers to keep. If he's ever found with the gun, we're covered by the burglary story. But he's long gone. What we got to make sure of is that we find all the tapes he might have made. And by god you are going to help me search the place. Tonight."

"Tonight? What do you mean?"

"I mean were going out to the farm and turn that place inside out until we're certain there are no more tapes."

"Jesus. Not tonight. I'm bushed."

"We got to do it. Tommy Johnson is executor of Horst's will and one of these days he'll be out there taking an inventory for probate. We got to go through that place before he accidentally finds a tape and gets curious. Art left a note in the plastic bag with the one I found. What if he has put notes in other places to lead to hidden tapes? Rogers wasn't dumb. He'd have thought of some clever way to spring his trap by leaving a hint of where the tapes are."

"You and your big development deal. All turned to shit, didn't it?"

"You're a great help, you are. Get something to eat because in an hour it'll be dark and we're going to go out to that house and you're going to help me stay in the clear. Once this is all over I don't give a shit about how important you think your career is. Or our marriage. But I by god am not about to lose everything I've worked for over the years. If being State's Attorney is all that's left for me, it's what I'm going to hang on to."

Jim Henslow could not shake the feeling all during that night as they searched frantically the Horst Henslow farm house that his wife was dangerous. He promised himself that he had to watch his back.

Sunday visitors' hours were posted on the bulletin board in the waiting room of the public entrance to the State Penitentiary. It was thirty minutes after the nine a.m. opening hour. Jack Traid sat quietly reading a newspaper, waiting to be called to an interview cubicle when Clarence Rogers was brought there. Jack had indicated on the visitor's request form "friend," being a simpler designation than admitting to be a Sheriff's Department investigator for Chautauqua

County. That, he reasoned, might have triggered alarm bells in the warden's office arranged by Jim Henslow.

Clarence Rogers sat on the other side of the plate glass barrier dressed in prison white overalls, a frown creasing his brow. Rogers picked up the phone set, waiting.

"Good morning. I'm Jack Traid," Jack offered into the phone on his side as he sat and faced a man he'd never met.

"Do I know you?" Clarence asked. "They said you were a friend."

"Let's put it this way. I might be more of a friend than a stranger before we're done. I didn't want to tell the official folks here that I'm a deputy sheriff from Chautauqua County concerned about your brother."

"Well, I don't know nothing about where he is, if that's what you're after."

"I didn't expect you to tell me, frankly, but I had a hunch that you could tell me more about how Art got involved in torching Horst Henslow's shed two weeks ago."

"And why the hell should I? That State's Attorney of yours come down here and took all my cassette tapes because there was one in there proving he bribed Art to do the fire."

"Now, that's very interesting. Want to tell me more?"

"Sure. Art got himself a tape recorder when Jim Henslow proposi-tioned him. For protection, like. He recorded Henslow twice. Once Henslow told Art to wait on doing the fire. The other time Henslow told him, clear as anything, to set the fire early on Saturday night. That would attract lots of attention in town, he said. And he told him to leave a gas can with a swastika painted on it. It's all on the cas-settes. He left one with me when he visited last time."

"Cassettes? More than one?"

"Yeah. More insurance, like, in case Henslow tried to get cute and set him up. Art said he was going to give Henslow a virus. When Art visited me the week before, he told me that Henslow was trying to scare his old man off the place."

"And Art agreed to help him?"

"Sure he did. Because Henslow said he'd get me paroled if Art would cooperate and do the fire."

"Yes. Well, Art got enthusiastic and did up *two* cans. Painted both of them with swastikas."

"Yeah. I saw the picture in the papers. It was all Jim Henslow's idea. And he won't be helping me none, now, you can bet."

"So, where do you think Art is now?"

"I don't know. He said he'd let me know where he was going if he had to hide. He's pretty smart, Art, is. He promised to send me a post card from Aunt Harriet when he found somewhere to hole up. But I haven't got nothing."

"When did you last hear from him?"

"He sent a letter just last week. He mailed it from Chesterton. Said Henslow—he called him the recording artist in case the screws got interested in our mail. Art said the artist had arranged for him to take a 'vacation' at his family's country place because unfriendly folks were coming out to my place to visit him. Art wrote that the recording artist was going to get some money together to pay his vacation expenses. His whole letter was written like that. Like I'd understand what he was hinting at. He underlined the sentence, 'Never got to meet the artist's old man, no matter what anyone says.' That means Art didn't shoot old man Henslow."

"When'd you get the letter?"

"Same day Henslow came down here and searched my cell. So you can ask Henslow where Art is hiding."

"Fits together, Jim Henslow protecting Art to protect himself. If Art wrote that he was going to the Henslow country place, that would mean he was going to hide out at the Henslow farm, where no one would look for him. The Henslow saga is getting a lot clearer. You said there is more than one copy of the tape cassette. You don't have another copy, do you?"

"Sure wish I did. Should of made one myself. But Henslow and the warden stripped this place when they searched my cell. Took all my tapes. I'm surprised they even let you in here to talk to me. Warden said I'd have no visitors for awhile. Someone goofed."

"You mean you are being isolated?"

"Call it that. Warden said that State's Attorney Henslow recommended I be restricted to my cell except for exercise because of a case in Hamilton."

"That was ordered right after Henslow took the tapes?"

"Yeah. Guess they wanted to make sure I didn't squawk about Henslow being the recording artist. Someone ought to get that bastard."

"Did your brother say anything else about tapes? Where they were hidden?"

"Nope. Figured if Henslow got aholt of his letter, it wouldn't help him none. But he left me a hint, when I get it figured out."

"A hint?"

"Well, at the bottom of his letter he added a couple lines from a poem he must have learned in grade school. Like we all had to memorize. If I can remember exactly, it went 'Under the spreading chestnut tree, the village smithy stood…'"

"Sure. Longfellow's 'The Village Blacksmith.' Do you think he meant to refer to the recordings."

"Yeah, sure. What else?"

"Okay. Since Art was the village blacksmith at Pioneer Village, that little poem might help if we can figure out what he meant by it. Now if you'd tell me where Aunt Harriet is likely to send a post card from?"

"I'd guess Texas. Art spent time there in the Army. Fort Hood and then Fort Bliss in El Paso. He could slip into Mexico easy. Knew his way around there."

"Well, okay. I appreciate what you've told me," Jack said, concluding the interview.

"Get that s.o.b. Henslow. That's all I'd like you to do."

"We'll see about that," Jack said, standing to leave. "I'll let you know what I find out about Art once I've worked through what you've told me. Guess I owe you that much."

The guard on Clarence's side of the interview room motioned for Clarence to get up. Jack gave Clarence a quick nod and turned and left the room.

Since it was a sunny, warm Sunday, Jack did not feel like driving Interstate 29 north to Hamilton. The State Penitentiary sat right next to U.S. Highway 77 that went north to Dell Rapids. Jack decided to take the slow route home. The picture of the Henslow matter was nearly complete. Since the beginning he had believed that it had been a crime scene with too much evidence, too many hands involved. And so it was. Now it was clear. There was the hired arsonist. There was the fervent youth Jonah trying to make a statement about Nazi horror. And there was the chief law enforcement officer of the county heading up a conspiracy in an attempt to get his stepfather's farm. All that seemed clear except for how Sheri Henslow was involved. Was she helping her husband try to frighten Horst Henslow or did she have her own agenda? How did she know exactly where the A.R.-initialed knife was hidden if she hadn't been in the barn that night? And as he thought about the medical examiner's judgment that Horst died of a massive heart attack, he could not get the picture out of his mind of the blood that had oozed from the dead man's wounds. That didn't quite square with his experience. What would a gun shot wound look like during a person's heart fibrillation? Maybe it was murder, after all. That wonderment required a visit to the medical examiner soon.

Cars passed him as he drove north at forty-five miles an hour, windows rolled down to admit the smell of mowed hay. He was thinking of how much he liked the rolling prairie countryside, and wishing that Mildred could share with him the sense of quiet and space which he had found since coming to Hamilton. How were they

going to accommodate both of their needs? She had to have a place
for art and for showing her work. And she would want to continue to
teach art. And then there was his own teaching. He didn't want to
give up the non-demanding academic life he'd carved out for himself
and the challenge of being with young people. Teaching basic courses
was adequate and promotions were unnecessary. At Hamilton State
he enjoyed a measure of gratitude expressed by the administration at
his contentment with his role. It had freed him to work on creating
letterpress books and monographs and trying to hold together a
Dixieland band. There was room for creativity. With Mildred back
into his life, there was the excitement of having recovered all of a real
life.

As he was thinking of Mildred, her studio and his print shop and
bookbinding, Jack was entering Dell Rapids on the bridge over the
Big Sioux River. Slowly turning up the main business street he
admired the pink granite of the old hotel seeming to glow in the
noon sunlight. The granite was also used to build several of the other
buildings. It was evidence of the once thriving quarrying operation
east of town. This village, he realized, was just half way between
Sioux Falls and Hamilton, and today it seemed to shimmer with
promise in the warm September sun, appearing anything but ordinary. For a moment he saw it as if it were a magical place he had just
discovered, like some Dakota Brigadoon. He had to tell Mildred that
simple fact. Perhaps, he thought, he was driving through the place
where they would stake out a life together, she close to Sioux Falls, he
within easy driving distance to Hamilton State.

The image of their establishing studios and their own house in the
pleasant river town filled his mind on the rest of the trip back to
Hamilton. He decided he had to call Mildred that night, as he had
every night since his return, to tell her of his discovery. Yes, he
thought, it was as if he'd seen this little town for the first time,
although he had driven past it hundreds of times before. There it
was, a place that could give them access to both their worlds:

Mildred's need for the urban, his desire to hold on to what had began to bring him peace of mind in Hamilton.

Jack reached home at two in the afternoon. After several calls he located Dan Morris.

"Clarence Rogers told me Art made a recording of Jim Henslow arranging for him to set the old man's shed on fire," Jack said, getting to the center of things.

"Jeez!" Dan exclaimed. "So there was a conspiracy."

"You got that right. But Henslow got the warden to search Clarence's cell with him, and they took all the tapes Clarence had, including Art's recording which he had hidden."

"So we got nothing?"

"Except Art made more than one copy. He gave Clarence a hint that he was hiding out at the Henslow farm. Clarence thinks he hid extra copies out there."

"How we going to get at that? Should I get a search warrant from the court?"

"Why don't you call Tommy Johnson. Tell him we got some important information that fits in with the boys' confession. We better meet with him as soon as possible."

"Okay. I'll call you back."

When he had fed Rasputin and settled into his easy chair to catch up with the Sunday newspaper, he was presented with another piece of the Henslow puzzle. There on the front page of the Local Section of the *Argus Leader* was a full-page spread of photographs Sheri Henslow had taken of the Aberdeen tractorcade protest by wheat farmers. A sidebar article with a picture of Sheri reviewed her career as a news photographer. The picture showed her with a camera at the ready. She was dressed in jeans and wore a World War II bomber jacket. It was a jacket, he realized, that would have been dyed with the older dyes of the 1940s which the Crime Lab had analyzed on the scrap of leather Dan Morris had found on the stall door. Sheri Henslow knew what she was talking about when she told Don Fogel where Art Rogers' knife had been found.

Dan Morris called to tell Jack that Tommy wanted to meet with them that evening at five in his office. They agreed it was urgent that they both make the meeting.

As Jack returned to his newspaper and the picture of Sheri Henslow, it had become clear that Jonah Bickerson's confession and Clarence Rogers new evidence about the tape recordings pointed to Jim and Sheri Henslow's conspiracy. Maybe Tommy Johnson would know how to stop Henslow from proceeding with a grand jury before it got started.

CHAPTER 20

*J*udge Nelson frowned a dark scowl upon the gathered delegation sitting in a semicircle before his desk. It was an irregular, and he feared, an improper and deeply disturbing procedure that Tommy Johnson had talked him into. It was Sunday evening and nearly seven o'clock when his favorite prime time television shows were beginning. Yet Johnson had said it was urgent. And there they sat, Attorney Johnson, Acting Sheriff Danny Morris, Jack Traid, Jake Bickerson and Hank Severson. It was disturbing to Judge Nelson that Bickerson and Severson had been included since they were the very persons to be subjected to the grand jury investigation. State's Attorney Henslow had said he would present evidence to the jury implicating them. And why was this college professor Jack Traid included here? It seemed especially irregular that a former cop from Dallas, deputized by Sheriff Taylor a week ago, should be included. It was outside the official family and had all the aspects of a slap-dash effort to get around a regular proceeding. Such thoughts raced back and forth in the judge's mind as he worried about how long this session was going to take.

"You know most of these men here, Judge," Johnson began. "Dan Morris is, as you know, acting sheriff of the county for now. Mr. Bickerson and Mr. Severson have an important bearing upon what I am going to request of you this evening. And Jack Traid, as I explained earlier, is helping the sheriff's department as a deputized officer."

"Before we go any further," Judge Nelson interrupted, "let me tell all of you that I don't like the irregularity of this meeting. I agreed to meet with you out of respect for Counsel Johnson. But I believe, Tommy, you ought to be handling your concerns with formal petitions to the court if and when indictments have been filed."

"Yes, your honor, I appreciate your concern," Johnson began in muted tones. "I don't intend to prejudice the court in any way regarding the substance of the Henslow matter as it may come out eventually in a trial, but when I learned that Jim Henslow is a party to the conspiracy at the center of the events on the Henslow farm, I just had to bring forth this profoundly disturbing evidence. The details have turned up in the last few days, in fact in the last few hours relating to Jim Henslow personally and the real purpose behind his asking for a grand jury."

"All right. I'm going to let you start with your story since you claim it is a truly urgent matter weighing on law enforcement in this county and the subject of the events on the Henslow farm. But let me warn you, I may stop you at any moment if I think we are entering improper areas, and I might just ask you to leave and utilize proscribed petitions."

"Fair enough," Johnson replied. "I understand your concern and only wish to set out to the court in a confidential way, facts that have come to light which you ought to know about before allowing a grand jury to proceed along the lines of Henslow's charges. Henslow is proceeding on the basis that the Pioneer Village board, and specifically these two gentlemen here, Bickerson and Severson, were involved in a conspiracy to wrest the Henslow farm from Horst Henslow, and more seriously that they may have hired Art Rogers to set the fire at the Henslow farm. Jim Henslow also claims that these men are responsible for the threats to Horst Henslow's person.

"The State's Attorney," Johnson continued, "has made it public that he believes there was a conspiracy among Village board members to harass his father, already damaging the reputation of these two men. He is correct about there being a conspiracy. In fact there have been two conspiracies, and the evidence, including two signed confessions, which the Sheriff's Department has in hand, prove that the actions on the Henslow farm were in no way connected to Jake Bickerson or Hank Severson."

"Now wait a minute," Judge Nelson said. "Severson here, according to Jim Henslow, has confessed to sabotaging Horst Henslow's tractor. Isn't that right?"

"Yes, your honor, it is."

"I admitted I done that, yer honor," Severson injected. "And that is all I ever done to Horst Henslow."

"But that prank," Johnson went on, "was not prelude to the other events which took place on the Henslow farm on which the State's Attorney is building his case for the grand jury. What I hope to reveal to you is Jim Henslow's real motive for taking these trumped up charges to the grand jury. May I continue?"

"Dammit, Tommy. This really upsets me. Any evidence you have in this matter should come before a grand jury. You know damned well that I can't just stop the jury from receiving evidence."

"Normally I would agree absolutely, but Jim Henslow will avoid bringing the evidence we have before the jury. There are serious extenuating circumstances in the case which the court should know because they could result in a terrible miscarriage of justice, and further damage the reputation of these two men. I am thoroughly persuaded that a grand jury proceeding on Henslow's theory will become the principal element in a cover-up. I'm hoping you can prevent that by persuading Jim Henslow not to proceed and to let the Sheriff's Department file the legitimate evidence."

"Proceed, then. But let me warn each of you. Nothing of what goes on in these chambers tonight is of record, and if any of you attempt to use this court in some way to avoid correct procedures you can be damned sure I'll find you in contempt."

Judge Nelson's face and scalp had turned crimson, under-lighting the thin white hair combed carefully back from his forehead.

"Danny, I guess you better take it from here about your Department's investigation."

"Okay," Dan said hoarsely, nervously clearing his throat to begin. "There is little doubt that Art Rogers of Chesterton is the prime suspect in the torching of Mr. Henslow's shed. When he was seen fleeing from the fire, he was shot by Miss Gloria Miller, housekeeper at the Henslow place. The pellets taken from Rogers' left arm by veterinarian Brasley match those of the kind of shells given to her by Horst Henslow and which she was using in the 20 gauge shotgun the night of the fire. Also, the condition of Rogers' jacket, which I found hidden in a barn on his brother's place, as well as the Sioux Falls hospital records of treating his wound, point clearly to him as the person running from the fire and being shot by Miss Miller. He is further implicated by the match of the paint on the gas cans that were found in his shop in Chesterton."

"Why can't that evidence wait until there is a trial on this matter? Maybe Rogers was hired by the board members, as Henslow claims." Nelson spoke with irritation.

"Normally this evidence could wait," Johnson said. Speaking to Morris he added, "I think we better jump to the heart of the matter, and then give the judge any details he might want to hear to substantiate what we believe."

"Certainly," Dan replied. "Jack, you have put the pieces together. Why don't you lay it out."

The delegation was on thin ice, Jack realized. Nelson was risking a lot allowing this meeting to proceed. His shifting from elbow to elbow signaled his mounting doubts and displeasure with what he had heard so far.

"I learned today, your honor, that State's Attorney Jim Henslow is the author of the conspiracy to harass his father and…"

"Wait a minute, now," Nelson nearly shouted. "You realize what you're saying?"

"Yes sir, I do," Jack replied, "and I'm well aware of the consequences of making such an accusation, but at the same time I believe that if State's Attorney Henslow proceeds with a grand jury on the basis of what he is claiming happened on his father's place, a cover-up will be perpetrated that might well obscure or pervert the evidence that the Sheriff's Department has assembled. Evidence exists which will prove conclusively that Jim Henslow sought to scare his father off the farm by hiring Art Rogers to set the shed on fire and making it seem that Horst's past as a guard in a Nazi concentration camp had come to visit revenge upon him. He prepared for that by having Horst's Nazi past included in a news story."

"And what is that evidence you say you have?" Nelson asked. "Are you telling me that Jim Henslow was out there painting the side of his old man's house with swastikas?"

"No, and that is an entirely separate matter," Johnson interjected. "We have the confession of two young men, one of them Jake Bickerson's son, who did that. They also admit sending Horst the threatening letter which was found on his body. Charges will be brought by juvenile authorities on that matter and your honor apprised of all the facts regarding the painted message on the side of Horst Henslow's house."

Johnson turned to Traid. "Why don't you continue, Jack."

"You realize, your honor," Traid explained, "that the State's Attorney is claiming that Hank and Jake here did that painting, and he is claiming that that act was central to the conspiracy on the part of the Village board to manipulate Horst Henslow into willing his farm to the Village. But with the confession of the two young men Mr. Johnson just mentioned, Jim Henslow's theory becomes pure fiction, and we believe, a diversion to prevent the real story from getting out.

It is his effort, I am convinced, to stall, to buy time because he can't explain where he was at the exact time Horst died, nor can he explain how he has a trust agreement with Horst's signature on it dated the very same day that Horst was in Mr. Johnson's office signing his will before witnesses. And underlying these serious matters is fact that Jim Henlow hired Art Rogers to set the fire."

"Now how do you know that?" Nelson snapped.

"Art Rogers gave his brother Clarence a tape recording of telephone conversations, made by Art of Jim Henslow, ordering him to delay setting the fire, and then later telling him to do it on that Saturday night. The recording also has Henslow telling Rogers to leave gas cans with swastikas painted on them. The conspiracy is on that tape recording."

"You have the tape, I trust."

"We don't because Jim Henslow went to the penitentiary and with the help of the warden confiscated all of the cassette tapes in Clarence Roger's cell. The warden can verify that."

"But you have no specific proof, then, of what was on an alleged tape which a convicted felon claims exists. Not very good evidence in South Dakota, I might say, regardless of what they might do with it in Texas."

Judge Nelson's sarcasm threatened to end the meeting.

"I appreciate that, your honor," Jack continued, "and I realize that Clarence Rogers is not a very credible witness, but we believe we will have a copy of that tape soon because Art Rogers made several copies and hid them in various places in the community."

"Hurumph!" Nelson sighed, looking at the ceiling.

"There is further evidence" Traid went on, "that Jim Henslow or his wife fired the .32 caliber shots into Horst's body. That is the same caliber as the revolver Jim Henslow bought the day after the window in his house was shot out. Bought it at Mork's Hardware. Then we learn that the knife with Art Rogers' initials on it was in Jim Henslow's possession after the tire slashing episode that was reported in the paper."

"I read that," Nelson said."

"Well," Dan Morris interrupted, "Henslow reported the knife missing after he learned that I had found it in the barn near Horst's body. He claimed Art Rogers must have broken into his house because he knew that Jim had it. But, and this is the crucial fact, it wasn't until a week later that Henslow claimed his .32 calibre revolver was stolen at the same time. This was after the Crime Lab determined that Horst was shot with a .32. I have notes of the meeting in the sheriff's office when he reported the knife stolen, and he for certain didn't report his gun stolen at that time."

"My god, you fellows are making mighty serious accusations on pretty sketchy, and I must say, confusing evidence. If this is all just a trumped up story you fellows are bringing in here, I promise you there is going to be hell to pay."

"It isn't, your honor," Johnson pled, "And I'll take the consequences if you'll just give Morris here a bit more time to gather the key evidence and bring charges before a grand jury is sent on a wild goose chase by Jim Henslow where no evidence warrants it, especially in the light of the confession we have from the two young men who painted the swastika on Horst Henslow's house. It absolutely wasn't Jake and Hank who did that as Jim Henslow is claiming. He has no evidence of a conspiracy on the part of these two men. I think Dan, here, and Mr. Traid, will have all the evidence necessary if you will just give them a little more time by delaying Jim Henslow from going before a grand jury with accusations against Jake and Hank."

"I don't like this one bit," Nelson said. "You should know that. And," he continued, rising from his high-back, leather chair, "I'll think about your request over night. Don't count on anything from me. And if I were any of you, I'd forget this meeting ever took place."

Johnson, Morris, Traid, Bickerson and Severson filed out of the judge's chambers silently, descended the stairs to the first floor of the court house and exited the front door. Johnson spoke first.

"It might not have worked, fellas. As you could see, the judge hated the irregularity of what we were asking. We just might be in for a round of dirty work before the grand jury."

After Bickerson and Severson drove off to their homes, Johnson invited Dan and Jack to his office to consider what had happened in the judge's chambers.

"So you don't think Nelson will try to talk Henslow out of going to the grand jury," Dan said.

"Just as I said. Nelson hates any irregularity, and tonight was about as irregular as it can get for him. Laying evidence of a crime before the judge before any charges are brought, by-passing procedures carved in stone. It's obvious he hated it."

"If Henslow goes to the jury," Traid offered "we can expect him to make a desperate effort to string the process out. Henslow has to give Rogers all the time he can to get far from Hamilton, and according to Art's brother, maybe all the way to Mexico. No lie or trumped up evidence will be too wild for Henslow if he gets before that jury. He's in a bind about what he was asking Rogers to do. And if you ask me, he forged the trust agreement to keep the Minneapolis outfit interested in the Henslow property while he figured out how to get control of it. Everything he has is at stake and my guess is he's desperate."

"So, what are you fellows going to do?" Johnson asked.

Dan looked to Jack.

"Two things, no matter what the judge decides," Traid replied. "Get back to the medical examiner about the exact condition of Henslow's heart when the bullets entered his body. Did the ME just take the easy way out because the autopsy evidence was a bit confusing? Confronted with questions about his findings, will he reconsider? Because it is bit more serious a case if Jim Henslow, or for that matter his wife Sheri, shot the old man while he was in the throes of his heart attack."

"You mean there may really have been a murder." Johnson exclaimed.

"Yeah. Wild shot on my part. But if we get a copy of the tape that clinches the case of conspiracy to commit arson, it will show that our State's Attorney was open to any kind of desperate action. Then if we prove that Sheri Henslow's flight jacket, which can be seen in the article in today's *Argus*, matches the leather bit Dan found snagged on the stall door in the barn, we will have a better idea of what happened in the barn that night. Husband and wife working to get the old man dead. Looks like we'll just have to confront them about that, sooner or later. And then too, where is the revolver that Jim Henslow bought after his window was shot out? Rogers didn't burgle Henslow's house, in my opinion. Either Henslow or his wife planted that knife in the stall, and Sheri Henslow knew exactly where it was found when no one but Dan and I knew that. So, she was there, or Jim was there and told her. So the gun is probably hidden somewhere, if not still in Henslow's possession. When we find it we'll get a match with the slugs out of the old man's body, count on it."

"You know," Johnson mused, "I can't picture Jim Henslow standing over his old man, pumping a couple shots into him, whether Horst was alive or dead. I knew he was getting desperate about the Chautauqua Acres development deal because he wasn't getting any takers from Hamilton money. He didn't know when he was trying to sell us on investing in it the night of the fire that I already knew that Horst had willed the place to Pioneer Village. He might have been desperate enough to try to scare the old man, but shoot him? I don't know. Sad, in a way. Jim's promising future, and all that."

"We have to find a copy of that tape," Dan said. "That will clinch the Jim Henslow-Art Rogers conspiracy."

"We suspect," Jack said, "from what was in Art's letter to Clarence, that Art was hiding out at the Henslow farm at Jim Henslow suggestion to him the day Dan went out to arrest Rogers. Some of the tapes he said he made must be out there."

"Well," Johnson said, "as executor of Horst's will, it is my duty to make an inventory of the property. We better get on with that tomorrow morning. You two give me a hand?"

"Sure," Dan replied.

"I have a class at nine in the morning, but I could be out there by ten thirty. And by the way, Clarence said that in the letter he got from Art, which was mailed from Chesterton the day he went into hiding at the Henslow place, there was a hint of where one of the tapes might be hidden. Art quoted the beginning of Longfellow's 'The Village Blacksmith.'"

"Seems out of character for Rogers," Johnson commented.

"Except," Dan said, "Art *is* the village blacksmith in Chesterton and at Pioneer Village."

"Which suggests," Traid added, "that while we search Horst's house tomorrow, we keep in mind that Art Rogers meant something by quoting the poem, out of character or not. Sometimes the roughest of appearing thugs will call up some tender things from childhood something meaningful that bitterness in life has squelched. We better take another look around Art's shop in Chesterton, too."

"Okay," Johnson concluded. "Dan and I will be at the farm at ten. We'll see you as soon as you can make it Jack."

As Jack Traid drove through the quiet streets of Hamilton, the street lights sent diffused rays up into the elms and box elders. It was a tranquil village settling in for the night. Certain as he was now about what had happened at the Henslow farm during that week, he worried that everything they claimed they had as evidence against Jim Henslow was, as of now, circumstantial. That a jury would buy the story that the notorious Art Rogers was an agent of the popular chief law enforcement officer of the county was too far fetched. He and Dan's urging Tommy Johnson to get the meeting with Judge Nelson had been a wild throw of the dice and snake eyes might come up tomorrow. They better have some luck finding a copy of Art Rogers' tape.

CHAPTER 21

$\mathcal{A}$ Dakota September is an uncertain time, temperatures soaring into summer peaks, the air saturated with Gulf of Mexico moisture, only to plunge to near freezing as an Alberta clipper cold front sweeps across the high plains and prairies. Thunder storms soak corn and soy bean fields to the frustration of farmers. Blazing sun over a weekend raises the spirits of those same farmers as they prepare to harvest their crops as October arrives. For those who reflect on such things, there is a sense of abundance in the country. The harvest proceeds with determination. Combines crawl across fields both day and night, their lights in distant fields appearing like visitations from other realms. Yet, in these first days in October,1995, much of the population of Hamilton focused its attention not on the abundant gifts of the land but on headlines in the *Times*: "Prosecutor Questions Autopsy," "Fugitive Still Sought," "Nazi Past Haunts Pioneer Village." The Tuesday, October 3rd issue's story about the grand jury was relegated to the bottom of page one, it's simple headline "Grand Jury Still Out." The newspaper was marking time with the rest of the community.

The clear, brisk October weather was in sharp contrast to the strained and frustrated mood in Attorney Tommy Johnson's office Tuesday afternoon where Dan Morris and Jack Traid were meeting with Bickerson and Severson's lawyer for yet another strategy meeting.

"I was with Jake yesterday when he was called to testify," Tommy was explaining, "to advise him, you understand, since that is the only role counsel can play. Can't argue. The jury foreman seems a competent enough guy. It appears that he runs the show about as well as you could expect. I think he's taking Judge Nelson's charge to heart. As I told you when the judge turned down our plea that he try to stop Jim Henslow from going to the grand jury, he decided he would charge the jury when it was sworn in. He said he cautioned the members in the strongest terms possible about being very critical before accepting as true any theory presented by anyone, including the chief law enforcement officer of the county unless supported by facts—hard evidence. He told me later that he had not wanted to attempt to stop regular procedures regardless of our suspicions about Henslow. He thinks what evidence we have, without the tape recording, is too flimsy to implicate Henslow. In his mind Henslow had to be allowed to carry out his duties, even if it turned out he was involved somehow. Anyway, the hopeful sign is that even if Jim Henslow has tried to lead the jury into accepting his theory that Bickerson and Severson conspired to harass Horst Henslow, the jury's questions to Jake, and the gentle manner of the questioning, seem to indicate to me that the members haven't bought it yet. Henslow's theory that the harassment of Horst Henslow was a conspiracy brewed by the Pioneer Village board isn't producing much evidence. Hank's confession about sabotaging Horst's tractor is about it. If anything, I think the jury may be getting irritated at not being able to resolve the thing and get out of there. Half of them want to get back into the field. They want to bring an indictment or ask for a dismissal, but Jim Henslow keeps promising to bring more witnesses. It seems to me he hasn't produced anything that convinces them. The delaying tactic is getting obvious."

"Can't the jury just end it then?" Dan asked.

"Could. During Jake's appearance the foreman asked him if he knew who painted the swastika on Horst house. Jake told the jury that his son and the Marritz boy had confessed to painting the swastika, and to sending the threatening letter, and that the juvenile court was handling the case. He explained that the boys acted on their own. At least that got before the jury. But the jury didn't pursue those questions very far, except by their manner I could tell that Henslow has suggested that Bickerson persuaded his son to do those things, as part of the conspiracy. Henslow also keeps escalating the charges the jury is to consider in order to keep their interest whetted. At least that is my guess. He's now hinting that there is evidence that Horst was murdered. He leaked that to the press, saying there is a medical expert prepared to testify who will refute the M.E.'s autopsy report."

"Isn't that curious," Traid interjected, "the guilty bastard is buying my suspicion about Horst being in the throes of a heart attack when he was shot."

"Well, if Henslow is guilty of anything it's obfuscation," Tommy replied. "As to the murder theory, the jury hasn't gotten into that, from what I can learn. And it was kind of clear when Jake and I were in there that Henslow has kept putting off calling the unknown medical witness to make the case."

"And the jury believes he has a witness?" Dan asked in disgust.

"No telling, of course, since their deliberations are in secret. Nevertheless, I don't think so. But how are they to know for sure? You have to understand that the States Attorney can guide the jury's investigation. After all, they are lay people with a huge legal burden of which they only vaguely perceive. When they are deliberating in the jury room, they are alone, without legal counsel or the prosecutor. All they have is what evidence is placed before them and ideas the prosecutor has put in their minds. And we have no idea of what the total picture is that they are being given by Henlsow. They can be, and are led where the prosecutor is clever enough to take them."

"And he is desperate enough to try anything," Jack said. "Henslow is buying time. But he must know there isn't enough time left in the world to rescue him. Eventually the tapes both he and we are trying to find will show up. And maybe Art Rogers will end up being able to tell his story."

"Incidentally, as to the murder rap, Jack," Tommy asked, "have you anything further about your theory that Horst might have been suffering heart fibrillation when he was shot?"

"I called an old buddy in Dallas who is one of the medical examiners in the coroner's office there. He thinks it could have been possible that the wound would look as it did if fibrillation was going on when he was shot, but wasn't very hopeful that we could prove it conclusively. He thinks our ME probably did his best with the autopsy. Seems to me that even if Henslow is trying to make sensational news with the idea, and lead the jury on, when we spin this out to the end we may have every reason to believe that a viscous murder was committed. But we won't be able to prove it."

"So, where are we with our plan?" Tommy asked

"As you know," Dan explained, "the Department of Criminal Investigation people are in the county, as we requested, to investigate Sheriff Tom Taylor's involvement with the PCB oil dumping. The county commission agreed with me that it would be better to have the DCI give us a hand with that. They will do an objective, thorough investigation. So far, the DCI guys have been very thorough about the case. For example, Acme Transformers in Worthmore will have some explaining to do about deals with Taylor when the case comes to court. But I haven't told the DCI yet about our suspicions about Jim Henslow and the tape connecting him to Art Rogers. I thought it would be better to keep them out of it until we have a copy of that tape. Solid evidence."

"Yes. I think so," Tommy said.

"I've got all the other evidence together," Dan continued, "to give them when we are finally ready to prepare a case against Jim Henslow and Art Rogers. With the hard evidence we have against Rogers, we'll be ready for them to wind up the case and bring an indictment against Henslow as well."

"And Sheri Henslow, don't forget," Traid added. "We know for sure that she's involved. Might have been in the barn when Horst was shot."

"Well we weren't very successful in our search of Horst's house, were we?" Tommy said. "And you didn't find anything when you went back to Art's shop in Chesterton, Dan."

"But we know that someone got to the Henslow place ahead of us," Dan replied. "Stuff thrown all over the place."

"And you know who it had to be," Jack added. "The question is, did Henslow find all the tapes? Or is there still at least one out there to convict him?"

"Rogers will tell us when he's finally arrested," Dan offered. "If for no other reason than to get even with Henslow."

"If, in fact, he hasn't disappeared into Mexico as his brother suggested, never to be seen again," Traid added. "We still don't know what Art meant by his quoting lines from the 'Village Blacksmith' poem. No doubt in my mind that he meant it as a code, a direction. If you didn't find anything at the village blacksmith shop in Chesterton, there is only one other village blacksmith shop we haven't checked. The one at Pioneer Village."

Johnson's phone rang and he picked it up and listened, then said, "For you Dan."

Morris listened for a minute and said, "I'll be out there as soon as I can. Don't let anyone in."

Handing the phone set back across the desk to Johnson, Dan stood and explained the call.

"Speaking of the Village. That was Jake Bickerson. They opened the blacksmith shop this morning. He said that they've been getting the Village ready for Pioneer Days this weekend. The Village board arranged for a substitute to run the blacksmith demonstrations.

Some relative of Carter's. Anyway, they took a bolt cutter to Art Rogers' padlock on the shop. Inside they found Art's pickup crammed into that little shed. Wherever Rogers is, his truck didn't go with him."

"Let's go take a look," Traid said, getting up from his chair.

"Let me know what you find, okay?" Tommy said as Morris and Traid were leaving the office.

"Sure," Dan replied.

Ten minutes later the two investigators stood at the wide open double doors under the newly painted sign "Village Smithy" examining Rogers's Ford 150 which had been forced into the narrow space of the rude board-and-batt shed.

"Whoever drove this into the shop was in one big hurry," Dan said. "Knocked down that bench and those acetylene tanks. Just crammed it in."

"Looks like you'll have to take this place apart piece by piece. If Art took time to stash his truck here before taking off in some other vehicle, he might have hidden a tape too. You might want to see if there are any fingerprints on the truck besides Rogers'."

"Right," Dan replied. "First we'll put up our police line tape. The Village might have to skip a blacksmith demonstration this weekend."

"I suppose it makes sense that Art would flee in something other than his own truck. But the truck being here bothers me. It suggests that after Henslow hid him at the farm he provided him with another means of getting away. Too complicated."

"How's that?"

"Seems out of character for Henslow. Too much trouble for him to arrange. You know, Dan, I keep thinking we have to put Henslow under pressure."

"What do you mean?"

"We know for sure that he got Art Rogers to set the fire to scare Horst, even if we don't have the tape yet. And he and Sheri must know how Horst was shot. If they think we know all about their involvement, they might panic and make a mistake.

"And run?"

"Not likely. Jim Henslow is wrapped in too much respectability. No. My bet is that he'll try something foolish and show his hand."

"Okay. What do you suggest we do?"

"Don't know yet. But I think it should be something that won't involve the Sheriff's Department officially. Let me think about it. Then I'll let you know. Okay?"

"This the usual Dallas police procedure?"

"Only when driven to it."

❦   ❦   ❦

Twenty-four hours later the readers of the Hamilton *Times* knew that Art Rogers had not been on the run in his own pick up. The *Times* reported that his pickup had been discovered hidden in the Village Smithy at Pioneer Village. Acting Sheriff Dan Morris reported, according to Carla Garza's by-lined story, that no fingerprints were found on the vehicle. It had been wiped clean. Morris would not conjecture on why.

The Henslow's had hardly touched their Wednesday evening dinners of microwaved "Kind Diet" stroganoff, avoiding each other's eyes in the tension-filled room. Jim Henslow read the story, shaking his head and muttering about the fools in the Sheriff's Department. Sheri listened to her husband's complaint with detachment, absorbed in the phone call she'd had that afternoon from Derrick Holmes telling her she was being put on permanent staff at the *Argus*. Regular salary and steady work, he had promised. She was her own person again.

"Maybe the truck is the new evidence I need. Makes sense that Bickerson and Severson hid it out there. Without something I can't keep that jury forever," Jim said bitterly. "Sooner or later the jury is going to make a decision."

"Then you can take the Village board into court," Sheri replied absently.

"You aren't listening. I'm telling you that it isn't going well. That bunch of farmers might just report to the court that there isn't enough evidence against the board members. Especially after what Judge Nelson told them."

"Nelson?"

"I told you, goddamnit, he charged the jury when he swore them in, and as much as said they weren't to believe anything I said. They're as skeptical as a bunch of virgins at a beer bust."

"So? What if they don't buy your idea that the Village board hired Art Rogers? Then what?"

"That leaves me with charging Rogers with arson and suspicion of murder. But he isn't going to be around to talk any time soon. But we'll try him in absentia. Unless of course one of his tapes show up. Then we're cooked."

"You are," Sheri snapped.

"No, my dear," Jim said in a flat, angry tone, "we are. You are in this up to your ever loving rear end. You killed Horst and thought you could get me out of the way, using my gun."

"That's damned ridiculous, so quit saying that. I told you he was dead when I got there. I was just trying to help and make it look like Art Rogers did it. Besides, you sure as hell didn't know how to get the old fart off the farm."

"Well, don't think you're out of it. Like it or not, we're in this together and we better figure out what we're going to do if the jury asks the court to dismiss my charges against Bickerson and Severson."

"So?"

"So everything is screwed up. The Chautauqua deal is as good as dead. The Carpenter Group heard about Horst's willing the farm to the Village. They say they can't wait on a law suit to settle the will, unless I can produce the original trust agreement with Horst's signature within a week. So I'm up a creek."

"Too bad."

"Too goddamned bad because you shot the old man. Otherwise we'd just have a little case of arson to pin on Art Rogers and half a chance of successfully challenging Horst's will. But now…"

"Quit bellyaching. You got us into this with your big-ass plan to turn the farm into gold and then fumbled everything."

"I didn't plan on shooting the old bastard. That's when you got us into deep shit."

"Rogers did it. That's your story. Stick with it. I left the knife. Enough evidence to let you prove he did it. Then you can go on and break the will."

"Maybe. It's a long shot. Maybe I'll find something in those letters of mother's we found when we searched the house."

"But no tapes."

"I think Rogers was bluffing. He had to be. I bet he only made three tapes. The one he gave Clarence that I confiscated, the one I found in the can of grease in Clarence's kitchen, and the one he gave me when I paid him off. I've got all three."

The doorbell rang, three steady, prolonged rings, startling the couple at their table.

"Who the hell…" Jim exclaimed, getting up and going to the front door, opening it to the unexpected and threatening aspect of the meddlesome college professor.

"Sorry to bother you at supper time," Jack Traid said, his voice stern, his eyes fixed on Jim Henslow's, "but I have something important to discuss with you that can't wait until tomorrow."

Henslow paused a moment, not opening the door wider, thinking what to do.

"It won't take but five minutes," Traid said without looking away from Henslow's eyes.

"You could have made an appointment," Henslow complained.

"But I didn't," Traid shot back, watching for the defensive reaction.

"We were just finishing dinner."

Traid pushed the door aside and stepped past Henslow. In the foyer he waited for Henslow to shut the door.

"You're not welcome here," Henslow said. "I could get you on breaking and entering."

"But you won't because you wonder why I'm here."

Traid waited, his body tense.

Henslow turned and led the way into the living room. Sheri Henslow was standing in the archway between the dining room and the living room.

"Missus Henslow," Traid said, acknowledging her with a nod.

"What's this all about?" Jim Henslow demanded, turning to confront the imposing figure of the ex-cop. "Want to sit while you explain this intrusion?

"I'll stand," Traid said. He stood with his feet apart and his body still tense. Unarmed he still felt as he often had as he moved in for an arrest alert, ready for a violent reaction. The purpose tonight was only to arrest the attention of two people who had the answers to the tragedy of Horst Henslow. He intended to pry them open. A chancey move, he admitted to himself, but a little panic in the Henslow household might be all that was needed to open things up.

"I thought you would like to know, Mr. Henslow," Traid continued, "that as a deputy sheriff I have been following up on Clarence Rogers' telling me that his brother Art made a recording of his telephone conversations with you, a tape he had in his cell but which you confiscated."

"A goddam lie. A felon's way to…"

"Don't tell me about motives of criminals, Henslow. I've had one or two years more in that field than you."

Traid's unblinking stare at Jim Henslow did not miss the movement Sheri Henslow made to retreat down the hallway.

"Missus Henslow," Traid called sharply. "Why don't you just stay in this room? What I have to say applies as much to you as to your husband. I'd appreciate having your both where I can see you."

"For christsake, what in hell do you think you're doing?" Henslow said. "You think you can arrest us?"

"That will come later," Traid said, watching as Sheri went to the couch and threw herself at the far end. Traid took a step back to better keep them both in front of him and the foyer and front door just behind him. The move would make them nervous since they didn't know if he was armed or not.

"I'll get to the point quickly so you know what is about to happen. I found another copy of the tape Art Rogers made of your instructions to him."

Traid paused, letting the lie penetrate the frantic minds of the Henslows.

"It's the tape you didn't find when you ransacked the farm house. It will convince any jury that you initiated a conspiracy with Rogers to commit arson. Second, it is pretty clear that you are both responsible for the death, if not the murder of Horst Henslow, your stepfather."

"Get out, goddam it," Jim Henslow shouted, making a step toward Traid.

"I'd not try that Henslow. I've taken men twice your size."

"Goddamned college teacher isn't going to come into our house and accuse…"

Henslow lunged at Traid, fist raised. Then his arm was behind him and he was on the floor, with Traid's knee squarely in the middle of his back.

"Listen carefully," Traid growled, "because I am going to spell this out only once whether you like it or not. First, I know and can prove that you, Jim Henslow, initiated the conspiracy to have Art Rogers commit arson. Second, either you or Missus Henslow got Miss Miller off the farm and went out there to kill Horst Henslow. We have evidence connecting Mrs. Henslow to the scene because she left a piece of that famous bomber jacket of hers snagged on a stall door."

"Bull shit," Sheri screamed, sitting bolt upright on the couch.

"That…that," Henslow stuttered, his face pressed against the carpet, "that happened weeks ago when we were looking at the barn as a place to keep horses."

"Sure," Traid replied, getting up off Henslow and backing toward the front door, "and no jury will believe you when it considers all the other evidence. Like, I know that one of you planted Rogers' switch blade knife in the barn. It was probably you Mrs. Henslow. Maybe you'll tell me if the old man was pleading for help when you shot him, Mrs. Henslow. Was that the way it was?"

"Don't say a goddamned thing Sheri," Henslow shouted, getting up from the floor. "This son of a bitch is making it all up. There isn't any of it he can prove."

"The crime lab will make the match when you hand over that jacket for testing."

"No damned way are you getting my jacket," Sheri shot back.

"Sooner or later you'll have to give it up. Better to let me have it now and then take time to think up a better alibi than a sudden desire to keep horses on a farm where neither of you were welcome."

A heavy silence permeated the room. Let it hold a minute, Traid thought to himself. It will deepen the shock.

"It's about over, isn't it Henslow? You can't keep that grand jury out indefinitely. Besides, you'll soon be answering charges in court. Oh yes, there is also a little side detail that embellishes the story which you'll have to answer to. After you killed Art Rogers, where did you hide the body? You were in quite a bind, weren't you?"

"Get out, goddam it."

"Your mistake was wiping the pick up clean. It was obvious to me that you thought you could erase all connection between you and

Art. But, in fact, the clean truck said it loud and clear you'd gotten rid of Rogers. The question is how you did it and where."

"You're crazy. So get the fuck out of my house."

"My guess is that neither you nor Mrs. Henslow are going to enjoy this house or the Henslow farm all that much while you're in the state pen. And," Traid drew out the syllable,"now that I have told you what the sheriff's department knows and will act on in the next few days, I'll take my leave."

Quickly, before Henslow had decided what to say, Jack Traid was at the door and half way through when he turned to the State's Attorney of Chautauqua County and said, "You might decide, Henslow, that you were not involved in your wife's killing Horst Henslow. Unless it was you who encouraged her to make the phone call to Miller and then went out yourself to kill your step-father. But if she did it on her own, you'll only get sent up for conspiracy to commit arson and one murder. Not as rough as being sentenced for two murders."

Traid stepped into the cool night and slammed the door on the sounds of two raging suburbanites shouting after him. He hurried to the battered Toyota and once inside made a U turn to leave the cul-de-sac. Big gamble, he thought. Now he just had to watch what the Henslows would do with the burden he had put on them. And, too, he thought, he would have to watch his own back for awhile, until he did find where Art Rogers had put the golden piece of recorded evidence and where poor old Art was himself.

On the seat next to him as he approached his house was a copy of "The Favorite Poems of Henry Wadsworth Longfellow," which he had picked up at the library on his way from Pioneer Village to the Henslow residence. Tonight he would need to explicate a poem for answers while the guilty scurried around for a way out.

✤   ✤   ✤

"You're not plying me with this date just to find out what's going on with the DCI coming into the county, are you?"

Dan Morris spoke quietly as he and Carla glided across the room to the smooth sounds of Sammy Gail's big band at the Wednesday benefit dance in Sioux Falls.

"What other reason could a struggling girl reporter have?" she replied, pressing closer to Dan. "There seems to be no other way. Since the state investigators showed up, you have become a deaf mute."

"Come on. I told you about our finding Art Rogers' pickup. That was something. It had been wiped clean. No finger prints. So we're still digging around in the blacksmith shop for evidence of how and why it got there."

"Okay. Good for one story. But that's about all you've told me in the past month."

"Haven't I told you about my going insane? Yeah. Batty. I wake up in the middle of the night thinking about you."

"Sure."

"I mean it. Stark raving mad. There is only one remedy, you know."

"Whoa there, sheriff. I hear an invitation for a sleep over."

"Smart girl. You read my lips."

"You're mumbling, though, and what I choose to hear is that we are going to take our good time, have no regrets about some big prize after the first date."

"But there will be other dates?"

"What do you think?"

"That I'm turning lucky."

"It might even get more interesting when I know you better. Like where you are going."

"Going?"

"Well, yes. For example, I'm going to work for a major daily. Soon. This job with your dad wasn't just a summer job for the fun of it. I'm getting on with my profession and I'm darned serious about it."

"I know that. It isn't only your beauty that's attractive."

"And you? What are you going to be serious about when you get over being dumped by that college cheerleader?"

"I told you about Cynthia. How about I get serious about you? Is that an answer?"

"No. Something serious. You could excite me with a little bit of ambition."

"You are serious."

The piece ended and they walked hand and hand back to their table and cocktails.

"Maybe it's my background," Carla began as they sipped their drinks. "My folks sacrificed a lot to get me through college. My dad works for the City of San Antonio. It was the most important thing in their lives to have their kids succeed and prove that Hispanics can play responsible parts in the mainstream. I mean to satisfy that dream for them."

"And you see me drifting?"

"I see a neat, kinda spoiled guy who can't make up his mind to do something important. Something he thinks is really important."

"Fair enough. I won't argue with you. I guess my only answer is that I'm looking for a place to make some kind of commitment but haven't found it."

"With a law degree you could help people who can't afford expensive lawyers. I know that is true in San Antonio. Kids in trouble. Poor folks confused by debt and harassment. They can't afford to walk into posh law offices and get help. They depend on public defenders, outfits like the Texas Defender Service."

"Yeah, I know about those outfits. One in Sioux Falls. Never thought much about it."

504   The Albino Stag Witness

"When I go back to San Antonio, you come down there and I'll show you what I mean."

"What do you mean, when you go back?"

"I've been offered a job on the *San Antonio Express News*. City hall beat. Which will be a good beginning at the edge of the big time."

"When is this going to happen?"

"First of November I have to report for work. Don't tell your dad just yet. I want to give him notice personally in the next couple of days."

Dan reached over for Carla's hand.

"Okay, then. If you're asking me, I'll be in San Antonio as soon as this Henslow business is over with."

"Promise?"

"It's a promise."

❈   ❈   ❈

After pulling down all the blinds as a precaution against a desperate Jim Henlsow, Jack Traid microwaved a pasta dinner, fed Rasputin, and settled down at the dining table with William Wadsworth Longfellow. There was a pleasant calm at his dinner table, an old feeling he'd often had as the chase was coming to an end, the loose ends tied tightly around the truth. He was reading the poem for the second time when the telephone rang.

"Jack. This is Ann," Ann Faregold announced. "We're making plans for the tailgate cookout at Pioneer Village Saturday noon."

"Great. I know we talked about it, you and Ellie. But maybe you should know that Ellie and I have agreed to just be buddies because…"

"Don't explain, for gods sakes. I talked to Ellie and know all about it. I also called Mildred and asked if she could come and be with us. And she said 'yes.'"

"Well, great. I talked to her last night and she didn't say anything about it."

"Because I called her this morning. You have to pick her up at the Sioux Falls airport Saturday morning. 9 a.m. Okay?"

"Sure. Wonderful. I'm going to call her tonight."

"And don't worry about Ellie. She has a date. She's bringing Clyde Masters to the cookout. He needs some diversion."

"Yeah. I understand."

"So, all that meddling of mine is okay?"

"You're just great, Ann. I look forward to Saturday."

"Okay. Pick up Mildred at 9 a.m., lunch at noon, Tractor Parade at 2. Got that? Oh, by the way. Ellie said you're supposed to phone Gordy Easton. He wants to ask you a favor."

"I wonder what that might be."

"Ellie didn't say. Guess it's between you guys."

"I'll do it soon as we hang up. What can I bring for the meal?"

"Yourself. Everything is set. See you later."

"Thanks Ann. That female old-gal network seems to be in high gear."

"Don't you forget it, either."

When he had hung up the phone he dialed the Easton farm to hear Ellie's familiar voice. It sent a brief pang of longing through him, as if a pleasant memory had reappeared after having slipped away.

"Hi Ellie. Jack. Ann Faregold told me I was to phone Gordy. Everything all right?"

"Oh, sure. He just wants to ask a favor of you. As a friend. Here, I'll get him on the phone."

Jack's sense of loss evaporated as he warmed to the declaration of friendship. It was with an unaccustomed eagerness he waited for Gordy's voice."

"Hello. Jack?"

"Yeah, Gordy. What's up?"

"I was wondering if you'd ride with me in the tractor parade. I got my dad's Allis all ready to go and it would be really neat if you'd ride along on the draw bar."

"Sounds like fun. What's the deal?"

"The parade sponsors want each tractor entry to have a guest. You know. Someone important in town. I'd like you to be my guest."

"You really flatter me, Gordy. I'm just an old college prof."

"Mom says you're mor'n that."

"Your mother is too generous for her own good. But sure. I'd love to go with you."

"Okay, then. I'll tell them because the *Times* is going to publish the line-up with names of the tractor, the owner and the guest. So we'll be printed up together. Thanks Jack. Here's Mom."

"Jack," Ellie said, "I just need to know if my coming to the cookout when Mildred is there is going to be a problem for you. You know, considering."

"Not for me. I explained to Mildred about us. She says she's looking forward to meeting you. Ann's idea of the cookout is going to take care of that."

"Wonderful. And Clyde needs some fun in his life. Saturday's cookout will be a great break for him. Incidentally, I was wondering how the *Pioneer Voice* is coming. You and Mike Wilkins all set to print the first edition?"

"The final press run will be Friday in order to have papers ready for Saturday. We got the special story about Horst Henslow's gift. Banner headline in old style type. Ought to be a sensation."

"I can't wait."

"You're a wonderful person, Ellie. It will be a good day for all of us on Saturday."

"Yes. I'm sure. See you, Jack."

When he hung up Traid read for the third time the last stanza of the "Village Blacksmith" from the book that lay open before him on the dinner table:

Thanks, thanks to thee, my worthy friend,
For the lesson thou has taught;
Thus at the flaming forge of life
Our fortunes must be wrought;
Thus on its sounding anvil shaped
Each burning deed and thought.

"Each burning deed and thought," Jack repeated to himself. It was the anvil that held the secret, the anvil where the village blacksmith taught his lesson. While the Pioneer Village press ran tomorrow, Dan Morris and he would have in hand the burning deed Rogers' anvil was about to reveal.

Taking a pillow and blanket from his bedroom, Traid went out through the gallery-breezeway into the darkened print shop. He didn't need to turn the lights on to find the open space between two presses where he would spend the night.

CHAPTER 22

Chautauqua County State's Attorney James Henslow did not report for work on the Thursday or Friday before Pioneer Days at Pioneer Village. There were preparations he had to make. He had phoned his secretary Mary Pettigrew to tell her he was ill. It was not far from the truth. He had hardly been able to eat for twenty-four hours after Traid left their house Wednesday night. A raging head-ache was unrelenting as his wife shouted at him and the memory of Traid throwing him to the floor had released adrenaline into his bloodstream. He shook nearly all night long. Scotch whiskey would not calm the angry frustration.

In his confusion he could not at first think what to do about Jack Traid's invasion of their house. The old detective knew too much, or thought he did, about Rogers. But did he really have the tape? The question was whether to confront Traid and demand the tape or arrange that he'd have a serious accident? Then again, probably bet-ter not to be that direct. It might be best just to wait it out in case Traid was bluffing. When Sheri and he had searched the farm house they had found no tapes. Rogers had to have been bluffing. Traid had to be bluffing—didn't really know anything.

All during Wednesday night and early Thursday morning the fight with Sheri raged as she packed two suitcases. Neither she or Jim got any sleep. It was sun-up Thursday when she lugged each of the suitcases to the garage and put them in the trunk of the Continental without his help.

"I'm out of here," she muttered as if to herself as she loaded the last suitcase into the car. "I tried to help and what do I get for it." She squinted as she looked him in the eyes. "You threaten to indict me for murdering your old man. You've turned into a crazy bastard. You never did know who your friends were and now you haven't got any."

Jim Henslow stood in the hall doorway to the garage, exhausted with shouting. A deep calm had come over him. It was inevitable, he thought to himself, that it would end like this. The years of her bitching, undermining him, hating everything about their lives in Hamilton could have no other end. Let her go. When the legal process unwound she would have to answer to the fact that she had gone to the Henslow place with his revolver and had shot the old man. If nothing else, he thought, she's guilty of trying to mislead the authorities. There'll be plenty of charges to make against her when the time was ripe.

"Okay," he said quietly. "Have it your way. But don't you believe for a minute that you're going to slip out from under your involvement in my father's death. No way. If that ex-cop actually has one of Rogers' tapes, there'll be ways to get around that."

"I bet," Sheri shot back. "You said yourself that the tape has your voice telling Rogers not to set the fire one night but to wait. Then you tell him to do it Saturday night. How're you going to get around that?"

"Simple. It was a put up job. Faked tape by my political opponents."

"Jesus, you're nuts. What political opponents?"

"The ones who don't want me to run for any office. You and everyone else know damned well that I'm up for State Senate. But to hell with Tommy Johnson and the rest of the bastards and their dirty tricks. I'm going to reveal everything, including the fact that I had a wife who tried to help them by setting me up for a murder charge."

"Good luck, buster. You'll screw it up like you did the Carpenter deal, and the agreement with your old man. No one's going to believe you."

"Go to hell," Jim shouted, the calm of a moment earlier was lost in frustration.

He watched as the garage door opened and the Lincoln backed down the driveway into the street. Sheri did not look back at him. The Lincoln's tires threw loose gravel from the macadam surface as the car lurched forward. He pressed the switch to close the overhead door on a soured marriage.

Against the opposite wall was the four by eight-foot piece of plywood that had covered the shattered window. It now suggested to him what he had to do. Campaign signs would be the beginning of his defense against any story Traid or Morris or Johnson might try to bring against him. With a sign painter's lettering, this and other boards would become the first campaign posters for James H. Henslow, Republican Party primary candidate for the United State's Senate. The campaign would start with an announcement today and the signs that would hang on his farm wagon during the tractor parade during Pioneer Days at the Village.

Hurrying to his bedroom and his computer, Henslow typed out a news release. Short and sweet, he thought. Henslow announces candidacy for U.S. Senate. He didn't have time now for the stepping stones through the State Senate. Dirty tricks by his enemies were not going to trap him.

❧   ❧   ❧

"I tried to reach you last night," Traid complained to Dan Morris. It was seven in the morning and he couldn't wait for Dan to get to the office.

"Date," Dan said sleepily.

"Hmmm," Jack mused. "Our investigative reporter?"

"The same."

"Look, I've arranged for someone to take my classes this morning. You and I have to get out to the Village pronto. I think I know where Art hid the tape."

"No kidding. How'd you figure that out?"

"From the letter he sent Clarence. It's in the Longfellow poem. I'll explain when I see you at the Village. I'll drive my own car."

"Okay. Fifteen minutes, at the Village Smithy, then."

When they both had reached the board-and-batt shed it was still wrapped in police line tape, its double doors padlocked with a Sheriff's Department lock. As Dan fitted a key into the lock he brought Traid up to date.

"The DCI and Crime Lab guys went over the whole place for me. Dusted the pickup and found nothing except evidence of blood on the truck bed. Sample sent to the Crime Lab. Otherwise, the truck was wiped clean."

"Yeah. So the paper reported. You know what that tells me."

"I guess not."

"Rogers would have no reason to take his fingerprints off his own truck. But Jim Henslow had every reason to do it to hide the fact that he killed Rogers."

"Jeez. You sure?" Dan said as he swung the doors open to reveal the truck as they had found it two days before.

"You don't try to remove your fingerprints if you haven't something to hide. What is it the person who drove this truck in here had to hide? Simply that he drove it here and not the owner, Art Rogers. Why? Because Art Rogers was unable to drive his truck. My guess is that the blood the DCI guys found will match Rogers."

"So you think Henslow drove it?"

"Sure. Who else? He'd hidden Rogers at the farm. We know now what Henslow was up to. Sure he drove the truck in here after he got rid of the body. But he was in too much of a hurry to think of everything, like the truck bed."

"Okay. I believe you. How we going to prove it?"

"Let's back this thing out of the way," Traid said, indicating the pickup. "We need room to get a close look at Art's anvil."

Dan got into the truck and backed it slowly out of the shed. Returning to the interior, he and Traid stood over the massive anvil mounted on a steel base.

"I better tell you now what I did Wednesday evening while you were courting that beauty of yours. We have every reason to believe that Henslow conspired with Art Rogers to commit arson in order to scare Horst Henslow. We just don't have the proof. But if Clarence Rogers is to be believed, it was Jim Henslow's plan to have Art burn down the shed on the Henslow farm. And we know that Sheri Henslow is in on what happened in the barn that Saturday night. She was either there with a gun to kill Horst, or knew that her husband was. So I made an unofficial visit to their house Wednesday night and told them a little lie about our having a copy of the tape, proving the conspiracy with Rogers. And after reading your report in the Times, I told Henslow I knew he'd killed Rogers. Sheri Henslow would not give up her jacket. You can attend to that later. At any rate, I figured a little panic would cause them to make a mistake."

"That's wild. If Henslow is as desperate as we think he is, wasn't that a little dangerous?"

"Well, maybe. I took a couple of precautions, just in case he came to my house that night. Slept out in the print shop instead of in my bed. But nothing happened."

"And if we don't find the tape?"

"But we will. Help me unbolt this thing from the base."

"All four bolts are loose," Dan said as he took a wrench to them.

"Art didn't have time to tighten them the night he came over here from the farm."

By hand Dan unscrewed the nuts from the bolts under the frame and removed the four bolts. Together the two men lifted the anvil from the base and lowered it upside down on the dirt floor. Stuffed into a cavity in the bottom was an oily rag. Dan pulled it away to reveal a tape cassette beneath.

"Voila," Traid said. "I think if you and the DCI fellows play that you'll have enough evidence to indict Jim Henslow. And, incidentally, blow his grand jury caper sky high. But until the DCI is ready to follow up on your investigation and take action, we should play it cool. Maybe Henslow will lead us to where he's hidden Art Rogers' body."

❦   ❦   ❦

Andrew Pettigrew III and Tommy Johnson stood opposite each other across the conference table in their law offices, staring down at the front page of the Thursday edition of the Hamilton *Times.*

"State's Attorney Announces Candidacy" the headline read, under which a sub-head explained, "Henslow Claims Opponents Smear Him."

"He doesn't say it," Johnson said with irritation, "but the clear implication is that persons in the party are doing the dirty tricks to implicate him in his father's death."

"I haven't read the story yet. What in hell is he up to?" Pettigrew asked.

"We all agreed that Jim would make a good candidate for State Senate," Johnson replied. "Told him we'd support him. Get him in there. That was before all this business about a Chatauqua housing development, and Jim going to the grand jury with a case against the Pioneer Village board. Now he's decided on his own that he's a candidate for the U.S. Senate. Nobody's talked to him about that. It's crazy. He's crazy."

"Get him on the phone. He better just withdraw that announcement or we'll have to disown his candidacy for any office."

"Let me read you the quote from his statement. 'In the coming weeks the public will hear dire and totally untrue accusations against me in an attempt to discredit my campaign. Former legal colleagues afraid to pursue justice wherever it might lead, have attempted to taint the evidence I have brought before the grand jury in the case of the murder of my father. I will not be deterred in my quest for justice in this case.' He knows that we are certain he has no proof against Jake Bickerson or Hank Severson. He's trying to cover-up his own involvement with the fire and death of his father."

"I don't understand."

"Well, I have meant to brief you about the words Jim and I have had about his going to the grand jury with his theory. The truth of the matter appears to be that Acting Sheriff Dan Morris, with help from that ex-cop from Dallas, Jack Triad, has reason to believe that Jim was scheming with Art Rogers to get Horst off the farm."

"But Horst left the whole kit and caboodle to Pioneer Village."

"Yes he did. He signed his will in this very room. But Jim is claiming he was promised the farm. And the most disturbing thing is that he says he has a trust agreement signed by Horst on the very day he signed his will."

"Impossible," Pettigrew spit out.

"Of course. Our partner, it appears, has gone off the deep end."

"Get him on the phone. Tell him we're going to have a partners' meeting and get to the bottom of this."

"Certainly. But I wouldn't hold out much hope of getting his attention this weekend. Monday be soon enough?"

"Whenever. Just let him know how upset we are about this whole mess. And tell him to forget about the U.S. Senate, for godssake. We know darned well who is likely to get that nod to stand against Senator Tom Daschle, and it sure as hell isn't Jim Henslow."

CHAPTER 23

On highway 43 east of Hamilton slow moving lines of cars from both east and west waited for highway patrolmen to permit them to turn onto the gravel road leading to Pioneer Village. From where these Pioneer Days attendees were edging forward could be seen a column of thick smoke arising into the clear, cool October sky from an unseen steam engine. It was a signal that the Village of the past had come alive. The pillar of steam and smoke arose from a demonstration wheat field at the far side of the pretend town.

In a hay field turned parking lot opposite the entrance to the Village young men and women on nervous horses directed automobiles down long lanes to form neatly laid out rows. All morning the traffic had eased off the highways and into an idealized representation of life on the prairies at the turn of the Twentieth Century.

The brisk, sun-filled day animated the stream of people walking from the parking lot into the bustle of the Village. Mid-morning Saturday, the crowds milled around demonstrations of old time skills—the weavers at their warp and weft in the school house, a stationary steam engine powering millstones grinding wheat into flour. Men wandered down to the tractor sheds to watch the steam tractors being fired with wood and coal. Once pressure was up they would be driven off across the reservoir dam to line up in the Henslow farm fields for the major attraction of the day, the tractor parade that featured these steam behemoths.

It was with disappointment that people found the Village Smithy doors closed, the shed wrapped in yellow police tape. A hand-printed sign advised, "No Blacksmith Demonstration."

Inside the Village Print Shop Mike Wilkins was explaining to a group of children how lead type had to be set by hand in order to make up a page of a newspaper. A pile of the four-page *Pioneer Voice* lay on the stone table near the entrance to the shop. A printed notice said: "Take One—Free." Under the masthead of was the inch-high headline: "Village Willed Henslow Farm," under which was printed a statement by the Village board of directors explaining the gift of land made in Horst Henslow's will. The article went on to announce that Horst Henslow would be "recognized and memorialized" in today's tractor parade as Grand Marshall. His Avery steam tractor would be driven by board member George Carter at the head of the parade which would begin at 2 p.m.

True to his promise, Jack Traid had set and printed on the front page the article by Minnie Morris about the Chautauqua movement in the United States and in Hamilton. The headline read: "Chautauqua an Educational Movement."

A pile of the Hamilton *Times* "Pioneer Days Special" lay next to the *Pioneer Voice*, its front page featuring a schedule of events. On the back page of the edition was a list of the tractors and their owners who would participate in this year's tractor parade. Next to the name of each owner was the name of a prominent member of the state or local community who was to be honored as a special guest of the village. Among those listed were U.S. Senator Tom Daschle, State Senator Andrew Pettigrew III, Hamilton College President Franklin Adams. Named as guest of the last steam unit in the line-up was States Attorney James Henslow. Far down the list among the gas-powered machines which would bring up the end of the parade was Gordy Easton's name followed by that of Professor Jack Traid.

It took twenty minutes for Traid and Mildred Singer to drive from the Sioux Falls airport to the Highway 43 exit. Traffic had already backed up to the intersection from the entrance to Pioneer Village a mile away. It was only eleven o'clock when they got into line to make their turn into the Village parking lot.

"Plenty of time to find Ann and Roger," Jack was explaining. "They said they would try to get a parking spot against the far fence where there will be more room to have the tail-gate cookout."

"Ann said she was going to do her famous boiled dinner which she does in a converted milk can," Mildred said.

"I know. It is really great. Everything in it. Sausage, corn, potatoes, carrots."

Mildred put her hand on Jack's arm and looked across at him.

"I have the most wonderful feeling that we're really starting our lives today, this very minute. It all seems so right."

"It was great that Ann persuaded you to come. These are old friends of yours, too. You'll feel comfortable to be back among them."

"Except I haven't met Ellie Easton, yet."

"That trouble you?"

"I'd lie if I didn't admit I'm a little jealous of those months you two were going with each other. But, no. Everything will be okay."

"And you'll be glad to know that the Henslow matter will soon be over. Solved."

"Oh? Did they arrest Art Rogers?"

"No sign of Rogers yet. But Thursday morning Dan Morris and I followed Rogers' hints in a letter to his brother about where he hid the tape recording I told you about. We searched the Village Smithy, right here in the Village, and found a cassette stuffed up under a hollow in the bottom of the anvil. Dan checked it out with the Department of Criminal Investigation guys and says that the tape is a clear recording of Jim Henslow setting up the conspiracy with Rogers to burn down Horst Henslow's shed."

"And he shot his step-father?"

"That is yet to come out clearly. To tell you the truth, I think Sheri Henslow did that. Whether or not they planned the killing together will have to come out in the trial. The medical examiner's autopsy said Horst was dead before he was shot. Maybe. But why he was shot if he was already dead will be interesting to learn."

"So you have evidence enough to convict Henslow?"

"Of a conspiracy to commit arson, without a doubt. But we haven't got what we need to prove he killed Art Rogers. I'm certain he did it. But forget that. We're about to celebrate your homecoming with a picnic. Then tomorrow we're going house-hunting in Dell Rapids. Right?"

"Your idea is terrific. It will be fun, Jack. The nicest thing I've ever been asked to do."

Directed to a parking space half a block from where the Faregold suburban was parked, Jack and Mildred walked back down the line of automobiles.

"I never knew they got such big crowds," Mildred said. "This is the first time I've been to a Pioneer Days celebration."

"The estimate is that more than ten thousand people will be here today," Jack replied.

Ann Faregold waved them into the circle of friends, reaching out and giving Mildred a hug. Roger Faregold had arranged a buffet on the tailgate of the suburban where dishes of prepared food were displayed. Jack introduced Mildred to Ellie Easton and Gordy. The Reverend Clyde Masters shook hands with both Jack and Mildred. Minnie and Elliot Morris arrived at that moment and joined in the greetings.

"Hope you like the way your article came out," Jack said to Minnie, handing her a copy of the Village Voice he had kept for her.

"Wonderful," she exclaimed. "See, Elliot. The *Times* is being one-upped."

"It's a nice job, Jack. You hand set all that type?"

"Mike Wilkins and I."

"We'll have to stop by and take a look at the old flat bed press," Elliot said. "But I'm sure glad we are out of the hot lead process."

"Kid's coming into the shop are fascinated by the old presses, and the pieces of type," Jack added, "We tell them that letterpress lasted five hundred years and transformed human culture."

Roger Faregold had opened the steaming cream can and with a pair of tongs began to serve each of the picnickers. Heaped on each plate was sausage, potatoes and corn on the cob. Parked at the end of a line of cars, the Faregolds had arranged a semicircle of folding chairs on the clearing along the fence line.

"The big story in the *Pioneer Voice*," Elliot Morris commented, "is the Henslow gift."

"How sad," Minnie added, "that it came out of so much strife and Mr. Henslow's death."

"And you don't know exactly how he died, do you?" Roger directed the question to Jack Traid.

"Coroner's report says Horst Henslow was dead when he was shot, and that conclusion will probably not change. Despite that, I think murder may have been committed."

"Really?" Elliot exclaimed. "What do you know that we haven't got in the paper yet?"

"I think you're going to have a big story for Monday's issue. But I better let your son handle how that comes out."

"How mysterious," Minnie said. "And our son is in the midst of it all."

"Does that have anything to do with the surprising announcement by Jim Henslow that he's a candidate for U.S. Senate?" Morris continued. "The news release he handed out claims he's being smeared by political opponents making false charges about him."

"I think you'll discover," Traid replied, "that Mr. Henslow is trying a new tactic, since the grand jury hasn't accomplished what he wanted."

"Which is?" Roger asked.

"To buy him more time."

"I don't get it," Ann interjected. "All this political wrangling over this Village."

Traid changed the subject to Gordy Easton's tractor to avoid explaining more than he wanted.

"We ready to go with your Allis?"

"Sure am. I even fixed a little platform on the draw bar. It will be easier for you to stand behind me."

"Great. I'm honored to be your guest, Gordy."

"We're supposed to cross the dam after all the steam tractors are lined up on the other side. Gasoline models are last in the parade."

"Yes, I gathered that from the list in the *Times* Pioneer Days special."

As they spoke the shrill call of steam whistles echoed across Pioneer Village.

❧   ❧   ❧

The hay wagon waiting at the end of the tractor shed to be hooked up for the parade displayed a freshly painted sign on either side: "Henslow for U.S. Senate. Your Law and Order Candidate."

Within the three-foot high sides of the wagon were bales of hay on which half a dozen children sat, small American flags in hand. Impatient, they were calling out to friends over the sounds of blowing whistles, steel wheels crunching along the gravel street, men shouting instructions to the tractors beginning to move toward the dam.

Jim Henslow stood talking to Carl Martin, owner of the Hart Parr steam unit that was backed up to the wagon. The din made it necessary to shout.

"In the cab with you?" Henslow said loudly to Martin.

"Sure. Plenty of room. Kids will be fine in the wagon."

Once tractor and wagon were hitched, Henslow climbed up onto the canopied operating platform, positioning himself on the left side facing Main street of the Village. Bystanders already gathered along the parade route along the main avenue waved as Henslow waved.

A parade coordinator directed Martin's tractor into the line of machines edging its way across the hundred yard long dam. The gate at the far end of the dam was opened wide and the ponderous line of creaking, huffing steam engines snaked across the open field in a wide arc. Parade coordinators directed tractor drivers to form parallel rows facing the dam in preparation for the parade. It was one forty-five in the afternoon and Pioneer Village was about to display its greatest treasure, a veritable history of American farm tractors.

❦   ❦   ❦

"It's about to begin, folks," the public address system blared from four corners of the Village. "The 1995 Pioneer Days Tractor Parade is about to start."

"Golly," Gordy gasped. "We got to get going Jack."

"Okay. Let's go. I'll follow you," Traid replied. He turned to tell Mildred he'd meet her at the Print Shop when the parade was over but she was deep in conversation with Ellie Easton. Jack got up from his chair and hurried to put his plate on the suburban's tailgate, then called back to all as he followed Gordy, "See you at the Print Shop after the parade."

Gordy had broken into a brisk trot toward the open field behind the steam tractor shed. Most of the gasoline models had made their way across the dam and were being lined up behind the steam tractors in the Henlow farm field that sloped gently to the reservoir. To the crowd waiting along the streets of the Village across the lake, the scene suggested a military maneuver from the last century. Ribbons of steam and smoke rose into the warmed October air, the din of engines, whistles and lumbering steel wheels enforced the image as the first tractor, Horst Henslow's Avery, moved onto the dam's crest toward Pioneer Village.

George Carter was at the controls of the Avery, its cab festooned in red, white and blue bunting. Newly painted signs under each of the cab windows declared: "In Memory of Horst Henslow, 1995 Grand Marshall, Pioneer Village." As Carter proceeded across the dam he pulled the cord to the steam whistle every thirty seconds, the shrill blast answered multiple times from those steamers following.

"We're late," Gordy was saying frantically as he climbed up on the freshly painted, orange Allis Chalmers tractor that was the legacy from his father.

"Take it easy, Gordy," Traid said. "We can get by the parade if we just go around it on the down side of the dam."

"Sure," Gordy said, as the tractor jerked into motion. On the narrow platform on the draw bar, Traid gripped the steel seat to keep his balance. The lead tractor had come off the dam and was turning down Chautauqua Avenue to the delight of the gathered crowd. The blast of its whistle started the crowd even as they anticipated it.

Slowly Gordy steered the Allis along the side of the gravel road that stretched across the crown of the dam. The earthen dam was grass covered where he and Traid hurried forward. Men at the controls of the advancing giant tractors shouted encouragement at them.

Near the far end of the dam as they approached the open gate to the marshalling field, the left rear wheel of the Allis sank into a soft spot and began to spin.

"Damnit all," Gordy cried out. "We're stuck."

Jack Traid looked down over the left fender at the soft rut into which the tire had sunk. The spinning wheel and thrown wet earth back of it.

When he saw a human hand and arm slither under the tire he shouted at Gordy, "Stop, Gordy. Turn off the engine."

Traid jumped to the ground just as Carl Martin's Hart Parr, pulling the Henslow campaign wagon, turned onto the dam and was proceeding across. As Traid knelt at the back wheel of Gordy's tractor, he could see from the corner of his eye Jim Henslow leaping from Martin's tractor and running toward them. Gordy was at Traid's side.

"Geez," Gordy exclaimed, straightening up as he realized that a partly decayed body had been uncovered.

"Get that tractor out of there," Henslow shouted, as he approached at a run.

"Gordy," Traid said firmly, "Go get Dan Morris. Tell him to bring a CDI officer. Quick. Fast as you can."

Traid stood as Henslow came up to him.

"What's this?" Henslow asked.

"You know what it is, Henslow," Traid said. "I thought you had probably hid Art Rogers away somewhere nearby—after you killed him and carried his body here in his own pickup."

"No goddam way," Jim yelled. "This is a matter for my office Traid. Just butt the hell out."

"Won't work, Henslow. Art Rogers is going to testify after all, since we really do have the tape he hid where you would never have looked."

"You're bluffing," Henslow shouted above the roar of engines along the road above them. "No one can prove I killed Rogers."

"My considered guess is that we'll discover that Art Rogers was killed with your gun. The slugs will match those that went into your father's body. And after they hear the tape of you instructing Rogers to burn your father's shed, no jury will have trouble putting it all together. Although, you might tell me whether it was you or your wife who shot Horst. That still isn't clear to me."

"You're full of shit. It's all a dirty trick." Henslow shouted, turning back to Martin's tractor which had paused above them. Martin's honored guest and primary candidate for the U.S. Senate clambered up into the cab and took his seat at the window, waving to the crowd again as the Hart Parr and farm wagon with flag-waving children turned off the dam and moved down Chautauqua Avenue.

The parade of tractors passed over the dam, wound its way through the streets of the Village, and found its way back to the tractor sheds. Left behind on the face of the dam was one Allis Chalmers tractor with its left rear wheel stuck in a shallow grave.

Dan Morris and two plain-clothes officers hurried up to where Jack Traid stood at the back of the tractor. The three of them knelt at the disturbed grave under the tractor wheel.

At the Village end of the dam Gordy Easton was returning to his tractor.

"Don't come out here, Gordy," Jack yelled to him. "We'll take care of this. I'll get your tractor back to you later."

Gordy stopped ten yards away from Traid.

"Go tell your mom and the rest of them what happened. Tell them that we found Art Rogers' body. I'll be there in a few minutes."

Gordy turned and broke into a run. Traid turned to Dan Morris who straightened up from the grave.

"Well, Dan. That's the end of it. You and the CDI can put it all together, arrest both Jim and Sheri Henslow. I'm resigning as your deputy as of now."

"Sure. I understand. Looks as if your hunch was right all along. Henslow had to eliminate every tape, and finally Rogers himself in order to survive."

"What he never realized was that his fiction could not absorb all the facts which reality kept thrusting at him. The first lie uncoils the noose," Traid said. "And I'll leave it to you guys to tighten it around State's Attorney Jim Henslow's neck."

❦   ❦   ❦

By the time Acting Sheriff Dan Morris and agents of the Department of Criminal Investigation had moved Gordy Easton's tractor off the shallow grave and removed Art Rogers' remains, the sun had gone down and security lights had flickered on throughout Pioneer Village. Most of the crowd had dispersed without knowing what the confusion on the dam had been about during the tractor parade.

Jack Triad agreed to help Gordy retrieve his tractor once Morris and the DCI gave them the okay to go back out onto the dam. The security lights of the Village cast shadows where they stood at the end of the tractor sheds waiting, but a bright harvest moon high in the sky illuminated the reservoir, dam and the Henslow fields beyond. As Traid and Gordy started toward the Allis Chalmers, which had been driven up onto the road over the dam, Gordy suddenly stopped and pointed to the top of the hill where a grove of trees stood at the edge of Henslow's field.

"Look!" Gordy exclaimed.

"What?" Jack asked, looking at Gordy.

"On the hill near the trees."

Gordy whispered his excitement.

"The albino."

There in the white light of the moon stood the buck deer, its flanks seeming to glow, its antlered head held high as it sniffed the air. Like a marble sculpture whose creator had frozen a moment of tense awareness, the stag did not move. Gordy and Traid stood motionless, unable to speak.

Neither man nor youth could say afterward how long they had stood transfixed by the sight of the deer—a minute, five minutes? Slowly, majestically the creature turned it head as if to better focus on the near-empty village across the lake. It eased itself into the copse, moving deeper among the trees, its white flanks flashing ghostly shapes back to the intent watchers.

"Gee," Gordy said.

"That was something, wasn't it? Just as if that albino buck has been a witness to murder." Jack replied.

CHAPTER 24

*T*he most determined of Hamilton's little children, herded by gallant parents, braved the first snow storm of the year Halloween night as they trudged head down from house to house in the neighborhood of Hamilton State College. These miniature ghosts, werewolves, and monsters from a crypt were in pursuit of sweets, unaware they were celebrants of man's darkest, primordial fears of an inexplicable nether world.

Automobile traffic slowed as grown-up revelers on their way to the Hamilton College Scholarship Benefit waited for coveys of these fearless treasure hunters to cross an intersection. Patient adults wearing coats and stocking caps for the first time this year hurried them along, then hung back as the costumed troupe approached a lighted porch. "Trick or treat," the children's voices called out, the joyful sound muffled by the accumulating snow that had begun to blanket the quiet town.

The parking lots on campus were white with the new snow, automobile tracks of the first arrivals marking the way to the party. By eight in the evening most of the lots were full with vehicles lightly dusted with the still-falling snow, their costumed occupants scurrying against the rising wind toward the Student Center Auditorium. At the entrance of the auditorium a large poster announced "Scholarship Benefit Dance featuring the Dakota Dixieland Ramblers."

The spacious auditorium had been transformed into a nightclub. Lights were turned low, and along the walls of the room shimmering spirit forms danced in blue light. The ceiling was festooned with black and orange streamers, under which lighted jack-o-lanterns served as centerpieces on tables that circled the dance floor.

A six foot-eight ghoulish monster with a voice that was changing this season greeted arriving guests, directing them to reserved tables. Elliot and Minnie Morris's table had been arranged for weeks in advance. Their invitations to their guests for the *Times*-sponsored table announced that the benefit dance was also to be a farewell party for Carla Garza, who was leaving Hamilton for her native San Antonio, Texas.

Elliot and Minnie Morris, dressed as 1930's farm folk, were among the first to arrive and were already seated and sipping Witches Brew Punch when Jack Traid and Mildred Singer entered the auditorium and approached the table. Elliot stood as the couples greeted each other. Mildred was costumed as a witch, Jack as a Keystone Cop, outfits Mildred had found in a party shop in Sioux Falls.

"Mind if I abandon you for ten minutes, Mildred," Jack said. "I need to check the PA system once again and be sure members of the band have all their charts."

"Go," Mildred ordered. "Elliot is going to tell me all about your riotous years at the U. of Iowa."

"Elliot and I have a pact," Jack returned, smiling at these friends, "so you'll learn little. Better that you tell them about the glorious digs we're buying in Dell Rapids."

With that Jack Traid hurried across the dance floor to the stage, his silent-film, jaunty shuffle suggesting he was now free of old cares. He had given himself permission to play the character he portrayed this night.

"He's doing what he loves best and not feeling guilty," Mildred said to the others as she watched Jack mount the stage and confer with the drummer who was already at his place.

"What's this about a place in Dells?" Minnie asked.

"We found an old warehouse on the banks of the Big Sioux in Dell Rapids. A nice river view but a disaster, except that the foundations and walls are sound. Needs a new roof, but after we get that and the place cleaned up, it will make two beautiful studios and a roomy apartment. We're getting help with plans from a Sioux Falls architect."

"Sounds like work," Elliot said.

"But affordable," Mildred replied.

"And lots of fun," Minnie added. "I think its great you two are doing this. So, you'll teach in Sioux Falls?"

"And Jack here. Mid-America College was eager to get an art teacher and made me a nice offer. We will both have easy commutes."

"And Jack's print shop?" Elliot asked.

"When we get the warehouse converted, we'll move it all there, to his studio. Mine will adjourn his."

As Mildred was describing the plan, Dan Morris and Carla Garza arrived at the table, arm in arm. Carla, in her bright, flamenco dancer's costume, attracted the attention of those at adjoining tables. Dan wore a bowler hat, a black and white checked suit with vest of a vaudeville performer.

"The honoree," Minnie exclaimed, greeting them warmly. "And I suppose Danny is going to abandon you while he plays tonight."

"He promises me the first dance," Carla said. "After that, I guess Mildred and I are band widows."

"There'll be guys eager enough to dance with you two," Elliot said.

From the stage came sounds of a trumpet trying phrases, the drum brushes whispering anticipation. The volume of laughter and conversation rose as the costumed crowd rapidly filled the tables in the auditorium. The Morris's table began to fill as Delores and Tommy Johnson arrived dressed as Little Bo Peep and Jack Horner. Patricia and Andrew Pettigrew III were next to arrive, she costumed as a 1920's flapper, he as a fraternity man of the same period, white trousers and blue blazer asserting his status.

Elliot Morris's annual contribution to the college scholarship fund mandated in his mind that the Johnsons and Pettigrews be his guests at the benefit dance since they and he formed the nucleus of the town support for the college. Andy Pettigrew was recognized as the state legislator most able to rescue Hamilton State from any moves to diminish or eliminate its mission.

At intermission a buffet luncheon was served to the party-goers and the Morris's table caught up with the news published in this day's *Times* as well as news yet to be published.

"I want to offer a toast to our guest of honor," Elliot announced, standing at the head of the table. "Carla Garza, in the eight months she's been with the *Times* has proven herself a dedicated journalist. She served the paper well and we wish we could have kept her here. But she's ready for the *Express News* in San Antonio. We'll be watching as she rises in the field. Carla, from all of us, thank you! The Times is pleased to give you your Christmas bonus early," with which he handed Carla a sealed envelope.

Carla stood to respond.

"I can only say how grateful I am for the chance you gave me, Mr. Morris. And for the support of the staff at the paper. It will be hard to leave the peace and quiet of this small city."

Laughter erupted around the table.

"Yeah, hardly anything happened while you were here," Danny said.

"I began to think," Carla replied, "That Hamilton was like that all the time. Crime wave after crime wave. Again, my sincerest thanks."

"And I have a little announcement to make," Dan said, rising and standing next to Carla and putting his arm around her. "When I've finished as a witness for the State Attorney General in the Art Rogers' murder case against Jim Henslow, I'll be going to San Antonio and…"

"Danny, you never said a word," Minnie Morris exclaimed.

"Carla made the challenge and I have arranged to join the Texas Legal Defense Group. It's time I put my law degree to some use."

"Bravo," Elliot offered. "Decision time, then."

"Guess so," his son replied. "I'll miss the old home town. And the Dakota Dixieland Ramblers. But it's time to move on. Besides, I have to be able to report back to you about Carla, don't I?"

"And Carla can report about you," his mother added.

Elliot Morris turned to Tommy Johnson and asked, "What's the schedule for Henslow's trial?"

"Judge Nelson scheduled it for December 15."

"But I understand that Sheri Henslow won't be indicted," Morris said.

"Despite Jim Henslow claiming that she killed his step-father and Art Rogers, the Attorney General's office believes all the evidence Dan and Jack assembled points to Jim," Johnson explained. "His revolver was found on Rogers' body, you know. Crime Lab ballistics prove it was the gun used to kill Rogers, and the one that was used to shoot what the medical examiner says was the dead body of Horst Henslow."

"The fact that a piece of Sheri Henslow's leather jacket was found in the barn," Triad added, "is being dismissed as too circumstantial to indict Mrs. Henslow. Guess finding Jim Henslow guilty will have to do for justice this time around."

"And why don't you take over our sheriff's department?" Andy Pettigrew asked of Traid.

"Oh no! Mildred and I have books to create, paintings to paint, new adventures to share. Now that Sheriff Tom Taylor's law enforcement career is ended and he's serving his two years of probation, the county ought to get on with getting a young professional lawman and provide him with a staff this county deserves. But I did agreed to do my bit by volunteering to be probation officer for Jonah Bickerson and David Marritz for the next year."

"Too bad you won't take the sheriff's job. There's going to be a new sheriff's department office and jail," Elliot added. "The paper is going to nudge the county commission to get on with the plans to fund the up-grade of that department."

Intermission over, Jack Triad and Dan Morris returned to the stage and the Dakota Dixieland Ramblers. At the microphone Jack announced the next number.

"This next piece is for a very special person—Mildred Singer. "Love is Here to Stay."

Applause rose from the Morris's table, followed by general applause as the band began to play. Jack put down his saxophone and came off the stage, skirted the dancers on the floor and went to Mildred.

"I believe this is our dance," he said as the two of them embraced and glided into the midst of dancers.

About the Author

Robert Feragen was born in Minot, North Dakota, and reared in Sioux Falls, Dell Rapids and Madison, South Dakota. He served in the U.S. Army during World War II, including one year in the European Theater, after which he attended the State University of Iowa where he received a graduate degree in English from the Iowa Writers' Workshop. He and Madlin Ann Melrose were married in 1950. The couple has five grown children, six grandchildren.

After being graduated from Iowa, Feragen taught English and directed student creative writing projects for nine years at two colleges. Leaving academia, he went to work in public relations for rural electric cooperatives in the Dakotas. In 1971 he was made manager of the Northeast Public Power Association and moved to Massachusetts. He became General Manager of the Massachusetts Municipal Electric Company in 1974. In 1978 President Jimmy Carter appointed him Administrator of the Rural Electrification Administration, in which capacity he served until January, 1981. Feragen returned to Madison, South Dakota, in 1981 to work for East River Electric Power Cooperative. He was appointed general manager of that system in 1986. After retiring in 1990, Feragen turned to writing and publishing poetry and fiction. *The Albino Stag Witness* is his first novel.

0-595-22255-2